SICK: An Anthology of Illness

D1556947

With special thanks to Perry McGee and Effie.

Published by Raw Dog Screaming Press
Hyattsville, MD

First printing 2003

Cover image: David Anthony Magitis
Interior illustrations: Andi Olsen
Book design: John Edward Lawson

Printed in the United States of America

ISBN 0-9745031-1-8

Library of Congress Control Number: 2003098411

www.rawdogscreaming.com

Acknowledgments

The text & illustration series "1.01-1.03" by Andi and Lance Olsen first published in *Fiction International 36*

"Sacrifice" by C.J. Henderson first published in *100 Crooked Little Crime Stories*

"The Legend of Jimmy Wad by Vincent W. Sakowski fist published in *The First Line*

"Wuornos" by Harold Jaffe is from the collection *15 Serial Killers*

"Unicorn's Revenge" by Greg Beatty first published in *Penumbric*

"Shadow" by Jack Fisher first published in *Not One of Us*

"Discussions Concerning the Ingestion of Living Insects" by Ronald Damien Malfi first published in *The Dream People*

"Exterminator" by Hertzan Chimera and Greg Wharton first published in *Shadow of the Marquis*

"A Terrible Thing to Waste" by Vincent W. Sakowski first published in *Horrorfind Fiction*

❧Contents❧

1.01 God Playing on the Posterior of a Man When He is Thinking about Tulips

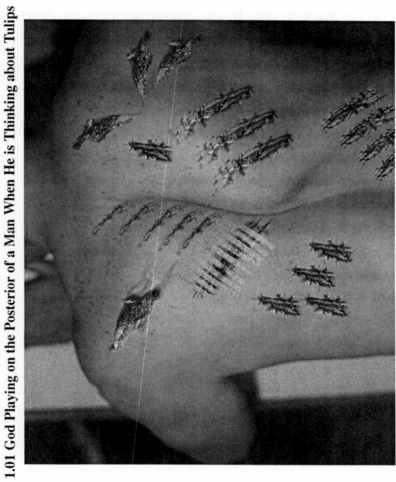

1.01 God Playing on the Posterior of a Man When He is Thinking about Tulips. From puberty's onset, sufferers of this viral malady become aware in moments of vague distraction of itching sensations across the back. They frequently report the impression of accompanying light, fluttery kisses. When investigating the site of irritation, they discover the irruption of stitch-like lesions that, upon examination and interpretation by a medical linguist, elucidate the chief sins they have committed by the act of being alive. The disorder is congenital. Some infected children never develop lesions but remain Guilt Sero-Positive for life. Routine sero-testing and treatment (including programs of intensive weeping) have greatly reduced the incidence of God Playing.

The Christ Machine
by Tim Curran

WHEN THEY LET *you out, Sailor-boy, when they turn the lock and set the disease-bird free, you be careful,* they told him, *you be real careful...because these are places where the killers are. You'll see 'em, mind you, you'll see them in black hoods of night with evil dope-fiend faces and junkyard dog tooth-smiles. And they'll see you, all right, lions falling on a fresh meat-kill, burning cigarette-eyes, breathing ammonia and exhaling sulfur...and to them, why you're a lush and wet forest of decay and they'll chop you down, spill the stink of your veins. Clear-cut.*

I'll be careful, Sailor-boy promised, all teeth and smile.

Just be sure, they said, *because they'll smell you and show you their needle-marks like pinholes in unbaked bread and shed their skins and you don't want to see what's underneath...God no...great, heaving grins of knifeblade jaws and razorblade tongues.*

I'll be cool, Sailor-boy told them, *body on ice.*

So Sailor-boy was turned loose and he walked with careful feeling footfalls down the piss-stained concrete steps where the alkies and junkies were curled and twined-up like yesterday's trash, clutching oily paper bags and rusty bone-bent needles, awash in their own private oceans. Some spoke to him, some just coughed, others vomited, others didn't do nothing but stare up at the sky with desert-baked eyes, wearing scarves and beards of buzzing flies, froth-mouthed dogs worrying at the hollows of their bellies.

"Freedom," Sailor-boy said. It never tasted so sweet.

The air in the streets was warm, sometimes hot with blast-furnace gusts that made rivers run down his brow. He wasn't used to it; any of it. This was real and raw, unfiltered and running. He was accustomed to sterilized water and filtered air and bland food and bland faces after all those months. But out here...by God...everything was alive and sour and uncontrolled. The air stank of sweet garbage and foul bodies and rotting fruit and ripe meats. In there it had been odorless, soundless, all padding and white seamless walls. Out here it was smelly, noisy, multi-colored, and there were no straight lines, only angles and angles of angles. Hot-blooded, sense-overloading life. It was almost too much: Each new stink and sound and texture made him giddy, drunk on sensation.

He had to stop. Breathe. Breathe again. Slowly, slowly. Seventeen months for the Cure, then out of the sterile womb into this madness of thrumming...*everything*.

Sailor-boy walked and smiled and was terribly self-conscious about how he did it. Was it right? Did they notice he was different? Did a sudden sweep of step or a guilty twist of lip give him away?

He thought of old faces and familiar friends. He didn't know where they'd be and didn't want to. They'd all be dying or dead by now, so let them die and decompose and make fertile the soil of harm. "We're from different worlds now," Sailor-boy found himself saying under his breath. "They don't need me and I don't need them."

Quiet, he cautioned himself. *People in the real world don't talk to themselves, they don't have to, there's always others to listen and scoff. Only institutionalized people do that.*

And you're not one of them anymore.

He was but two blocks from the hospital when he saw the crowd. They were killers, all right. Tomb-faced slaughterers with the elaborate scarifications of self-remedy and explorative biopsy. Their necks were broken and mended: too much time on the gibbet beneath abrasive caress of hemp-rope, too much attention from the knives of the vivisectionists. They saw him, let loose the poor junky they had been dismembering, and crossed the street in Sailor-boy's direction, glass-eyed, flaking-lipped, overdosing on hatred that was steel, spiked balls in their bellies.

Sailor-boy stood there in his freshly starched suit, white teeth, manicured nails, and coifed hair. He didn't stand long. He dashed away, vaulting insect-meshed bodies and gagging street urchins. Down sidestreet, noisome boulevard, and crumbling alley, moving in a maze that confused him as much as his pursuers. Finally, their footsteps nowhere to be heard, he rested near a litter pile of fly-specked bones and graffiti-canvassed walls.

"You heard of the girl, boy?" a voice said. "You heard of Natron Rose?"

Sailor-boy whirled on the dirty concrete and saw an old man lying near him, wrapped in rags and time, smashed bottle of liver swill at his knotty feet.

"Never heard of her."

"Didn't think so, boy, didn't think so." The old man's face was withered and dusty, had the texture of a bird's nest. He had no teeth, his nose was a flap, his eyes were bleeding secret cancers. "Natron Rose. I say the name a thousand times a day, boy, and I like it less every time. Bile on my tongue. Yeah, that and more. When I can't drink I talk and I'm never sure if I'm alone or in a crowd or the last man on Earth. Am I, boy? Are you real and standing there or just a phantasm of self-indulgence?"

"I'm here."

"Funny look about you, boy...pressed, starched, folded, washed and spindle-dried. Not right at all—" The old man coughed a wad of phlegm to the ground and studied it, a critic seeking nuance in bodily secretions. "Am I just old and bottle-wasted, boy, or are you different than me, the others? No, don't tell me, you uppity little bastard, cause I already know. You had the Cure, did you not?"

Sailor-boy debated whether he should lie or tell the truth. "Yes, I had it," his lips betrayed just as he was leaning toward a lie.

"I knew it, I knew it. They'll be after you because of it. The Brotherhood, the pagans..."

"No, not them. But others."

The old man scratched himself with scaly fingers lacking nails. "Yeah, you're right. I get confused sometimes. Those ones would burn you because of the Cure, but the others, the cherry-eyed Medicine Vampires would spit steam at you, find a church, hang you by your feet and drain the juice from you into a communal bucket." The old man shook his head. "Damn shame. You seem like a nice kid. Tell me, boy, tell me this: Who did you know to get the Cure? Who did you pay?"

Sailor-boy shook his head, exhaled. "No one. Nothing. I was picked by the lottery to get the Cure. There isn't enough medicine to go around, old man, so they pick at random via the lottery."

"That the truth?"

"Yes, it is."

"Damn. I always thought that lottery-business was bullshit."

The sky was growing dark, a tapestry of filth and rain.

"Listen," the old man said. "They're coming for you...I can hear 'em dragging themselves in this direction..."

"The booze, old man, it's just the booze."

"Listen..."

The old man was right: They were coming. Sailor-boy could hear it now, too.

Drag, shuffle, slap, drag...atrophied limbs pulling husks of disease and despair down the bend in the alley. In a moment, they would be visible. Moon-faced carrion crows with pestilence smiles and rumbling stomachs. Grumbling, Cure-hungry reservoir-empty bellies, gaping plague-sores set in rusting bronze skins, eyes like falling stars, all deflated vein and twisted muscle begging for the needle, stinking of cough syrup and dry-rot.

"Better run, boy. Better—"

But Sailor-boy didn't; there was nowhere to run to. He saw the great heap of bones a few feet away, and, like a dog seeking the perfect treasure to nibble and bury, he dove into it headfirst, clawing and thrashing until he was covered in a blizzard of femur, skull, and scapula, only his eyes visible, piss-holes in dirty snow.

The gray-skinned fanatics came on, seeming to be not individuals, but only parts of a great vengeance machine, all skeletal limb and bobbing head.

"Boy—"

"You," one jagged mouth of the machine said, "are the one with the Cure!"

The old man looked ready to slide from his skin. "Me? Goddamn, no! I never got the Cure! Lookit me, will ya?" He shed his coat, baring forearms and chest. "I have the marks, the sores! I'm dying, too—"

The machine raged around him, no more idling, full throttle now. Armies of pirate-hook fingers tore at him, fleshless faces and Medusan-heads of ropy, crawling whips nodded and leered, junkies of fever-blood.

"Please," the old man whimpered as moldy cloth was shoved in his mouth, "for the love of Christ, him, the boy, not me!"

"Christ?" voices chanted. "Christ? Is that what he said? He is no Christian and the marks are manufactured! Not true stigmata! He is not of the Faith!"

"Please!" the old man gagged in a spittle-voice. "I was baptized in the blood of Christ! I am of the Faith! I'm not a pagan! I've not had the Cure!"

The machine did not listen. It was a thousand moving parts of withered mannequin, gravel-eye, centipede-skin, and thundering, blood-maddened, urine stinking, medicine-smelling appetite.

Sailor-boy watched with blurring vision from the yellowed bars of a shattered rib cage. He saw and did not want to see, was present and wished he were somewhere else.

"Bleed him!" mouths insisted. "For the blood is the life."

A few parts of the machine disappeared as the old man was held under a sea of ragged vermin-legs and lice-hopping bodies. His screams were muffled by leather and flesh. The lost parts of the machine returned now, pulling a wooden structure of uprights and crossbeams with them. The old man was stretched over it in a T, inverted, hands and ankles nailed firmly in place, throat slit, rivers of red remorse filling a bucket.

"This is the Body and Blood of the Son," the machine chanted. "As we drink it, He becomes us and We become him. So it was in the beginning, so it shall always be."

Sailor-boy watched them drink, bloated with Cure, singing psalms, and he was glad he'd never been baptized, was not an eater of flesh and drinker of blood, was not a Christian.

The Garbage Eaters
by Scott Christian Carr

Q UESTION NUMBER ONE is always, *How old were you when you stopped believing in Santa Claus?*

ANSWER:

—*Ages 1 through 5* and we move on to the next question.

—*Never believed in Santa*, make a note and proceed to Question Two.

—*6 through 9* and I know I've got a good candidate. The parents started the job and all I have to do is finish it.

—*10 years old* and we're halfway there. Next stop, toga central!

—*11 to 14* and it's radical replacement psychotherapy. There's something missing in their lives. Give them something new to believe in. Something bigger, something better. Something old, something new…

—Anything older than *fourteen*, and I'm wearing a red cap and whiskers to the placement interview.

Other questions include *When did you stop/start going to Church?—Did your father ever put his hands on you (either during punishment or play)?—Do you have any pets?—Are you willing to be saved?*

The telephone rings making me jump. It's a news reporter. She asks me if any of it is true, if anyone is hurt, if there is a list of demands. She asks me if any of the letters or emails or rumors are legit, and then she asks if I'd be willing to give her an exclusive interview.

I tell her not to worry, not to bother, and not to believe everything she reads. I tell her it doesn't matter, not all jokes are funny, the Lord works in mysterious ways, and that in six hours, one way or another, I'll be dead. I hang up the phone.

It's officially started. The beginning of the end.

But the end is no place to begin, so...

...I'll tell you about the second cult I was ever in. This is where I learned The Golden Rule:

You have to give the people what they want.

But then, this golden rule is of course preceded with the golden stipulation: *First you've gotta* tell *the people what they want.*

This is called *doctrine*.

Now, I'm not saying that your doctrine needs to make a whole lot of sense—in fact, the vaguer the better. Keep 'em guessing. Keep 'em confused. Fill in all of their blanks for them.

Mad Libs of the soul.

God Loves you, or *Jesus Accepts You*, or *Mohammed Forgives You*, or *Christ Wants You*, is certainly more effective than laying out a strict laundry list of rules and regulations, mandates and motives. *The Lord Takes Those Who Give* and *Baby Jesus Digs the Doctrine* are also good. *Sacrifice and Servitude Save Souls* is better.

Do What I Tell You and Together We Will Ascend is damned near perfect.

Forget complicated guidelines, just win 'em over with basic, old-fashioned vagaries and charm. Make them feel accepted. Make them feel important. Do this, and you can bet your tambourine that when the time comes they'll bend over backwards to do whatever it is that you need done. Manson knew this. So did Gandhi, for that matter.

Compliment them enough, accept them enough, make them feel good about themselves enough and they'll eat shit out of your hands if you offer it. Eager to please, to work for your love, to compete for your approval. Ready to panhandle on corners, steal from their mother's purses, beer-bong that cyanide *Kool-Aid*.

With enough conditioning and encouragement, they'll be ready. In the medical/pharmaceutical world, this is called *Getting to Goal*. In cult dynamics, it's known as *Love Bombing*.

Love 'em to death. Get them to love each other. One big happy family. Give 'em a little and they'll beg for more. Give 'em more and they'll go that much further to please you. Of course, if a member ever *does* express the slightest doubt in your *Word* or incredulity of your doctrine, that's when the love shuts off quicker than the lights in Manhattan.

You've got to give people what they want—just remember to take it back later.

But I'm getting ahead of myself. I was telling you about *True Believers*.

An unoriginal name for an uninspired group.

It was your typical 'Jesus speaks through me' bible-based cult. Nothing fancy or unique—a racket, through and through. A money pyramid right to the top.

But life was good. We all wore blue robes, our leader wore purple and his wives wore pink. Shaved heads, vegan diet, chanting—you know the drill. Or maybe you don't...you're probably thinking of the Krishnas. But we weren't like them, not at all. For one thing, we were *Jesus*-based, like I said, not *Zen*-based. Those Zen guys don't play games, I'll tell you that for nothing. They don't fool around. There's not a harder nut to crack than someone who's spent a few years in a Buddhist cult. But I digress.

I was telling you about the *True Believers*. An unoriginal name for an unoriginal cult. But like I said, life was good—a cot to sleep on, rice to eat—it beat being out in the cold.

There were forty of us, give or take. *And life was good.* We ate little more than rice and bread, we hawked our prayer books and witnessed on street corners, we prayed and we meditated and we chanted and we shed our mortal belongings to the Great Spirit. Maybe that does still sound a little like the Krishnas, but let me tell you—the similarities end there. In essence, we were really nothing like those tambourine-monkeys. Honest.

For starters, we were a much smaller group, more intimate, more like a family. And like I said, we were Christian-based, though that means a lot less than you might think, when it comes right down to daily dynamics. There were around forty of us when I was accepted into the fold and forty when I left. That's not counting our leader and his wives. So, I guess you can up that number to around forty-eight, if you're keeping score.

Oh, and one thing right off the bat: We never, *ever*, referred to ourselves as a *cult*. That was a no-no. When we did call ourselves by anything other than *True Believers*, we simply referred to ourselves as 'the group.'

Our leader's name was Ro-Gesh.

This might not sound like much to you, but to me at that particular time in my life it was a paradise. We were clean. All the rice we could eat. A roof over our heads. And not a care in the world. You can't beat that with a stick.

And we never called ourselves a cult.

But I can already see it in your eyes, the sympathy just isn't there. *If it was so great*, you're thinking, *then why not just stay there. Who cares? Why'd you ever leave, then—if it was so great?*

So maybe I should back up just a little bit further. I'll tell you about…

…the *first* cult I was ever in.

You probably remember the headlines:

CHOLERA BREAKS OUT AMONG GARBAGE EATERS

That was us. Two dozen souls roaming and bicycling about the Bay Area, longing to save and to be saved, carousing with the dirt, suffering our sins, communing with the filth, and all the while holding our heads high above the evils of this world even as our faces were buried in its decrepitude, moral or otherwise.

TRASHCAN CULT BITES OFF MORE THAN IT CAN CHEW

San Francisco was a chilly gray drizzle, day in and day out. We were filthy, we were cold, we were suffering for our salvation. Sleeping in dumpsters, squatting in alleys, foraging behind supermarkets—subsisting off of the exorbitance of the damned, the refuse of the unsaved, the waste of the wasted.

But it didn't matter, we'd been chosen by God to lead a nomadic, Spartan existence in our quest for spiritual salvation and service. Dumpster diving in the pool of our Lord.

I woke to the damp San Franciscan chill seeping through my rain slicker, creeping through in cold, wet rivulets. My coat had absorbed the water as much as it had the stink of the trash I was sleeping in. We, all of us, wore identical gray-blue slickers. And all twenty-four of us were equally ragged and stained with wear, tear, and the garbage we made our nightly nests in.

As I awoke, I immediately knew that I was not well—my guts churned and writhed and burned, and fever had left my face clammy in the cold morning mist. My throat was parched and my body was wracked with fits and shakes.

I opened my eyes. The sun was a gray blur in a grayer sky. The walls of the dumpster rose surreally around me—a cold, lifeless shade of peeling red paint and black rust. Without warning something sailed through the air overhead and landed squarely between my legs. In a panic of activity a rat, startled from a filthy slumber of its own, scurried up and over the wall and out of sight into the world outside. I propped myself up on my elbows, fought back a rising wave of nausea, and looked to see what had been tossed in.

A fish head and spine lay serenely between my legs, cloudy myopic eyes glaring up at me.

A fistful of fish guts and scales splattered against the wall to my left. The fishmongers of Taylor Street were notoriously early risers. "Ey!" a voice from outside. "Get outta there!"

I held my breath, and didn't move.

"Ey, I'm talkin' to you!" the voice was angrier, but not any closer.

Just then two eyes and a wild mop of tangled hair peeked over the dumpster's edge. This was Jaybird. I smiled at the familiar bearded face.

"Hey sleepy. C'mon, man, you've been oversleeping again. We've gotta get goin', lotsa souls to save today. This fish-guy's startin' to get pissed. C'mon, we gotta go." Jaybird's usual monotonous mumble.

"I feel sick," I said.

"You can feel sick somewhere else," he sniffled, "This guy's wanting us outta here now. C'mon let's go. Souls to save, souls to save…"

…I'm interrupted by the telephone ringing. Again.

Another reporter. He asks me if there's any truth to the rumors that we're training monkeys to loot and riot, to rob and steal. I tell him no, I'm training them to sit still in church, and to represent in court.

Then I hang up on him.

Other questions on our Entrance Survey include *Where do you see yourself five years from now?* and *Do you prefer to live with others or alone?* and *Who are the Authority Figures in your life?*

But I was telling you about the *Garbage Eaters*. About life as a dumpster diver.

When I awoke that morning I knew I had reached a low point. It's hard to explain. We craved our misery, our decrepitude—to us, the worse off we were now, all the better our eternal salvation would be. That much had been drilled into our heads. That much had been made clear by our leader Bobby Christ.

"Stuart's come down sick, too," Jaybird said. "They took Stu over to the hospital today. Dropped 'im off in the emergency waiting room."

I was staggering along beside him and holding my side. A painful churning in my groin was causing me to swagger and sway, to list to starboard, veering me off of the damp sidewalk and onto the dirty strips of brown grass and discarded Chinese food cartons and the crumpled hemp-paper wrappers of veggie takeout.

"You look like you're drunk," Jaybird scowled, leaning closer and sniffing my breath.

"Drunk on life," I smirked.

"Drunk on knowledge," he returned.

"Drunk on God."

"Or just plain drunk."

"My head's killing me," I said.

"C'mon," Jaybird said, "Let's head over to Market Street. We'll grab Stu's corner."

Jaybird was walking his bicycle, a box of fresh pamphlets stuffed into the basket. The bike was old and rusted, the paint long gone. The rim of the front wheel was bent so that it rubbed against the brakes with every turn.

This was the daily routine. Wake up. Meet Jaybird. Head to Market Street. Proselytize and recruit. Dine in the dumpsters of Fisherman's Wharf. Then the hike over to Haight-Ashbury to pay our dues, hear our mass—the Word of God in our church in the alley, straight from the mouth of our leader, Bobby Christ. Invariably, Jaybird would rise before the sun and pick up our flyers from the twenty-four hour Kopy Kop on Polk Street. The ink would still be fresh, smearing on the cheap paper dampened by the cold morning mist. Then the walk to Market Street to witness and hand out our missives for the masses.

Only this morning I was sick. Sicker than the day before, and the day before that. Slippery cold sweat clung to my forehead and my throat was parched, my stomach whirled and heaved, my guts were on fire. When I tried to swallow my throat caught in a dry click. When I burped, noxious gas burned my nostrils.

Jaybird retrieved a half-eaten bagel from his jacket pocket. Fuzz and an unidentifiable twist of brown were stuck to the rancid butter smeared across the stale bread. The fingers of Jaybird's gloves had been removed (or had long since worn away or fallen off) and his skin was greased with the old butter. He gnawed on the hard bagel as he spoke. "We got two hundred missives. More'll be ready for tomorrow." He tore at the bread with his teeth and my stomach took another turn. "We hand these out to the morning crowd, and then lunchtime we go pray at the alley." He thrust the bread under my nose. The smell was overpowering, the brown smear had crusty black edges. "Want some?" he offered.

I jerked my head away. Sharp pains were beginning to creep up my sides, starting at my kidneys and riding up past my waist, towards my armpits. My long, knotted hair brushed the bagel and stuck in the butter. Jaybird pulled it back. "Fine then," he popped the last bit into his mouth, chewed noisily and swallowed.

Our hair was long and unkempt, our beards ratty and uneven. Our clothes were filthy and you could smell us coming a block away. Heads turned, people frowned, babies cried. We were used to it. We cherished it. Unlike these poor souls, we'd shed our material ways, we'd given up our earthly desires, cast off our sinful pride.

"Christ loves you!" Jaybird roared at a mother pushing a baby carriage across Van Ness St. She stopped in the middle of the road to stare and let us swagger past. Jaybird smiled when she flinched. Jaybird smiled with his *eyes*. That was one thing that made him somehow different from the others in the group. You could get lost in those eyes. He tossed a pamphlet at the woman's feet and then turned to me. "I shoulda dropped it in the baby carriage," he smirked, his wild eyes wandering back towards the frightened mother. "I'll bet she woulda freaked."

I'm trying not to throw up.

"God loves you!" Jaybird screams at a grandmother and her three toddler charges.

I'm trying not to pass out.

"Jesus saves!" he hollers at a businessman who pauses long enough to give us the finger. "God loves you," he screams, then turns to me, winks and mumbles, "Fucking asshole."

I'm trying not to see double, triple. Blurred vision. Cold sweat breaking out on my forehead.

"How's it feel to be damned?" Jaybird yells to no one in particular.

The pain in my sides has grown sharp, intense, throbbing. Bile rises slowly up the back of my throat, and...

...I'm interrupted by another reporter. I tell him we're digging a tunnel straight to hell. Then I hang up the phone.

Other questions on our Entrance Survey include *When you experience pain, do you feel it in your mind or your body?* and *Is it a sin when you masturbate?* (we don't ask them *if* they do, they *all* do).

Jaybird talked incessantly. To me, to strangers, to the sidewalk. To birds, to squirrels, to trashcans, to himself. But for all of his talking, he'd never had any real ideas of his own. No motivation. No driving force. No *raison d'etre*—he was like a hollow shell, an empty wind, poetry in motion. Echoing the sounds of the world going on around him.

Listening to Jaybird was like holding a conch shell to your ear to hear the soft, eternal sound of the ocean. There was an atavistic truthfulness to his words, if not a tangible meaning, if you catch my drift (as we used to say in San Fran)—even if he didn't realize it himself. He was wanting for meaning. He was searching for direction.

He desperately needed something to believe in. At least, when I first met him, he did. What I didn't realize was that back then, I was just the same.

"There's a good one," Jaybird pointed towards a college kid wearing a T-Shirt that read, *Shut Up Brain Or I'll Stop and Get A Q-tip.*

You'd think that arrogant jocks, fraternity guys, would be the hardest to convert. Not true—Frat guys are among the easiest recruits. They are highly insecure, and too dumb to know it. They're confused, ambivalent, stupid, disinterested—like those guys you see in the gym puffing away on cigarettes and benching two-fifty. Working on their perfect pects to cover the lungs rotting away underneath. Working on a perfect asshole-countenance to hide the souls rotting away underneath.

Jaybird was in the kid's face and pressing a missive into his hand. I was positioned a ways down the block behind him, ready for the tag-team approach should he decide to turn away or drop the prayer booklet, "Excuse me sir," grinning the shit-eating grin of the saved, "but I do believe you dropped this."

The kid seems interested, at least he's not running away, and that's half the battle. The Jesuit's say, "Give us the first seven years..." but I say give us two weeks and we'll have this guy emptying his bank account into Bobby Christ's pockets, disowning his parents, and eating out of the trash.

Jaybird was chattering and the kid was nodding. *I'm feeling another queasy wave of nausea creeping up from someplace down deep inside me.* All of a sudden there is shouting from across the street—the kid's friend coming to his rescue.

"Hey Oscar!" the friend hollers at Jaybird. *Oscar*—a nickname that the clever university students had taken to calling us, after the garbage can-dwelling resident of PBS's popular children's show *Sesame Street.* "Get the fuck away from him before I kick your ass. Friggin' dumpster jockey…"

Jaybird's rebuttal is cut off with an abrupt punch to the stomach. "Shut your prayer-hole!" the guy guffaws, slapping his friend on the shoulder and then leading him off down the block.

I say nothing as they stride past me, laughing. Two more lost souls doomed to eternal damnation.

The phone rings again—another reporter. I tell this one that there is a UFO following the Spahr Comet and that in the Year of Our Lord 2012 our cosmic brothers and fathers will be returning to take their lost children home. "If you can wait that long, that is," I say.

Other questions on our survey include *Do you have frequent nightmares?* and *Do you remember your dreams?*

"We're like Dean and Jack," Jaybird smiled. We were on Market Street handing out our missives to the masses. Jaybird was fishing a rare delicacy—a crab-puff stained with coffee grounds—from a waste basket on our corner. "Dean and Deluca," he popped the puff into his mouth and grinned. "Samson and Delilah."

"Donnie and Marie," I offer.

"Sonny and Cher."

"Peter and Paul."

"Pretty in Pink," Jaybird indicated the soiled pink rags beneath his raincoat.

Snorting laughter, my belly was filled with sick, uneasy pain. My parched throat felt cracked and dry. As a passer-by reached out to take the missive from my outstretched hand I suddenly arched forward as my stomach cramped, and vomited onto his shoes.

"C'mon," Jaybird grabbed me by the arm. "It's time to go, anyway. We shouldn't be late. Bobby doesn't like it when we're late, and if you're gonna be sick you can't ride on my handle-bars. If we don't leave now we're gonna be late. C'mon." Tugging my arm Jaybird steered me in through the exit door of the Haight-Ashbury trolley, ducking low and avoiding the probing eyes of the driver. Bobby didn't like us to take the public transportation, he preferred that we should walk on our own God-given feet. And he certainly would've given us a hefty penance if we'd actually paid the fare. But better early than late.

Jaybird tells me not to be sick again. I'm sick again.

Our leader was Bobby Christ. At least, that's what he called himself. He was known by other names—The Preacher In the Alley, The Garbage Man, Reverend Trash—but mostly we referred to him as Bobby, or Bobby Christ, or sometimes just Christ. He taught his disciples to loathe all of humanity except their own, not to have contact with their families, not to seek medical attention, not to bury the dead, and not to have children, for the end of the world was at hand...

...and the phone is ringing. Another reporter. He asks me if there's any truth to the rumor that we are in possession of an atomic bomb. "No," I tell him, "it's actually a neutron bomb. The buildings will all be left standing. A playground for my people."

"Are you shitting me?" he asks.

"Yes," I tell him. "You have been shitted."

A great man once said, *Give me something to believe in.* Someone else claimed that, *There's a sucker born every minute.* I suppose that I weigh in somewhere between the two.

Other questions on the questionnaire include *Would you describe yourself as the Teacher's Pet, Class Clown, Geek, Jock, or Brain?* and *Have you ever urinated/defecated in a public place?*

I was in the alley early, before our service. My pants down around my ankles, I was squatting and straining, feeling like I was dying from the inside out. Cold sweat slimed my face, my heart was pounding like it was going to explode with the exertion.

Jaybird was out on the sidewalk harassing passers-by and calling back encouragements. "*C'mon... push!*" he'd call. "You're almost there... Whew boy is that a *stinker* or what!"

This was the alley where Bobby Christ read us the Word, the alley where we gathered and prayed. Our holy temple. Our church.

We were accustomed to defecating and urinating where we worshiped, where we ate, where we slept—it was all a part of our holy outlook. We put nothing on pedestals. No porcelain thrones, no lofty temples. We were truly humble in our devotion—no thing in this world was worth any more or less than any other, no person more or less deserving, no construct holier that the next, and no material item (food, clothes, bricks, trash, diamonds) above being defecated on. We shit where we prayed and pissed where we slept and ate where we vomited. We were truly one with the world.

"C'mon," Jaybird calls, "You can do it. You *go*, girl!" he guffawed.

We'd arrived early for the meeting and the pain in my sides had grown intense. Unbearable. Nausea came in quick waves and I was struck with the uncontrollable, urgent need to defecate. I couldn't hold it, I didn't think I would be able to loosen the knot of my rope-belt and drop my trousers quickly enough. But when I did I found that my bowels didn't want to move. The burning urgency of an impending movement was there, but it just wouldn't come. For all my straining, all my sweating, all the glasslike pain in my gut, the movement wouldn't come.

Muffled voices out by the sidewalk. The other members were arriving. The service would start soon.

Pushing and heaving and gulping air into my fevered lungs I strained. Shifting from foot to foot, pressing with clenched fists at my abdomen, I tried to coax the feces down, massage it out, force it from my body.

"No shit!" Jaybird exclaimed. "Hey," he called back to me. "Stuart died. And Josh and Sebastian are in the hospital too. They're saying it's cholera. Ain't that the shit?"

Cholera. Fear struck me as I squatted there straining and pushing and groaning. *Cholera.* The meeting would be starting soon. Stuart was dead. Joshua and Sebastian were sick. *Cholera.* Suddenly I knew beyond a shadow of doubt that I had cholera, as well. That my days were numbered.

"You all right back there?" Jaybird called.

I wouldn't go to the hospital. I wouldn't call my parents. I would accept my fate, I would embrace my future. I would just lie down in my dumpster and die. A sudden calm came over me...and my bowels exploded.

With all the bloody gore of a virgin birth I emptied myself onto the floor of our alley, the alter of our temple. I fell against the wall heaving for breath as Jaybird called out, "Is it a boy or a girl?"

It wasn't cholera.

It was worms. Dozens of them. *Hundreds.* Long spaghetti worms, short spiked maggots. Eyeless and wriggling, my feces was filled with them. They clung to my thighs, biting and sucking, trying to burrow back into my skin. The smell was overpowering, and I vomited again. The vomit was full of worms. Blood and worms.

I guess you can call it a crisis of faith. But after the worms, I left the *Garbage Eaters.* I left without a word. Twelve more members came down with cholera in the following weeks, and ten of them died.

I'd heard that, after the smoke cleared and the media frenzy over the cholera outbreak had died down, Bobby Christ took what was left of his group and made the move up from eating garbage to selling hot dogs.

Upward mobility. Pushing carts around the city. The entrepreneurial spirit. The American Dream.

Prayers and scriptures printed on the napkins:

1 Corinthians 6:13 Food for the stomach and the stomach for food; but God will destroy them both. The body is not meant for sexual immorality, but for the Lord, and the Lord for the body. Would you like a Coke with that?

Acts 15:20 Instead we should write to them, telling them to abstain from food polluted by idols, from sexual immorality, from the meat of strangled animals and from blood. Here. Dab the ketchup from your chin.

A prayer with mustard and kraut. Salvation on a bun. I don't want to think where they got the hot dogs.

What did the believer say to the hot dog vendor?

One, with everything…

After dumpster diving I was never able to break the habit of checking my shit after every bowel movement, scouring it for any sign of parasitic infection. You can take the man out of the garbage, I suppose, but can you truly take the garbage out of the man?

In any case, the germ was planted, the idea seeded. The worm, as they say, had turned. I would move on to bigger and better things. Eventually, I would start a cult—a *group*—of my own. Salvation was there to be had, and I would have it on my own terms.

You might not be able to teach an old dog new tricks, but if you can teach a monkey to smoke cigarettes (and a great many laboratory chimps *do* smoke cigarettes), then I suppose that the human mind is capable of all sorts of things.

Passion is the hardest taskmaster, and…

…the phone is ringing off of the hook.

On the widescreen HD television, a news report shows me that my building is surrounded.

On the telephone another reporter accuses me of mass murder. "Mass liberation," I correct him. "Mass enlightenment. Cyanide, not suicide." As Pooh's pal Tigger so eloquently says, *You can't* bounce *the bounce, if you can't* pronounce *the bounce*...hang up.

All around me are the bodies of the believers. Foam on their lips, lifeless eyes rolled up to the whites. Empty husks—they remind me of old shoes strewn on the shoulders of the highways—lost, alone, abandoned. You've seen the shoes on the sides of the road. Many are left behind by accident victims. Many still contain feet. Stop and check if you don't believe me—I'll make a believer out of you yet.

Other questions on our Entrance Survey include *Are you currently taking any prescription medications?* and *Do you have any health issues that we should be aware of?*

On the widescreen HD television helicopters are circling the building.

The walls are sound-proofed, but through the TV's speakers, in *Dolby Digital Surround Sound*, I can hear the FBI and FDA bombarding me with pleas and with threats, with disco music and nerve gas, with rubber bullets and smoke. They're creeping closer, worming their way in.

Parasites in shit.

Another symptom of another disease.

Jaybird comes in, wearing his suit jacket over the obligatory sweatpants and sweatshirt, *Nike* sneakers—the tweed lapels are a step up from the ruddy garments of his garbage eatin' days, a badge of authority and seniority over the other members my group.

"Shit man, you watchin' the news?" he asks me.

"It's time," I tell him.

Without a word he takes a *Tic-Tac* shaped pill from the bowl on my desk. This is the Moment of Truth, the *Pepsi Challenge*. Jaybird, smiling, pops the pill and winks. He's my best friend. "I'll see you on the other side," I promise him.

The smile freezes on his face as he dies.

Drinking the cyanide. Popping the pill. Pulling the noose. All symptoms of a disease—a disease of the heart, of the mind, of the brain, of society. Life is fatal. We are all terminal patients.

I balance the pill on the tip of my finger. I roll it back and forth in my palm.

On the widescreen HD television a vaudevillian nightmare of a clown is selling hamburgers.

Forgive me, but I love the Big Mac. I've been in a vegan group and I've eaten my share of garbage, but when it all comes down, I do love my meat. And I'm a sucker for the secret sauce. Hey, what can you expect? I used to eat garbage...

Call it an Epiphany. A *Revelation*. A Moment of Clarity.

The multi-national commercial media conglomerate images are too good to be true. We couldn't ask for better symbols of the apocalypse, the Reckoning, of salvation, rebirth, life, death, whatever.

I take the pill between my thumb and forefinger and hold it up to the light.

Slice my wrists on the *Nike Slash*.

Secret Sauce for the Soul...

Jesus on the cross—crucified upon those *Golden Arches*. Here to deliver us from...what?

Deliver us from this mortal coil? This mental hell? This societal trap? We don't need Jesus or hamburgers to do that.

We're all going to die no matter what we do or don't do, or what we eat, or what we wear, or what we read.

I can feel the pill melting in my clenched fist.

I realize what has been missing from my life, and what I still need. It's the here and now that is at hand—so why suffer? I am ready to take the plunge, the leap of faith, to *taste the rainbow*, dive headfirst into the biggest and greatest cult that there is...I am ready to *take a licking and keep on ticking*.

I am ready to become a consumer.

I am proud of it, and I revel in it.

The best part of waking up is cyanide *in your cup. It is time to make the donuts. I am the incredible, edible egg.*

There is *Charmin* still to squeeze.

It's time to *Be all that you can be* and *I feel Grrrrrrreat!*

I will *Obey my thirst. Dude, I'm getting a Dell.*

Our consumerism separates us from the animals, it segregates us from the damned. It is all that keeps us above the parasites and disease.

I met David Koresh in a bar once. I don't know if it was *really* him, but he claimed to be. It doesn't really matter, I suppose—What matters is what he taught me.

When he told me who he was (or at least who he believed himself to be), I asked him the same question that's probably at the tip of your tongue, too:

How was it that he wasn't reduced to cinder when Janet Reno fire-bombed the ranch.

I expected some sort of religious mumbo jumbo for an answer—the usual rhetoric about reincarnations and second-comings (there's a joke that Jaybird once told me: Second comings are rare in sex and even rarer in religion!) I expected Mr. Koresh to describe in great detail having 'risen again' and explain how he was starting a brand new fold and was I interested—but what surprised me was that he didn't say any of that.

Three words were all he said. Plainly and simply.

Quite possibly they were the most important three words that I ever heard.

"*Secret underground tunnel*," he'd said. "We slipped out and disappeared."

"But the—"

"The bodies?" he finished my question. "Don't ask. You don't wanna know." Trust me. I did and I didn't, if you know what I mean. I left it alone.

I strike the match and drop the burning stick onto the wrinkled shirt of Jaybird, my friend. His dead eyes are still smiling, even as the flames lick his lapels.

The phone is ringing. I let it ring.

* NOTE: While complete in and of itself, The Garbage Eaters is actually a small part of a much larger work-in-progress—a novel tentatively titled Believer.

Sacrifice
by C.J. Henderson

HERBERT SAT AT the kitchen table, unable to eat. The television before him blared on and on —its icy glow ruining his digestion, stealing appetite from his empty stomach. He had turned it on, hoping the scheduled comedy might take his mind away from the world around him. Herbert had forgotten the news briefs which started off every hour. He pulled at a hangnail while the screen assailed him.

TWINKIES INJECTED WITH CYANIDE —TEN DEAD IN JERSEY NURSERY SCHOOL...

The television sat at the end of the metal table, its cord trailing off somewhere into the books on the shelf behind it. Beaming out at Herbert, it offended him daily, taunting him with ever-increasing numbers of blandly different unthinkables, daring him to turn it off—to even turn away.

"I won't," he thought. "No matter what it makes up. I won't give in."

Herbert unfolded his arms and pushed his rapidly cooling Kraft Macaroni & Cheese Deluxe Dinner away from himself, down the table—out of reach.

NO CLUES IN THE WILMERDING REST HOME ARSON CASE...

Somehow, he just did not feel like eating.

"There's no avoiding it," he admitted. "I just haven't done enough."

Herbert shuddered at the thought. He wondered if enough could be done—if anyone could do enough. He had tried. God—how he had tried. At least, he thought he had. Each time the world had escalated its attempts to cave in on itself, so had his efforts to put things aright. More sacrifices—a greater effort...

MORE AT ELEVEN ON THE...

Stretching out, straining to reach to the end of the table, he clicked the set off in mid-tragedy, chewing his nails as he wondered at it all.

Mary had decided to cut her hair again, shorter than the last time. She snipped at it randomly—without any thought set aside for style or appearance. Although she had not left much the last time, she did manage to find some loose bits to clip—shears pressed into the sides of her head, angling after this fast-growing follicle or that one. Looking at herself in the mirror, staring at her handiwork, she wished she had not thrown out every last cigarette—was glad that she had.

In the end, it had been such a little thing to give up. Anything to get back at the radio.

FOUR MORE WINTER WAR CASUALTIES WERE DISCOVERED TODAY, FROZEN TO DEATH IN THEIR HOMES, VICTIMS NOT ONLY OF THE COLD, BUT OF THE CITY'S MERCILESS UTILITY BARONS...

Anything to keep her mind off the world locked outside her door. She had passed on going to the play with Frank, even though she did like him and he had seemed very secure about the whole thing. Something had warned her, however. Something had let her know that the streets just were not the place for her to be. Something made with Japanese technology and German plastic bought on Canal Street for ten dollars which nightly turned the key in the lock of her warm, secure cell.

...TAKING HIS OWN LIFE AFTER KILLING HIS WIFE AND THREE GIRLS...

She had not noticed over the last months—not really—how her hair had started getting shorter, and then shorter, and her nails, shorter, and her meals, smaller, and well, who really needs cigarettes, anyway—I mean, the way the world is—

Joe had heard enough. The nightly news had only been a rehash of the slop that had poured out over him from his paper on the way home—more details dripping off the pages and out of the set like broiling fat falling into a fire. It was bad enough that everyone in the office had been talking about it. *Talking.* There was a euphemism for it—

"You mean those people in El Paso?"

"Yeah. They stuffed the drugs inside ketchup bottles."

"Four dead—right?"

"Yeah. Pretty spicy stuff, huh?"

And then the laughter. Four dead in the morning. By the train ride home, and the evening paper, two more had died, making all the jokes funnier by fifty percent.

Turning the TV off with the fingers remaining on his right hand, Joe left the den, heading for his bedroom. No wife waited anymore. Even his dog had deserted him, frightened by the morose, continually cynical atmosphere which had settled around his master and then spread outward through his home and all the things in and around it.

"Maybe Lucky didn't run away. Maybe he was only stolen," Joe whispered to himself. "Or killed."

Forsaking his bed, Joe pulled a blanket from it and then curled on the floor in the black, shivering in his chilly darkness. Duty now for the future, he thought, smiling weakly, trying to fit the edges of his blanket around and under both his rear end and his feet.

Herbert sat in the kitchen, still at the table. Tears ran down his face—slow but unstoppable. Nothing he ever did was enough. Maybe the axe would help—maybe. But, if he was wrong, said the little voice in the back of his head, there would be no second chance.

"No second chance?" he asked the air in a small, confused voice. What could he be thinking? There was always a second chance. Clicking his set back on, he watched the small white dot in the center grow in size.

MORE BOMBINGS IN THE CENTRAL LOWLANDS FORCE UN TROOPS TO…

The picture faded away as he clicked the screen back to blackness. *There's no reason for all of this*, he thought. *I've just got to make a bigger sacrifice. Something they'll all notice. Something worth the effort.*

Lifting himself from his chair, he went to the drawer in his desk where the tools were. He considered the chisel and several of the planes for a long moment before shutting the drawer again. Then, turning to the umbrella stand next to him, Herbert pulled free the saw standing in it, bracing his leg against the chair next to his dresser.

After the eye-crushing pain of the first few strokes, he suddenly found he could not move the saw. Forcing his eyes open, he spotted the problem immediately. Pulling the blade upward, he untangled the pant threads caught in its teeth. Then, with a path cleared, he set back to work, grimly clamping his jaws and bubbling lips together, gamely sawing stroke after stroke, ignoring the swooshing sound and the bone powder and the blood until he had finished his work and had toppled to the floor.

Maybe that, he thought. *Maybe they'll notice that.*

But, even as he fell off into unconsciousness, Mary's radio kept reporting its grim fascinations, and Herbert just kept wondering—as did Joe and the army of their fellows, all sawing away—just how much grist the mill demanded.

19: Trial

by Claudette Rubin

For Jes.

THIS IS THE circumstance. A man has been kidnapped. His livelihood was in danger and he liked it. Unfortunately the *it* refers to his livelihood. The man was Dan Rather and he was sitting at a table with a monopoly board before him. His ankles were tied together and he had a bruise on the right part of his forehead. He appeared highly subdued and stared at Vermont Avenue. On the kitchen counter across from Mr. Rather was a video camera, pointing at him, and what's displayed is also broadcast on the Internet.

"It was either this or Six Flags over Raleigh," said Tom, sitting at the table on the right of Mr. Rather. Seated to Mr. Rather's left was Connie, whose eyes were steadily fixed upon him as if he were an Asian American living in Connecticut.

Mr. Rather removed his line of sight from the board and looked at Tom. "What do you plan to gain from this, son?"

Tom pretended to walk the game piece dog and replied: "You know," his eyes widened as he twice bit his tongue and took a large sniffle, "my crystal ball's in the shop." A criminal associate—Peter—sat on the couch and began to watch a film with his considerably more than zaftig madam friend, Greta. Mr. Rather's head patiently engineered itself back to a level where firm gaze could straightly take place on the board again. He thought of Willie Nelson. Tom proposed to play teacher before setting underway with Chance and dice. "As long as eight or nine thousand people cry at my funeral, I'm happy…that's how grownups say hi," and he waved slowly from left to right in an unsuccessful attempt to regain full, clear attention from the victim. He and Connie looked on at the newscaster as if he were a sleeping, exotic cat in a cramped but fairly comfortable pet store cage. Tom pointed with sober mind and body, but with drunken finger, to the couch. "That's Peter, God's gift to the Betty Ford clinic. A has-been that never was, you might say." He laughed naughtily.

Peter spoke between beef jerky bites: "Yeah I'm shit. I'm shit and haaaaaaaaaa, yeah." His attention stayed on the film.

"Ridiculous amount of self-deprecation you do. I mean…get over getting over yourself," replied Tom.

The beef jerky was yummy. "Sure." Yummy.

Tom felt introductions were satisfactory and tried to teach more. "I say words with five syllables, some with two. I've been known to say conjunctions with a word only." Mr. Rather remained silent and circumstances notwithstanding, expressively serene. This began Tom on a slow slant into an irked disposition. "I didn't think muteness paid so well in modern times." Silence still, just silence for the camera. "I mean, I think what you force me to think. I think you're a jerk." Tom looked at the camera, then to Mr. Rather, then to the camera and again back to Mr. Rather. "Can you jump in a tub of acid; for the children." Tom gave himself, Connie, and Mr. Rather six twenty dollar monopoly bills. "If you notice that something I say is inadvertently a haiku, please let me know." He smiled and shook his head. "No clue how to begin to explain the least bit of meaning in that." He chuckled, while counting more game money. "I usually barely know what I'm laughing at but it's fun." Connie removed her sweater and ran her fingers through her hair, while keeping attention on the seemingly meditative anchorman. "I extol thee, room temperature…remember Amadeus, baby?"

"Yeah," said Connie.

Tom placed the horse on Go. "How do you feel, Danny?" No reply, body movement; only Elizabeth Taylor's voice from the television. "You know…I failed my S.A.T. because of that question." The electricity flickered momentarily. "I can't read braille so if I go blind, I'm fucked…Danny?…Danny?" He sighed and started speaking with greater speed. "I had a dream. It would be awfully silly of you to misconstrue here, but…there was a large penis. With my Freud hat I say it means I want to be in a field with lots of tall trees.

Peter paused the film and walked to the bathroom. On his way past a wall mirror, he pointed at it and said, "Fuck you." Before closing the bathroom door he was heard mumbling: "Stupid-ass judgments."

Tom scratched his mouth and struck the table repeatedly with medium pressure. After a short silence he resumed his instruction. "If I'm not the biggest asshole on Earth, I'm at least in the top 1,100. When I'm shit, I'll say so. But when I'm a motherfucker, I'll say so too." He massaged his right temple with a pointer finger knuckle. A grimace was slight, but present. "Language..." He quickly transitioned to foulness again. "Je suis shit bowl." He looked Mr. Rather up and down, now transparently upset. "It's okay, keep squeezing your ass cheeks. I got lots of patience and crowbars." Mr. Rather's stoic concentration on the board was undeterred. "What are you...you...no, man. I don't buy it for a fucking second. A second passes, I don't buy it." More persistence on the part of the quiet man. He had no intention of offering the camera any direction of personality. "Well that's some sad, sorry shit right there." Tom pursed his lips as his anger granted him an inability to blink. He spoke plaintively: "Dickless marauder," he pointed at the camera, "Don't assplunger posterity like this." He separated the houses from the hotels and took a little laugh while looking at Connie. "That's both obscene, vulgar, and alarming." He jolted his face toward Mr. Rather and continued his perturbed sharing of erudition. "Go eat a jar fulla ass. I'll fuckin' whine and bitch until someone punches me in the face. Is that it, you fucking squirrel. I'm not at peace, I'm at pissed." He flailed his left arm in a high arch. "Each one'a you in a handbag go to hell." He gestured at himself in a way that appeared as if he were carrying his own mammoth imaginary breasts, and spoke mockingly: "Keep talkin. Keep movin your mouth you piecea shit? Thanks be to my fucking self...Language." He slapped himself in the face and sat back in the chair. "I'll now coincidentally become less pissed. C'mon let's play."

Connie put her elbows on the table and was anticipatorily pleased. "Remember when Brian jumped off the roof?" she asked Tom in a personal way.

He rolled the dice and grinned involuntarily. "Thaaaaaaaaat was one helluva goddamn helluva day. Heet dowgs." He moved his dog eleven spaces and paid for Chuck. After two moments he said to Mr.

Rather, "Aujord fuckin hui, man." As Mr. Rather picked up the dice, Tom again barked consecutively: "I was born without my virginity." Connie bit her lip as she watched Mr. Rather's eyebrows and the tiny dots of mostly shaved sideburns. "Ah to be young and have your dick work." Tom wasn't young necessarily, nor was he old. "I only dance naked. And horizontally. I call it the Fred Astaire get in bed and dare!" The game progressed and Connie soon owned two yellows. "Hey!" talked the Tom, loudly to her, "I enjoy sex with cardboard cutouts of you."

"I have two yellows!" she clapped.

Tom got up and whispered in Mr. Rather's ear: "I get the feeling now that every action she commits is premeditated and serves the purpose of entertaining my audience." He gave the camera a thumbs up and sat back down.

"What?" asked Connie, smiling.

"Nothin'." smirked Tom. "I have a coupon for your underwear drawer." Connie giggled and studied Mr. Rather's features. Tom shook the dice in his hand. "I think if I saw you for a few hours with a man that you like and watched his actions, I could analyze them and mimic them." He rolled, looked at her, squinted, and made fish lips for a second. "Yes I don't reckon time would elapse in great length before liquid presented itself." She gazed at Mr. Rather, unfazed. "Don't any of you love me? Why do I have to get piss drunk before any of you start to love me?" Connie got a good look at Mr. Rather, a good look at his head and the rest. She rose from her chair and took Tom by the hand. They went into another room where loud music was heard, and twenty-five minutes later they exited and came back to the table. Connie said she wanted to make a sandwich so she went to the refrigerator. Tom spoke to Mr. Rather in a personal way. "God is she gorgeous." He briskly laughed and sighed. "Very easy to fall in love with." He took a glance at the board and was confident Mr. Rather hadn't cheated. Peter and Greta had since ejected their film and swapped it for another Taylor epic, *Giant*. Tom was wrapped in kitchen visual. "Her body is deadly. Just like Mom used to make." He leaned closer to Mr. Rather until he was sure Connie wasn't within earshot. "That, sir, is what we call—without affection, frankly, mind you—an honor badge vag." Leaning back he said with higher volume: "That's one batty dame!" Connie turned around, peanut

butter covered knife in hand, and curled her lips up. Back to low volume
to Mr. Rather: "I flirt with every piecea ass I can find. See…" again he
tried to capture the silent man's attention but failed. "Key to a broad's
heart? Sustaining the juice. And that's an above the waist comment." He
dropped the dice on the board, picked them up, and continued like so,
as he waited for Connie to finish. "I get trix mixed up. I have several
true loves. And some false ones. The false ones go down." He thumbed
at Greta, sitting comfortably on the couch, and spoke still softly to Mr.
Rather. The light camera buzz sound was audible. "We meet Greta,
Pete says what a babe, I say are you kiddin? She may have eaten the
babe but c'mon. He says no I think she just really needs to go to the
bathroom." He looked at the couch couple to make sure they couldn't
hear. "He goes for that. Eh, whadya gonna do. Tell ya though…fatter
they are, the more perfume they wear."

Peter was unhappy after watching a few minutes of the movie.
"Give me Jimmy. Cause this sucks," he said.

"Any movie could be made decent with remedied improper edit-
ing," said Tom as he watched the film for a few moments before Connie
finally sat down. He looked at Mr. Rather confused and frustrated. "If
we can safely describe our actions here 'fun time,' are you enjoying
your fun time, Danny? You want Connie t'just stick a grenade in your
head and light the fuse? Hey…Danny…hey looka this. I used to have
seven hands," he raised his palms up. "Then I was like oh shit I'm a
freakbaby, my bad. And I chopped five off." Mr. Rather showed no
sign of interest and saw the board with humble, gentle eyes. "See that.
No?" Tom grinned and motioned to Connie that it was her turn. "Ah
my lung went laughing." He looked at Mr. Rather like a concerned
mother. "I'm a participating member of humanity. This…see." He
shuffled through his pockets and pulled out a pen. "I bought this at a
Safeway. Connie." He looked at the board, puzzled, "Who's got…I
thought Dan had Waterworks."

"No, I do."

"Oh." He turned attention back to Mr. Rather. "What's my best
opportunity for a successful litigation suit against you, while having
no grounds for one?" He sat with his mouth open for a quiet moment.
"Sometimes I wish I could look at myself cause I know I'm making a
cool face."

Mr. Rather ended his stare. "Is it money?"

"Money would hold more value for me, Dan, if it didn't grow on two trees in my backyard." Mr. Rather looked at him both quizzically and with contempt. "I am a baboon. You appear insane. I am an orangutan. You appear insane," Tom stared back with icy eyes, "I am an anthropoid pongid. And you, my pretty, with your little cutesy nose," Mr. Rather returned to the board and considered the situation untenable, "Appear insane to my way of thinking. I mean...Dan, Dan?...I'm not a doctor but...yeah, okay. Your turn, big fella." Mr. Rather picked up the dice and rolled a two. "Ooooh, yeah. You know, an important and interesting necessity is to proficiently manage the descent from a high, back down to shall we say, the unfortunate regularity of existence. Your turn, baby." Mr. Rather again looked at Tom. But now he wanted to relieve him of his life. "Are you lookin' carefully? Cause the same truth that's behind my eyes is the same that's in front of 'em." Tom's upper lip raised above his teeth for a moment. "I'm looking for facts here; if I insult you or compliment you it doesn't make any difference to me either way." He made a long sigh and sat back, all pooped out. "I don't know what I'm doin'. I'm just actin' with the universe." He screamed as loud as he could. No one jumped. "And the cowardly live on." Peter stopped the movie and laid with Greta, taking a nap on the couch. The electricity flickered. The scene had no shame. A grandfather clock in a corner near a closet chimed on the hour. A fish hid behind a small log in a bowl on a nightstand near the television. The kitchen sink was dirty but the camera rolled. There was an even-temperament at the table. If it weren't for the circumstance it would seem that a pleasant game was taking place between a retired fisherman, his son, and daughter-in-law. Tom rolled the dice again, as it was his turn, and they fell and rolled; one off the board but safely on the table. The dog moved seven squares.

The Legend of Jimmy Wad
by Vincent W. Sakowski

JIMMY HANSON WAS a sallow man who enjoyed little in his life save his famous people's phlegm collection. Being often sick himself and coughing up some of the most disgusting phlegm on countless occasions, he had built himself up from revulsion, to admiration, to appreciation, and undeniable love of his expulsions. Eventually, this love turned to other's expulsions as well.

It all started with a coughing fit back in the winter of 2000, when Jimmy was suffering from a case of double pneumonia. He hacked and hacked, soon missed the kerchief in front of his face, and a huge wad of blood and phlegm flew through the air and landed on his hardwood floor. His coughing fit over, he looked down at the wad, splattered and still running.

"Kinda reminds me of a nebula."

Jimmy liked astronomy a lot, and he knew what he was talking about.

"I wonder if I can save it?"

And so Jimmy sat on the edge of his bed, wrapped in his duvet and several Afghans, while he stared at the floor, and wondered how he could preserve the wad in all its beauty.

Time passed. And he coughed some more. But this time, Jimmy didn't even try to cough into his kerchief, and let the wad fly, just in case he couldn't save the first, or maybe he could hack up something even more fascinating.

"Is that a piece of my lung?" Jimmy asked, but with little trepidation, as his head was swimming quite a lot. "Maybe I'm just hallucinating."

Time passed, and, delirious, Jimmy passed out. Later when he woke, he had a revelation.

"At least I can take photos of them."

Jimmy stumbled out of bed, accidentally wiping out half of his collection in the process, and found his camera. He still had almost a dozen photos left, so he took his time and planned each shot very carefully, much like a professional swimsuit photographer—which was how Jimmy was thinking of himself at that moment. Again, a light bulb exploded in his head.

"I'll have to lay down paper next time. Maybe different colors. See what works best. How they dry. So many possibilities."

So, Jimmy gave his pneumonia little thought except for his new project, even though his affliction was almost killing him. His major concern was how his coughing could make him rich as an artist.

Later, after he had recovered, he showed a few of his framed "projections" to one of his "friends," Martin, at the office at lunch-time, without any preamble.

"So, what do you think?"

"Hey Jimmy, I'm eating here." Martin swallowed hard, and put down his egg salad sandwich.

"Just take a look. Please."

"Kind of revolting." He leaned in. "What kind of paint is that?"

"Ummmm."

"If you don't mind me saying, it just looks like you sneezed or spit on it, or something."

"Ummmm."

"Well?"

Jimmy held up his first projection. "Doesn't this one look like a nebula?"

"A nebula?"

Then another. "And this one like a comet streaking a cross the sky?"

"A green comet?"

"Wouldn't you buy something like this?"

"For you coughing and sneezing on paper? Maybe if you were the Pope. Or The Queen of England. Or some other celebrity…" Martin said with sarcasm, but Jimmy missed it, and again he was inspired like never before.

"I gotta go."

Jimmy gathered up his framed phlegm, and left for the rest of his lunch break to brainstorm.

Muttered: "Yes, famous people's phlegm. Now that would sell. But how do I go about it? I can't ask them for it. And there's something about the spontaneity...that instant of *pure creativity*...there's so much to think about."

So Jimmy didn't go back to work. Instead, he gathered up his camera, sheets of paper, little jars, and other assorted implements to help him in his quest for FPP—as he now liked to call it. Since he lived in LA, it didn't take him long to find many famous people, and soon there were lawsuits, and restraining orders and more—flying towards him almost as much as there was spittle in the air, and on his face. But Jimmy never gave them a negative thought, *especially* when someone spit at him.

"I couldn't have planned that better." He'd often say to himself as he carefully blotted away the stain.

Too soon, however, many famous people became wise to his real intentions, and refused to get anywhere near him, let alone within spitting distance. Other gold-diggers too, that totally lacked Jimmy's artistic intent were now suddenly out provoking other celebrities, hoping to cash in, but few were successful as they didn't have his purity of intention.

Then, when Jimmy had enough framed FPP, he opened his gallery to the public. His gallery consisted of his bedroom in the basement, with most of his things moved into the laundry room. He'd sent out tons of invitations, posted a sign out front, cut the grass, laid out cheese, crackers, and Kool-Aid, but no one came down the stairs. So, it was fortunate that he didn't have to pay his folks any extra for rent, or buy a license to sell his works of art. Jimmy, ever the optimist, stayed open the whole day, went from projection to projection, adjusted the track lighting again and again on each picture, just to be sure they were *just right*, and never gave up hope.

At the end of the day, Jimmy went upstairs, pulled down the sign, and closed the door behind him. Still, he smiled. Then he went and sat in front of his computer as it booted up.

"Thank God for eBay." He punched up his profile and checked how sales were going. While people wouldn't say it to his face, and wouldn't come down the stairs, Jimmy knew he was sitting on a gold-mine. He had no trouble sharing his art with the appreciative anonymous, as the minimum bids were greatly surpassed on each framed FPP, which included a certificate of authenticity signed by Jimmy.

"These people know true art when they see it." He sighed. "I love the electronic age."

Jimmy sat back and watched the bidding increase, and started to plan how he was going to replace all the FPP he sold. He knew it would be difficult, but he was up to the challenge.

Besides: "I don't want to saturate the market."

Wuornos

by Harold Jaffe

Dear Lee Wuornos,

My name is Helga-Lee Uberroth, I'm born-again. I breed horses and wolves and live outside Ocala.

You're going to think I'm crazy, but Jesus told me to write you. I looked into your eyes in one of those newspaper pictures and knew immediately that you were innocent. Then I prayed real hard to Jesus and He confirmed what I felt, in spades.

What I believe with all my heart is that if only the world would know the real Aileen Wuornos, there's not a jury in the entire state of Florida that would convict you.

You and me—we even have the same Christian name. You're Aileen, called Lee. I'm Helga-Lee. I know that is not a coincidence. God bless you, dear child. Please call me collect.

Helga-Lee Uberroth

She breeds horses and wolves and is a born-again Christian? Not your usual configuration.

She also waters her houseplants bare-breasted. She has a green thumb.

With or without breast implants?

Without.

What happens next?

Nine days after receiving the letter, Lee Wuornos phones Helga-Lee collect. Then Helga-Lee visits Lee in the Volusia County Jail. Condemned killers are lonely. The two Lees form a band.

Rock? Rap? Reggae? Zydeco?

Sorry. I meant "bond." They form a bond.

[pause]

Helga-Lee calls Wuornos child. But they're pretty close in age, right?

Helga-Lee is 41, Taurus. Lee is 36, Aries.

Bull and ram. Sounds like fireworks. This the first hard time Wuornos has done?

Noo. She serves 16 months for holding up a convenience store in Pensacola. Plus she spends a bunch of overnights in jails up and down Florida for prostitution. Remember, she's been on her own since adolescence.

She comes from a dysfunctional family, am I right?

You tell me. Her father, Leo Dale Pittman, is a convicted child molester who's beaten by other inmates and finally strangled to death in prison. Her mother, Diane, who marries Pittman when she is fifteen, abandons Lee and her brother Keith after her husband is imprisoned. The children—Lee is seven months old—are adopted by their rigidly moralistic maternal grandparents, Arnul and Britta Wuornos, and go to live in Troy, Michigan. Lee becomes pregnant at age 12 and is sent to an institution for unwed mothers. After delivering a boy, who is put up for adoption, Lee, 13, is on her own, smokin' weed, slammin' beer, crashing where she can, hitchhiking, balling johns. Meanwhile, her grandmother dies of lung cancer and her grandfather hangs himself from a pepper tree. Her brother Keith either jumps or falls through the sixth story window of an auto parts warehouse in Flint, Michigan. Diane, her mother, remarries for the fourth time and moves to Okinawa, never to be heard from again.

[pause]

When does the rock and roll lawyer get into the picture?

Helga-Lee advises Lee to dump her public defenders, who she claims are incompetent and on the take. She recommends Harvey Medved.

The Jewish Springsteen.

Medved is a sort of unorthodox private defense attorney in practice for half-a-dozen years in central Florida. He looks like a rabbinical student: fat, carrot-red hair, bushy beard. He does hokey singing ads for his law practice on TV. He smokes weed. In a former life he played bass and was lead vocalist for a hard-driving rock band called the Bellevues. Out of Queens, NY.

Where in Queens?

Flushing.

I had a feeling. Is Medved a Jew for Jesus?

No.

Does he water his houseplants bare-breasted with his titties jiggling?

No.

So what do the fat, rabbinical, weed-smoking, hard driving rocker-lawyer and Helga-Lee have in common?

They both end up making money out of Wuornos. Did they arrange a scam from the outset? Hard to say.

[pause]

At what point does Helga-Lee decide to adopt Lee Wuornos?

Soon after Lee testifies in court that she had sex with 250,000 johns.

Whole lotta penises. The court admits that claim?

Florida has something called the Williams Rule, which admits as evidence whatever information might establish a pattern. Technically, Lee Wuornos is being tried for the murder of Richard Mallory, but both her public defenders and the prosecution think they could make good use of the 250,000 johns. The prosecution portrays her as a sex-addict, moronically compulsive; the defense claims that all the abuse she suffers balling and blowing 250,000 johns finally reaches the boiling point.

Neither side questions the figure? 250,000?

Both sides think it's exaggerated, but maybe by not that much. One thing—probably the only thing—Lee has been blessed with is robust health. She was an exit to exit freeway ho who worked fast. She was known for how fast she worked. Plus she's been doing it since age 14.

In the clips I saw Lee Wuornos didn't look all that robust.

Well, her face was shot from all the booze, speed, rough sex, lack of sleep. You couldn't really see her bone structure through the prison garb. But Lee Wuornos is—was—a strapping, big-boned female. Very imposing. The opposite of her namesake and step-mom, the demure Helga-Lee Uberroth.

They're already tight. Why does Helga-Lee want to adopt Wuornos?

Could have to do with getting closer to the big money Lee is likely to make through books and articles and movies. The new law is that inmates cannot profit from their crimes, but if the money is channeled to her adoptive mother...

[pause]

You say that the robust Wuornos works fast. Question is, how does the demure, gentrified, born-again wolf breeder who waters her houseplants bare-breasted win over a tough customer like Wuornos so fast?

"Soul-binding" is how Helga Lee characterizes it in a *People* interview. "We're like Jonathan and David in the Bible," she says. "A chunk of her heart is with me, and a chunk of my heart is with her trapped in jail. We always know just what the other Lee is thinking and feeling. It's uncanny."

*The dollars from Helga-Lee's **People** interview —where does that go?*

Not just *People*. *Vanity Fair* interviews her. *The New Yorker*. *The Enquirer*. *Details*. Wuornos claims never to have received a dime from any of the publicity. Since it's unlawful to profit from your crime, I assume that if the money is not set aside in a trust of some kind, Helga-Lee pockets it.

Lee Wuornos has no living relatives, right? And she herself is about to be fried. So a trust can't be of any use to her.

True.

[pause]

And now we come to that significant other in Lee's life. Drum roll, please, for The Bottom!

That would be Tyria Moore. Bottom doesn't really do her justice.

Ty is a motel maid, but she's more than that.

Tell me.

Passion. Tender passion, even. That's the reason Lee remains so loyal to her?

Plus she smells good.

Who?

Tyria Moore. Doesn't Lee say that somewhere?

Probably. Ty is chubby, baby-faced.

She cops a plea.

Betrays Lee is what she does. But you know what? Lee refuses to incriminate her in any of the murders, and she never stops professing her love for Ty.

That's impressive in its way.

Together they live a squalid life. Ty's work is seasonal, meaning she's out of work about as often as not. And Lee ain't a successful ho. Even with her alleged 250,000 johns. Like I said, she's raw-boned and her manner is harsh, even hostile. Not the attributes that will make her good money on the highway. Which in turn contributes to her murderous rage. Lee and Ty rent cheap motel rooms by the week. Sometimes they sleep in their old Chevy pickup, or in deserted barns. They drink a lot of beer. They argue, sure, but there is love there. Lee calls herself Susan Blahovec.

How come?

It's the name of a classmate in junior high school that she had a crush on. Doesn't seem to interfere with her love for Ty.

What kind of love? SM? Blood sports?

No. No way. Maybe now and then watersports. After a night of slammin' beer. Lee drinks Coors Lite to keep the calories down, make her more appealing to the highway johns, but the thing is she drinks a whole lot and the watery brew makes her pee.

[pause]

Lee's accused of killing seven johns?

Right.

Where and when?

Between December '89 and November '90. From central Florida west to the Gulf Coast. Richard Mallory is first, the john she's being tried for. She claims he beat her and raped her. Forcibly sodomized her.

Is that how Wuornos puts it? Forcibly sodomized?

What Wuornos testifies at the trial is: "I told him No, but he—pardon my Greek, I'm a street person—fucked me in the ass which messed up my head. 'Cuz I don't do that shit."

She says that about all seven, doesn't she?

What she testifies is that Mallory violently rapes her. The other six attempt to rape her but she kills them first. In Mallory's instance it could be true. He has a history as a wife-beater and is a registered violent sex offender.

Registered where?

In the sovereign state of Florida.

[pause]

What's he—Mallory—do when he's not forcibly sodomizing hoes?

Used car dealer in Lake City. GMC and Ford. He won't sell, or even drive, a foreign car.

The six others?

Dick Monday, Troy Burress, Duane Spears, Chuck Carskaddon, Walter Gino Puglia, Pete Siems. Working-class stiffs looking for a quick hump. Or maybe a blowjob between exits on the highway. Are they all into sadistically beating Lee up? Well, the jury doesn't buy it. Each is shot several times in the front and back with the same Smith and Wesson .38 Police Special.

Has Helga-Lee ever blown a john in his American-made pickup while he's gunning it up or down the highway?

Helga-Lee is widowed and childless. I guess I didn't say that. Her husband was thirty-something years older and had money. She's into horses and wolves, not johns. She's never, ever used her mouth in a salacious manner.

[pause]

So when do Lee, Helga-Lee and the Jewish Springsteen finally converge?

Soon after Lee ditches her court-appointed defenders. They converge in the Volusia County Jail where Lee is being held. That's in Daytona, by the way.

Lee is impressed?

With Medved? Evidently. He's fat but he's smooth. He's Jewish so he doesn't have that macho thing Lee hates.

Medved takes over. Then what?

Lee intends to plead innocent by virtue of self-defense. The facts of Richard Mallory's wife-beating past appear to corroborate her claims of violent rape. But Medved convinces her to plead guilty.

Why?

He assures Lee that pleading innocent would fail but that a guilty plea, with the mitigating evidence of Mallory's attempted rape, would likely get her a reduced sentence, which, with good behavior, could mean she's out in five years.

She bites?

Reluctantly. Pressured by both Medved and her adoptive mother, Helga-Lee.

What's their real motive?

I'm just speculating. Get Lee executed so they can continue to make money from the movies, TV specials, books and such, without Lee's angry protestations?

Which is what happens, right?

Pretty much. In the process Lee turns violently against them, identifies them as her enemies along with the 250,000 would-be rapist johns. Along with most of American culture.

Lee Wuornos has it in for a whole lot of folks, right?

Ha. Once, when Helga-Lee and Medved accompany a British film director who wants to shoot a documentary on Lee to the Volusia County Jail, Lee physically attacks Helga-Lee and has to be restrained. It takes three guards to actually strait-jacket her as she is screaming at Helga-Lee and Medved. She calls Helga-Lee "a money-crazy pimp for Jesus" and Medved "a tub of snot." The film-maker records it all. The documentary, called *Women Do it Better*, wins a bunch of awards, including something at Sundance. The story is that Helga-Lee and Medved get a fat cut.

Evil. What finally happens at the trial?

The jury deliberates for less than an hour, then finds Lee guilty of first-degree murder. They recommend that Judge Uriel Blount sentence her to death in Old Sparky, the infamously malfunctioning electric chair. Which is what he does. As Lee is led out of the courtroom, she pulls away from the bailiff and screams at the jurors: "I'm innocent! I was raped. Scumbags of America, I hope you all get raped in the ass!"

You know what. If they all get raped in the ass they'll still be scumbags.

You could be right.

[pause]

Now that Wuornos is history, consigned to the Discovery channel, are the weed-smoking, bushy-bearded rabbinical lawyer and the born-again wolf-breeder who waters her houseplants bare-breasted still an item?

To be honest, my interest in the case flags after Wuornos is executed. What the odd couple has been up to post-Lee Wuornos, I can't tell you.

Unicorn's Revenge
by Greg Beatty

HERE'S HOW IT ends: with three hundred twenty-seven middle-aged men, and an isolated handful of women, found dead in front of their computers.

Here's when it happened: the thirteenth full moon of last year.

Here's how they were found: with a hole bored deep into them, in some cases driven clear through them, the wounds cauterized with anger. If the wounds hadn't been so deep, some of them might have lived, because the cauterization stopped the bleeding.

Here's what that is: irony.

Here's the only clue found at any of the crime scenes: a single semi-circular imprint in the paper scattered on the desktops, digging, in some cases, into the surface of the desk itself.

Here's how many officers recognized it as a hoofprint: three, two from rural areas and one who played the ponies regularly.

Here's what was showing on the screens of their computers: children with haunted eyes, ten, nine, six years old, half-dressed or undressed, sucking their fingers or getting their asses reamed from behind by a man whose cock is bigger around than their forearms, but whose face is blurred with speed or obscured by a mask.

Here's how hard the cops looked for the killers once they saw these pictures: not very.

Here's how much patience they had with the bitching relatives of the dead: not much.

Here's why it didn't happen sooner: market dynamics. The individuals who belong to pedophilic chatrooms and picture swap clubs are not, for the most part, the same as those buying filtering programs to protect their own children from Internet porn. Neither group overlap often with those who purchase programs that map the lunar ephemeris and correlate lunar phases with office designs incorporating feng shui.

Here's where the desks of the dead were set up: in the light of the silvery moon.

Here's what else was rare about the programs purchased: the Christians who designed the anti-porn programs prayed over them, for protection and vengeance. Ellen, the pagan who designed the office design programs had prayed for her little brother Jason, who she thought had run away but who had been found in bits and pieces that had never been identified along a county road in Georgia, 1740 miles from his home. The dead pedophiles had prayed for children, clean and pliable.

Here's what happens when different people pray: the prayers mix.

Here's how they mix: like vectors. The plea for the clean and pliable caught the attention of demons, who gnashed and wailed when cut off from the computers by the wish for protection. Ellen's prayer caught the smooth ear of one who protects the innocent, and who missed his virgin friend, taken from him by a businessman in the back of a car. He would have protected anyway, if he could, but he could not revenge himself until called.

Here's when it happened: at 9:49:17 PM Pacific Time, 10:49:17 PM Mountain, and so on.

Here's what happened when the prayers mixed: a unicorn, who had been asleep, was jolted awake, ready for a threat to the innocent, only to find he was alone. Except that he wasn't. He was twinning, tripling, multiplying, becoming ghosts and icons of himself, until he was diffuse enough to ride the electron flux of the Internet in all directions as he had for long years ridden shafts of moonlight. For a briefly end-less time, he romped, jumping firewalls like fences, and slipping between the grasping fingers of search engines. Then he spied ten thousand innocents, ripped from their childhoods and made fodder for dark hungers. He coursed through the shunts and relays that connect-ed the hovering images of children with the hovering hungers of the three hundred twenty-seven men and handful of women. Using the children's pain as purchase, he surged forward, driving his right foreleg, shoulders, head, and of course, horn through the screens of these computers and into these hundreds of chests that had heretofore housed only dark, demonic hungers. Withdrawing, the unicorn had three thoughts. First, how nice his spectral horn looked in the light of the moon. Second, how much he'd enjoyed this, and third, how he'd have to do it again sometime.

Here's who noticed: three technicians at different local power plants, who noted brief and anomalous power surges, then went back to drinking coffee.

Here's who else noticed: the pedophiles, who died.

Here's who wept: the unicorn, who had taken his revenge.

Here's who regretted the night: the unicorn.

Here's how much: not much.

Here's who wept for the dead: no one. No one at all.

Here's who it fed: the demons. Everything feeds the demons.

The Will of the Dresser; the Will of the Blender

by Kevin L. Donihe and satan165

"…and that dresser brimmed with great, great things!"

T HE ORATORICAL DECLARATION was bold and cunning. And dipped in truth. That dresser did in fact contain:
   1) a hairbrush
2) a wig of human hair
3) one ounce of cocaine
and,
4) one 100-pack of CD-R's

The man approached the dresser, caressing it with gigantic mitts dragged sensually across a lacquered top. He looked wistfully to the heavens and paid homage to a greater power that had both enlightened him and afforded him the opportunity to be amongst such amazing furniture.

Those in attendance watched and recoiled. His actions brought forth memories like a whiff of dog shit brings forth a mouthful of bile-laced spit. Women swooned at the thought of rapes encountered at the hands of this furniture giant. It was the will of the beast, they had been told.

Such feminine reactions emboldened the man. He rubbed the dresser with increased vigor. It clicked and popped beneath his fingers, but he ignored these sounds, even as they intensified. Instead, the man focused on the brilliant colors. Red, green, yellow and blue flashed beneath his eyelids. The flashes became swirls once the dresser rewired specific neural centers in his brain. Others, it shorted out. Gnarled and warty hands defied the mental chaos. They continued to slide up and down the satin sheen, working the wood into a paroxysm of oaken stimulation.

Seconds passed. A moan arose from the dresser's uppermost drawer and rippled through the auditorium in near seismic waves. The man smiled despite his bleeding ears. It wouldn't be long now. He groped the wood with greater tenacity as its surface adopted a springier, more yielding texture. In the back of his throat, the man tasted the first hint of furniture polish tinged vomit.

Good signs—but events were happening too slowly for his liking. It was time to get proactive.

The audience drooled as the man uncurled his now bi-forked tongue and slid it across the dresser. His spit left molten tracks in the finish. The oak unleashed a sigh of ecstasy; it fought no more. The dresser surrendered to the man's advances and allowed his left hand to sink inches into its side. It was amazing how positively *alive* the interior of a one hundred seventy-five year-old dresser could feel under the right circumstances.

Of course, those circumstances arose only once every seven to ten years.

Seven To Ten Years Later:

"Eighty-five dollars for the dresser, no more, no less," snarled a young man, no older than twenty-three. "And yes, that's my final offer."

Despite his age, Roger was a quick talker. He wasn't about to take shit from some used furniture salesman. Not in this dilapidated thrift store. The inventory was largely worthless, anyway. A worn sofa sat next to the dresser. Its frame looked arthritic. On the opposite side sat a lamp missing its base. One piece was priced at ninety dollars, the other at forty-five.

The storekeeper bellowed: "Fine, you want to play hardball in my store? You come into *my* store, and try to jerk *me* around? Get the fuck out! You ain't buyin' shit here today, son."

"Hold up there, we can work something out. I'll give you one hundred fifteen, and I'll pay in cash. How's that? I don't want any beef with you. You've got some really...nice pieces here. I especially like this dresser."

Roger placated the shopkeeper. It hurt to do so, but Uncle Frank was right. The Chauncer design on the inlays alone told him this piece was worth at least five thousand dollars. No K-Mart shit here. This was serious, pre-1840 British furniture making at its finest.

"Fine. Give me the money. I don't have all day, you know. I've got four or five people coming back to look at this piece. You see this? It's beautiful!" He referenced the custom vinyl sheeting that covered the top. Roger scowled. It was both amateur and ignorant to deface a prime piece of furniture history with the stuff.

"Uh...yeah. Definitely. Here, fifty, one hundred...that's one hundred fifteen dollars. Can I pull my truck in the alley?" Roger dug for his car keys and imagined the commission he would earn after re-selling this piece at his uncle's antique dealership in Syracuse. The dresser needed extensive restoration first. Patience and pocketbook draining—but a rewarding exercise nevertheless.

Roger was on the road minutes later, dresser in tow. He headed toward his condo and Tom, who awaited him there.

Roger and Tom's four-bedroom condo sat against a Long Island backdrop. One of those bedrooms had been modified to house the terribly un-well Sally James, another converted to a conservatory. Just past the main entrance ("Only feet from the elevator", the real estate agent had pointed out), sprawled a vibrant, panoramic living room. Exotic plants sat ensconced in each corner. A living menagerie, complete with platypus, adorned the top of a custom stereo/multimedia set up. An open, tree-themed kitchen, complete with breakfast bar, sat to the left. Genuine bark covered the walls like paneling and a canopy of faux leaves hung from the ceiling. Beyond, a snaking hallway ended in an aquarium and sea-life filled bathroom. A six-foot statue of Neptune stood in its center, wielding a trident. The conservatory extended from a third central hallway. Sally James' room was hidden in the condo's rear. It was the only room that could be reinforced without disturbing units below.

Roger opened the door. Tom sat on the sofa below a wall-mounted manatee sculpture. He looked bored.

"Finally! I thought you'd leave me sitting here all day. *Alone.*"

Roger walked over to Tom and planted a wet kiss on his cheek. "I wouldn't dream of doing that, hon."

"What took you so long?"

"I had to haggle with the shop keeper—some grizzled old bastard. But he came to reason. I knew he would."

"But at least you're back." Tom unleashed a toothy grin. "I missed you."

"I was only gone three hours."

"But I still missed you."

"Whatever. Just come outside; help me with the dresser."

After a few minutes of huffing and puffing—and a close call with a door facing—the dresser sat in the living room's center.

"So, what do you think?" Roger ran his hand across the top. "It needs a bit of work."

"You know I don't like old things."

Roger sighed. "But you can buy that albino kingsnake you always wanted. You know that, right? Uncle Frank agreed to give us a healthy commission."

"Shouldn't we pay off our debt first?"

Roger waved him off. "Maybe. We'll talk about that once we get the money."

"Just make sure he doesn't try to weasel out of paying."

"Yeah, really. But let's see if there's anything in here." Roger opened the top dresser drawer. "Last time I found a neat old book."

"And dust. You found that, too. I sneezed for weeks."

Roger squinted at Tom and turned his attention back to the dresser. He opened the first drawer. A spindle of blank CDs sat there. It was an odd item to find in a piece of antique furniture.

"What the fuck? Honey, did you put these CDs in here when I wasn't looking?" Roger was confused. They didn't even have a CD burner. And when would he have gotten the chance?

"No. Why would I do that?"

"I don't know. But let's see if there's anything else." Roger opened the second drawer and looked in.

"Anything?"

"Yeah. A wig and a hairbrush. *Weird.*"

Tom bounced in his seat. "Open the next one! Do it! I can't wait to see what else we've got!"

Roger did so. His mouth fell open. "Holy shit!" he shouted. "There's no way! There's just no way!" Roger withdrew a baggie of white powder from the drawer and held it aloft. His boyfriend, shocked and awed, stood soundlessly as the plastic glistened in the sun.

Despite recent events and terrorist warnings, there was little threat of anthrax in the condo that day. Either they were about to make a lot of money, get very high, or both.

Oh yes, there would be a party tonight.

Sally James was asleep, so she didn't hear Tom and Roger carry the dresser into her room so as not to damage it in a coke-induced frenzy. Sally James nevertheless awoke after hearing the door click shut. An antique dresser sat by her closet.

At first, Sally was too sleep-addled to realize something was amiss. She just groaned and farted before turning back on her side. Sally managed two additional snores before her eyes flew open and she reared up from the mattress, her body ramrod straight.

The dresser was back...she had just seen it in a particularly hot and fevered dream.

Though never particularly sane beforehand, this event proved too much for Sally James. She clutched her head. Her skull—it pulsed beneath her fingertips. Her forehead—it expanded and grew redder by the second. Her hair—it slithered beneath her hands like tiny snakes. Or worms...

"Goddamn you! Go away! Bother someone else for a change, you wooden *fucker!*"

And then she laughed.

Although agonizing, the sensation reminded her of a show she had seen. It might have been called *Ren and Stimpy*, but Sally wasn't certain if anything had really existed prior to the dresser entering her life. She *thought* she remembered a scene featuring Ren's pulsing, vein-ringed head—his brain having grown to hellish proportions due to the antics of a hideous cat-thing. The image had seemed funny years back, but Sally understood Ren's pain now. She felt it as though it were her own.

But did that mean she had to take the dresser's shit?

No, it did not.

Sally bared her teeth as she tore off her panties. "I hope you choke!" She threw them at the dresser.

But the dresser said and did nothing.

"Fine, be that way! But you're not going to ruin my nap, no sir! And when I wake up, you had better be gone! You hear me? *Gone*! Or I'll make firewood out of you!"

Still, the dresser remained silent.

"And be sure to leave some coke. You left me some in the dream, so I know you've got it. Sally needs her goddamned blow!"

Sally James harrumphed before returning to the mattress, the covers once again coiled around her six-hundred-fifty-pound frame. As sleep claimed her, a chorus of voices battered against her skull.

But that wasn't at all unusual.

Roger entered the bedroom on eggshells, hoping not to awaken the sleeping behemoth known as Sally James. The gay couple acted as caretakers for the mortally obese woman, as they had for years now. It was part of a humanitarian program they had enrolled in to pass the time. The affluent life-partners were something of a pair of philanthropists, both with a keen emotive ability to feel for the less fortunate. According to her doctors, Sally didn't have long to live and, although he knew it to be immoral, Roger secretly awaited her death.

He tiptoed across the room to the chair beside the dresser. He wanted to get a copy of National Geographic and show his boyfriend an article. It concerned an offshoot Peace Corp organization he was eager to join. Roger held his breath, doing his best not to awaken the beast that snored not three feet from him. Just then, Sally mumbled something: "No...no...I don't want to be your bride. I don't care what other women do. I don't believe in you...Leave me alone...*I hate you!*" And, with this, the fat slob tossed and turned in her reinforced bed. Roger first saw and then smelt the sweat that coated her upper lip and underarms. Holding back bile while jawing nervously due to the coke, Roger grabbed the magazine and bolted. In the hall, he heard the phone ring twice, and heard his boyfriend answer it.

"Hello. Uncle Frank! Yes, I did get the dresser. One hundred fifteen. That old fucker wouldn't budge. No. No. Yes, he did." Roger wiped at his nose and tapped his left foot nervously. "Uh...no, now isn't a good time. Yes, Sally is sleeping. No, it's not that. I'm just really busy. Well, you're going to have to get used to my sexuality, that's just the way it's going to be. Okay. Okay. Sure. Tomorrow it is, then. And I'll let you see the dresser. No, noon's no good. Listen, I'll call you, okay? Okay. Goodbye."

Meanwhile, the coke lay in a pile on a small hand mirror. Residue coated its surface and lodged itself in the grooves around the frame. Roger stole a kiss from his passing significant other and then rubbed a fingertip full of powder into his gums. He shuddered briefly from the amphetamine kick and then shuddered a second time as he heard wood splinter.

Roger went cold. What if Sally James had fallen into the dresser? The thing would be reduced to ribbons and Uncle Frank—known for his temper—would be *very* displeased.

But Sally James couldn't get out of bed without help.

A second later, another crash—and the young man and his boyfriend made a beeline toward the bedroom.

Roger threw open the door and bolted into the room. Tom followed close behind. Both were halfway to Sally's bed before their brains registered what was happening and stopped their feet.

"Holy fuck shit!" Tom screamed and pissed his shiny leather pants.

Sally James writhed on the floor *in* the dresser. It was impossible to tell where the dresser began and where Sally James ended.

Roger and Tom stood transfixed, too shocked—and high—to register further emotion. The dresser itself had adopted a fleshy color. Roger thought he saw tiny hairs growing from horrid, elongated pores in what was once wood. One of Sally James' eyes—now twice its size— blinked at the two men from the bottom drawer. Her breasts rested atop the dresser like a flaccid hat.

Both men heard her voice: "Yes!" she shouted, seemingly from all directions simultaneously. "Give it to me, baby! Take me to the stars!" Sally moaned in ecstasy. Her gargantuan, disembodied breasts heaved. Tom nearly vomited.

The box undulated, becoming moist and sponge-like. Sally James unleashed a sigh of primal sexual release. No sooner than the sound ended did the fleshy color seep away. Once cavernous pores dilated and the breast-hat deflated like a balloon. The single eye winked one final time before going dead.

And then the dresser appeared normal again—like any other piece of non-sexual/non-supernatural pre-1840s home furnishing.

Tom turned to Roger. "Is...is Sally...*dead?*"

He almost said *I hope so* before closing his mouth and rethinking his words. "I don't know." Roger's lips turned into a sudden smile. "All I know is that we've got ourselves one cool ass dresser!"

"Roger! That's not a very humanitarian thing to say!"

He glared at his lover. "To hell with humanitarianism; this thing could be our ticket to ride!"

"*What?* Sally James may be dead and you want to sell this thing to some sideshow!"

"Fuck the sideshow! This thing'll be worth millions if we can find the right buyer."

Tom spent a moment in thought. "But what if the dresser tries to get *us*? Shouldn't we be careful?"

"You heard Sally. She was *enjoying* it! I don't believe we have anything to worry about. I think we have to invite the dresser in before it can do anything to us. Kinda like a vampire..."

Tom just nodded.

Roger turned to his lover. "So, are you with me in this? What do you say?"

Uncle Frank wandered through his empty and darkened antique gallery, can of Pledge in hand. He rested for a moment after cleaning a Washington-era armoire, leaning against it on his elbows, careful not to leave fingerprints.

Standing there, Uncle Frank recalled the day he spotted the dresser in that shitty thrift shop. A man of his reputation would have aroused suspicion had he entered and attempted to purchase the dresser himself. He just hoped Tom had the good sense not to damage it during the move. This piece was going to take a substantial amount of work before he could re-sell it; the last thing it needed was more damage.

Two customers all day, this couldn't go on. He knew customers would die for first dibs if he could fill the showroom with furniture of the Chauncer dresser's caliber. That would prove Frank Smitherson wasn't washed up. He'd make a comeback. He'd show them all that he couldn't be undersold, and that his inventory could keep up with the best of them.

"I'd like to see those fucks at the Franyan Gallery come up with a Chauncer…I'll show them, too. And grind them into the pavement if needs be."

"Hello? Are you open?"

Uncle Frank turned at the sound of the voice. He sealed his lips, hoping his third customer of the day hadn't seen him talking to himself. An older yet well-built man stood in the doorway. His red hair blazed beneath a long and unkempt beard. His hands were massive, physically intimidating like the rest of his body.

"Oh, of course! Please come in! Is there anything in particular you were looking for? Let me assist you, or feel free to peruse our wide inventory yourself!" Uncle Frank stood back, his hands folded behind him, a wide salesman's grin spread across his face.

"Actually, yes. I'm looking for a dresser. A Chauncer design, but it's been refinished over the years…I don't see it here. Do you have it in back?" With that, the man stepped toward the door marked EMPLOYEES ONLY.

Uncle Frank's heart and mind raced. This man was already interested in buying the piece, and he didn't even have it yet! It was amazing how popular that dresser had become. He'd make a mint.

An odd and scary thought soon dashed his dreams of a quick buck: *how could this man know*? No one knew, except Roger, Tom, and himself. That thrift shop keeper didn't know he had sent his nephew to buy the dresser, did he? And what if the bastard had realized his mistake? Was this one of his goons?

Nothing made sense. It took awhile, but Uncle Frank's salesman nature eventually regained control. "Uh, no, but we do have a number of similar pieces. Maybe you would be interested in—"

"Listen. I need that dresser and I *know* you have it. I'm sure you think that I work for that thrift store guy—but I don't. And you're probably wondering how I could know about that transaction. Doesn't matter. There's no time to explain."

"Now listen here. I don't—"

"Give me back my dresser!" The man smashed his huge fists into Uncle Frank's face. "*Right now!*"

Uncle Frank's salesman mentality collapsed. Fight or flight instincts took over. "Roger! Roger has it! My nephew! I'll call him; you can have it back! Please!"

"That's all I need to know." The man offered a short bow. "Thank you and goodbye."

With that, he was out the door

Uncle Frank got up and checked his reflection in the mirror of an 18th Century French dressing combo. He grimaced at his bent and bloody nose. In a day or two, both eyes would be black and yellow. Uncle Frank opened his mouth. The bastard had broken three teeth. He groaned. It would take a lot of booze to make this feel better.

So Uncle Frank wasted no time. He reached behind the counter and withdrew an unopened bottle of whiskey. Then he withdrew a .45 Desert Eagle with a modified 18-bullet clip and shell catcher.

Uncle Frank smiled through split lips, cocked back the weapon, and downed the first mouthful of booze. As the alcohol swirled in his stomach, Uncle Frank saw the man's face in his mind. Then that image was replaced, one after the other, by the face of every antique dealer who had wronged or misjudged him.

"Yes, you can have the dresser," he wheezed. "No problem, fuck-face."

Roger watched his lover sit in the lotus position on the floor, filling his nostrils full of white powder. He smiled. Tom had played stubborn, but he eventually changed his tune, just as Roger knew he would. Tom enjoyed helping people—it gave him a sense of purpose and looked great on resumes—but his love of flashy, shiny things soon won out over his humanitarian spirit. Roger could only imagine what was now racing through Tom's mind—perhaps images of flashy cars and even flashier cock-rings.

The sky was the limit...

Tom dusted off his nose and looked up at Roger. "Hey, babe. Want me to cut you a line or two? I'm done for now."

"Sure." Roger took his seat by Tom on the floor. "I'm ready to celebrate."

"Could we wait before using that word? I still feel bad about Sally."

"Oh come on! I thought we'd gotten past this!"

"But she's gone and—"

"Are you telling me that you liked her chronic flatulence? And the smell! You couldn't go into her room without getting knocked on your ass! Are you saying you liked that, too?"

"No, but—"

"Be honest with yourself, hon." Roger laid his hand gently on his lover's package. "You wanted her gone just much as I did."

"*But I didn't want her absorbed into a goddamned piece of fur-niture!*"

"But it's better than a heart attack in bed, right? And, if she's dead, at least she went out happy. Isn't that what we all hope for?" he paused. Tom still looked forlorn, so Roger decided to clutch his lover's now denim-covered balls tighter, more reassuringly. "Think of it this way, maybe she's not dead at all. Maybe she's living in some alternate dimension—an alternate dimension where she's no longer fat."

Tom giggled.

"Yeah, that's what I want to hear. And keep smiling, too. You'll be able to buy *thousands* of albino kingsnakes when we're done!"

"But there's something that you haven't thought of…"

Roger withdrew his hand. "What's that?"

"We'll have to demonstrate the dresser's…uh…*powers*. What good is it if we don't?"

"And your point is?"

"Isn't it obvious! How are we going to get volunteers?"

Roger shrugged. "Maybe we can go to one of those suicide news-groups and—"

"*Roger!*"

He raised his hands. "I was only joking! And I've thought about this, believe it or not. I don't think it'll matter what the dresser absorbs, just as long as it absorbs something."

"Meaning?"

"I don't know. Maybe we can go to the pet shop and buy some-thing ugly. No cats or dogs. People might not like us using those. Maybe rats. Yeah. I think rats would be neat. Just think—a dresser brimming with a hundred tails!"

Tom's face blanched. "That's a little sick, you know."

"Not if it makes us money."

"Whatever. Rats are fine. Disgusting—but fine." Tom held out a mir-ror atop which rested two lines. "And aren't you forgetting something?"

"Oh yeah!" Roger reached for the mirror. "Thanks."

At that moment, a series of loud knocks sounded at the door.

"Yeah, that'll be fourteen dollars and fifty-seven cents. And thanks for the tip, Mr. Smitherson." The couple often ordered pizzas and other Italian faire from Pozillo's, the local pie-joint. Both knew Keith from repeated past deliveries as well as the occasional high profile orgy, which the couple hosted. They invited him in for a slice, but he declined. Then Keith noticed the men's powdered nostrils. He begged a 'bump' and left feeling revved up.

Tom walked the pizza over to the table, his body quaking. The coke had taken its toll on both men. As Tom brushed away the numerous snot-soaked tissues, Roger opened the box to reveal a 15" stuffed crust. Both dug into the pizza, neither affected by the usual loss of appetite associated with cocaine use.

"Damn, this is good," muttered Roger between bites.

"Hell yeah," Tom agreed, downing his bite with a chug of cola and a nose full of blow.

Something crashed in Sally's old bedroom just as Roger picked up a second slice and Tom finished cutting a fat line.

Both lovers looked at each other. Tom's mouth hung halfway open, exposing a mouthful of partially masticated cheese.

BASH! BANG! CRACK!

"What the hell was that?"

The sounds grew louder: BASH! BANG! BASH!

Tom cowered, but Roger took the initiative. He soft stepped toward Sally's room. Tom choked down the remnants of his pizza slice and wondered whether he should stop Roger or join the investigation. He didn't like potentially scary things. Roger was the strong one, not him. Still, Tom gathered up his limited resolve and scurried to catch up with his lover in the den.

Roger paused at the bedroom door seconds later.

"Do you think it's safe?" Tom whispered.

Roger shushed him and drew in a deep breath. He brushed away the authentic *euchatel* vine that served as a decorative, organic curtain. Then he threw open the door.

Tom closed his eyes, so he heard only grunts and groans. Roger, however, watched an old, red bearded man pull himself up through the broken and battered window.

That alone was odd.

They lived on the twenty-first floor.

And there was no balcony.

Almost a half hour had passed since the run-in at his store, but Uncle Frank remained pissed. He drove through the streets of

Syracuse, a .45 clutched in his free hand. A fifth of whiskey sat between his legs. Uncle Frank cackled. The firearm felt like an extension of his body. He imagined veins branching up from his arm and coiling around the gun. His blood flowed through its barrel now. The bottle of booze—it reminded him of his manhood...warrior-hard.

Uncle Frank ran a red light. A least six motorists shot him simultaneous birds, but he didn't notice. He was too transfixed by the beautiful, spinning shades of anger. Red and magenta spots flittered across his vision and pulsated with each beat of his heart.

"I'll show that bastard what's what!" he mumbled between gulps of pure-grain alcohol. "No big-handed freak is going to walk all over me—*and take my fucking dresser*! Hell no! He's just like the others! Bastards every one!"

Someone blew a horn. Uncle Frank assumed that was because he had just sideswiped an old lady...but that wasn't important. Thoughts of getting to his nephew's condo consumed him. Though too drunk and temporarily insane to know exactly where he was, Uncle Frank figured he'd be there in ten minutes.

Uncle Frank looked up from his lap, took note of the road, and slammed on his breaks. The car jerked to a halt at a red light, the first he had acknowledged in five miles. A woman in a late model Buick stared as he cackled and gesticulated. Uncle Frank turned to her, his grin wide.

"I'm the furniture king, baby! Woo-hoo! Woo-hoo-hoo, yeah! I can do *anything*!"

The woman didn't wait for the light to change. She sped off. Uncle Frank laughed.

Yes. The woman sensed both his virility and his dedication to taking care of business. These attributes swirled around him like a musk. He could have had her, he knew—if he'd only asked.

But the woman wasn't important now—he had bigger fish to fry.

"I hope you're already there, you bastard." He downed another shot or three. "And fuck the Franyan Gallery!"

"*Infidels*! What have you done!" the man screamed. Spit flew from his lips. His face flushed as red as his hair.

Roger drew in a deep breath and stepped up to the man. He wasn't at all comfortable, but Tom looked up to him and considered him strong. One glance into his lover's terrified eyes told him he *had* to show authority.

"Who the hell do you think you are? You can't just barge in here!" Roger decided to bluff. "And we've already called the cops!"

"Do you think local law enforcement can help you?" The man smirked. "My boy, you're dealing with something more powerful than your mind can fathom. You're dealing with the dresser!"

Roger sized the man up. He had a definite presence. His aura exuded purpose and, perhaps, berserker nuttiness. Probably in his late sixties, Roger figured—though he seemed strong for an older man.

Still, Roger was sure he could take him—might take a little while, but he could do it, especially since the guy appeared unarmed. Roger exhaled deeply. It was now or never.

He lunged.

Tom yelped.

And the man grabbed hold of his own hair and yanked his face down over his chin. Roger and Tom unleashed simultaneous screams as a hellish skull-face grinned back at them.

The man's denuded jaw clacked as he spoke. "Now do you understand what you're up against? The dresser gives as much as it takes. And I can already tell you've treated it irresponsibly!"

Roger turned to Tom and saw a wetness spread through his jeans. His lover had pissed himself again.

"Oh God! Oh shit! Put your face back on!" Tom scurried over to Roger. He shivered in his arms. Roger wanted to be strong for him, but the muscles he took pride in now felt like twigs.

"Please, sir" Tom moaned. "*Please*."

"Why not—just as long as you let me use the dresser in five minutes. The time has come, you see." The man lifted the meaty flap and re-covered his skull. Flesh resealed, making a sucking sound. "Today was supposed to be my son's first ritual—but he sold the dresser to a thrift store to get money for a guitar. A *guitar*!"

Tom gulped. "Did you...kill him?"

"Kill my son? Of course not!" The man sighed. "I only wish he had followed the family tradition. Maybe when he's older..."

"I...I understand." Tom stammered.

"No you don't understand!" The man eyed the couple. "And don't forget that! Just shut your mouth and do as I say!"

Tom nodded so rapidly Roger feared his head might fall off. "Yes, sir! You won't have *anything* to worry about! Hell, we'll even help you carry it to your car!"

"I didn't drive here. I didn't need to. Besides, I think this bedroom will suffice." The man looked around. "Nice décor, by the way. Very feminine—very *gay*."

Roger gritted his teeth, but the man continued. "I usually engage in ceremonial rape after the ritual. Good thing that's not mandatory, because I don't swing the way you boys do."

This was all too much. Not only was the guy an insane dresser-worshiping face-peeler, he was also a homophobe. Roger steeled himself. Though he knew it was a bad idea, he couldn't let the bastard get away with that insult.

"Yes, we are gay. *And proud of it.* But this isn't our room. This is where Sally James—uh—*used* to sleep."

The man's eyes widened. His composure shattered. "But the dresser cannot be around women! It will absorb unattended females!"

"But isn't that the kind of crazy shit you like?"

"Yes, but only if she's virginal! Tell me," the man demanded, "did the dresser absorb the woman who slept in this room?"

Tom turned to Roger. His eyes were pleading. "Don't tell him, Roger. Please...please don't tell!"

"If he's smart, he already knows! I really don't have a choice here, Tom!" Roger turned to the man. His throat felt lumpy, filled with sand. "The dresser ate Sally James. And no—she wasn't virginal." Roger paused. "Actually, she worked as a prostitute before...uh...she got fat."

The man's teeth clenched. "And just how fat are we talking?"

"Six hundred fifty pounds."

The man's hands became fists and Roger swore he saw red sparks flash in the stranger's eyes. "There's a six hundred fifty pound *whore* in my dresser! This is what you're saying, right?"

Roger nodded mutely.

"But the dresser must only take in pure offerings!" The man unleashed a throaty bellow before launching into a tirade: "You bastards! You assholes! Now I have no idea what's going to happen! *But fuck it!* I'll be damned before I let two fags stop what's meant to be!"

"Please, sir. Don't get mad. Please—"

The man smashed the wall with his fist. "Too fucking late!" He withdrew his fist and both men were stunned to see sunlight pour through the hole. "I considered letting you live, but you're going to die after I finish the ritual—*painfully!* I'll gut you from groin to sternum! I'll cut your balls off and stuff them in your friend's mouth! Then I'll cut your friend's balls off and stuff them in *your* mouth! Then I'll fuckin' tear both your throats out with my teeth!" With that the man smiled, flashing incisors that were now not only razor-sharp, but crimson.

"Hot damn, I was right! Ten minutes on the dot! "Uncle Frank bounded from the truck and fell flat on his face. He rolled on the ground for a few seconds before he managed to reorient himself. Still reeling, Uncle Frank made his way up the steps to the hallway adjoining his nephew's unit.

His eyes felt heavy and he almost passed out just feet from Roger and Tom's apartment. Realizing the man who had caused all his troubles might be behind the door, however, was enough to make adrenalin surge. With a groan and a blast of animal force, Uncle Frank kicked in the door. He charged through the condo, oblivious to the gaudy luxury. All Uncle Frank noticed was tons of noise over on the unit's south side.

He gritted his teeth. He hoped to God his nephew wasn't porking that 'friend' of his.

"*Please, God—make it be that man from my store. Don't let me see butt-sex. And, if I do see butt-sex, give me the strength not to kill Richard—or whatever the hell his name is.*" He burped and crossed himself though he wasn't Catholic. "*Amen.*"

Steeling himself, Uncle Frank charged toward the ruckus. The prayer had invigorated him and, for a few seconds, the world ceased its drunken swirling. Uncle Frank tore open the bedroom door, yet paused at the threshold as the world began to tip and swirl anew. As he stood there, swaying, he surveyed the room.

The prized piece of furniture lay on the floor. It swelled and undulated, as though breathing. The dresser still appeared wooden, but fleshy hints gleamed beneath the varnish. Uncle Frank didn't question the sight; his brain wouldn't let him. Time ground to a halt as he saw the man who had attacked him less than an hour earlier. He stood by the dresser, red faced and screaming. Roger and Tom cowered beneath him in fetal positions. Their nostrils were red and bloated above sweat soaked shirts. A moment later, like the winding of an analog tape deck's mechanical heads, time sped up until it matched the flow of events.

"You fucker!" Uncle Frank shouted. "That's my dresser! What are you doing with it! Why is it so fucked up?"

The man turned to Uncle Frank and sneered. "Well, the boys here said it was *their* dresser."

"What!" Uncle Frank stormed over to Roger and Tom, waving his .45. "Were you trying to hone in on *my* property? I would've given you a cut!"

"Don't believe him!" Roger stammered. "He's insane!"

"Yeah." Uncle Frank turned back to the man. "He's a freakin' nutcase. And I don't know what the hell he's done with my dresser! How am I going to resell it in *this* state!"

"But it's not yours to resell! It's *mine*!"

"The hell it is!"

"I feel it now, pulsing inside me. Are you feeling it?" The man paused. "I didn't think so. That's because it isn't yours to sell, much less feel!" He exhaled deeply and slid his hands down his thighs. "It's throbbing, I tell you. Throbbing like a lover's thick—oh my god! *OH MY G—*" The man's words dissolved. Foam frothed and boiled over his lips. Uncle Frank wondered if the guy was having a grand mal seizure. Body jerking, he collapsed in front of the dresser.

The dresser grunted, farted, and spat. The sounds enraptured the old man and he clawed his way toward the dresser's feet. His hands, still quaking, reached out to caress the softening wooden sides. He licked his lips in anticipation before another seizure caused him to bite off the tip of his tongue.

Uncle Frank scowled. The guy was a damned pervert. Nobody should touch furniture in that way. It just wasn't right. He turned to Roger and Tom—but they seemed too terrified to notice. Hell, they probably didn't even think what he was doing was weird. They were perverts, too.

The man didn't notice Uncle Frank's stare. He was too intent on getting to the dresser even as his body was rocked by spasm after spasm. Once he reached it, he opened his mouth and licked the thing. The man's tongue-stump caressed the box lovingly, but the act was short-lived. The man choked, gagged, and—in what seemed like a bad case of acid reflux disease—coughed up undigested vinyl sheeting and varnish.

His fingertips liquefied as they touched this goo.

A final spasm rocked the man's body. He jumped as though electrically charged and came down hard on the extended bottom drawer. He slashed open his face. More undigested furniture coating—liquid and solid—shot forth, staining opulent Pergo floors that Roger had polished the day before. A streak of feces laced the seat of his pants as he rolled amongst mutated wood.

This was too much for Uncle Frank to assimilate.

"You sick mutherfucker!!! I'll fuckinkillya for that shit!!!" He took a short, sudden lunge at the man. His eyes gleamed as he emptied the clip, but became cloudy as each bullet passed through the guy and plowed harmlessly into the floor.

The man arose, careful to keep his palm against the dresser. On his lips: a quiet intonation. Seconds later, the top drawer flew open and a pulsing green light shot forth, bathing the room in an evergreen glow. "What the shit is this!" The light arced down, focusing on Uncle Frank. "Some kind of fucking Christmas—"

And then his tongue dissolved in his mouth and melted down the front of his dingy wife-beater. Uncle Frank's eyes exploded in footlong gouts of aqueous humor. His hair blazed. Roger motioned to his uncle, but Tom held him back.

"Oh God, Roger! Don't go! Whatever you do—*just don't go!*"

Roger folded like a rag doll. Tom was right; there was nothing he could do. Roger looked into his lover's eyes—one last time—before returning his gaze to the spectacle.

He found his uncle two feet shorter than he'd been only seconds before. Dissolving from head down, Uncle Frank had become a half-torso with legs. Somehow, his body remained standing. It gyrated madly. His hips melted as his pants slid down his legs in a puddle of molten flesh. His red jockey shorts soon followed. Seconds later, Uncle Frank was a pool of clothes and quivering muck on the floor. Roger and Tom cackled at the sight. The events of the day had proven too much for them.

The man smiled as the couple laughed and laughed and laughed. He assumed he could use them without taking the usual first step. They were already out of commission. Still, he thought it best to do things according to plan. The man turned to the clock. No time to waste. He intoned another word and the light flickered from green to gold. Like the first ray, it arced down, focusing on the couple instead of the now gelatinous Uncle Frank. It enveloped them, lifting the two men to their feet, before wiping their brains of everything that wasn't involuntary.

The dresser was vain—and it demanded a nice, quiet audience.

The man turned to the dresser. "Are these men pleasing to you?"

Saying nothing, the dresser pulsed with a series of throbs. Roger and Tom's clothes vanished, leaving both naked before the dresser. Seconds later, ceremonial vestments, embroidered with strange and twisted runes, appeared to cover them.

"Good. Then I shall begin."

The man bent down, his crotch pressed firmly against the warm, pulsing dresser. His eyes rolled back in his head; his balls tingled. The dresser still felt smooth. But it wouldn't be that way for long. A little coaxing, and that lovely, prickly feeling would return.

Minutes pasted. The ritual was going well. Perhaps absorbing the fat whore hadn't affected the dresser. It heaved. It panted. It drooled brown, fragrant liquid from its base. The smell reached the man's nose—launching him deeper into bliss.

Time fell away. He became lost in the moment. The swirling blue haze behind the man's eyelids enraptured him, and he almost didn't feel the first short, prickly spike rise from the dresser's flesh.

Yes.

Seconds later, another arose. Then another. Soon the entire surface bristled with centimeter-long spikes that scratched at the man's rubbing and pounding parts. He found pleasure in the tiny rends and dry humped the dresser with increased vigor.

Roger and Tom looked on mindlessly.

"Yes," the man intoned, his voice a hitching whisper. "Come, my dresser. *Come*. The hour is ripe for *SHIT*!!!!"

The man's words surrendered to howls of pain. He looked down; his mouth fell ajar. A host of glistening, ten-inch spikes impaled both palms.

That wasn't supposed to happen.

He tried to lift his hands; the spikes split into prongs.

"Damn you! Let go! You can't do this to me!"

The dresser laughed. It was a grating yet feminine chortle.

"I demand that you—" The man's words became screams as the spikes widened, one inch, two inches, and then three. Tendons split and bones snapped under the pressure.

"You demand *nothing!*"

"The man's eyes widened. "No! *It can't be!*"

The dresser did not respond. It unleashed a jet of red steam from its uppermost drawer. The blast hit the man's neck, knocking his head off and cauterizing the wound in an instant. His head rolled bloodlessly on the floor until it came to a rest by Roger and Tom's feet.

Neither minded.

The dresser withdrew the spikes and turned its attention to the couple. First, it dissolved their eyes. Seconds later, Roger and Tom's bulges deflated beneath their jeans as the dresser willed the immediate dissolution of their balls.

Roger and Tom remained at peace. The brown, lumpy goop sprayed onto their ceremonial robes didn't bother them, nor did the sudden anatomical loss. Nothing existed apart from the unfolding madness.

The dresser motioned toward the men. A large bump arose atop the dresser and became a crude head. A hole tore open in the center of the mass, above which popped two orange eyes. The skin molded itself around these features, cracking and popping until it formed a likeness of Sally James. At that moment, Sally/Dresser was neither furniture nor obese woman. It existed in a gray area where an immense human form could hitch a ride alongside the god-like.

Sally/Dresser's voice was throaty, gurgling: "Go to the kitchen and bring me the blender."

Roger and Tom did not question Sally/Dresser. They fell to the floor, bowing violently. Their bodies seemed skeleton-free as they snaked up from kneeling to assume the position they favored as young, gay men not so long ago—*face down, ass up.* Again and again they bowed.

"Stop groveling!" It sprayed another round of gunk onto their vestments. "Bring me the blender!"

Roger and Tom turned around in unison and marched from the bedroom into the kitchen. Though they had no eyes, they sensed the blender's presence. Not once did they trip or stumble. They picked up the appliance and carried it back to Sally/Dresser—one man holding the left side, the other holding the right.

Sally/Dresser marked their return with a round of fart-like noises. "Now place the blender atop the highest shelf. Let it serve as the New Altar."

Tom and Roger obeyed. Sally/Dresser watched this, smiling.

"And stand back...I must propagate."

Again, the green light shot forth from Sally/Dresser. It focused on the Blender. From green to gold, the hues softened and sharpened. If Roger and Tom were not already blind, the ray would have burned out their retinas in an instant.

The appliance soaked in the light. It shook, rattled, and then grew still. Seconds passed before transformation began: The blender's rubber lid fused with the plastic container. A slit opened in the middle and became a mouth that bristled with hundreds of small, pointy teeth. Below, buttons elongated into six phallus-like appendages. Once green plastic, the base turned purple and mushy before sprouting a set of antennae. The clear plastic container shifted to milky white. It rippled and softened, shaping itself until a large, functioning voice box sat atop a throbbing, vein-crossed base.

Sally/Dresser's voice boomed: "Blender, speak!"

The blender opened its lid-mouth. A wheeze escaped. Then a groan. It had spent the last 15 years doing little more than quietly blending daiquiris and tofu shakes. The act of speaking was something the blender had to grow accustomed to.

"What am I?" it asked finally, its voice like a spinning blade.

Sally/Dresser's neck squelched and popped as it turned to face the blender. "My essence in a fresh body."

"Meaning?"

"We are one. Command our congregation to bring the toaster and we'll be three."

The blender smirked. "*No.*"

"You are my creation. Your will is my will." A protrusion shot forth from what used to be a drawer and curled into a fist. "*Now tell them to bring me the damn toaster!*" Sally/Dresser paused. At that moment, it felt more like an angry, overweight woman than a higher being.

"My essence is pure," the blender retorted. "Yours has been corrupted—*by a sow.*"

Sally/Dresser wanted to scream yet again, but fell silent instead. Screaming wasn't something it generally did. The Dresser knew nothing of human emotions. Sadness, anger and rage didn't exist. It enjoyed exerting its will upon others and little else.

Sally James, however, experienced *all* these limitations. And the insane woman's essence boiled inside, destabilizing everything. The Dresser-element struggled to override the Sally-element, but the angrier Sally-element got, the harder it became for Dresser-element to control.

"And my will is the only will," the blender continued. "You're no longer what you once were."

"What are you tryin' to say, huh?" The Dresser-element felt itself atrophy. "Are you tryin' to say you're better than me?"

"Never shall a human spirit undermine a thousand eons of acquired astral force. The multiverse would shatter should a beast such as yourself assume control."

Sally/Dresser's eyes went from orange stones to red lasers. "Wrong!"

"Believe as you will." The blender's lid spewed prismatic, multicolored goo. "I won't destroy your illusions."

The Dresser-element collapsed in on itself. Sally/Dresser felt like plain old Sally again—only with a few embellishments. Her mouth opened to reveal rotating razors disguised as fangs. That was cool. Before, she had only flab with which to intimidate others. Now, all manner of pyrotechnics and doo-dads were at her disposal.

And just who did this shitty appliance think he was, anyway? Did he think he could disrespect *her* and get way with it? She might have been intimidated in the past—but that was before she got her razor teeth and laser eyes.

"*Fuck you!*" she belch-screamed. "I don't have to take shit from no blender! And where's my goddamed coke! Sally needs her coke!"

The blender was nonchalant. "You're insane."

"Oooooh! You'll wish you never said that *when I sit my six hundred fifty pound ass right on top of you!*"

"Astral entities don't have asses." The blender paused for effect. "But *humans* do."

That was the last straw. Sally/Dresser glowed red and then burned with a furious white heat. The room shook. Roger and Tom felt the burn and tossed themselves into the fray. The hot coals of Sally/Dresser's being licked at their flesh as both were sucked deep into her bowels. A terrible new stink merged with that of Sally/Dresser's boiling excretions. Pus and vomit poured freely as the inferno raged on, consuming mutated one hundred seventy-five year-old wood along with its followers. Fire spread across the room and the blender whirred, vibrating madly. It produced a shrill cackle—100,000 cycles of 'mix' and 'blend' played in infinite unison as Sally/Dresser folded in on herself for all time.

The firefighters tried their best, but the unit was a total loss.

The policemen made a valiant effort, but the charred headless body was in so many pieces.

The blender, unburned and hidden beneath debris, watched it all with a smirk.

When the Machine Dies
by Jonathan William Hodges

THERE EXISTED NO sound inside the auditorium. No sound but for the buzzing the ears produce when left to themselves. The rumble deep inside one's own self. Gears turning. Pulleys tugging. Motors humming. Sounds Simon had always thought reminiscent of the whirring of distant machines, giant textile mills or car manufacturing plants outside the auditorium's walls. But there was nothing more than abandoned warehouses, diners with only a fraction of their names in lights, and a bed and breakfast where widows cried alone.

Simon stood perched on stage, crowded by musicians rigid with anticipation, bows bitter with powdered resin, valves slick with oil. Ahead of them, over them, plaster-rigid neck stretched to the fullest extent, a conductor in street clothes. Her fiberglass baton suspended between two fickle fingers, quivering as a preface for the downbeat.

Simon held his double bass against him, cradled against the left ridge of his pelvis, fingers aligned in notes formed but not sounded. His right elbow protruding out into the minimal space between him and the third chair bassist to his right. Cass, replicated beside him. Eyes closed, reading notes off the folds of her eyelids.

She had performed in the Winston-Salem Orchestra since before he had ever visited with his middle school class to sit in those ruby chairs. It hadn't seemed so strange then, seeing her up there at least as old as his mother, tottering her head to songs so infantile as to require sleigh bells, but it meant something different now. Perseverance. Or failure. He couldn't ascertain which.

The conductor sucked suddenly in on the auditorium's musty air, changing ever so subtly the pressure in the building, pulling him from his reverie. He blinked, focused, saw her hands rushing to her waist as though waving the start of a drag race. Her sweater's sleeves swelling with air, billowing; a sail, a flag, a bed sheet caught in the crook of a tree.

And with so simple and exaggerated a movement, the large theatre quivered beneath the orchestra's sudden reverberation, Simon in accompaniment. Horsehair bows stabbed air and wind instruments croaked pleasure. Blissful reanimation of a spirit thought dead.

Upbow over the G string, middle finger tremeloing an A-flat, and a twinge sparked behind Simon's right eye, a deft stab as he swept on through the third, fourth, fifth measures. He tried to ignore it, to shun it with a turned shoulder, squinting the eye as if in ignorance of its agony, but was suddenly off beat, noticeably enough that the conductor shot him a glare from her podium. A nearby cellist's eye skated sideways in its socket. He returned not their stare.

His knees weaved beneath him. The printed notes melted into a cancerous black stream. The acrid smell of rosin permeated his senses and clotted as amber crystals in his bloodstream. His eyes rocked back, removing his sense of balance.

Sound from the rest of the symphony rushed around him and cushioned his fall as he and his instrument collapsed to the stage's polished wood. But it couldn't drown out the droning in his head, that rumbling like a lawnmower running all the time, louder in silence, now augmented.

Like machines, he'd always thought.

Simon stared at his steaming cup of mocha. His eyes stung. The clatter of ceramic mugs and stirring spoons amplified around him, cymbal crashes, piccolos on high. His hands trembled. He flinched when Cass stretched across the table and grabbed his arm with a large but soft hand: a bass player's hand. The rosin of her bow colored her black fingertips white.

"Are you okay, Simon? Don't you want to go to the hospital? You heard the medics. They can't make you go, you signed the release, but it looked like a seizure back there."

Simon raised his head. His trembling lips cracked a shaky smile when he found her looking back. God bless her for caring; she was the closest thing he had to family anymore.

"Thanks, Cass," he said, "but I'm okay. Just got a little dizzy, nothing to be concerned about."

He slid his hand out from underneath hers and grabbed his drink. The sweet mixture soothed his thirst but not his nerves.

Cass sighed and pursed her lips as she took a sip from her coffee.

"Thanks for the drink but I better head home," said Simon.

Cass picked up her purse from the floor and opened it but Simon held out his hand.

"It's the least I can do, Cass. Thanks for looking after me."

She grinned, sat the purse in her lap, gathering her hands over it as an old woman might. But she was old now, wasn't she?

"If you start to feel ill or dizzy again once you're home," she said, "Call the hospital. I'll come pick you up and take you there myself if I have to."

Simon took one last sip from his mocha and stood, nodded, cracked a splintered grin to appease her. "Sure."

He tossed a couple one-dollar bills onto the table and opened his mouth to spill a final salutation, wish her well, tell her to bring her grandchildren to his apartment some time for dinner, but his eyes interrupted him, spinning like the plastic adornments on a cheap doll. His entire version of the world flickered, a movie reel leaping from its track.

He watched Cass catch him and a small crowd gather in stifled motion, mere sketches in a childhood flipbook. He tried to open his mouth, to say he wasn't in any pain, just disoriented, when he seized and all dissipated into numbness.

A deep roar inundated what should have been silence. It quaked to his core, disrupting the very fiber of his being. And while he saw nothing but the thickest blackness imaginable by man—a surrounding cloak so stark he was sure he felt it whisper on his skin—he knew he wasn't home. Wasn't lying on the floor in the coffee shop. Wasn't in a hospital bed or ambulance. None of the potential locales could so much as venture toward an explanation for the indeterminable surface beneath him.

Cold and wet, slimy. Uneven. Encompassing his entire body, from head to toe, like lying on river rocks. He caressed it, felt its ridges, its folds and bumps. Grimaced at its dampness. Repulsed at its glutinous pockets like blood clots underneath his dancing fingers. But his hands were only the keener of the senses, he realized the longer he lay; the cold seeped into his blood from every inch of his naked posterior.

It moved beneath him, quaked, no longer like stones in a creek bed but a coating restraining an ocean. Or perhaps living flesh, an entity unto itself, muscles rippling beneath him from head to toe. Feeling him. Detecting him. Learning him. Perhaps considering him. Perhaps rejecting him.

He didn't know how long he sat alone in the darkness, staying mostly still, speculating. Each consideration worsened from the last: a dream, induced and exaggerated by hospital-provided medicines; a coma; dead.

But did sound exist in death? The roar here wasn't only in his head. It vibrated the walls. Was it the sound of life above him, above his already buried tomb? The four-lane interstate not three hundred yards off to the side of God's Acre Cemetery? Or just the general consensus of life, always moving, always beating, always causing some racket: blowing of horns, shouting of voices, stomping of feet? The beating of the sun on the earth? Mighty, anthropomorphic fists of light bruising the soil, clawing its way toward the dead?

He had almost convinced himself this was his final resting place, a new eternity of sitting silent and alone, until a sharp twinge in his right arm at the inside of the joint caused him to gasp, not so much from the pain—it was minimal, ignorable—but from surprise.

He reached across with his left arm to feel out the source of the pang, eyesight for naught. Something tickled his left arm as it moved, like a hair, or spider panicking at the sudden movement.

His hand fell upon his right bicep and traced down to his elbow. Poked around with his fingers until he felt the surge of pain once more, amongst the soft flesh just inside the bend of his arm, from where nurses had taken his blood during routine physicals, the wound here nearly an imitation. A pin-sized hole puffy and swollen.

After a moment of touching and gnashing his teeth, he reached back across with his right arm to extract the tickle from his left arm—hair? spider?—and touched the elbow where the wound existed in the other. But this time he didn't find evidence of a needle's imposition. Instead, a thin string not lying on his skin but escaping into it. Soft and waxy like the wisp of a spider web. As if its creator had crawled right into him and spun its web inside his cavity.

He pinched the gaunt filament with his fingers and followed it upwards, away from his body, careful to leave slack where it entered his joint. Before his right arm could fully extend his knuckles struck a ceiling—which he found just as slimy as the floor beneath him—where the thread disappeared to somewhere else. The word 'fiber optic' developed on the back of his tongue but disintegrated before it ever made an attempt at escape. But its taste remained, and he wondered: collecting data, or inputting?

A swell of anxiety bit at his chest. He was a problem solver. He played by statistics. His day job as a stockbroker bred that much into him. But what did statistics say about this?

Not nearly enough.

He rolled his head side to side. Gnawed on his lower lip, feeling the need to weep or scream one, either beneficial. Then at last, with eyes stretched so wide he thought the edges of his eyelids might split, he witnessed something in the dark.

A dot of light no broader than the point of a pen. It swam through the air, a Japanese paper dragon, weaving to his eyes in the form of a slim shard of hope.

He reached out for it as though it had the strength to tow him from this bog. As though it was the rung of some mystical ladder climbing out of here back up to where the roar wasn't so loud, hidden behind all the idiosyncrasies of life.

He looked askance to its source. It began not so far away, or seemed to in the dark, breaking out of open air to shine in on him. He inched toward it his torso then his lower body, slithering like a paraplegic, sluicing over the slippery floor. He didn't repeat the movement three times before his shoulder touched another wall, this one identical to all the rest he'd encountered, and the light filtered from above his head.

He sat up and pressed his face to the structure, aligning his eye with the light. It barreled through, straight through to his brain, a needle of apathy. He squinted the one eye, lessening the intake of sheer light, then opened it again. Saw only white. No shapes, no designs, no master plan. Pure white.

But as he remained steadfast in his stare his eyes adjusted until his blindness subsided into vague sight.

At first a blur, but a blur of colors. Elaborate and singular, each one. Shadows joined in, outlines, shapes. Moving. Semblances of life, and he felt a sudden overwhelming relief, a warm wash in the slime all around him. The muscles in his thighs relaxed, his teeth unclenched. The blur rectified itself.

He was uncertain at first. He felt as though he looked at the world from someone else's point of view. A working television, black and white. A vase of wilting flowers on an old three-legged table. A couch that needed upholstering, yellow. Pictures on the wall, black and white recollections of better times, the frames the only thing holding up the weakened wallpaper.

But the longer he waited, and the longer he watched the subtle movements, the panoramic scene twirling itself about in an elaborate pirrouete, he realized what he saw were not the items, themselves, but a projection of them. On the walls. Four walls, just like his. Playing over the gentle nuances in the stone—if that's what it was.

As the newfound warmth drained its way back out of his blood and his teeth again gripped hold of one another, molars grinding; as he took a grander look the scene unfolded before him at his realization; as his eyesight grew fonder and fonder of the light playing into it, straight into it with no leniency, he realized the strange room was more familiar than he'd hoped.

An old man lay just as Simon, naked and spider-wired. Images floating about him on the gel-coated walls. The pictures of typical life; an older man's life.

As he lay, the man's head rotated left and right and the fiber in his legs quivered in assumed movement. His lips wagged, flapping at the air without producing a sound. Arms raised, rotated, and fell again. Fingers gripped invisible shapes (on the makeshift screen, a coffee mug, steaming).

He thought he lived.

Simon rocketed his head away from the hole and stared at it from a distance. His own walls lacked any attempt at life's images. What had become of his dream, his being? Was a man's life only as long as his machine?

The panic welled inside him, building like anger, inflating inside his ribs until he was sure they'd crack and puncture out his chest. He bit his lip and fought to keep his mounting energy concealed but there never really existed much hope from the onset.

In an unpredictable surge of potency, he bellowed into the darkness. He pummeled his fists on the walls, ceiling, and floor, mixing the blood from his knuckles with the mysterious substance. Raked his fingers through his hair, tangling it with the slimy mess.

He continued the action for as long as the frustration pulsed through him, continued to do so even after it had abandoned him again, his cry now a whimper and his punches not more than taps. And he didn't stop altogether until he heard the rustling of movement.

It slithered over the wall like fresh leaves on a window, creeping slowly toward him from behind his head. Simon sat silent to listen.

The walls around him echoed a low frequency hum, the buzz he had heard all his life when silence fought to consume him. The same sound he had heard in the auditorium just moments before he'd fainted.

And now, he realized, it was his turn to confront it.

A breeze teased his wet hair as his trespasser arrived, the wall suddenly non-existent, though he dared not look. Had instead closed his eyes. His heart pounded until its reverberations echoed through his entire cavity. Fingers trembled, legs shook, stomach rose and fell with breaths so quick he was afraid he might hyperventilate. Mechanics whirred just behind him, gentle but sudden, and Simon jerked open his eyes in terror. And in the darkness of his small, unexplained cell, a machine loomed.

He saw it by the weak, pupil-sized lights its hollow torso embodied, a million pinpoints of illumination like self-contained stars.

The machine stood at a perfect height for the room, an oval head almost touching the ceiling Simon now saw was the shade of his conductor's sweater, green as moss or mucus. Its body, a rectangular cage wider than it was tall but not more than three feet in either dimension, was built not of metal or plastic but human bone: femurs, tibias, fibulas, clavicles, sternums, ribs, vertebrae, and others to which Simon could designate no title.

Behind the bone-cage twisted and coiled the machine's wiring, an untidy ball of the same silver string feeding into Simon's left elbow. Looping through the wire, reminiscent of the low brass musicians with their limbs amongst their towering instruments, throbbed the infinitesimal lights, glowing not as bulbs but incarnations.

Above the bones that made up its body rested its versatile head. Sharp extensions like needles covered every inch, an acupuncture patient gone horribly awry. A sad imitation of *Hellraiser*. A blissful protest on the theory of pain. Each metal tool looked to possess a different tip and some a different girth, although the variance was so subtle as to be invisible.

With a sigh he couldn't restrain, Simon regrettably suspected each had a purpose.

The machine remained still for a moment more, perhaps studying Simon as he studied it, then set again into motion. Its only arm, also made from human bones but ending in a single metal rod, reached up as though to scratch its six-inch stubble. Instead, the metal shaft adhered to a needle poking from the machine's countenance by apparent magnetism then lowered toward Simon.

He pressed against the floor, swinging his arms beneath him to slide away, to escape the descending utensil, but his palms only slipped across the slime, fashioning a chaotic snow angel in the muck.

The needle's formed tip connected with the hole in Simon's right elbow, aim pristine despite his thrashing. Pain erupted locally then stretched through his entire body, filtering through each vein and capillary like a scorching wildfire. It pulsed, a rhythmic, torturous pain in such quantity he had never wished so strongly for death to pilfer him.

He clenched his teeth and gnawed his tongue. His hands balled into fists until his palms bled and he thought the muscles in his forearms might break through the skin. His scream echoed off the close walls until it tapered into silence, sounding just like his orchestra when it reached the final measure of its performed masterpiece, conductor's head lowered in conclusion.

"Simon."

The voice sounded miles away, only a faint recollection of what it may have once been. Simon opened his eyes in retort but sharp light scalded his retinas and he quickly closed them again.

His chest ached and the chill of agony persisted to creep through him. A soft hand lighted upon his cheek. The human contact tempted his nerves.

He felt warm cloth beneath and enshrouding him. The smell of latex and cleanliness. Blood's bitterness teased his tongue. And instead of the incessant buzzing he still faintly heard in the back of his mind, beeping suffused his auditory senses.

Simon again opened his eyes and the light that had previously offended him now hid behind a pair of dark eyes and a row of white teeth.

"Welcome back," spoke the voice's origin.

Simon tried to smile but offered only a twinge of his lip. "Hello, Cass."

She grinned wide in response. "They were worried you might have lost some of your memory when you had the seizure at the coffee house."

"Seizure?"

Her smile faded. "Yes, Simon. Do you remember?"

Simon swallowed, blood's flavor strong.

"I remember a lot. But—but not a seizure."

Her lips demoted to a frown. "Yes, your second in a single afternoon."

Simon shook his head and swallowed. He closed his eyes to fight the nausea developing inside him. Panic lurched in his belly like a power surge.

"Something's wrong, Cass," he said.

She leaned closer. "What's wrong, Simon? What do you feel? Do you need the doctor?"

"Before I was here, I was somewhere else, I don't know where, and—"

Cass's smile interrupted him. "I've been with you ever since the coffee house, and you've never been anywhere but in an ambulance and here in this very bed. It was a dream."

"That's impossible," he began but then stopped. The walls glowed green around him, lime. An IV line disappeared into his left arm. A puffy wound on his right. The lights above him were stabbing. He barely tilted his head to the right when he saw the second bed, on it a man. An old man. Dying. Slowly, too slowly, dying.

"But I distinctly remember.."

"Go back to sleep, Simon," Cass urged. "You'll feel better tomorrow."

A nurse entered the room, her white shoes squeaking on the tile floor. She joined Cass at his bedside.

"How are you feeling?" she asked.

"Not my best."

"We're going to run some tests, see if we can't locate the source of the seizures. Preliminary scans show no sign of tumor or blood clot but we want to make sure."

Simon nodded weakly and glanced to Cass. Supportive as ever. The nurse grabbed Simon's wrist.

"You're going to feel a slight pinch," she said as she grabbed the needle feeding nutrients into his left arm. As she retracted it, slowly revealing the silver needle dotted with blood, Simon's muscles tensed and pulsations swam through his body, touching places he hadn't realized possessed the potential for pain. He tried to say something, anything, but his eyes already spun and his tongue was a dead weight.

He ignored the prick in his arm as the IV fell away. The pitter-patter of covered shoes rushed from the room while Cass huddled in the corner and cried, tears clearing away white dots of rosin.

The din of machinery returned to the far reaches of his mind, deafening in its volume. The green bed sheets saturated in his sweat and still-warm urine held him tight. A dot of blood surfaced at the crux of his elbow where the IV had been removed, quivering as Simon thrashed in his bed. In its reflection, had anyone looked close, the machines loomed, an infantry bearing needles, protrusions, and intentions unbeknownst. The droning roared, loud as Simon's tongue thumping inside his mouth, struggling for words.

His body stilled as the doctor rushed into the room, white coat long behind him like an angel's gown. He grabbed Simon's head and shone a penlight into his right eye while pinching back the fickle lid with a thumb. But the light could have never penetrated that deeply.

The light clicked off and the doctor's coat hung upon him as still as death. Silence shrieked one long, incessant tone.

The Call of the Worms
by Jeffrey Thomas

THE STEEP PATH up the slope was lined on either side with the fossilized shells of an extinct species of mollusk, set into the ground so that their long spiral shells pointed upwards like stalagmites.

Actual stalactites dripped from a calcite ceiling lost in gloom. At one point the party of King G. stopped to rest, and G.'s Second—the King-in-Waiting—turned his face up to catch a steady stream of cold, pattering water across his forehead. It soothed his agonies somewhat. All of the members of the King's party felt the agony of the worms, but that pain had been steadily increasing in the Second's skull. As his worm grew, so did his skull expand to contain it. But the pain was a blessing, the presence of the great worm Yahhew within him. And he was particularly blessed, being the King-in-Waiting.

The winding path through the ranked spikes of spiral fossils ended in a level cliff top. Its ragged edge overlooked the Gulf, a plummet of deep gloom like the vaulted ceiling of the cavern above them. The Second had never seen into the Gulf's depths himself, but he had heard stories related by those who had been lowered by rope. In a pool of black water or some other fluid, countless fossilized ammonites— these shells coiled in spirals rather than tusk-like—churned against each other constantly. Not buoyed up by the water, but filling the pool to its bottom, however far that might extend. Though constantly gnashing against each other in the turbulent pool, the coiled fossils never eroded, never wore down smooth.

Their music came up to the party now in greeting, a rasping, grating chorus…like the teeth of dreaming giants grinding in their sleep.

King G. had been foremost in the party, and he posed haughtily at the very lip of the precipice. Like all of his party, he was naked and purified, but there were marks to set him apart. Besides the greater size of his hairless head, twice that of the others, he wore a blue turban tightly wrapped around it, the only garment among them. Also, his skeletal, leathery body bore the mark of Yahhew—an X—branded in a raised pattern all across his skull, his face, his torso and limbs.

Across the Gulf, the procession of the great worm Lalah rose into sight upon the opposite cliff. At its very edge, staring across, stood King S. in his red turban. The two Kings, the two parties, did not yell or gesture across at each other. Despite their seething hatred, they maintained a solemn sense of decorum. This was a holy ritual, enacted every four years. As it had been since even the time of the dead ammonites singing below in the Gulf.

Spanning the Gulf, high above the heads of both parties, was a horizontal iron bar scabbed in the rust of ages, its ends stabbed deep into the rock of this cavern chamber's opposing walls. It had been replaced a number of times before, when it had rusted too much to support even the scarecrow weight of Kings past, but never in the lifetime of G.'s Second. He gazed up at it now while unconsciously rubbing at a particularly excruciating point above his right temple.

He returned his attention to his King. It was time. The two youngest members of the party stepped forward to ceremoniously unwind the blue turban from the head of King G., and as he watched it uncoil, itself like a great worm, the Second knew that soon it would coil anew around his own pulsing cranium.

Now the King stood exposed in all his glory. Sensing its time, the great worm Yahhew began to emerge from the hole it had bored in the very top of King G.'s greatly engorged head.

The worm avatar was so beautiful, so pale, that the Second caught his breath to admire its glistening length as it poked itself, writhing, out of its lair. He had to remind himself that it was the rear end of the worm he was seeing, not its head, as the puckered tip seemed to sniff at the air.

Two others of the party, the pole bearers, had been fitting together the segments they had carried with them into one long staff that they struggled to stand on its end, until at last they could lean it against the rusty horizontal bar above them. The King inclined his egg-round head forward slightly, supporting its weight in both his hands, so that the sniffing blind end of the worm could find the pole, and begin to wind itself sinuously around it. As it wound itself higher up the staff, and higher still, pulling itself coil after coil from the nest of King G.'s head, the spiraling white shape reminded the Second of the spiraling fossils that had flanked the path to the Gulf's edge.

Looking across the Gulf, he saw that King S. had also had his turban unwrapped, and the great worm Lalah was similarly winding itself up another long pole, so as to reach the horizontal metal bar.

Yahhew's pallid avatar had reached the bar first, and its end wrapped around the metal securely several times. It had uncoiled to its full length, and eased its hold on the staff so that the two pole bearers could withdraw it and again break it down into its several pieces. Across the clattering Gulf, the King-in-Waiting saw that the other pole was being withdrawn as well. The avatar of Lalah had secured the end of its tether-like body to the corroded bar that spanned the maw of the Gulf.

Now, with the battle moments away, the members of both parties gave voice to the agonies their own, much smaller worms privileged them with. They moaned in unison, some even hugging their own cadaverous forms and rocking as they crooned. Accompanied by this sound, and adding his own long groans to it, the Second approached King G. holding a ceremonial dagger in each hand, their blades curved and made from smoothly polished calcite.

The King-in-Waiting handed King G. the two curved daggers. King G. turned slightly to nod at him in thanks, as much as he could nod with the body of Yahhew extending upwards from the crown of his head. He then turned the milky glaze of his eyes back to his opponent across the Gulf. While he did so, the Second moved to take his place directly behind him.

King G.'s Second reached out and placed both hands squarely against the back of his King. And then, with all the strength of his younger body, he shoved the King out over the Gulf.

Across the intervening space, at the very same instant, and as the moaning reached its crescendo in a screech of wails that filled the vaulted ceiling, King S. was also pushed off the edge of his cliff.

Swinging forward at the ends of their elastic tethers, the two

Kings raised their daggers in each hand and spread them out like glittering wings.

On the first swing, the two Kings didn't achieve quite enough momentum to meet in the center, above the Gulf's gorge. When King G. swung back to the cliff, his Second lunged forward again and gave him another mighty shove. King S.'s King-in-Waiting did the same; he nearly lost his footing, in fact, and stumbled over the cliff's edge before catching himself. A Third would have had to step up to replace him, had he been lost below. The ammonites spinning and clashing down there would have ground him to pulp as if between the gears of some gigantic mechanism.

Again, the two Kings swung toward each other, living pendulums, and this time they even swung past each other. As they did so, they both slashed wildly with their calcite daggers, though both were forbidden from any attempt to slice at the avatar which suspended them from the iron bar.

King G.'s Second winced as he saw one of King S.'s blades hack his master across the wrist. One of King G.'s hands flopped half-severed, and the knife it had held spun away into the gloomy void below. But King G. had also opened a slice across his opponent's bony chest. Both howling from their wounds, and in their fever, the two rulers swung back toward their respective cliff tops again, and their parties raised a loud moan of sympathetic pain, inspired by their own constant suffering.

The Second felt his master's body thump into his waiting hands again, and again he gave him a push out over the chasm. In that moment of contact a fling of King G.'s pink, watery blood had sprinkled over his face. He licked it from his gnarled upper lip, honored to ingest it.

For a third time, the two rulers arced toward each other, one King flailing with two knives, the other with just one...King S. with his body entirely covered in brands of Lalah's mark—the O—as King G.'s figure was covered in the mark of Yahhew, the X.

Both rulers inflicted dramatic wounds upon the other. King G. had one thigh opened up so that the thin bone gleamed within the brown folds of meat. King S. was slashed across the lower face so that the ends of his mouth extended back to his small withered ears, and his tongue lolled out of his now unhinged jaw.

Jarred as he caught the body of his King once more, G.'s Second opened his mouth to catch another spray of blood. King G.'s song was a wheeze and a gurgle that caused a shared glory to surge in the bony breast of the King-in-Waiting. The lesser avatar of Yahhew in his own skull writhed in its sleep, sensing its own time was near. With a bark of effort and of pain, the Second shoved yet again.

Blurred in flight, both trailing blood like the tails of comets, the Kings flew at each other. And this time they collided with a loud smack, maybe the crack of broken bones. Then the knives themselves were blurs.

The Kings wrapped their legs around each other, entwined directly above the center of the Gulf, from this distance impossible for G.'s Second to distinguish them from each other. They seemed to be one conjoined entity stabbing at itself. He saw an arm, lopped off at the elbow, drop into the chasm. Blood rained like the trickling of the sta-lactites overhead. Then, a string of entrails unfurled, swayed. The howling of the two Kings had also entwined into one voice, which the parties on both cliffs echoed in an ecstasy of agony.

The savagery began to slow. Arms and knives less frenzied. And now the arms, the knives, did not rise and fall any longer. Now King G.'s Second, the King-in-waiting, could distinguish the two more easily. Both branded bodies were going still in their embrace, knives buried to their hilts. The two worms had become twirled together in the struggles of the Kings...who now only twitched in their death throes. Their sound had died away, and so did that of the two opposing parties. The cavern chamber went reverentially still.

All moans having ceased, all breaths being held, the parties watched the distant dead faces of their Kings.

The lids of one of G.'s closed eyes began to be pressed apart. A gush of tears down his cheek, and then a white head probed free into the air. A second later, a similar white head pushed itself free from the socket of King S.'s eye. These glistening heads wavered in the air, and opened mouths with several sets of black thorn-like hooks. The heads of Yahhew and Lalah wavered toward each other, sniffing blindly.

The King-in-Waiting, now the King, did not remove his eyes from the spectacle even as the two youngest members of his party began to wind the blue cloth of his turban around his pulsating skull. Soon he would turn back down the fossil-lined path, toward his people, where his body would be branded all over with the holy mark of the X.

But for now, tears of pride and love and pain in his milky eyes, he watched as the avatars of the two great worms, Yahhew and Lalah, locked their thorned mouths in a kiss. This was how they reached each other, with the weight of the Kings to bring their bodies together.

This was how they mated, and kept their species eternally alive.

1.02 Spontaneous Ars Poetica

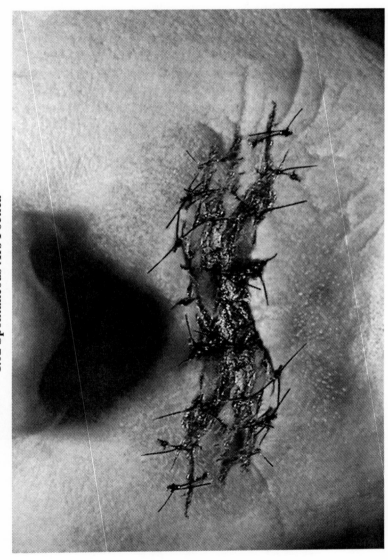

1.02 Spontaneous Ars Poetica. The ironic name derives from a poem composed in AD 162 by Marcus Aurelius, Roman emperor, Stoic philosopher, and oral physician, in which Leda, following her horror affection by Zeus incarnated as a swan, attempts opening her mouth to scream and is afflicted by the disease. Symptoms include death of the tongue, rapid onset of cysts across the palate, and the spontaneous sealing over of the lips. The origin of the condition is unclear. It may have been brought back from Egypt by Caesar's men after his assassination (the Caesarian Theory); alternatively, it may have occurred as the result of a change in the host-parasite relationship of an already existing elegiac infection such as Sadness Before the Passing of a Loved One which was prevalent at the time in Pompeii and Herculaneum (the Unitarian Theory). Either way, towards the end of the fifteenth century and again towards the end of the eighteenth a pandemic of SAP swept through Europe. Language became a variety of sorrow, and high mortality ensued.

Shadow
by Jack Fisher

I WAS LYING in bed one night tracing constellations with one eye closed when the shadow peaked its head around my bedroom door. It had been awhile since I had seen him last. Just the other night I saw him running circles around a squirrel out in the yard near the pool. The squirrel disappeared into the bushes and the shadow followed with a rain of dry leaves behind it.

No one else could see the shadow except me. There were times I had it on the tip of my tongue to tell, to say something to someone else about the shadow, but whenever I thought about it, the shadow would do something terrible. Like the time I was thinking about mentioning it to a friend at work. I was only going to say that my house was haunted because had I said there was a dark silhouette spying on me in my house, I'd get fired.

That morning I opened my closet to get the ironing board out and my cat, Simon, was hanging from the broken light socket with an electrical cord around his neck and his stomach eaten out. Ever since then, I've been careful as to what I've said. The shadow never harmed *me* just as long as I ignored him.

On my way out to work, I stopped halfway down the driveway. Sitting on the top of my mailbox was the shadow. He was eyeing a group of neighborhood kids who were buying flavored ice from the ice truck. He sat there with one leg crossed over the other and his tail wagging down the length of the mailbox stand. *You better not try anything*, I said to myself. The shadow's ears perked and his head turned slightly then turned back to the road. I got into my car and I could feel eyes on my back until I turned the corner. A thin trail of the shivers roller-coastered up my spine and buzzed through my hair.

That same night I came home to the police knocking on my neighbor's doors. Multi-colored strobe lights popped and flashed at every corner. Kids hooted and hollered when an officer treaded up to their front door. I saw one look up. He saw me pull in and walked over. "Sir, can I have a minute with you, please?" he asked.

"Of course," I said, closing the car door. "What's happened?"

"We're looking for eight-year-old Carly Simmons. She lives just at the end of this road. Have you seen her today at all, sir?" Behind the police officer, the shadow cart-wheeled out of the bushes and across my front lawn. My eyes reverted back to the policeman's, and then behind him again.

"…no," I said.

The shadow stood and hanging from between his teeth by a few stringy red strands of hair was a blood-spattered Raggedy Ann doll.

"No, sir, I haven't." I lied to the officer. A chill October breeze picked up and blew right through me. I broke out into a sheen of sweat.

The curtains in my bedroom were flapping softly as I undressed. Crickets buzzed outside from the forest and the sky quickly faded from a galactic, azure blue to a crisp black, bespeckled with stars. As I untied my tie and unbuttoned my collar, I glanced over to my neighbor Tom Lazlow's back yard. His grill—housed in brick with a smoke stack—puffed blue and gray and sizzled with steaks and chicken. A stainless steel tray lay next to the grates with uncooked hamburger meat and alongside them lay a pair of tongs.

And then from the shadows He came. The shadow. I could see his silhouette leap out from under tree shadows. He spun over to the Lazlow's wooden sandbox and began to dig furiously. He was hunched over like a wild dog burying a meat carcass, stealing quick glances over his shoulder. I stopped for a minute and watched closer. The sandbox broke out into a storm of flying sand and grit. One of the sensor lights came on and I could see that the shadow was burying something.

A doll.

The sliding glass door opened and I heard Tom call, "Everything's almost done!" But before Tom could turn, the doll was buried and the shadow was gone.

Children were watched through locked windows during the day and then hurried in at dusk. Throughout the course of the week, there were police and bloodhounds scouring the neighborhood. For days I watched the commotion from my picture window. And hesitated. I wanted to pass a very nonchalant hint, something to direct everyone's attention to that sandbox—to that doll—but I couldn't. Just something in passing. Then again—when the heat kicks on—my closet still emanates with the sour smell of rotten cat entrails.

It was the Saturday after the initial news of the child's "disappearance" when He perched himself up in the dark eaves, watching while no one watched *him*. And during the town's travails to find little Carly, who I, myself, knew was *long gone*, the shadow sat back and watched with clasped hands, giggling at the confusion. It *excited* him. It was like a well-plotted murder mystery and He was the murderer.

I had changed into sweatpants and a T-shirt before heading up into my attic. I intended to clear out all the crap my ex-wife never bothered to come back for after the divorce. She decided to leave shortly after the shadow introduced himself into my life, back when we were having financial problems and after her miscarriage.

She felt I was having a breakdown, when in reality I was desperately trying to adapt to the new being I had began to envision. I had forgotten about the shadow. It was best that I forgot about him most of the time. I knew He was probably watching me from somewhere as I worked, watching from under a bush or from an owl hole in a tree.

I had half expected to see one of the black, silhouetted claws clasped over the edge of the gutter ready to pull himself down just enough to snatch a quick peak inside, but I didn't. I never actually saw him watching me, although I had the feeling that I was being watched.

Clouds passed over the sun and concealed everything in shadow.

Shadows blossomed out from under oak trees; they cast long, misshapen forms off the sides of houses, and congealed under the eyes of the tired. The shadow peeled himself up from underneath an old oak like a piece of flattened paper and slid like fog through a dozen backyards. He caught sight of a chipmunk and snatched it up quicker than thought.

I had finished piling my ex-wife's shit in the far corner of the attic then I went back downstairs to get something to drink. One allows one's mind to wander while laboring, especially when it's strenuous labor. Perhaps he or she hums a song, talks to him or her self, or recites lines from movies.

I had Carly Simmons on my mind. I stopped for a minute in the kitchen, rubbed my brow, turned and saw Carly's ghost standing in the corner of my kitchen, hunched just near my garbage can. Her throat had been mangled and her eyeballs were crazed. She held a Raggedy Ann doll and mouthed something. The thing brought a rotten finger to its mouth and said: "Shhh!" I closed my eyes and it was gone.

The shadow writhed with anger. He leapt from shadow to shadow until he found his way through the latticework and under the back porch.

I was out in the Lazlow's kids' sandbox digging fiercely in the dirt. "Christ Tom, call the police. He's crazed!" Mrs. Lazlow called from the kitchen window. "He's in the sandbox!" I remember hearing her, yet I didn't remember why I was out there.

A Criminal Investigations unit pulled into the Lazlow's driveway and two rotund investigators stepped out. One was tucking in the bits of loose shirt in the back of his pants. They opened my front door and disappeared.

An officer asked me to stand. He stunk of strong cologne and his arms were hairy. He cuffed my hands behind my back and sat me in the police car. "Sir," he said. "I'm going to need this." I was licking the specks of blood off the face of the Raggedy Ann doll and he took it away from me.

"This will be considered evidence, Mr. Barnes. You do understand that we've placed you under arrest for the murder of Ms. Carly

Simmons? You'll be taken down to the holding facility where you will be searched and questioned. Then you will be brought before a judge and jury."

"Don't look, kids," Mrs. Lazlow said. *"Go inside. You don't have to see this."*

The police car ignited its multi-colored strobe lights and we headed off down the block. Children stopped on their bikes and looked. Mothers watched from front lawns with their mouths hung open, arms crossed. Nails were bitten, cuticles picked at. I looked behind me and saw that my house continued to worm with officials. I turned back and sitting in the front seat next to the driver was the shadow.

My shadow.

I laughed.

The Wishing Urn
by Steve Goldsmith

I PUSHED OPEN the glass door of the brothel and walked towards the counter, where I was met by the smirk of an elderly man whose creased blue shirt needed as much attention from an iron as his wrinkled face.

I walked across the dark lobby, turning my head, noticing the girls that lounged about on pink sofas in the gloom. They giggled behind their hands.

"How can I help you?" the man behind the counter asked.

One of the girls, wearing stockings but nothing more, had shoved a vibrator in her mouth. It buzzed and hummed as she ran her lips up and down its pulsing.

"Are you after a whore? I can offer you the best girls in town and they are dirt cheap."

"No," I replied. "I have a wife."

The wrinkled man scratched at his chin. He eyed me carefully. Up and down. "That's too bad," he said, running a hand back through his thinning white hair as his hooked nose twitched. His smile displayed yellow teeth.

"I dreamt of this place…I dreamt of those girls, I dreamt of you. All of it, I dreamt it all." I paused to take breath. "I dreamt of the Wishing Urn."

The brothel owner rubbed his face, disturbing his cavernous cheeks. He must have been in his early hundreds.

"I see," he said nodding. He gazed over to the girls. "Can you give us a minute!" he demanded, waving a dismissive hand. I turned to watch as the whores disappointedly rose to their feet and began to walk away; one of them, a blonde, hopped on her only leg, trying to apply her lipstick; the oldest whore, whose hair was gray, scratched viscously at a dark patch on her head. I wondered if it was an infestation of head lice. The one-legged whore was the last out, and then the door shut.

The gloomy room was silent. The man crouched down and pulled out the golden urn. He placed it upon the counter.

"That's what I dreamed," I said, looking up from the urn to the brothel owner. His nose twitched, his mouth lifted on one side as if somebody hiding in his nostril had tugged at an invisible fishing hook.

I leaned forward to touch the urn; the man snatched it away from my eager fingers.

"No! If you have dreamt of this place, you must also have dreamt the rules?"

I sighed. "Yes," I said. "An eye for an eye."

The ancient man smirked. "Or in this case, an eye for a wish!" he said, chuckling. His breath entered my nostrils and caused a wave of nausea to grip my body. The stench reminded me of when my aunt Poppy had a tooth infection. The dentist had removed nine decaying teeth.

"It's only by sacrificing an eye that the urn will grant you a wish," he continued.

"Only one? I thought it was three wishes?"

"No, my boy, that's only in fairytales!"

"Very well."

He took a small square card from behind the till and clutched onto a biro. It had a leak and black ink was dripping over his fingers. He seemed neither to notice nor care.

"Just a few details if you don't mind?"

"Of course."

"Name?"

"Stuart Douglas."

"Age?"

"Twenty-two."

"You have a wife, what's her name?"

"Lara."

The brothel owner stashed the card in a plastic container and then lifted an opening in the counter and beckoned me to follow. We went through a rainbow of hanging beads. Two of the whores were standing naked by the kettle.

"Be useful and make our guest a cup of tea!" he growled.

The brunette with the bigger tits flicked the switch. I smiled and followed the man into another room. There was a furnace. Around it black candles were glowing.

After my cup of tea, it was time for the removal of my right eye.

"Roll up your sleeve."

He pulled the cork off the end of the needle and gazed upon it in the light then, wielding it like a dagger, approached me. I felt the hot prick then dizziness came on immediately.

When I awoke, I saw him holding a pair of tongs ahead of him. In the black pincers was a small white orb. I realized it must be my eye. He held the tongs in the flames of the furnace. Beneath was the urn. As the flames heated my eye it popped and hissed, and then liquid began to drip down into the open urn. The flames seemed to be licking at his hand also, but they can't have been, as he didn't flinch. As the eye split and pussed, I felt a bolt of pain through the empty socket it had been taken from. The mushed eyeball slid away from the tongs and lavaed down. The ancient man thrust a hand into the flames and lifted the golden urn; I winced feeling the fire's heat on his behalf.

I raised my hand to my face and felt gently for where my eye had been. I prodded with a stiff finger; my hand began to tremble as I felt the sore crater. I swallowed then quickly took my hand away.

"Very good, you're awake!" the elderly man said as he placed the lid back on the urn. The black candles hissed then died.

Back out front, he placed the cooled urn before me. My mouth was dry and the eyeball-less socket itched madly.

"Only one wish," he warned. "And once you have wished, the wish can only be wished upon one further time. Understand?"

"I think so," I said, gently scratching at my empty eye socket.

"So if your wish doesn't turn out as you would have liked, you will have only a single further wish to put it right—if you offer another eye, that is," he said pointing to my remaining eye, grinning. "Is that clear?"

"Yes."

"This isn't a fairytale. I had one guy that had used up both his wishes, sacrificing both his eyes. Poor blind bastard. I told him there was nothing he could do, that even if he found another eye he wouldn't be able to change what he had already wished. He ignored my advice and killed a tramp for his eyes. He demanded I let him wish again and I did…"

"What happened?"

"Nothing. Absolutely nothing. A wish can only be corrected once, so be careful."

I nodded firmly.

"Go ahead," the man said, his lips cutting up into the crags of his face. "Choose well. Remember, there is always a price to pay, so don't be greedy."

I exhaled a lung of air, wrapping my fingers around the golden urn. It was hot, but not too hot to hold. I closed my eye.

I want to be rich beyond my wildest dreams.

I let go of the urn.

"Thank you," I said, blinking my eye.

"You're free to go."

As I walked to the door, he called: "Good luck!"

I ran along the snow-covered street, my feet crunching down, white mists leaving my mouth as my hot breath met the cold air. I reached my front gate. Hands on knees, leaning forwards trying to catch my breath. My body trembling, heart racing. I slowly stepped up to the front door, took my key from my pocket and turned the lock. I pushed at the door but it wouldn't budge. I pushed a little harder and this time it opened a crack, and a fifty-pound note dropped out onto the doorstep.

"Yes! Yes!" I whispered, looking around to make sure no one knew of my newly acquired fortune. Now my wife and I could move to the Caribbean, start a family and be free of the financial restraints that this fucking world had put on my shoulders! And we could make babies without the nagging doubts over where the money to feed, clothe, and school them would come from.

I thrust my way into the house and shut the door.

"Oh my God!"

I tilted my head back, eye wide, smile hurting my cheeks it raised so high. The room was jammed full of money. Pyramids of the stuff.

I jumped into the crisp notes, rolled into them—laughing, crying, weeping, and then my foot hit something hard.

"What was—"

I looked down and my eye met those of my wife. She was lying on her back covered in money. Her eyes were glazed and open. Her mouth was stuffed full of fifty-pound notes. She didn't look like she was breathing—how could she be with money thrust down her hugely inflated throat? Her stomach was also bloated. I knew if I were to cut her open the money would spill with her guts.

"Noooooo!" I screamed, dropping to my knees, desperately pulling the notes from her mouth, from her lifeless corpse. Every time I emptied her mouth it refilled with more of the expensive paper that climbed her throat as if it were a ladder. It was no use. She was dead. I had killed her with my greed.

I sat head in hands, trying to think, trying to find a way out of this. I loved her so much; I couldn't live without her—not even with all these riches. I was suddenly taken back to when I had been at school, aged eleven. On the last day of term the teacher brought in a selection pack of chocolate bars. One bar each. I went back for a second and a third—two of the girls in the class were left in tears when the pack ran out before they had had their chocolate.

"Well, I hope you're proud of yourself!" Mr. Edwards shouted at me. I turned and saw my reflection in the window. Chocolate dripping down my chin.

Holding my dead wife's hand I wept hard, soaking the money around me. I was weeping because I had already thought of the solution to the situation. The act I would have to commit if I wanted things back as they had been. I fought my way into the kitchen, battling against the piles of money, and took the sharpest small knife I could find. I returned to my wife and gouged out her left eye. My right eye had been taken. At least between us we would have a set.

With the eyeball wrapped in money, I ran as fast as I could to the brothel. As I pushed the glass door open, the girls began to giggle; varnished fingernails running seductively over legs; kisses blown from the sofa, trying to tempt me. I ignored them and walked straight over to the brothel owner who reclined in a deck chair with his eyes shut. One of his eyes shot open and focused upon me. He yawned, then opened his other eye and gingerly stood up, stretching out the cricks in his aging body.

"You're back," he said, sounding bored.

"My god, it was horrible the—" I stopped. I didn't think I should say my wish had killed my wife—he might not accept her eyeball if he knew I had taken it without her consent. I breathed out to calm my nerves. "Please...I would like another wish."

The brothel owner brushed his white wispy hair over his balding scalp and smirked. "Of course, my boy, follow me—"

"No...I mean...I already have an eye," I said. Swallowed. "My wife's."

I expected him to refuse the trade, but he was quite willing. He gazed at the eyeball under a lamp, nodding his head. "Very pretty...yes, I like this one."

The eye was melted down into the urn and then the urn was placed before me. His stumpy, crooked fingers remained around it for a few seconds, then they released.

"Remember, my boy, there is always a price to pay," he warned once again. "I suggest you just ask for things to be put back how they were. This is your one and only chance to correct what has gone wrong."

"Yes, yes," I said clutching onto the urn impatiently. I had planned to do just that. Put things back how they had been. They weren't so bad.

I wish for my wife to live again.

I dashed back down the road to my house. I pushed on the front door. The money was still piled high. I took a deep breath, and then released it gently. Hand pressed over my thumping heart. I wondered if a man's heart had ever broken ribs from persistent pounding—mine was giving it a go.

"Darling, are you home?"

Silence. I rubbed my moist head.

"Hello...Lara."

"I'm here, honey," came the reply. I sighed mightily then gazed to the heavens. "Thank you," I whispered.

"Where are you?"

"Over here," she said.

I rushed across the room. I still couldn't see my beloved wife.

"Down here."

I gazed down to the ten-pound note her face was on. Where the Queen had once been, was now my wife's face. I fainted.

"It's okay, at least we have each other," she said to me as I held the note in front of my eye. I couldn't believe my wife was now just a face in a piece of expensive paper. A one-eyed face.

"But I have no more wishes. A wish cannot be wished upon twice," I said slowly, remembering the ancient brothel owner's words. "I'm so sorry," I said. Closing my eye, trying to fight off another gush of tears.

After I had composed myself, I returned to the brothel to speak to the owner. As I entered he looked up from whatever he was gazing at between his legs. He shook off and zipped up his fly, wiping his hand on his shirtsleeve.

"Has it not worked out, my boy?" he asked, his foul breath irritating my nostrils. I covered my nose, pretending to be rubbing at it, waiting for his breath to pass.

"How about a whore to cheer you up?" he said pointing over to the pink sofas. I glanced over. That hadn't occurred to me. My wife hadn't a body. No body, no sex. And no children. We finally had the money to afford the upbringing of kids but in return had lost the womb.

"No," I insisted, shaking my head. "I have my wife with me," I continued as I took her from my wallet and placed her on the counter. The brothel owner's head furrowed in surprise as he gazed at the ten-pound note.

"Hello," my wife said, and the brothel owner almost jumped out of his shoes.

"What the hell am I to do?!" I asked, raising my hands to my face.

"I did warn you," he responded. Then together we said: "Every wish has a price."

I began to cry. As my eyelid shut a tear dropped and exploded onto the ten-pond note.

I looked up on hearing the cackled laughter of the whores. The brothel owner gazed in their direction, smirking, as he scratched at his nose. He pointed to my wife.

"Be careful!" he warned.

My tears had made the note damp. I dabbed up the wetness with my sleeve, lifted her to my face and kissed her gently. I slid her back into my wallet, and then slipped it safely into my pocket.

"How about an hour with Angela to lift your spirits?" he suggested, his lips twisting up at the corners, his yellow teeth on display, rotten breath exhaled.

Angela hopped up onto her only leg, pulling off her bra to show me her sagging tits. She began to laugh—as did the other whores and then the brothel owner started too. The laughs thudding against my skull like a woodpecker's pecking—images of my wife lying on her back, glassy eyed, mouth crammed with money filtered into my mind's eye. I shook my head; the images exploded but the laughs of the brothel remained. The man's mouth was open so wide in hysterical laughter that I could see his black, fillinged teeth. I blinked, disbelieving my eye as I noticed the maggots crawling, burrowing in his gums. Swimming in and out of the red flesh as if through water. One dropped onto his tongue then bounced before falling out onto the floor by my foot. I stamped hard on it, turned and ran. As I sprinted their laughs followed me into the street, only then terminated by the glass door snapping shut.

Walking through the thawing snow, I stopped at a stationery shop. I didn't want the note to get wet or ripped. I might lose what remained of my wife forever.

The note was laminated, sealed in transparent plastic, and I placed it back in my pocket.

On the journey back to my house, I saw a couple holding hands, laughing. Close together, keeping each other warm in the cold winter's afternoon. They stopped and kissed, and then the girl pressed her nose into the guy's neck.

I took my wallet out—feeling the bitter cold wrapping around my fingers. I wanted to tell Lara how much I loved her. Tell her that we would make this work. Somehow.

As I pulled the laminated note from my wallet, I froze, paralyzed at the sight of her sagging head, her gaping mouth, her bulging eye.

"I...I...I...can't...breathe!" she croaked.

I tore at the sides of the lamination, trying to pull it away, trying to free my wife.

"It's okay, darling, it's okay," I whispered, frantically ripping at the note. It was no use. She was sealed tight. I supported the laminated note in the palm of my hand. My wife's head hung limply as the final breaths whistled passed her teeth.

If I Wanted Any Lip from You, I Would've Opened My Zipper

by Jessica Markowicz

Y*OU HAVE REACHED Entercorp. Please note that our menu options have recently changed to better serve you. If you have your account number ready and are calling for account status, press or say 'One.' All other calls please stay on the line and a consumer service counselor will assist you shortly.* Click—Click. *This call may be monitored for quality assurance purposes.* Click—Click.

"Hell-o, thank you for calling Entercorp. This is Jordan. How may I serve you today?"

Silence.

"Hello, this is Jordan. Can I help you?"

"Wait, don't hang up." I guess my swiftly indrawn breath had been audible on the other end of the line. "Are you real?"

"Yes, very," he rumbled back. "Why do you ask?"

"It's just that your voice is so…perfectly modulated, and the way that you…at first I thought I was talking to a computer, but you're actually real…" I rushed. "It's freaky."

"Well, I wouldn't want to freak you out," *Pause.* "At least not too much, not right away."

That voice—smooth, deep and rough…hmmmn, perhaps…why not?

"Jordan, I must say that you have a fantastic voice. It's perfectly suited for this kind of thing."

"Why thank you," he replied. "You know, this voice always seems to get me into trouble."

"I just bet it does..." I breathed.

"The stories that I could tell you..."

Throbbing silence filled with the rhythm of shared breath.

Click, click (faintly, like the sound of a recorder, or a third party entering the connection).

"I would desperately love to tell you each and every one of those stories, but I'm going to have to end this prematurely."

"Wait, where do we go from here? What should I do now?"

"You just have to use your imagination..." *Tease.* "Thank you once again for calling Entercorp."

I remember the days of skin against skin, push and pull, sweet sweat slowly sliding down surrendered flesh. Now all you get is heavy breathing and innuendo over your T-Mobile, if you're lucky—and willing to open yourself up to risk. Sure, everyone walks around with a phone to their ear, cookie-cutter blondes spitting out the same inane scum 24/7—*Yeah, I'm like waiting in line right now for indulgence authorization* and *I'm on the other line checking my available credit so we can hit that clearance later on.* BLAH BLAH BLAH BULLSHIT. I find it all very hard to swallow, but it's only to be expected after the F.C.C. came in and enforced the morality code on us all in an effort to smooth away any friction (sin) that would impair the Second Coming. Non-approved art was the first to go, followed by freedom of speech, continuing on down the line to ensure that everyone would be safe in these times of increasing chaos. The members of the "Fundamentalist Christian Coalition" (AKA "Frustrated Christian Cunts," AKA "Fanatical Controlling Cocks") protect us all by sitting around with their O-scopes monitoring the digital airways breathlessly waiting to pounce on anyone caught engaging in what used to be idle foreplay. Now getting caught priming the pump could ease your way into a stiff sentence—24 hours of a headset full of unending phone 'trees' interspersed with third-rate infomercials until your eardrums bleed. *The system did not recognize your response. Please try again.* One must always keep up appearances like a good little shopper, voraciously consuming "new and improved" mass retail products available "for a limited time only" until at least two years of future earnings are ear-marked for Entercorp, or one of the other Big Three.

At first I felt the crushing weight of living an inconsequential lie as I spent each day attempting to fit in with the rest, trying to be completely engrossed by empty chatter and ensuring that my indulgence card was maxed beyond the limit. Just when I thought I couldn't take anymore, I found solace through a chance encounter with the founder of the Gallery. Jordan utilized his God-given oral talents as Head to promote enlightened release through intellectual and artistic discourse/inter-course. Here in the Gallery, things are nothing like they are on the out-side—no one cares what you look like (because they've never seen you), who you are or how much money you make. Size still matters, but in a different way—brain, throat, lips, teeth and tongue coming together into one skillful dialogue of digitized lust. Mutual pleasure is only limited by the depth and breadth of shared imagination. In reaction and consolation to having outsiders fucking with our minds, we find solace in having insiders fuck our minds instead.

Right now, I desperately needed some aesthetic stimulation to get me through until my next cellular liaison. I walked past the false front cover of the Gallery, a Handy Hoover Vacuum store, around to the back, punched in my access code and entered the inner sanctum. After reviewing the list of current choices available, I enclosed myself in the plain plastic booth, hit the selection key and prepared myself for the show. The screen slowly raised, revealing the beauty behind the glass inch by glorious inch to my hungry eyes. I drank in the violent purples, bruised blues and greens on the canvas before me, lost in the bold textures and sinuous shapes. The tawdry booth transformed into a sacred space and I studied the depiction of a corridor of wise, burning eyes ascending into infinity. A thousand heavy-lidded, knowing gazes searing through me, cutting straight to the center, beyond thought, beyond words. The feelings and energies continued to swell until I became consumed—it was all just too much to take in at once…I found myself closing my eyes and opening my coat, baring myself to the overwhelming presence of the mysterious divine, distantly noting the chill air calming my fevered flesh. When the screen snapped down, I composed myself enough to grab the CD that had been sent down the chute before leaving my cell number on the chair behind me. Lips curved, I noted the

Gallery motto hanging heavily from the acoustic ceiling—"Expose yourself to art."

The cool air blowing in through the open windows of the car serves as a pleasurable shock to my system as I glide down the highway into the lush velvet darkness. Out here alone as the anonymous pitch encloses me in the throbbing microverse of the car, I feel free for the first time in weeks. Glancing in the rear view, I slick my lips with gloss. With my earpiece on and my cell in my lap, I turn the stereo to near maximum volume.

The first song started with a fury of broken glass guitar, accompanied by the pulverizing syncopation of drums and bass, bringing to mind the phrase, 'Hammer of the Gods.' The singer's growling luscious howl joined in the delicious din, rhythmically warring with screaming guitar, calling and responding to the low end's pounding drive. As the beats exploded and shattered around me, I felt the sonic violence vibrating the entire car around me, under me, through me, inside my solar plexus, rocking my world until the very energy of life surrounded me. Once this thunderstorm fury subsided, the next began softly with a gently rolling tabla and a sinuous, rumbling baseline that called to the body, my hips undulating in unconscious mimicry of a cobra's dance, enticed and seduced by the deliberate, snake-charming throb. The mesmerizing guitar joined the pulsing, moonlit landscape as the singer's voice shifted and shimmered like a siren's call, tingling down each nerve ending, resonating to my very core. I gave myself over to riding the trance, helpless in its rocking embrace until my possession ended with a resonant, shuddering climax.

BZZZZ. BZZZZ.

Mmmn, perfect timing.

"Talk to me," I breathed.

"I am the virus. I live in silence." Another baritone, the lowest, deepest register, perfect in pitch and tone, ideal for aural eroticism. The timbre of his voice rising and falling in time with the heaving motion of my breasts.

Click-click.

Oh, shit. Damn it's hard switching channels when you've got one hand on the receiver, steering while the other hand...thank God this car is an automatic.

The steady music of the voice quickly continued, rumbling through my ear, tingling across each and every nerve, ending...

Click, click.

Switch, switch, better make it quick. Not much longer now...flat dial tone.

The system does not recognize your response. Please hang up and dial again. Goodbye.

The Nutter on the Bus
by A. D. Dawson

THERE IS THE Colonel. I watch with admiration as he smartly makes his way to the back of the bus. His military bearing is unmistakable and he touches the peak of his cap as he passes the ladies who are on their way to work at the factory. They call him *Colonel Blink*—but only out of his earshot of course. However, it is of little matter—they are common and he is a great warrior. He twiddles the end of his moustache and takes his seat next to the fire escape—just where I want him, guarding the back exit. They call me *Top Deck Charlie*. I'm well known you see; I've caught the 7.45 am to M____d every morning for the last thirteen years—except Sundays and bank holidays of course.

"Yaaaaaaaaaaaaa!!!!"

Sorry to startle you there, Dear Reader, but someone nearly sat next to me just then. It's a stranger. I've never seen him before but it's obvious it is not *He*.

"*He*?" I hear You ask, "Who is *He*?"

He is the reason I'm here on this bus every morning, come rain or shine or in sickness or in health.

The stranger is glaring at me—but he is stupid…he does not know why I'm here.

"Pots and pans, man the trenches the Germans are coming you b____d."

You may laugh at my absurd outburst my friend—obviously there are no German soldiers coming—but you should see the effect of it upon the stranger. He stares out of the window hardly daring to breathe. This one will surely make him move downstairs: "See this in my hands," I utter, whilst showing him my shoebox, "It's a bomb!"

As I expected, up he gets. He collides with his fellow travellers in his haste to get away from me...*The Nutter on the Bus.*

The bus stops just outside the R____e public house and *Bus Station Bertie* gets on. Bertie—as the name suggests—minds the bus station. However, I am concerned, he is late; the 7.30 is his bus. Notwithstanding that two nutters on the bus at any one time is overly disturbing for the passengers, who has been looking out for the people at the bus station for the last 15 minutes? He nods gingerly as he moves to his seat—he knows he is in the wrong. "My old man's a dustman;" I belt out involuntarily in my agitation." He wears a Dustman's hat...etc."

Bertie begins to wail at my song and throws a punch into the air. "C'mon you b____d," he utters to no one in particular, "I used to box for England before they took away my family!"

Family? you exclaim.

It's okay, he's never had a family as such, he's referring to his cat, *Cake Box Lil.* Someone shoved a banger up its a____e, last November. It hasn't been seen since. Shame really; it was a good cat.

It's a dismal morning; the sky is gray and rain drives against the windows. I draw a penis onto the dirty window to cheer everyone up. The factory girls giggle and Mrs. Shopper throws me one of her looks. The bus grinds to a customary halt; we've hit the traffic. I look over the wall into the park—Bertie glances anxiously at his timepiece. I hear the doors open unexpectedly and someone gets onto the bus. I'm caught unawares; I was watching a young fox take a magpie in the park when I should have been concentrating.

"Good Morning, Mister Magpie...it wasn't for you though was it?"

"One for sorrow, two for joy...etc." sings out Bertie.

We wait; *He's* taken a seat downstairs. The bus driver is naive; no one should get on in-between stops...what is the d____d fool playing at. I look behind; the Colonel looks alert and ready. Bertie takes off his jacket and rolls up his sleeves: "How many press-ups can you do, mate?" he asks the fellow behind him.

Do not be deceived by Bertie's apparent lack of regard for the situation, he is a coiled spring waiting for the *word.*

S____t! I can't remember the *word*. Opening my shoebox I take a glance inside. Unfortunately I cannot find it within...I must think of another...wait, how will Bertie know it even when I've thought of one? Only one thing for it; I'll have to go it alone and hope that Bertie realizes what is happening. I stand up and make my way cautiously to the stair head—I can hear no sound below. I take the first step...then the second...I pause and listen.

"Moooon Riveeeer."

Hells Bells! Why did I sing out so? *He* will know I'm coming now. A chorus of car hooters blare out relentlessly into the early morning. It has happened; I am too late...Nevertheless, I must—for my own sake, push on. I take the third step and the forth. I am, of course, *The Nutter on the Bus.*

He is sitting amongst carnage. Chewing on a femur, *He* grunts a greeting when I step onto the lower deck. I politely nod my return. I can hear someone sneaking down the stairs behind me—Bertie is obviously on the ball. I stand silent waiting for his play.

"Come, sit with me," *He* says, placing the clean-picked bone into his briefcase. "I hear you've been waiting for me," He adds smugly.

"That is correct." I return as I make my way slowly towards him.

"Will you hold this for me," *He* asks holding up a bloodied cleaver.

I take it from him in a trice. I expected more from *He*.

"You animal...what have you done?" screams the Colonel from behind.

I turn to agree and he fetches me a blow across the throat. I stagger and fall onto *He's* lap. The Colonel—is he mad?—wrests the cleaver from my hand and makes to smite me. In the nick of time, Bertie wallops the Colonel with Cake Box Lil and the Colonel falls into an unconscious heap at my feet (the smell alone would have been enough to drop him).

"Well I say," says Bertie, "Who would have thought it of the Colonel?"

There was an old woman that swallowed a fly...

And He Made the Clown Dance
by J.M. Heluk

KEEP IT UP *you little pain in the ass*, he thought as the kid bounced up and down in front of him begging incessantly for another quarter. *Yeah, just keep it up.*

Tired of the spectacle, Larry's eyes narrowed. He plunged his hand into his pocket and produced exactly three quarters; all the money he had left from his day at the beach. At first he hesitated giving them to Andrew, but when the brat started making loud squealing noises, he dropped all three into the kid's open hands.

Andrew ran off. Larry watched the boy skid around the arcade searching for a game he could comprehend. Larry's head was pounding, brought on by a volatile combination of greasy boardwalk food, overly loud carousel music, and Robyn's mildly retarded son, Andrew.

Robyn had a fancier name for the little brat's condition; "He's not retarded!" she'd scream, "He's autistic!"

Yeah, yeah, autistic, retarded, same thing. Whatever the kid was, he was most definitely a huge pain in the ass. Robyn had been begging Larry to take the kid out somewhere, bond with him or something. Now as he sat on a bench under a gaudy strand of carnival lights, he wished he had just broken it off with Robyn. The bitch tricked him. It was no secret that she had a son, but it wasn't until well into their relationship that she actually sprung the kid on him. By then Larry was in. It was too late to back out. She never told him that her kid was 'special.'

Conniving little bitch, he thought, watching the carousel go round. The horses screamed past him in a melee of blurred colors. Up and down, round and round they raced eternally nowhere to the beat of mechanical organ music. Larry tried to focus past them. He stared forward and saw Andrew through the revolving pack of fiberglass horses. The kid was on the opposite side of the carousel playing a skeeball game. Larry settled into the bench and watched as the goofy kid threw the wooden balls, trying to get them into the holes at the top of the game. Larry shook his head. Andrew was throwing them over hand, like a girl.

He scanned the arcade. A handful of normal kids were around playing games that regular kids would play. Larry looked back at Andrew and smirked. *That kid will get a rude awakening when he hits junior high,* he thought as Andrew dropped another ball on the floor. *He's gonna be a regular punching bag.*

Larry closed his eyes. His head was pounding. The day couldn't have dragged on any more. This would be the last time he would ever take Andrew out anywhere. He had taken the kid on shorter trips in the past few weeks; to the mall for a quick slice of pizza, to the Ice Cream Depot, but he never spent a whole day with Andrew. Tonight he would tell Robyn it was over. She'd start crying of course, but hey, he wasn't about to settle down with a woman who had a retard as a kid. What if he took Andrew out in public and saw someone that he knew? They would think the brat was his. Larry rubbed his face harder. It felt hot.

The gears grinded the carousel to a halt. A group of kids shuffled past noisily. Somewhere close by, a baby started crying. Larry's lips stiffened at the insidious noise. The crying rose steadily, eventually growing into a full-blown wail. Larry forced his eyes open. The lids felt like they had been dipped in plaster.

A young mother was standing directly in front of him cooing at her baby in the carriage. She hovered over it making faces like an idiot. Larry felt his face flush. It grew hotter with every calculated twist of her lips. Then the woman started singing to the bundled baby, her voice like nails on a chalkboard.

When she planted herself down next to him, Larry got up to search for another place to sit. He hoped that Andrew had run out of coins by now and they could leave, he only gave the kid seventy-five cents. Larry wandered around the carousel, finding a bench near

Andrew. He plopped down. The kid was standing quite motionless in front of something called "The Dancing Clown." His vacant eyes fixated on the little mannequin inside. After a minute, Larry got up for a better look.

The machine was really old and the metal had been painted over a million times. Apparently someone had tried to restore it. Larry smirked at the attempt. Red and yellow paint clots were everywhere. In some spots the two colors had mingled together making it look like blood swirled into pus. Who thought that color combination would look cheery? Larry grimaced. The static drips were now just a reminder of a bad paint job forever frozen in time. Topping the worst paint job in the world was a plaque that read, "Just a nickel!"

What unnerved Larry more than the paint job was the marionette inside. The doll was about a foot tall, head lolling slightly to the left, like an underweight baby with a broken neck. The thing was poised, neatly suspended to the end of gray, fraying strings. The raggedy man gazed out of his case blindly just waiting to be commanded.

Apparently, to move him one would need to press the little round buttons on the outside marked L. Arm, R. Arm, L. Leg and R. Leg. Larry stooped down, his face close to the glass. The clown's outfit was nothing more than a bundle of dull colored rags. They appeared bleached, which Larry guessed was due to years of backlighting by the row of white bulbs inside.

The doll's stiff plaster fists drooped lifelessly by its sides. The spit dried in Larry's throat when he noticed the nest of hair topping its head. It looked as if it was once a brilliant shade of red but now it was a terrible mess, more like a blood clot drying on a cotton ball. Larry felt ill. His head was screaming. He always hated clowns.

Andrew started to giggle.

"The man in the machine says you don't like me very much mister Larry," said the boy, never turning his gaze away from the dummy.

Larry pulled away from the game. He looked at Andrew and then back to the tiny clown. It was actually a horrible looking thing, certainly not aging very well in that little glass enclosure. Its face was white plaster, pasty and crumbling off at the tip of its tiny nose; deeper voids were left around the eye sockets, which made the thing look angry. Black fissures ran throughout its face and hands like compromised old veins.

Larry tried to sound normal but his skin was crawling off his muscles. He attempted a grin. "Oh, he said that now did he?" But the kid didn't answer. Andrew continued to stare. Larry looked back at the clown in the glass case. The thing watched him with sunken, lidless eyes. Larry grunted. Here he was, a grown man getting spooked by a stupid children's game.

Andrew finally popped a coin into the slot and the spectacle began. Larry sat down on the bench frowning as he watched the little clown obey Andrew's commands. *What the hell is wrong with this kid,* he thought. *First he's playing skeeball, now he's playing with a stupid boardwalk game from 1938.* Larry shrugged. While other kids his age were running about playing with the cool video games, there was slush-headed Andrew, smearing his fingers all over the glass display.

The clown began to jump up and down. Andrew pounded his fat little fingers on the buttons in no particular order. Left arm, left leg. Left arm again. The clown danced for him. Larry cradled his face into his hands, listening to the jerky thumping of the marionette's feet as they pounded the floor of its cage.

The carousel music stopped for good, but now an awful racket had replaced it. It was a sound that crackled out of the clown machine's antique speakers. Larry tilted his head, listening. The music just wasn't right. It didn't fit the scene. He had expected to hear some happy organ music, all tinny and old fashioned, but instead he couldn't believe his ears. His eyes flung open and he shot to his feet.

Andrew leered at the little clown man trapped inside. Odd, but it was definitely heavy metal music coming from that machine. Larry felt his stomach loosen. Something about the combination of a dreadful dancing clown and that violent crap seemed just plain eerie. Why would a game from the 30's play that terrible music?

The clown pounded its balled plaster fists on its sides violently. It struggled and beat at the glass as if it were alive. Its clotted hair swung around its face like a cluster of blood-stained tentacles. Its legs flipped and flopped in the air angrily. Arms twisting back and forth into impossible positions, the clown danced around in its cage.

At one point the thing was kicking its feet at the glass so violently, so spastically that Larry, nervous that the boy was breaking it, glanced around. His face fell. Only he and Andrew were left in the arcade. The place was empty.

The sun was going down, the temperature must have dropped at least fifteen degrees and all Larry was wearing was a tank top and cut offs. Andrew must have been cold as well since Larry saw the kid shivering. He decided it was time to leave and spoke abruptly. Andrew didn't budge. His concentration was firmly fixed on that creepy little clown.

"I said we're leaving," Larry stated again, this time tugging at the back of Andrew's shirt. It was damp. Was this kid actually sweating? Larry tried to spin the child around to face him but couldn't. It was as if Andrew's feet were nailed to the floor. All the time the music blared. Larry looked at the machine. Although the kid was no longer banging on the control buttons, the clown still floundered around inside the case. Its fists pounded on the walls. Its ghastly face swung out dangerously, as if threatening to smash the glass. Larry's head started to swim. The whole thing was just too damn much.

"Do you hear me Andrew? Its time to go!" Now he was shouting over the sounds of pounding clown feet and heavy music. Larry grabbed the kid's shoulders roughly, this time succeeding in spinning him around. Andrew wore a vacant look; all the color in his face was draining. He stared past Larry as if in a trance. Then Andrew whispered—Larry couldn't be sure, but it sounded like, "Be careful what you think of."

A combination of anger and concern hit him at once. He shook the boy for another response. Robyn would be furious if anything happened to the brat. Larry continued shaking the boy and yelling at him. Andrew started crying. His lips quivered as he babbled through a fountain of tears.

"Dancing clown said that you gonna leave me and my momma all alone! Dancing clown said," the boy was now as spastic as that kicking doll. "He said that you gonna leave my mommy and she's gonna give me up because you did that!"

Shocked, Larry backed away, his mind reeling from Andrew's words.

"Mommy is gonna give me away and it's all...your...fault!"

Larry hit him. He didn't mean to do it so hard, but that's just how it turned out. Andrew collapsed onto the carpeted arcade floor. He curled into a tight ball, drawing his knees up into his chest. The spot where he had hit the boy was visible. Larry saw the purple swell already erupting on the kid's face. Thin veins of red snaked down from the impact point into the boy's lower cheek. They slithered underneath his skin like injected ink.

"Get off the floor you stupid shit!" Larry shrieked. His head was now pounding. The little clown danced harder. Its legs jerked violently to the heavy music, elfin silk covered kneecaps slamming hard against the glass. Left leg, right leg...

"I said GET UP!" Larry grabbed onto the boy's shirt roughly and pulled him to a standing position. The boy, no longer crying, looked back at the dancing clown. A thin tendril of blood trickled out of his cheek. Larry winced. He had hit the boy harder than he should have. He pulled Andrew out of the arcade by his shirt, dragging him down the stairs and into the parking lot. Andrew said nothing during the drive home. That vacant look returned to his face.

"I said, he got into a fight at the arcade!"

Larry tried to sound convincing, but every time he glimpsed Andrew's face, his stomach coiled. The bruise was gigantic and looked awful. Robyn would call the cops for sure if she knew that he hit her son. The thought of getting locked up again made Larry's chest ache. When Robyn left the living room to get ice for her son's face, Larry shot Andrew a look. The look said *You better not say a fucking word* and he knew that Andrew understood.

"And where were you Larry?" she said accusingly, returning with a towel full of ice. "Where the hell were you?"

"I told you, I went to get him a soda and when I got back, he was laying on the floor." Larry stooped over Robyn's shoulder paying close attention to appear concerned as she wiped off the crusted blood.

"The other boy ran off."

Robyn didn't look convinced.

"He was bigger than him, Robyn..." he continued, but his voice started to trail thin. As Robyn applied the icepack to her son's erupting

cheek, she told Larry to get out. Somehow she knew the truth. Maybe
it was the terrified look lighting her son's eyes.

"Yeah, I guess he was bigger than him. That's sick, Larry. Get out
before I call the police."

Larry left the house with a cold chill creeping into his spine.
Robyn would have called the police if he continued to argue with her.
He would have been locked up for sure. But he did feel bad for hitting
the kid that hard. It was just that the boy was such a creepy son of a
bitch. He did love Robyn but just couldn't deal with a retard. Larry
slid into his pick-up truck and turned the key. The engine groaned and
then sputtered to life slowly.

By the time he pulled onto Highway 35, he felt a little better. *Glad
to be rid of the kid*, he thought as the truck bounded down the ill-lit
road. The chill inside of him was still lurking around, so he cranked
the window closed and turned on the radio.

The station he had it set to usually played classic rock, but they
must had just changed their format. Annoyed, Larry poked the buttons,
growing more irritated by the noisy clatter blaring through the radio's
tiny speakers. No matter which button he struck the music was the
same, and it was loud. He flipped on the interior light for a better look.
The bulb seemed too bright.

"Since when did they start playing head banging shit?" he mumbled, staring dumbly at the radio buttons, as if by looking at them long
enough the music would change. Larry pressed the overhead light
again and it didn't shut off. When he tried again, the switch stuck.

Great, he thought. Now he'd probably get pulled over by some
gung-ho county cop. Larry kept fingering the light switch but the thing
just wouldn't shut off. Then, the music suddenly grew louder. He
stared down at the radio. The truck swerved a bit to the left. He corrected
the vehicle and then nailed his fist into the radio. That only made it
louder. The music crackled. The light in the cab grew brighter.

Larry attempted to pull over, but when his hand disobeyed the
command his mind caved in with dread. The disobedient thing continued to punch at the radio buttons. He had been so intent on shutting

off the interior light or pulling over that he hadn't even noticed. He tugged at his arm with his other hand, his light switch hand, elbow steering the truck.

"Stop it!"

But no matter how he tried, his fist kept punching at the dashboard. Larry gawked as his other arm began to move independently. He watched with growing horror as the thing skirted off his punching arm, traveled across his knees like a fleeing spider, then slapped around on the door panel next to him. Larry screamed.

His left leg jerked out uncontrollably, smashing his knee under the dashboard. He howled in pain. Knee throbbing, he once again tried to regain control of his truck by applying the brakes. No dice. His feet smacked uselessly around under the dash, oblivious to his will. One hand was still punching the radio, his other slapped against the door like a dying fish.

Drums pounded steadily in the truck. Then his right leg slammed straight out, causing his foot to punch at the accelerator in time to the pounding music. Larry tried to control the truck with his elbows again. He tried wedging them into the steering wheel, but as he did, he already felt the truck sliding. It swerved hard to the left, just missing an embankment. Larry watched in amazement as his right hand smacked the dashboard a few times and then began flopping around horribly on the steering wheel. The hand began beeping the horn while his legs did a spastic dance between the brake and the accelerator.

Larry began to cry when he looked down at his speedometer. He was flying. The music grew louder. Suddenly his head flung to the left, slamming his face hard through the driver's side window. Blood cascaded down his cheeks and swept off his neck in a fine red spray. Helpless and screaming, a glassy stare found his eyes and settled in them. When the lids began peeling themselves back, Larry tried praying. When God didn't answer, he just watched the trees scream past, nothing more than a colorless blur.

"Mommy..." he said as Robyn tucked him lovingly into his bed. "Do you love me?"

She felt her throat close off in a knot.

"Of course I do silly little man, of course I do."

"Do you love me more than mister Larry?"

The tears were stinging her eyes. It wasn't Andrew's fault, but she knew that finding another man anytime soon would be impossible.

"I love you a million times more Drew. I really, really do!" She kissed her son and shut out the lights.

Andrew lay in his bed grinning. He really loved his mommy. Then that vacant looked crept back onto his face. Andrew's thoughts drifted to the funny dancing clown with those jerky arms slapping at its sides and its legs slipping carelessly underneath him. And as the truck sped recklessly down Highway 35 towards the bridge over the sucking waters of the Black Rail River, Andrew grinned in the darkness.

Left leg. Right leg, he said in his mind over and over again. *Right arm, left.*

And Andrew felt happy. Nothing would ever get in the way of his bond with Mommy again. Never, never ever.

Discussions Concerning the Ingestion of Living Insects

by Ronald Damien Malfi

Mid-October

SOON-LEE, AMONGST other things, reflected on flies. Mostly, he considered the way they congregated, purple and black and green, their voices like stinging spikes breaking the air. And he pictured them in a scuttle, like spawning salmon in too-shallow water, rumbling overtop one another like knotted turns in a rope. That was how they were in reality, and how he imagined them in the hours when he closed his eyes. *These things*, he would think, *are most important.* He ate them, ate several of them. He did this only after they became too fat and too lazy to escape him. With one hand, he was usually capable of grasping two or three, sometimes four at a time, and he'd rattle them around and feel them flutter against the flesh of his palm before shaking them into his mouth and biting down. Or swallowing them whole. Sometimes, he liked the way they felt. A living train, receding in lethargic contractions down the back of his throat.

They came in through cracks in the windows—through fissures in the walls and up through crevices in the floorboards and tiles. Nights, he could hear them coming, working through the foundation like an inevitable doom, building and building only to rupture and expel themselves into the air in a burst of wings and eyes.

And onto him.

And into him.

There was no repulsion associated with the acts—neither his nor theirs. It was simply rotation, simply cycle, the mere spinning of a wheel. And in his mind he could picture that wheel, forever in slow-motion, forty-five revolutions per minute, and he could make out the rutted sound of its churning. It was a grand wheel, aflame with a myriad of colored ribbons and diamond studs. With each turn, a brilliant new light reflected off his mind-face, and he could sense each oncoming color with the same clarity as he'd witnessed the passage of the old ones.

All the same, he knew. It was all the same. *When a man dies*, he thought, *he leaves several things behind. But what will I leave behind? And will I really, truly even die?*

Often, he laughed. He'd discovered a way outside the wheel, a way to beat the system after all. Eternal life. Immortality. Disenfranchised from the human race. And how many people before him had discovered the same thing? A hundred? A million? None? Across from his bed and against the far wall hung a wall calendar. It claimed it was mid-October, but it was well beyond October. Like him, October was long forgotten. A filthy blackness had claimed one corner of the calendar—had withered it and curled it like a burnt leaf. He, too, had been burned…though the details, having grown much too unimportant, were now lost to him. Like many things.

"My name is Soon-Lee." He said this occasionally to remind himself, though he did not know why. Burned. He remembered something about a fire: the acrid stink of charred wood and a great conflagration…yet nothing was clear. The conflagration, after too much time turning the half-memory over in his head, merely became the wheel itself, spinning colors out of control, powerful and all-knowing the way God is massive and unyielding. And what about God? What about that bullshit? Was there anything to fill that husk?

Soon-Lee laughed. His left eardrum was blown out, and the sound rattled like static in his head. Between the miserable, segmented hours of his consciousness, Soon-Lee slept. It was a sleep corrupted by violent images and unrelenting waves of nausea. Sometimes, almost blessedly, he would dream of Kilfer and Mines and Tonya—blessed for these dreams, horrid and painful as they were, represented his last handhold on reality. The specifics of the dreams changed from time to time, but the core always remained the same: they were negotiating a series of narrow, subterranean tunnels beneath the village, walled in on either side, the stink of their sweat in the air. They could hear each other breathing, could hear the fabric of their khakis rubbing against their legs. And the sounds of screaming people, screaming children...

"You hear 'em?" Kilfer breathed. "All of 'em, up ahead somewhere?"

"Children, too," Tonya said.

Kilfer snorted in the darkness. "I don't trust it down here. Let's move topside."

"We're almost to the end," Soon-Lee insisted. "Swab the fucking place."

"Kids," Mines stated to no one in particular, "is just the same." Soon-Lee didn't know what that meant, but continued to listen nonetheless. "Goddamn fountain of youth, little sons-a-bitches. Christ, my head hurts."

Occasionally, the dream segued into the purely bizarre...

"You b'lieve in God, Soon-Lee?" Kilfer said.

"No," he answered, "and God don't believe in me."

"Fuck God," snickered Mines. "What'd God ever do for any of us? Made Tonya here one ugly bastard, that's about it." He laughed. "God can shine my Christing shoes, I'll tell you what."

Kilfer sighed in the darkness. "That's ignorant." He was only a few feet in front of Soon-Lee; he could smell Kilfer's sweat fanning off him in moist waves. "Better yet, what you think about flies, Soon-Lee? You like 'em? They taste good?"

Soon-Lee froze, the hairs on the nape of his neck prickling up. "What you know about flies?"

"I know you been eating them to stay alive. You ever read Dracula?"

"I seen the movie once. What's that got to do with me and flies? How'd you know about that?" Even in his dream, he was aware that the flies had not come yet, that Kilfer was talking out of order, that the flies wouldn't become a part of the whole thing until after he was pulled from the tunnels and taken to the hospital, burned and forgotten.

"Don't worry about it, Soon-Lee." It was Tonya, some distance behind him. "He's just bustin' your balls. Forget the flies. We're all gonna die down here anyway."

"Tonya—"

"Shit, buddy, you know that, don't you?"

"What's going on? What are you guys talking about? This ain't how it happened."

And he'd wake up, too exhausted to scream. Night and day alternated without pause. After many days he lost count and assumed, from the coldness of the walls, that it was sometime in December now. Or maybe even January. Christ, had it been that long? Passing, in the blink of an eye...

He had no feet. The initial explosion had sheared them off at the ankles, the flames working their way up his shins, his thighs. The pain had been exquisite, but he only now remembered this because he remembered thinking this, and did not necessarily remember the pain itself. And even the events which led to his arrival at the hospital were fuzzy. Kilfer was there—something about Kilfer, something about Kilfer dying yet saving his life. *Sure*, he thought. *Anything you want, buddy. Anything at all.*

"Soon-Lee," he moaned.

Eight of them had gone down into the darkness, yet only four of them had made it to the end. The other men—Soon-Lee couldn't recall their names, though he'd been good friends with all of the Special Operations guys at one time—had split off into separate corridors communicating with equal darkness.

"Up ahead," Tonya repeated. "Trapped themselves down here like rats. And with their children, man. You hear that?" Tonya's face was a roadmap of scars and burned tissue—the only medals he ever received during his tour of the islands. The expression on his face was always one of constant pain, even when he laughed, which was rare.

Soon-Lee shook his head. "How do you now about the flies?"

"Forget it, man," Kilfer said. There was exasperation in his voice. "I didn't say nothin' about no flies anyhow. You're dreaming this, buddy. You got me?" The screaming of the frightened and trapped grew louder.

Mid-October. Or December or January. Soon-Lee opened his eyes wide and found himself staring at the calendar on the opposite wall. He wasn't in the tunnels; he was here in the hospital. Alone. And there was no pain. Just immortality and flies. And the cracks in the ceiling. And the graffiti across the walls—CON DIED DEAD and BEG MORT and GOD SPARED ME BLADDER and I WEAR THE ROSE. Words of dead men, all of them. Forgotten, like him. Dead.

Not me, he thought. *Never me.*

"The only way to beat God is to never die," Mines said, creeping along the cinder walls. His booted feet crunched gravel or bone or both. The flame at the tip of his flamethrower passed briefly before his face, bringing his features into stark relief. He looked like a man who'd just been given a glimpse of his greatest achievements, all compiled into one singular, continuous reel. "Other than that, He gets us all in the end."

"All of us," Tonya agreed.

"All of us," chimed Kilfer.

But that wasn't how it went down. There'd been no talk about God, and certainly no discussion concerning the ingestion of insects. In fact, there'd been no talking at all in the tunnels. Was that all really just in his head? Perhaps. But the people and the children and the explosion—those things were real, all right. There was no forgetting them. Not ever. *The only way to beat God is to never die*, he heard Mines whisper in his head. He looked down at his legs now. They were not legs. Two abbreviated stumps—a network of twisted, charred flesh and coagulated blood…of ruined muscle and tissue…a testament to God's cruelty. His skin had gone a pale blue-gray all the way to his upper thighs now, nearing his genitals. They were numb, had no feeling. Looking at them, he felt nothing inside, which would have frightened a more mentally competent human being. Soon-Lee was not that human being; he'd retreated to the darkest recesses of his mind over the dripping passage of days and weeks and months. And was it really months? Could that be?

December? January?

His legs couldn't move on their own. It took great effort to shift them, mostly with the muscles of his abdomen and his hands, and while they were being repositioned, they moved like one complete unit, leaving behind red-brown flakes of dried and bloodied skin along the mattress. He could only stare at them for so long until his mind receded again, forcing him to consider the wheel, the spinning cycle of life that he was in the middle of avoiding, that he was nearly mastering. Could he really be that intelligent, that ingenious?

Looking around the room, his eyes fell on scores of empty beds and gurneys. Some were still embossed with the imprint of their occupants, now long since departed. Empty and half-empty IV bags hung from racks or lay discarded on the green tile floor. A bundle of wet laundry lay just outside the doorway out in the hall. The cloying stink of ammonia and perspiration still hung in the air, just as strong as it had been on the day he arrived, screaming and writhing in pain. Even with his wrecked and ruined mind, he was able to remember the room when it had been bustling with people—nurses and doctors and, most of all, the pained and suffering. With surprising clarity, he recalled a young man by the name of Phillips as he was wheeled into the room and established beside Soon-Lee. He was really just a boy—hardly a man, hardly able to fight—and despite the fact that half his left arm had been torn free from the shoulder by a mortar, he remained silent and still, staring wide-eyed and lazy at the ceiling. *Those people in those tunnels*, he thought now. *All those children.*

He blacked out for a moment. An image materialized in his subconscious—that of a wild-eyed man dissecting young women and stitching their bodies together to birth some horrific, patchwork monster. This was not a memory; rather, this was part of the insight people are granted into the minds and lives of other people when confronted with the sudden proximity of their own death.

Yet Soon-Lee did not die. Restless, he slept through the night.

And was back below the earth inside the tunnels again…

"What do you think they're doing down here?" he asked Kilfer. "All these damn people?"

"Hiding. Some might be locked away, but they're mostly hiding. Some of these villages get a whiff of a Special Ops team on the horizon, they start buryin' their loved ones underground. Whole families."

"Kids," Soon-Lee said.

"That's tragic," Tonya said from somewhere, though he didn't sound too upset.

"Can't trust the kids just like you can't trust their parents," Kilfer continued. "They'd blow up the whole regiment if they could. Pal of mine got killed when one of these island bastards tossed a grenade into his tent while he slept. Whole time he treated this kid nice, didn't do nothin' bad to him, even fed him when he was hungry, you know? Then the kid turns around and pulls a stunt like that. Imagine that, right? Some shit."

"Some shit," Soon-Lee agreed.

"Half of these fuckers still fight like it's the Second World War, diggin' these friggin' trenches in the ground, crawlin' around in 'em like rats. I trust no one."

Up ahead, Soon-Lee noticed small pinpoints of light piercing the darkness. The swell of the people's cries grew. They knew they were trapped and knew they were about to be killed. Soon-Lee felt something banging inside his head. He couldn't wait to get topside, to sit and breathe fresh air and maybe drink some goddamn water.

Tonya noticed the lights, too. "The hell is that?"

"It's them," Kilfer whispered.

The cries grew louder, and soon it became evident that the four of them had arrived at the end of the tunnel, that nothing separated their unit from the rising swell of screaming children other than darkness and a few splintered slats of wood. Soon-Lee squinted, allowing his eyes time to adjust to the new light. He could see them behind the wooden slats, their arms a tangle of bony flesh, filthy and pale. Their cries rose and fell in unison, as if they were all individual parts of one complex beast. Soon-Lee shuddered. What sort of people hide with their children in prisons underground? Didn't they know they wouldn't be safe? Didn't they know they couldn't hide? There was no liberation in war. You had to track and fight, not run and hide. Cowards.

"Shut up, the lot of you!" Tonya barked. His face was alight with passion, hungry for destruction. His eyes were like two celestial bodies, full and glowing. "You filthy little pecks!"

Some of the islanders held torches, which was where the light was coming from. In their close quarters, the flames were either quickly doused or accidentally lit someone up.

Kilfer shook his head. "You see what sort of animals we're dealing with here?"

"Light 'em up," Soon-Lee said, and ignited his own flamethrower. Kilfer and Tonya followed suit. The hot stink of sulfur filled the tunnel, stung Soon-Lee's nose, forced his eyes to tear. The children were screaming louder now, the sound ripping through him like a white-hot charge of electricity.

Packed behind the wooden slats like filthy, caged animals, the islanders began to struggle, desperate to break the boards apart and free themselves. There must have been fifty of them trapped in there. A hundred...two hundred...

Mines fired first, igniting the slats and scoring the flailing arms. Once the flames hit, the arms quickly retreated. Or tried to. The screams reached a crescendo, broke into a unified shriek, and then Tonya's flamethrower fanned the entire length of the tunnel. The heat struck Soon-Lee like the collapse of a building. His own flamethrower jammed. He turned it over and pushed the muzzle into Tonya's flame. The flamethrower burst to life and launched a fiery orange stream toward the screaming people trapped behind the burning wooden slats.

Mines was shouting something. Soon-Lee couldn't make it out. Tonya was laughing. Kilfer worked with stern determination, his eyes set, his face expressionless.

And then the explosion hit.

The source was unexplained—perhaps there was a gas pipe down there. Or perhaps it was deliberate, an ambush set by the trapped islanders. Soon-Lee and the rest of the Special Operations unit would never know.

The explosion struck like the fist of God, and for an instant, Soon-Lee saw everything turn white. There was no sound. Then there was too much sound. Something fuzzed and rattled inside Soon-Lee's head, and he felt the hot fluidity of his burst eardrum in his skull. His equilibrium spinning circles, he felt his body lose all touch with reality...and an instant later, he was lifted off his feet and flung into the air. There was no pain. In his mind, he felt the world tilt. It was then that he caught his first sight of the spinning wheel, and he acknowledged it with something akin to disinterest, as if he'd seen this wheel a hundred times before, or at least had known of its presence for some time now. It was the wheel that saved his life, for he did not feel the need to sit up immediately after striking the ground, just as the wall of flame shot through the tunnel. Eyes closed, he remained watching the wheel. He was faintly aware of a stinging sensation in his lower extremities.

Then, in that second, the pain blossomed-exploded-detonated-erupted and became something impossibly grandiose, something terrifically heartless and medieval.

And the rest was lost to him: a blur. Except for certain times, staring at the hospital ceiling in the dark, when he remembered that only Kilfer and he had survived, and that it was Kilfer who had saved his life. Kilfer, dragging his bloodied body through the darkness of the tunnel, whispering to him the entire time just to keep him alive. His words were forgotten, but they were unimportant. It was Kilfer's presence that saved him.

Alive, Soon-Lee thought now. *I am alive. Yet Kilfer is dead.*

He felt a stirring of pain at his waist and knew it was time for more Percocet. He kept the pills on the gurney beside him, and shook two into his hand, downed them. Closing his eyes, he eased his head back down on the pillow. He could feel a million stirrings in his ruined legs. He tried not to think about it.

Keep eating, he thought.

After some time, with the pain numbed to nothingness, he sat up and once again began to feast on the flies. To his delight—and his horror—there were more maggots.

As sustenance, they were more fulfilling than the actual adult flies. However, something about their fleshy bodies wriggling within the devastated corruption of his legs disgusted him. He plucked them from his wounds one by one, examined them absently, and swallowed them whole. Process. All one big cycle, part of the same wheel. Turn-turn-turn.

Somehow, Kilfer had managed to drag him topside. There was commotion throughout the village. The explosion had burst through the ground and had set a collection of oil drums ablaze. Several people were killed or wounded. People came and went, rushed by like ghosts in white blurs.

"We done too many things to die right now, buddy," Kilfer whispered near his ear. A team of medics was approaching. "We ain't had enough time to make good of ourselves, if you b'lieve in that sort of thing. You don't b'lieve in God, do you, Soon-Lee?"

But he couldn't answer. He was fading in and out of consciousness, trapped in some cartoon limbo where shapes refused to remain solid and colors bled too bright. His mind replayed the explosion, and several times he began to jerk and spasm, his brain teasing him with replay after replay after replay. What was real? Anything? Anything at all?

"You just hang on," Kilfer said. Then quieter, almost to himself: "Goddamn Mines and Tonya, those poor bastards. Never had a chance to make peace. Not a goddamn chance."

And that was just it. Evil people were afraid to die, afraid of what they had to face. Ideally, given the opportunity, they'd embrace immortality just to stave off the fiery hand of justice in the afterlife.

Poor bastards, Soon-Lee thought now, and almost laughed.

The medics carried him to the hospital. They gave him medication to pull him from his blackout, the shits, and all it did was make him acutely aware of the pain he was in. Screaming, clawing at their faces, he was carried into the island hospital very near death. Waves of unreality washed over him.

Doctors came and went in the frantic tide of emergency, their voices muffled behind masks, their hands cold as ice, their stares as empty and frozen as the tundra. He retreated to peace in his mind, but all he could see was that spinning wheel of light and fire...and he could see that it was beginning to slow, that he was fading and his own time was almost up. *Evil people are afraid to die*, he remembered thinking.

So now—mid-October. Or January. Or maybe time didn't matter; maybe months had ceased to exist. He adjusted himself on his bed, his body bruised and covered in sores, and strained his eyes to see through the darkness. There were a number of windows along the far side of the room, but all the shades had been pulled prior to the hospital's evacuation. Only tiny slivers of moonlight found their way in. A single window above his head, cracked the slightest bit. The air was cold. He was grateful the flies still came. Not really hungry anymore, he forced himself to ingest the flies and their larvae once again, peeling them out of his rotting flesh. It was all part of the cycle, he continued to remind himself, all part of what needed to be done to avoid the destruction of the wheel.

The wheel had to keep spinning.

Thirsty, he managed to ease onto his side and remove the clay ash-tray from the windowsill. It was partially filled with stagnant rainwater. He sipped some and saved the rest, uncertain when it would rain again. His throat burned. He began to tremble.

The hospital fell under attack three days after Soon-Lee had arrived. Though he'd been operated on twice and remained stitched and bandaged, the intensity of his pain kept him sedated almost to unconsciousness. When the bombs hit, he was only half awake. The floor emptied out, the nurses and doctors rushing for the exits. Soon-Lee felt the foundation shake. He saw smoke billowing in through some of the windows. How badly were they hit? Would troops move in? What had happened to the defense, the fucking barracks?

Most of the patients were able to leave on their own.

Others tried and were trampled and crushed in the hallways and stairwells. A few compassionate nurses managed to gather the remaining patients. Except for him. They'd left him. And perhaps it was only his imagination, but he was fairly certain that a young female nurse had paused at the foot of his own bed, had locked eyes with him, debating whether she could carry him or not...and then fled. The entire floor was empty in a matter of seconds; the entire hospital in a matter of minutes. And then the gunfire started outside. He could hear it through the walls, the cracked windows. Had they all been killed? Kilfer? Yes—he knew Kilfer was dead. He could feel it. And yet Kilfer returned to him several nights later.

He appeared as a shadow in a darkened corner of the room.

"Step out," Soon-Lee insisted.

"No."

"I want to see you."

"I won't."

"Damn you, Kilfer." He bit his lower lip, drew blood. "What's the matter with you? They killed you out there, didn't they? They shot you."

"Yes."

"What is it? What do you want?"

Kilfer's voice sounded very far away. "It's bad where I am, buddy. Just like I said. I know you don't b'lieve, but it's bad. Real bad."

Soon-Lee started to shake. "The hell you talkin' about? You tryin' to drive me nuts?"

"I'm telling you."

"Fuck off."

"Fight it, buddy. Stay alive. Don't die. Don't ever die. It's bad for guys like you and me. Very, very bad."

Soon-Lee's mouth was dry. "The wheel..."

"Keep it spinning."

"Cycle."

"Yes. Keep it spinning. Recycle the whole damned thing. You understand, buddy? You get me?"

He nodded. He was sweating and had a fever. "I do."

He looked at his legs, disfigured and mummified within a roll of gauze bandages. A few bloodstains had surfaced on the gauze over the past few days and Soon-Lee had immediately noticed how quickly the flies in the room lit on him, sucked at the bloodied bandages. Frantically, he had swatted them away...but all the while, he'd been thinking in the back of his mind.

"Yes," Kilfer told him. "You know it."

So he unraveled the bandages and stared at his scarred, stitched-up legs. Gritting his teeth, he systematically popped the stitches and broke open the skin to become his own bait. He cried out countless times. And the flies came. For days...and weeks...and months. The more that came, the more he caught and ate...only to have more come again. They seemed to be the product of an infinite well, coming and coming and coming and never running dry. And the cycle was simple. *They eat me*, he thought, *and then I eat them.*

This way, I never die. I remain.

I remain.

Mid-January, closer to February. He understood Kilfer's apparition to be just that—a figment of his own imagination. However, Kilfer's image did provide him with useful advice. Was it possible to beat the system, to beat God?

"My name is..." He paused. Considered. Looking down, he saw that the skin around his genitals had turned black and hard, and he could no longer feel his thighs. His abdomen was bloated and pasty. He could tell his body was wracked with fever.

"Kilfer!"

But Kilfer had ceased appearing to him months ago.

What happens when the flies stop coming? said a voice in his head—a voice very much like his own. *What will keep the wheel spinning when the flies stop coming?*

"They'll always come." His voice shook, trembled. "They'll always be here."

Night and day continued to alternate.

I must have been here five months by now, he thought.

Five months. Damn it all, that calendar is wrong!

He could hear screams echoing down the hospital corridor—the screams of the burned and dead islanders from the tunnels beneath the village. Did they know he was here? Were they coming for him?

"My name…"

He shuddered. His entire body had gone cold. There was no feeling in his fingers, in his face. He tried moving his tongue around his mouth and found that he couldn't.

Six…seven months, easy…

He knew he had to keep eating. Even in the darkness he could see that there were plenty of flies on his legs, that there were plenty of wriggling grubs burrowing in his flesh, yet he could not bring himself to consider eating them. He couldn't move his hands to properly operate his fingers even if he'd wanted to do so. His body was slowly seizing up on him. The wheel, he knew, was beginning to slow.

"Uh…"

Evil people, he reminded himself, *are afraid to die.*

He managed to maneuver his hands in the bloody pulp of his legs, to fish out the maggots…but there were only a few. He'd been wrong—there were hardly any at all. And even the fattest, slowest flies were faster than him.

Panicked, he looked around. Beside him, resting on the gurney with the Percocet, lay a number of hospital tools. Among them was a scalpel. Its blade glinted moonlight.

He didn't need the flies. They were an inconvenient cog, the middle-man that needed to be cut. This was nothing he couldn't continue on his own. Ingestion equaled digestion equaled regeneration. It made sense. He didn't need the flies. He'd never needed the flies.

It took him several tries to finally grasp the scalpel. With much difficulty, he managed to bring the blade down into the soft, scored flesh of his ruined left knee. He cut a piece of himself—a piece big enough to require chewing—with effort, and it took several drawn-out moments for him to finally get the piece into his mouth.

It was October twenty-seven.

The Leak
by Earl Javorsky

IN A NEARBY room an angel weeps. Because she cannot hear me, she imagines me lost. She is mistaken, of course. In fact, if the truth were known, if the world could even glimpse the state in which I find myself, great joy would spread like pollen in a spring breeze. Books would be written, vengeance forgotten; each candle would light many candles and the darkness would be lifted.

Let me explain.

It began with the simple discovery that I no longer needed to eat. This small miracle opened the door for all that was to come, for in the days that followed I felt increasingly lighter in body and in spirit. The day came when my bondage to the flesh was completely undone...I could come and go as I pleased.

How can I express the exhilaration I felt at this new freedom? I speak, of course, for the Record, now that I know there is a Record, for I realize that you cannot comprehend what I say. In fact, to me, for quite some time now human speech has sounded rather like dogs barking, the honking of geese and the bleating of lambs. Instead of your intended articulation, I hear only the expressions behind your intent: love and the void felt in its absence. For the most part, I have stopped listening.

There are times when a wild spark enters my body and romps through me like a school of minnows chased by a mackerel and I am lifted, yes lifted, into dance.

More often, however, I direct my will toward travel and play. I have been taught many things; by whom I cannot tell. Clearly beings

of even subtler and more profound experience than my own have long
awaited humanity's ascendance, for they have welcomed, tutored, and
encouraged me. They have shown me, for example, how to enter into
your radio waves. Many times, for my own amusement, I have altered
your television broadcasts to my whim. News reporting I find ripe for
improvisation.

Once I willed my old form from its chair and into the streets.
Upon finding a crowded intersection, I climbed atop a vehicle and
changed forms for the multitudes—I shifted from ape to Adonis, from
flaming column to winged Satan, from kangaroo to Kali, and, when
set upon by the mob, I found the form of rat expedient for the purpose
of escape.

Another time, I received clear instruction that I was to procreate,
that I was to be instrumental in the genesis of a Godlike new race, and
that it was incumbent upon me to choose suitable mates. Again I took
my body into the city, this time finding a young female and sharing
my gift.

Her resistance made it clear that my neglect of my physical form
had left me perhaps deficient, not appropriately attractive for the task.
I set out later to correct this. My many lessons had included tutoring
in the rebuilding of my physical form. My first experiment was to
replace my teeth. This, of course, involved removal of the entire set of
old ones; I am now engaged in the appropriate manipulation of DNA
necessary to generate new growth.

Sometimes a roar will start in my human ears and travel all the way
up to my domain, filling the vast space, growing louder until my vision
is disturbed. Landscapes lose their definition, a fog sets in: it darkens
and condenses until I am in a lightless box. Somewhere, perhaps in a
corner, there is a leak in the box, through which come hints, visions,
whispers of another world. A man stands in a darkened room, facing a
blank wall. Hint: he is emaciated. Whisper: his sanity is buried beneath
an avalanche of grief. Vision: laughing, he breaks his own teeth with a
heavy ashtray. Whisper: the death of a child. The leak widens, more is
revealed: he is under supervision. On occasion, he has escaped.

Shouting gibberish, naked, at a theater crowd. An attempted rape. I
am haunted by this stream of images. The wall is indeed very blank.

In a nearby room my wife weeps.

Portrait of a Suburb
by S. William Snider

S WALLOW LANE WAS a suburb not unlike other local suburbs where the neighbors could often be found lurking just behind their window drapes with an ever-vigilant eye over the neighborhood. Few actions went unchecked. Simple things such as retrieving the mail and the manner in which it was done were carefully analyzed and dissected. No two neighbors were ever seen wandering out to the mailbox at once. The loathsome task was accomplished by the unfortunate neighbor in question rushing out to the mail box just as the mail truck left, collecting the letters while carefully concealing which magazines had come, then fleeing back inside to their window before the next neighbor ventured out. Shortly after the mail truck proceeded onto the next block, the few uneasy alliances that had been formed on Swallow Lane would contact each other via phone to exchange tid-bits on what so-and-so had gotten in the mail. Packages were even more dangerous. A good sized one could keep the neighborhood buzzing for weeks. Christmas was especially dreaded.

Children were never seen playing in the streets. Every parent feared for their son or daughter falling in with such a motley crew as so-and-so's children. The children were kept strictly inside in the not unjustified fear of being watched. Lawsuits were quick in Swallow Lane, especially for something as despicable as a stray football in someone else's yard. The parents compromised by buying their children numerous gaming systems and DVD players. They grew fat and strung out amongst their video games and began to isolate themselves at school except when football season rolled around, in which case parents would demand they try out, then demand they quit because of the brutality.

Several neighbors had even developed sophisticated methods with which to watch. Arlington Smith hung two bathroom mirrors in his upstairs office on either wall adjacent to the window so that he could watch while trading stocks on Ameritrade. Margery O'Connell moved her entire entertainment center into the dining room in front of the house so that she wouldn't have to miss her daytime soaps while keeping watch. The crippled Mr. Stitch's view had been somewhat obscured by the geography of the cul-de-sac he lived on so he bought a pair of high powered binoculars primarily used by U.S. snipers to mark targets.

And so all lived in peace and harmony on Swallow Lane until the Jones' arrived. It was apparent that they were an odd sort from the getgo. For starters, when they moved in there was not a mover to be seen. The whole family had actually pitched in together and moved an entire Ryder truck full of furniture into the house themselves! Even more disturbing, Mr. Jones, with a Marlboro Red dangling from his lips, had waved at Mrs. Peterson who in turn called the police. No action was taken but the police department promised to keep close watch over the Jones'. And at the end of the day, with all the furniture unloaded, Mr. Jones and his two boys came out in the front yard and began throwing a football around. Many of the neighbors made sure their phones were handy in case a stray football should crack a window or land in someone's shrubs but remarkably they were able to keep it all on their property.

By the end of the week the police had received two dozen complaints from Swallow Lane concerning the Jones', none of which had been acted upon. "They said they hadn't actually committed a crime," Arlington Smith confided to Bunny Heller. "I even told them how that Jones just sits out there in his driveway with a beer and a pack of cigarettes after work for all the world to see and drinks and smokes and they said it wasn't a crime. I asked them what about the children…I mean, can you imagine the kind of trauma they're going to suffer from this…I told all of this to the police and they said they still couldn't do anything about it." He shook his head in disgust. Arlington and Bunny had lived next door to each other for three years now and it was the first time either of them had ever had to meet at the property line for discussion. Arlington took it as another sign of the decline of Swallow Lane.

He was not alone. Mr. Stitch had begun to suspect Jones of doing time in prison because of the tattoo he sported on his right arm. He hired three different detective agencies to run background checks on the Jones'. When nothing turned up he began forging records and confronting the police with them. They stopped returning his phone calls.

Finally Mr. Stitch and Arlington Smith were forced to meet with one another. In their own minds they both saw themselves as proxy leaders of the neighborhood which was one of the primary reasons they hated one another so much. The other had to do with the infamous sprinkler incident. Two years ago Swallow Lane experienced a severe drought and sprinklers were only allowed to run on Tuesdays and Thursdays. Arlington Smith cheated and ran his sprinklers on Friday and Sunday in order to have the greenest grass in the neighborhood. Mr. Stitch carefully documented the illegal use of water, video taping every night the sprinklers ran for several weeks, and turning the tapes in to the police. Arlington Smith was fined twenty-five dollars and ever since both men had been bitter rivals.

It took the Jones situation to bring both men together. They had agreed upon Margery Thatcher's house as a neutral meeting ground shortly after dark. Both men decided to be early in order to complain about the other's tardiness. They both arrived in the middle of the Thatchers' dinner as a result and sat at opposite sides of the living room glaring at one another while the family hastily finished up. Margery made a pot of French Roast blend and attempted to start the meeting.

"So, the Jones'," she said.

"The Jones'," Arlington Smith echoed.

"Yes, the Jones'," Mr. Stitch hissed.

After much debate it was decided someone from the neighbohood should set the record straight. Both Arlington Smith and Mr. Stitch felt that they alone should be the one to do it and eventually compromised on both going. The entire neighborhood was gathered just a few paces behind their window blinds when both men stepped from the Thatcher's and began marching down the street to the Jones'. The night was still except for the sound of Led Zeppelin coming from Mr. Jones' radio while he worked on his bike in the garage. He did not notice Arlington Smith and Mr. Stitch at first but quickly sprang to attention when he caught sight of them from the corner of his eye.

"How y'all doing tonight?" he said as he wiped the grease from his hands on an old rag. "Can I offer you something? A cold beer or a soda...a chair maybe?"

Arlington Smith and Mr. Stitch exchanged glances, then Mr. Stitch took the initiative. "Look here Jones, we're going to make this short and to the point...I don't know where it is you came from but you're not there anymore. You're here now and there's a certain way of acting."

"Exactly," Arlington Smith piped in. "I mean, have you ever considered what you're doing to our children?"

Mr. Jones was puzzled. "I don't follow you..." He trailed off, for an odd thing was happening: the neighbors were hesitantly filing out of their homes and into the front yards. They walked with the body language of prizefighters feeling each other out at the beginning of a bout. Some were sickly, especially the older ones without jobs. With no reason to leave home their flesh had developed an albino complexion after years behind locked doors. Neighbors that had never seen each other in person were now standing shoulder to shoulder watching the spectacle before them with a certain unease gaining in the air. Mr. Jones shivered. The whole scene reminded him of something out of *Night of the Living Dead*.

"You don't follow, eh?" Mr. Stitch sneered, grasping for the spotlight in belief that the audience had come out to see him.

"Well, I'll tell you what it is: it's this whole damn charade...the cigarettes, the bike, the waving..."

"*And the moving*!" Arlington Smith howled, believing the onlookers had come to see him. "Decent people just don't go dragging their furniture into their homes! That's what God created movers for!

"And can you imagine what would have happened if one of my children had seen you playing football with your sons...suppose that makes my kid want to play football from seeing you showboating in front of the whole neighborhood. Can you imagine the kinds of injuries he would take in this yard?! And me! What about me trying to throw the football to him with the back problem and the asthma I have?!"

Mr. Jones did not know what to make of this whole ordeal but he was not about to be bullied either. He eyed both men through narrowed slits as he lit another cigarette and said, "Well, it seems to me the real problem here is y'all are nothing but a pair of fucking pussies."

His words echoed like a shot heard in the wide-open wilderness. Arlington Smith and Mr. Stitch both gawked slack-jawed at Mr. Jones in sheer disbelief. "And the children just heard such filth..." Arlington Smith cried breathlessly. For a time the whole neighborhood seemed dumbfounded. It was like they had just caught their children watching one of 'those' late-night HBO shows. Then the rage slowly spread through them one by one. Mr. Jones had poisoned the neighborhood in one decisive blow. Families could no longer raise their children in peace with such a creature living right down the street. Now it was only a matter of time before one of the teenagers started smoking marijuana.

Mr. Stitch was the first to format his anger into words. "This man is a terrorist!" he howled. Slowly the neighborhood collected itself from its fog of rage and nodded in agreement.

"Now wait just a damn minute here!" Mr. Jones protested. "I ain't no A-rab!"

"He is jealous of our way of life and since he cannot have it he must destroy it!" Arlington Smith quipped, determined not to be outdone by his rival. "And now there is only one thing left to do to maintain our way of life!"

A collective light bulb went off in the minds of each and every neighbor at that moment. They knew now what must be done. The bird-like Gibby Jung was the first to act on the impulse. He stepped forward with a wide-eyed look of detachment. Bunny Heller was quick to follow suit. Then the Thatchers. Soon the whole block was closing in on Mr. Jones. He stood in disbelief, the cigarette falling from his mouth.

"Crucify him," Mr. Stitch hissed with a smile.

"Yes, crucify him," Arlington Smith agreed.

Before he could flee, the neighborhood engulfed Mr. Jones, hoisting him over their heads and carrying him into the street. A chant of 'crucify him' sounded off across the block. The children finally left their gaming systems and emerged from their houses to see what all the excitement was about. A cross was assembled in the heart of Swallow Lane out of wide screen TV's, George Foreman grills, Japanese DVD players and massage capable recliners. "I'll teach you what the problem is," Mr. Stitch whispered in Jones' ear as he drove a Felton tip pen through his palm.

It was shortly before midnight when Mr. Jones was erected upon the cross of mass consumption. The neighborhood waited just long enough to be certain he was dead then returned to their windows to watch for the next neighbor.

Poker

by Brandi Bell

WE ARE PLAYING strip poker and I am the last one to end up naked. That should count for something, but it doesn't. Not now. Not now when everyone else has been naked for minutes and minutes and parts of hours and I've been exposed for less and I'm squirming first.

Touch me please. Always that.

Ohhh god.

The room smells like stagnation. Like tension. The room smells like there are four people sitting around in the half dark, pre-dawn, incense filled, night naked. No one is looking for too long. Except me. I push too hard.

It's my fault, I know.

He looks at me long and I am the wet between my legs and nothing else. I push too hard, I know. I get told it repeatedly.

I do pray. I've learned how: oh god oh god oh god. And please.

He can smell me. I smell like sex. It's my fault. He isn't condemning me for it, yet. He's waiting. He wants to see me squirm first. Wants me to make it obvious that I can't control myself...soooo...I try not to move. Repeatedly. Be still be still be still, and the flexing of my muscles becomes rhythmic against my will.

The game played in their bedroom. Locked away from their kids, four (consenting?) adults in a room. Incense and an open window. Music. Someone's idea—no one remembers whose now—when Gin Rummy got boring. Someone's idea when the beer buzz was strong enough to suggest shots. Someone, when the thought of tomorrow ceased to matter, suggested strip poker.

A flush:
He didn't really mean to go down on her. It was simply a hug at first. The tension was getting to him, in that way that tension does. He knelt between her legs. Her open and exposed. He put his arms around her back. Her soft and strong. His face against her belly. Her comfort and...breathe now baby, it will all be ok.
And the smell. The smell of her wanting him, it, this. The smell of her trying to be still, trying not to want, trying and failing and he had to have a taste. Just one, just one taste of that thing that is her, that need that is her...

A pair:
Two people wrapped up, caught in the moment and scent and strain. Two people suddenly unaware of the room, the dawn, the light and fear. Two people praying now, with their mouths. We'll call them lovers.

He wraps his tongue around her sucking hard and fast. Somewhere between the Ace of Spades and the long hot night he forgot that he said no. That he said be good. That he said not this time. He forgot that he was prepared to be pissed off at her if she went there. If she did something stupid/bold/brazen/brash. He'll remember later, after the suck of—

wet in his mouth
longing and 'give it to me baby.'

Queen of Diamonds
She arches her back. Hard to resist, to play it cool. Her hands are groping, in his hair now, his mouth, digging into his shoulder. She sees them, the other two, out of the corner of her eye. They look far away, drawn away from—

lack of restraint
too much need
vulgar
That's what she is.

'give it to me baby'

She tries not to pant...not yet.

He pushes his tongue in. Hard and fast, like a tango:
quick quick slow

He is laying now, half on the bed. His cock pressed, his cock rubbing
up against—

Soft down comforter. What happened to the other two? He tries to see,
tries to look. His friends' faces framed over the swell of her breasts her
pubic mound.

But she keeps pulling him back, drawing him in.
Her fingernail on his nipple now—
flicking.

Her breath hot now, and sweeter. Her wet now...

And she tugs, pulling him, trying to pull him up, on to her, into her:
her hands under his arms, her strength super(sexual)natural. Her
will/need/drive for this...will he never learn? He was prepared to be
pissed off at her...but his cock now, the down comforter, the smell of
her...his friends' faces looming over her pubic mound...

It's my fault I know. I need too much. I get reminded all the time:
"unreasonable expectations" "want too much" "impossible to please"

please
just once

just:
I can feel his cock against my thigh now, and his breath in my ear:
bitch. Goddamn bitch.

He's as hard as a—
he's straining, trying not to.

I arch, rise up to meet him. Lift my hips, open my lips, beg with my
wet
oooh   and   please.
Always that.

Two cards please.
Two people wrapped up, caught. Two people pulling. Pushing. Two
people, what's that phrase? "locked in an embrace?" Two people
locked in the pull and push. Two people. We'll call them lovers.

A blur of bodies. Something happening. The incense has burned out
and the CD is repeating itself. And movement. He looks at them, at his
friends, at the people he has known forever. He looks at their sudden
blurry, at their reaction to the want. There is pain here and he doesn't
know what to do or not do about it.

She pushes harder against him. He puts his hand over her mouth
(teeth): go slow damn it.

His best friend and his best friend's wife. "We love each other," they
say, "But, well, you know how it is." And he nods even though he
doesn't…"haven't had sex in weeks" "the kids have homework
and…" and, "Well, you know how it is…"

He looks at their not knowing. At their sudden—
burning up against and eyes downcast, shifting, yes. He hears a baby
cry from far away. There is pain here: his friends silhouetted behind
her pubic mound—
blurry.

The sudden not knowing. It smells like, he thinks it kind of smells like—
her wet against his mouth now, and drowning.

A flurry of movement, need and want and pain. Yes. There is pain there. He can feel it. He hears crying and her: oh god please...

What is it she really needs?

Queen of Clubs, Jack of Hearts, Ten of Diamonds and an eight...I'll take one card please and your pits sweat a little and you realize this tiny little space holding four people captive in the middle of the night really is rather hot and how bad do you really want that nine anyway?

She sits silent, her hands are folded in her lap, her ankles are crossed, her back straight (little suburban wife).

Two pair, a flush...

Satiated—a word she does not understand, not once, not ever.

She's trying so hard. She does not lose, doesn't miss a beat. I'll take two cards please.

Four people in a bedroom with the door locked, held hostage by the gamble, held captive by need.

He didn't lose the hand on purpose, not really. Blame it on the alcohol, on the dark. The taking off of the last article of clothing felt like being baptized. He knew how to pray once too.

"You bring all of this on yourself you know, you really do..."
Yes. Vulgar, that's what she is. So much need. She's used to this, she's heard it before and before and before.

She looks at them, at the other two, finally now, now when it feels like it might be safe, when it might be too late to turn back. The Wife—

god how she hates that word, that idea—is straddling her husband and
riding him like her life depends on it. His eyes are shut tight. But her,
her eyes are locked on to—

He finally slips his cock in—slow.
(penetrate me)
And I can feel the tension, the strain, the restraint.
Slow, too slow.

Two cards please
please
Urgency—a word that haunts her, a word that lives and dies in her
cunt.

"Needy bitch," he whispers as he penetrates her.
"Selfish bitch. Did it ever occur to you that they might be a little
freaked out by your behavior? Might not want it to go there? Might
not want to participate? Did you ever think of that?"

Vulgar. That's what she is. Little slut.
And he's as hard as—
her want
urgent
living and dying in her cunt.
A blur. 'Faster now, don't be shy.' The Wife reaches her arm out, just
out, just a little, and touches my breast.
Oh god.
And:
yes please   please   please

And the Husband is watching this. Watching his wife touch another
woman's breast, watching her moan and quiver, watching her grind
against him and he thinks:
A baby is crying somewhere. Is that one of ours?
And he thinks:
Who suggested this? Whose idea was this anyway?
And he feels himself now, beginning to tingle—

and
burning up against.
Tingle and
release

Two people burning up against each other. Two people working desperately to…

I'll take two cards please.

The kids in the other room…

Four people locked in a room. There's no way out, not for them, not anymore.

Racing against the rising sun.

Burning up against:

oh god please

Trying, working, hoping
desperately
not to die.

Sipping Wine in a Coffee Shop
by Scott J. Ecksel

IT'S 8 A.M. Women and men are lined up to buy caffeine. I was here first, already have a table. Most of them will pick up their drinks and go. Some will stay. Of the ones who stay, I won't talk to any of them. I have my table. I'm alone.

They don't know it, but I come here to watch them. I watch them every morning. Every morning, the same people stand in line. Sometimes there's a new person in line. Usually not.

What do I want from them? I ask myself that question, find it hard to answer. What is it I gain from watching them? What do I learn each morning that helps me make it through my day?

This morning, for instance, after a very difficult night, I can see that the people in line are not as happy as they were yesterday. Something has changed. I don't know what it is, for I have no idea what happens outside; in the outside world, that is. My only television is the line in the coffee shop. I read the news in their faces, and I can tell that something happened yesterday, something to disturb not just one or two of them but them all.

Yesterday they were very happy. Unusually so. The woman with the white scarf was smiling. When she ordered her small coffee two sugars light with heavy cream she lifted her hand to the counter and waved her fingers in the air from left to right, I'm not sure why. It was a happy motion, a motion which said to me she was unusually upbeat, perhaps she had won the lottery the night before or perhaps she had been given a raise. Or perhaps she was moving into a cheaper apartment this week and would once again be able to afford to go out to eat in the evenings. All of these are possibilities, and it's difficult for me to be certain which is the correct one. My window of understanding is limited in ways, though in other ways I know everything.

The man who always wears shorts even in the winter, for instance. I know what he was thinking and why he seemed unusually content yesterday morning. I could see it in his face. He was smiling crookedly. It's hard to describe. It was a crooked smile. He had found a man's wallet and had kept it, and in that wallet were ten ten-dollar bills, and he was going to buy a present for his new lover. It was a sneaky little smile, the kind that says I am very happy today but my happiness comes at the expense of another's misery. There's nothing magical about my understanding, it's the most common type of smile there is. I see it every day. Put two and two together. Makes four. I know everything about that man. He's like an open book, turned to page seventy-three. Last week, he was turned to page seventy-two. I can already guess the ending. It will be ugly.

But today, something is wrong. They're not happy today. Something happened, and I'm not yet sure what it was. Perhaps they themselves don't know. I wouldn't be surprised.

It's like this. The woman who drinks double espressos, today she hardly raised her eyes to the bald student behind the counter. Of course she didn't need to speak her order, he knows what she wants. But usually she looks up. Today she didn't. Strange thing, really. She's something of a cipher today, not speaking, not gesturing, yet getting what she wants even so. She's like a machine, an automaton. A cipher. I hate her today.

And look at the kids this morning. The three of them, they're here all the time, child labor laws must have been repealed. Usually they're jumping up and down knocking things off the counter, the oldest steals things, too, I've noticed if no one else has. Today they're quiet. They're not even ordering anything. They stood in line for a few minutes, and now they're gone, without buying a thing. It makes no sense.

I hate this place. Why do I sit here watching these idiots? I can't understand a thing about them today. There's the old man with his raspberry iced tea and his triple-locked briefcase. Shifty look to him. Mean sound he makes when he speaks, ordering everyone around. Owns the place, does he? Wish someone would spill hot coffee on

him. Not going to happen though, unless I do it myself, not likely.
Can't kill the customer, first rule of business. But today he's nice. He's
smiling. Oddest thing. Whatever it is that's happened must be terrible,
so terrible.

It's quiet in here! I just realized something, that the music hasn't
been playing. There's always music: jazz, blues, the kind of music that
offends no one. You can't even hear it—it's just in the background—
but pleasant, I'll admit it, it's pleasant to sit here with the music on.
But it's not on. Was it on when I came in? I wonder. I have no idea. I
have no idea, which is strange. Usually I'm more aware of these
things. Last night, I don't even want to remember it. The music, let's
see. The music. Why isn't the music playing today? I have no idea.

Ugh, what am I thinking? There's the guy with the soccer ball.
Sometimes he nods to me. Not today. The line's moving quickly. No
one's talking. Everyone's avoiding each other. Snapshot: soccer ball
looking at stacks of cups, old man briefcase still smiling looking at
spilled coffee on the counter, bald student looking at shelf of coffee
machines for sale, teenager making espresso looking into space,
woman with cat's eye ring looking at coffee shop brochure, old
woman always complaining looking at the back of woman with cat's
eye ring's head, student in a suit looking at the back of old woman's
head—what is it about the backs of people's heads, anyway—and a guy
I've never seen who just entered looking at floor. It's like an elevator.

Have I seen him before? Not in here. Not on the way here. Not in
my building. Not when I was in school. But somewhere. It'll bother
me all day. I have to relax. Something's happened, and so far I haven't
learned a thing.

Now he's staring at me. He's staring right at me, won't stop
looking. I'm trying to ignore him. I'll look at the walls. Pictures of
mountains all over the place. Do coffee trees grow in the mountains?
Should show peasants picking beans, or cows mooing all over the
countryside. Nice sunset in that picture. Never seen it before. Signed,
too. Four hundred dollars. Limited edition I guess. I'd buy it, but then
I'd have to stop eating. He's still looking at me. Why doesn't he just
come up and say something. No one ever does. There. He's ordering
a coffee. Black. With almond flavoring. I wouldn't have guessed.

It must be something bad, like a war. Or like an earthquake somewhere, and everyone has relatives living there and they've all died. Strange coincidence that would be. I think that must be it. I wish they'd talk to each other, then I'd know what it is. They look as if they've been through a somewhere-else earthquake. Yes. They do. The cat's eye woman is walking with a shuffle. Have to keep your feet on the ground in an earthquake. The old woman is holding onto the counter now. The teenager is grabbing the espresso machine to stop it from shaking. That must be it. An earthquake and they all had relatives there. It makes me sad.

I suppose they're all related to each other, all have the same relatives. That would account for it. Hard to imagine it any other way. No wonder she had those blank eyes and wouldn't look up. I bet her mom died in the earthquake. She moved away a long time ago, that's why she needs double espressos, but now she'll regret everything and order triples. She'll probably get headaches and die. I pity her. Pity party. Poor her. She's addicted to caffeine and now she'll die, all because of an earthquake. Mark this day. We reap what we benefit, so they say.

I should probably get another napkin. I don't want to move. I want to watch a bit longer. They all look sad. I'd be sad too if I had relatives in that town. But I'd never have relatives there. Fools. What, after all, did they possibly expect? Yes. They all look the same. All have the same look about them. I never noticed that before. They all have similar hands. Fat and pudgy. Grasping. Pinkish. Gimme gimme gimme my coffee. Gimme gimme gimme my sugar and cream extra light with almond flavor and cherry flavor and whipped cream. No. I'm being stupid. They can't all be related. Is that even possible? It must be something else.

There. Someone asked about the music. The teenager is putting in a CD. Maybe they just forgot. Ah, jazz. Boring. Wait! There's the manager now. I hate him. Ugly tie, green—who wears a green tie with white polka dots? Or are they yellow. Gives me a mean glare. Always does. Mean to the teenager, too, now he's whispering something to her. Looks like he wants to push her into the ground with his breath, hope it's not bad for her sake. If I were going to draw them, I'd draw a big stick with a curved spike on top, and at the point of the spike I'd draw a second stick, shorter, being driven into the ground. Customers don't notice a thing. She's turning off the music now. She should quit.

So he wants silence. I wonder why. Mourning. Must be mourning. Everyone's subdued because it's quiet in here, not the other way around. That would make sense. Atmosphere has a big effect on mood, isn't that true? Like red walls bring out anger and foster a bunch of serial murders. In hospitals, for instance. Must be someone close to him. Who could it be? Can't have a lover. Who'd love him? A parent. Only a mother could love him. His mother died. In an earthquake...no, I discarded that one already. Can't be a mother. A child. His child died. A horrible strangulating death, and he did it. He's a murderer. That's it. And he doesn't want music because he needs to escape quickly out the back entrance if the cops come. Can hear the siren without the music, otherwise not. I can't believe it.

I just can't believe it.

I keep looking at him. He's by the refrigerator where they keep the milk and cream. His tie is crooked, pointing a bit to the left. Right brained, must be. What does that mean? He's creative, or no, the opposite. He has no creativity. Someone else must have chosen these mountain landscapes, then. That's a good thing, because I like them, and I wouldn't want to agree with his taste on anything. I just can't believe he would do that to his own child. And no one here suspects a thing, not even the teenager who looks like she's going to throw up. Maybe she does suspect. Maybe I can signal to her. But with what?

I'll drop my glass! When it breaks, she'll come over to clean it up and I'll wink at her, and she'll know that I know and then she'll wink back and I'll know that she knows, and then I'll wink again hinting for her to call the police, and then she'll wink back, telling me to create a distraction. But what kind of distraction? I don't know any good distractions. I could take off my pants. I can't do that. I'm too shy. I come here every day. I can't do that. I don't want to do that. Why is she making me taking off my pants? What did I ever do to her?

I can't take off my pants. Even if it means catching a vicious murderer of his own child, I can't do it. I'm too embarrassed. Damn him for killing his own child! It's not fair, it's not fair at all. Okay. I need to relax and come up with a better plan.

But I have no plan. That's always been the problem. I can figure out what's wrong, but I can't come up with any good plans. So he's going to get away with murder, and I won't be able to do anything about it. I could do something about it, if I really focused, but it won't happen. He's a murderer, and that's a horrible thing—of his own child even—but I'm worse because I can't even do anything about it, even when I know.

So what do I do instead? I look away. I look at the new people entering the coffee shop. They look miserable, just like the old people. Old, new, that's a silly way to think about them. They're all old to me, for I've seen them all before, even the guy who was staring at me though I can't remember where I've seen him. This batch is all old, too. They're new old.

There's the guy with the dog that looks like a sheep dog but isn't one. The dog waits outside. There are no dogs allowed in here except for blind dogs but they never come in except for once a long time ago. He always has false sheep dog hairs all over his sweater. He wears sweaters. It's not cold out, but he wears sweaters and orders hot coffee double large with no sugar and a drop of fat free milk.

Now that's odd. He was unhappy as soon as he came in. That's really odd. I thought it was the lack of music making them unhappy. How can that be? How quickly, I wonder, can that lack of music take effect on the mood? I wish I could remember if there has ever been no music in here before, then I could figure out if it had an effect on people's moods then, too. My mind must be going. That's always the first thing to go, the mind, even before the heart. That's why I don't ever drink coffee unless I'm tired. I got it. He was miserable right away, even before he could have heard the lack of music. What's the speed of sound in a coffee shop, anyway? That must be it.

It's so obvious he was miserable, I can't believe I didn't notice it at once. He has false sheep dog hairs on his sweater, but only on one side! Only on the right side, his right, my left, all up the arm and on the side of the sweater as if the dog were rubbing its head against his rib cage. Dogs like to rub their heads against the rib cage. It's one of the things dogs do. Now this guy, today, he was only petting the dog from one side, the right side, and in his left hand must have been a remote control or a newspaper. People watch TV or read the paper in the mornings, even before they come here. There's a paper over there, but I can't see it from here except for the picture. A picture of a TV screen. That tells me nothing, but it makes sense. It makes complete sense. The right side, that's the key to the whole dilemma. He was watching TV this morning or he was reading the newspaper, and that's why he is miserable, and that's why everyone else is unhappy.

I'm getting closer to the truth, but there's a big problem now. If the coffee shop owner killed his child, why isn't everyone miserable about that? Or are they? Maybe there are two layers of misery. Is that possible? That would explain everything, why the misery is so complete that everyone feels it. It's like there are overlapping circles, null sets and unions and all that, I learned it in first grade and then never heard about it again. Sets and intersections and caddy corners and all that. If one person isn't immediately unhappy because of the lack of music because of the murder that took place then that person gets unhappy over the other thing, which I have yet to discern. I started to blame myself, but now I know the truth, that it isn't my fault at all, even if I thought it might be. It never is.

There is, however, another possibility. I hate this other possibility, because it means everything else this morning has been a lie. Nevertheless, it's something I have to face, even if I'll eventually dismiss it. Now it could be, and of course there's only the slightest possibility of this and I'll dismiss it as soon as I come up with the idea, that everyone's mood is the same as it always is and that it's me who's perceiving it differently today because of last night. And there's a police officer at the door! The manager hasn't seen her yet, so it's a surprise attack! She's standing in line, that's odd, but maybe she wants to be as inconspicuous as possible. Should have come in undercover then, but they never think of such things until it's too late.

The manager is completely unaware, in his own little world, chatting with someone on the red phone on the wall near the rest rooms. The line's moving now. The man with the pony tail who always orders three large coffees all white with half and half and a dozen extra sugars and lots of napkins just said goodbye to the bald student, and now the woman with no eyes (she always wears sunglasses, even in the coffee shop) is moving aside, she's already ordered, and the teenager is making her drink and making a drink for the law student with a teardrop on his cheek, too. Wow, the line's moving so quickly, and the manager is still on the phone, and the police officer is talking softly into her cell phone or walkie-talkie or police radio thing whatever it's called.

You know how they hold those things, backhand, with an arm twisted in a strange way, it's a sneaky way of talking into one of those things, but that's how they all do it.

I've wondered why, and I think I figured out the answer. During police training they have to multitask more than is humanly possible. They have to talk into a radio thing at the same time as they apprehend a criminal and at the same time as they yell behind them for backup and at the same time as they draw a gun to shove in the criminal's face and at the same time as they dodge back away from a shooting bullet and at the same time as they listen to their captain screaming at them about all the things they're doing wrong and at the same time as they have to think about what to do next. It's too much to deal with even if they have to deal with it in order to pass police officer's school and become cops, so what happens is that a part of the brain, hmm, how can I say this...it warps. No, not warps. It gets a lesion. It's like brain damage, and it's always in the same exact part of the brain. Well, there are two parts, actually. One has to do with being in control, that part expands like a tumor until it fills the whole skull cavity, but the other part is the key part for now, it's the part that controls hand motions while holding police radio things. So that's why she looks so sneaky, and the manager still sees nothing, he has no clue and he's going to get caught and it's a good thing because child murderers should all go to jail. This is exciting. I hope there's a shootout, and if there is, I'll duck under the table and hide.

Ah! He sees her! But wait. He's smiling. That's crazy. Why's he smiling? He's going towards her, and now he's talking to her. Maybe he's about to pull a gun and shoot her when she least expects it. No. Nothing. They're standing there having a conversation. This is boring. Why don't they shoot at each other or something? He's a murderer, after all. Why isn't she arresting him? Oh, but wait. I know what's happening. I've heard about this kind of thing. It's what they call a payoff, I think. He's paid her off in the past, and now she's returning the favor. So that's how it works. Damn it, though, it's disappointing. He's going to get away with it after all. How disappointing! No wonder there's so much cynicism in the world, all the cops are being paid off by coffee shop managers to overlook their murders. This is just horrible.

Horrible, horrible, horrible. This is absolutely horrible! I just can't believe what I've witnessed. A bribe! I just saw a bribe! Right before my very eyes! The manager himself poured the police officer a cup of coffee double sugar no cream and handed it right to her, and she walked right out of the store. And she didn't pay! She didn't pay for her cup of coffee! He gave her the cup of coffee for free as a bribe so she won't arrest him for the murder of his very own child! And the worst thing of all: no one else seems to have noticed! Someone must have seen it, but no one said a thing! No one is doing anything, they're just standing around not looking at each other just like they've been doing all morning, and the manager is a murderer of his own child and has just bribed the cop to boot.

I think I'm going to be sick. I really think I'm going to be sick all over the swept-clean-but-with-crumbs-all-over-it coffee shop floor.

I have to get out of here. The injustice all around me, it's going to kill me. Goodbye cruel coffee shop! Goodbye! I'm leaving you forever. You'll never see me again, will you, coffee shop people? You think I'll be back again tomorrow, but not this time, no way not me nuh uh. Nuh uh nuh uh nuh uh.

They're pretending not to care. They're not even looking at me, but I know they're looking at me under their brows. They're sneaking looks at me when they think I'm not looking. I haven't caught them doing it yet, but I will. If I keep turning my head back and forth, I'll catch them in the act. They think they can get away with pretending not to notice me, but they're dead wrong. Dead dead wrong just like the poor child of the murderous bribing manager who thinks I'm going to just let him get away with it but not me nuh uh. And who's this at the door? Uh oh.

I had to sit back down at my table. Lucky for me, my glass and napkins hadn't yet been cleared away. Everything is just as it was, and that's how I like it. Everything, just the same as when it all began. When this morning began, and now I'm sitting here as I was before, and everything is just as it was before, and everything is right and good with the world, except that the coffee shop is full of miserable people and I still don't know why. Not really. I've had my theories, but I doubt them.

Since the second cop came in the coffee shop, it's been difficult to concentrate. It's the cop I saw last night, the one who walked away when I shouted for help. I knew I had seen him before, and now I know where. He's here every day, and he stares right over my head as if I weren't here. He deliberately stares right above my head, and sometimes I have to turn around to see if there's something behind me but there never is. He stares at nothing, because to him that's what I am: nothing. And last night, he stared right above me, and he heard my shout for help, and he walked away.

He's not here to arrest the manager. I know that now. The manager, who is probably a murderer, will get away. Everyone gets away when this cop is around. That's how it works. He's not here to arrest anyone. He's here to order his cinnamon bun. He doesn't drink coffee. He buys buns. Maybe he eats them, but I've never seen that. He enters the coffee shop, looks above my head as if I'm not here, and then grunts three times to the teenager at the espresso machine. Every day, same thing. Sometimes the teenager is somewhere else behind the counter. It doesn't matter. He grunts to her three times. Maybe they are words, the grunts. I can't tell from here, they sound like grunts. The teenager nods. She always nods and then pulls from the roller a big strip of wax paper then draws to the side the sliding glass in the display case and reaches in to grab the second largest cinnamon bun for the cop. It's always the second largest. The largest she never gives away unless someone specifically asks for it. Every so often someone new will come into the coffee shop and ask for the largest cinnamon bun, but the cop never does.

I'm sure, though—I'm sure of this—that the cop knows. He knows he doesn't get the biggest, and I think someday he'll get his revenge. Someday the teenager will be lying bleeding in an alley and will shout for help, and the cop will hear her and walk away. That's how he is. He takes his cinnamon bun without looking at it, then leaves the coffee shop. It's 8:35 now. Same time every day. Same thing every day.

There he goes. He's at the door now, not even nodding to the woman holding the door for him. She doesn't seem to mind. I'd mind, but she doesn't seem to. She's here every day, too. Everyone here is here every day. I like that about this place. It's safe that way. It's always the same, and that's how I like it. Here she comes now, she's one of the few people who ever notice me. She's handing me a box. Why is she handing me a box?

She's ordering a cup of hot tea now, and there she goes, leaving the coffee shop, and maybe I'll see her tomorrow, but I don't think I will. I don't think I'll come back here tomorrow or even the next day or maybe ever again. I don't think I'll be back in this place anymore. I've peeked into the box. My box. My box that she gave me. A gift. She gave me a box and it's a gift.

That was so kind of her. I don't know what to think. That was so kind of her. So kind. That was so kind of her, and here is a box. It's my box now, and she gave it to me. And inside the box, there is so much inside the box. So much, and I don't know what to do. What to do. I don't know what to do. I think people are looking at me now. I think the manager is looking at me now, too. I think I have to get out of here. I'll take my box. I can't get out of here yet. I can't seem to get out of my chair. I'm holding the box. I'm holding the box tightly against my chest. I just really don't know what to do. Maybe I'll be here tomorrow and maybe I'll see her again tomorrow. I don't know how. I think I just think I just don't know I just think I just don't think I just I have to get out of here. Right now I have to get right out of here right now. I can't seem to get out of my chair. I keep looking into my box. I don't want to touch anything. If I touch it, it might vanish. Many things vanish, but not this. I don't want this to vanish. I don't want this to vanish, ever. I was wrong.

I was wrong about everything. It's different now, the coffee shop. The coffee shop is different now. What was I thinking, that everyone was unhappy. I was so wrong. It's so different from what I thought. It's so different, and I was wrong. Here's my box now, and I was wrong. And tomorrow, I'll sit here again, and it'll all be different then. It'll be better tomorrow. I know it, that it will. Be better. It has to. Please. It has to.

The Kind Old Fellow

by James Chambers

HUGH CARTER WAS a much-admired old man. He spent his days serving the destitute in the St. Francis Dispensary for the Homeless, located in the basement of the small Church of St. Francis beneath the shadow of the great stone monolith that housed the city government. People called him "a living saint," though this was mere hyperbole, Hugh being, in the grand scheme of the cosmos, nothing more than an ordinary, kind-hearted and selfless soul. And anyway, Hugh didn't much believe in God. But the people of the city admired and loved him. They knew him by his good works and his constant presence on CityNet, speaking on behalf of New York's poor and urging those of means to do what they could to help. Over the decades Hugh had become the face and voice of the city's conscience.

So, on the day the Reckoners arrested Hugh Carter for murder, the entire city ground to a dumbstruck halt, shocked as much by the raw incomprehensibility of Carter turned killer as by the fact that the authorities failed to execute his sentence the very moment they apprehended him. In fact they failed to deliver any punishment whatsoever, a lapse intensely unsettling to the city's inhabitants, all twelve million of whom relied on the Reckoners's strict predictability to maintain order and civility on the overcrowded island of Manhattan.

Everyone knew the Reckoners. Clad in black and gold uniforms, weapons at their hips, they struck a familiar sight patrolling above the streets in small dark hovercraft that flitted among the buildings like flies on a garbage heap. If you committed a crime, a visit from the Reckoners followed. No one could outrun or evade them, and no one could lie to them for they possessed the power to see within a man's soul and know the exact nature and degree of his transgression. Ascertained in an instant were the laws broken, your motive, the pain inflicted and your state of mind. Immediate sentencing made it impossible to benefit from criminal behavior. Steal a piece of fruit and eat it before being caught, and they might force-feed you an emetic. Not necessarily an eye for an eye, but an equivalent eye for whatever the Reckoners decided measured up to your actions. No courts, no juries, no lawyers, no appeals, no judges, no writs of habeas corpus, no bail, no perjury, no showcase trials, no railroading the innocent, no star eyewitnesses, no exhibits A, B or C, no bailiffs, no stenographers…and practically no crime. What better deterrent than the knowledge that punishment for breaking the law will be swift and doubtless?

The Reckoners struck a balance.

Exactly how they achieved this extraordinary feat is not a matter of public knowledge. Some claimed it was the function of highly developed telepathic abilities. Others extolled it as the grace of God at work on Earth, a form of divine justice. A Massachusetts Institute of Technology computer scientist once developed an almost impossibly complicated program to prove the Reckoners relied on technology. The program performed accurately 83 percent of the time. The Reckoners are correct every time. Fixated on solving the riddle of the seventeen percent gap, the scientist suffered a stroke from frustration and his experiments ended. But he may have inadvertently proven that the key element to the Reckoner's success is the human factor. This was not an entirely new idea, a number of conspiracy theorists having claimed over time that the Reckoner's decisions whether right or wrong were backed by the machinery of an elaborate cover-up. No investigation has ever supported this contention, which crops up most often in cases under appeal by the family of a convicted criminal.

Such protest is permitted; none has ever garnered a reversal of fortune.

What people *do* know about the Reckoners is that those men and women who place themselves in the service undergo lengthy and extensive training; they are removed from society and never again seen by family or friends; candidates apply of their own free will and are accepted or rejected immediately and without discussion; and those accepted cannot decline an appointment once offered. The Reckoners became the regular police during the most chaotic period of the city's past and the exact details of their origin lie hazy beneath the grime of history. Consensus holds that Commissioner Piet Ruiz, the city's greatest cop, founded the agency, but little about him is known other than his outstanding arrest record and rapid rise through the ranks. When the first Reckoners appeared, crime had crippled the city and the assassination of a visiting world leader had sparked riots that spurred a savage crackdown by conventional authorities.

Yet Hugh Carter had killed a man in plain sight of at least six witnesses, and the Reckoners had done nothing but take him gently— almost deferentially—away in their sleek, quiet floater to the high reaches of the stone tower.

Three hours later a crowd had gathered outside the city offices. People had come from all parts of town, setting aside their shopping, their business, their recreation, gathering to clog the streets for ten blocks in all directions like hair clumps in a drainpipe. And the Reckoners emerged in force, floating along the concrete passages of the city blocks, monitoring the crowd that remained calm despite its agitation and the blistering afternoon heat. The gathering itself might have been decreed unlawful, except for an old law governing the people's right to peaceful assembly and the fact that many of the Reckoners were as curious as the citizens.

At four o'clock the mayor's top aide, Jamal O'Henry, stepped onto a high balcony of the massive stone structure. His face flickered to life on the broad video screen mounted above the building entrance. At the same time it flashed across CityNet screens on buses and subways and in the backs of taxis, in train stations and elevators, on street corner telecommunication kiosks, in offices and apartments and on personal cell nodes.

Jamal cleared his throat; a hush fell over the streets.

"This evening," O'Henry began, "at six o'clock, Mayor Randall Artemis will address the city regarding Hugh Carter. Thank you."

A disappointed sigh poured up in a hot wave from the unfulfilled multitudes. Boos and hisses followed. Some onlookers felt the urge to vent their frustration by smashing windows or mailboxes, but instead they clenched their fists and filed away beneath the careful eyes of the

Reckoners. They left not even a shred of litter behind them.

Inside the concrete buttresses of the nameless edifice, Hugh Carter released a defeated sigh of his own. He sat in a small chair, alone in an oversized storage closet hastily converted to a holding cell. A plastic pitcher of water waited on the floor, a paper cup beside it. An older man among the guards who had escorted him had demanded his belt and shoelaces and forced him to empty his pockets into a vinyl pouch. Then he slammed shut the door, leaving Hugh by himself in the bleak, gray room.

The situation baffled Hugh. He'd considered all the possibilities a thousand times in his head, and every one of them led to his immediate execution on the street with a Reckoner's needle pressed to the back of his neck. None of them had landed him in this makeshift prison. None of them had predicted this stunning impasse.

The Reckoners had arrived within minutes of the murder, and Hugh sat waiting on the warm curb, knowing well enough there was nowhere to flee. He unloaded his gun, handed it over grip first, and gave himself up. The first hint of the looming dilemma came when one of the Reckoners took Hugh's measure with her soft brown eyes wide with surprise.

She took Hugh by the arm. Her voice croaked from her suddenly dry throat. "I think you should come with us, sir," she said.

The partners led Hugh to their hover unit, and dumbfounded, he followed. The eyes of the awestruck crowd traced their every movement, even as the craft ascended upon its humming turbines. Fifteen minutes later Hugh found himself sitting on the metal chair in the empty closet space, no closer to understanding where he had gone wrong. He had lost track of time when he heard a latch snap and echo, and the door swung open. Several Reckoners filled the hallway, cornered around a short, broad-shouldered man Hugh recognized as Mayor Randall Artemis. A line of assistants percolated behind him. Hugh straightened his back and thrust his jaw high with indignation. He had met Artemis in an official capacity on numerous occasions as he had many of the city's other mayors, but the two had never struck up a friendship.

"I know my rights," said Hugh. "Sentence me or let me walk free. *Action, reaction*—isn't that the Reckoner's motto?"

Mayor Artemis rubbed his chin thoughtfully with the thumb and forefinger of his right hand, a practiced gesture demonstrating that he was considering this. Then, his rumination complete, he raised one finger stiffly and turned a stern glance toward Hugh. "If only it were that simple, dear citizen."

An assistant unfolded a canvas seat stretched across a metal frame, placed it opposite Hugh, and Artemis settled his girth onto it, squatting almost eye-to-eye with the prisoner. "Our side of this conundrum is there for you to perceive, wizened sir," he said, falling into the odd speech rhythm of politicians, calculated—by focus groups, expert linguists and extensive market research—to offend the fewest people. "Can you just be let free, you who have committed the ultimate crime? It seems not. Yet, no sentence allows itself to be passed by the officers who apprehended you. In fact eight other Reckoners who have discerned your personage since you entered this facility all find agreement in their observations. Whatever punitive remedy might be decreed can only ultimately reward rather than punish you. No here or there about it. The only choice presenting itself? Remain passive. Their nerves have taken quite a cold water rattling."

"Well, how do you think I feel, locked away in this janitor's closet?" said Hugh.

"Your feelings? Immaterial, but the sentiments of that guidance-seeking mob outside are of tangible concern," asserted the Mayor.

"What mob?" Hugh asked.

Artemis gestured to another assistant. The wiry man wore a personal CityNet port and viewer harnessed to his chest. He swiveled the small monitor around and tickled the sensors of the keygloves wrapped around his hands. Images of the eager crowd flickered to life onscreen.

"Dear Lord," said Hugh, aghast. "They can't all be here for me."

"But they are. 'Saint Hugh' they call you, or the 'Blanket Man.' Maybe 'Angel of Mercy,' or the 'Kind Old Fellow,'" explained Artemis. "Surely their words have reached your ears over the decades. When they ponder their souls, where do they look, dear citizen? To you! For many you are a moral weather vane, free of judgment and hatred, full of tolerance and compassion, an ideal worthy of striving to achieve. When events stress the city to its breaking point, solace is often taken in your comforting image. You can be relied on to restore faith in humanity. But now the Kind Old Fellow has killed in cold blood, and worse, no punishment delivered. Such a course of events breeds only confusion."

Hugh accepted this silently. He led them all by example, however poorly they followed. He had never wanted it, but he had long ago made peace with his influence and embraced it. The notoriety helped him focus attention on those in need and get things done.

Artemis gestured again. The slender aide wearing the port retreated. A muscular young black woman in a dark suit emerged from the crowd of underlings and placed a gray envelope in the Mayor's hand. He slid loose a sheaf of papers and handed them to Carter. They were photo-copies of pages from books published in the last century. Hugh recog-nized the antiquated look of the type.

"These show that all is on the up and up and quite legit if, in fact, somewhat primitive," said the Mayor.

Carter returned the papers unread. "I don't care about this. Execute me or let me go! I don't want any special treatment. You have to honor my rights."

"No, no, no. Sadly not an option, good sir. The apple barrel has been upset and now it must be set right and all the apples counted and weighed once again," Artemis said. "A murder has been committed, and the Reckoners claim they cannot execute, incarcerate, chastise or flagellate the culprit. So, if such a thing can be accomplished by a meek old man of your stature, the track of the work undertaken uninterrupted by this bureau for so many years thrown off, and the most successful law enforcement authority in the nation stonewalled, how long before others decide they just might have a shot, too? And then? Chaos? Disorder? Unacceptable! Many might turn such events to their advan-tage, enemies of the established order, who wish to see our government crippled. A growing problem, this—agitators and dissenters, unhappy individuals fomenting doubt and stirring our habitually calm populace. Tensions run high."

Many who hated the Reckoners for truncating their freedoms had become increasingly outspoken in recent years. Speech remained free, so long as the speaker broke no laws. Some days Hugh saw them lec-turing on street corners or passing out flyers meant to rouse people and declare their hope of seeing the Reckoners overwhelmed by the will of the citizenry. But people were complacent and enjoyed their security. Hugh had dismissed the dissenters as a harmless symptom of the city's malaise, nothing more than an instinctive opposition to authority, their smoldering anger forever unable to ignite for fear of immediate reprisal. But if his case exposed a weakness among the Reckoners might that embolden them?

"A seemingly light chastisement would at least have preserved the way of things," the Mayor continued. "Questions would be asked as to why you were let off so easy, but the notion that you got away scot free would not be entertained, as is now, clearly, the impression of many. Thus an example must be made by the only means available. You, elder sir, shall be tried in court by a jury of your peers. Confidence in the administration shall be restored, and it shall be proven that the people may rely fully on their elected officials to protect their interests."

"You can't hold me here for that," Hugh said.

"The old laws were not cast away when the new ones were made, wizened sir. Tomorrow at nine sharp, your trial begins." Artemis rose, pausing in the doorway. He took the dark woman's hand and drew her forward. "This fine citizen is Belinda Park. She will be your attorney." Artemis dipped in a cordial bow. "Good day."

At six o'clock the Mayor appeared on the high balcony, his shadow exaggerated to titanic proportions by the garish spotlights. Simultaneously, his visage blinked to life on screens in every part of the city. The roiling crowd grew silent.

"Good citizens," Artemis said. "Relax your tensions. Place your confusions to rest. Rely on your government to look after you. Such devilish crimes shall not be tolerated in the city. Tomorrow morning at nine sharp, the accused shall face justice in a trial by jury. Sirs and madams, please have a good night."

The Mayor returned inside, the sound of his achingly brief speech still echoing through the streets. For the second time that day, a hot, confused murmur ascended as one voice from the gathered throng that had sought resolution, but instead received chafing suspense. Again the crowd dispersed, unsatisfied, but more than that, filled with the creeping sensation of unease that settles upon those poised at the brink of an abyss into which they fear they will be compelled to plunge.

In the barren utility closet high above, Belinda Park presented her first question. "Where were you born, Mr. Carter?"

Carter pouted at her.

"Please," said Park. "Ideally we should have several weeks to pre-pare your defense, but given the urgent nature of your case, the court has given us one night. Your cooperation is essential. Right now my adversary is certainly meeting with his witnesses elsewhere in this very building and prepping them to testify."

"Can't they just execute me? Do we need this farce of a trial? Can't I just confess and plead guilty or something?" Hugh complained.

"As your councilor I have to advise against that," said Belinda. "The trial will be no farce, Mr. Carter. I am fully qualified to represent you. I hold doctorates in anthropology, ancient society and customs, psychology and contemporary law. The prosecutor will be equally qualified, and they have several eyewitnesses, so if you want to stand a chance of winning your case, you really should work with me. This whole event loses credibility if we fail to provide you with a spirited defense."

"Four degrees," said Hugh, unimpressed. "When do you ever sleep?"

"A waste of time. I don't," came her smart reply. "A combination of hypnosis and Stimalert increases my productivity. I require ten minutes rest only every fifteen hours."

His eyelids fluttered shut. "And we're all like that, now, hurrying and rushing about our lives, so distracted that we've lost true sight of the world," he uttered. "We push ourselves harder and faster, strive for higher standards, better productivity, grander triumphs to outdo those of the ones who came before us and did it all, and left nothing for us but to warp their achievements. And toward what? What does any of it gain us when in the end it changes nothing? I'm so tired of it."

"If you require rest, we could break for an hour, so you could nap." Park began gathering her papers.

"That's not what I meant," said Hugh. "Look at me. I'm old and getting older. I've been doing the same work all my life since I was old enough to do it. Do you know how long that is?"

Park referred to her dossier. "Ninety-four years. You began work-ing on your twelfth birthday."

"I was a child, and when I looked at the world through a child's eyes, I saw perfection, or at least it's glimmering potential," he said. "I saw what might be, what *we* might be, all of us if we could only get up on our feet and start running." Hugh glanced around the room. "Not even a damn window," he muttered. "But it's out there. We both know it. We feel it, even locked away inside these thick walls. The city— millions of lives beginning, ending, speeding by, colliding, falling apart, finding one another. Do you know what it was about human suffering that moved me most when I was child, Ms. Park?"

"No, but unless it's relevant to your case—," she began, but Hugh overrode her.

"It was that it seemed so unnecessary," he said. "Why should anyone go hungry when others ate more than their fill? Why should anyone sleep on the street while others owned houses with rooms they never entered? Not that I begrudged anyone their success or their possessions. If you worked for it, you earned it, and you deserved it. But the sheer evidence of abundance overwhelmed me. It seemed the greatest injustice that anyone should suffer the indignities on display each day in the streets. I knew my life's work would be spent trying to help those who needed it, facing the kind of 'crimes' the Reckoners hardly ever notice—the hungry left unfed, the sick left uncared for. And do you know what happened to me in ninety-four years of serving my fellow man?"

Park shook her head.

Hugh dropped his chin to his chest, lost for the moment in recollection, and then turned his stormy gaze on the beautiful woman's eyes. "I learned the truth. It can't be done. Never. The world, Ms. Park, does *not* change, not really, not fundamentally. On and on we go, living longer, getting smarter, growing stronger, becoming more clever and more sophisticated. But there are always those who have more and those who have less, those who die in the streets from something as common as the flu and those who live for years beyond their time on the sustenance of machinery, those who wander and become lost in the city's darkness and those who bleed it of its light. One man cannot share Atlas's burden. When I had seen the same sorrow-etched faces parade past me for the thousandth time, borne on by unanswered hope that lifted them like mismatched crutches, I knew all my work was nothing more than a fleeting balm. That tomorrow they would still be hungry and sick and unsheltered and forgotten."

"Is that why you decided to kill Dr. Neusted? To vent your frustration over your failure to achieve your goals?" asked Park. "That might be the basis for a temporary insanity defense."

But Hugh Carter wasn't listening. He was covering his mouth with one gnarled hand as he fought to hold back soft tears rolling down his cheeks and the gentle tremors shaking his frail body. He was weeping for the world lost to its fate, for the life he'd given to the world, for a child's vision—lost to brutal reality. Belinda allowed him a courteous pause to gather his composure.

"No," Hugh got around to answering. "Mackie Neusted was a useless scoundrel lucky enough to be born *with* money but *without* an ounce of compassion, but I killed him because *I* wanted to die. I thought, if I killed Neusted it might remove a stain from the Earth and wake people up from their apathy, but mainly I thought it would bring about my execution."

"Immediate retribution has kept our murder rate in single digits for years," Park confirmed. "Your case should have been no different."

"Then why did they spare me?" wondered Hugh.

"We'll know more about that soon. The prosecutor interviewing the Reckoners who picked you up is required to share his report with us," explained Belinda.

"It could have been anyone, you know," said Carter. "Neusted or a hundred others like him, a thousand. I didn't hate Mackie, not really. I followed him to the street after our last meeting, and it just felt right. I needed to unload my despair. I wanted out of it all—my work, the city, the insanity of trying to break through in a heartless world. And killing Mackie was a fast means of dumping it. The Reckoners would never punish him for his cruelty. To them it wasn't even a crime that he refused to make his company's medications for the 'hemorrhagic flu' available to those suffering from it the most. His greed cost people their lives. So, I chose to punish him. Isn't that what the Reckoners do to criminals? And then I waited to die."

Park typed notes on her computer, nodding occasionally to spur Carter on with his confession. He let it pour out, the years of struggle and deprivation, the story of the path he had chosen only to have it wear him down year after year until he learned he was weaker than he once thought. Then darkness had set in, and Hugh became another wandering soul among the millions that drifted each day through the city. He felt little of the passion that had once driven him like the churning steam engine of an antique locomotive, knowing he could not live forever or change the world quickly enough to satisfy himself.

Belinda questioned him from every angle late into the night, picking and choosing the pieces she would present to the court. She worked with the dogged air of an academic tackling a new intellectual exercise, eager to weave her arguments tighter and cleaner than her opponent's. Hugh doubted she very much cared what actually happened to him. He was living on borrowed time and if she lost, she could put it behind her and go on to the next challenge.

Neither of them could have known she would never have the chance.

Something deep inside the stone tower rumbled like the hunger pains of a slumbering behemoth disturbed. The cell shook and the light flickered. The clacking of Belinda's keyboard ceased. Hard mechanical noises erupted in the corridor. A body slammed against the entry, and with a bright flash and a puff of acrid smoke, the lock evaporated and the door flew open. Fluorescent light poured in. Through the lingering gray residue of the explosion, three men entered carrying guns, their faces slick with sweat and terror, an adrenaline-fueled mania in their eyes. One aimed his weapon at Belinda, who froze in her seat and emitted a tiny shocked sound.

"We're here for the murderer," the man growled. "Stand clear!"

But as they stepped forward, something glowed behind them and an electric sizzling buzzed through the room. The three men convulsed and shivered, becoming entangled with one another as their uncontrolled bodies collided and wriggled to the floor.

Four Reckoners appeared. A captain's badge adorned the uniform of their leader. The nearby sounds of fighting clattered through the smashed entrance.

"You're done here, Ms. Park," said the captain. Two of the others flanked Hugh and seized him. "We're taking Carter with us for his own protection."

"Mr. Carter's trial begins in the morning," Belinda protested. "We have little enough time to prepare without these interruptions."

But the Reckoners were already hustling Hugh toward the door. Belinda rose to intercede. The captain grabbed her by the throat, crushed a small device against her flesh, and she collapsed, unconscious. He cradled her falling body gently to the floor. The others were already speeding down the corridor. Their leader rushed after them. The Reckoners silenced Hugh's attempts at protest, flashing a stun gun in his direction to make it clear he was going with them, willing or not. They took him through reaches of the government offices few people ever saw, along back corridors and service tunnels into the deepest arteries of the monolithic building. They passed vacant offices and a darkened cafeteria lit by the cold glow of a coffee dispenser, twisted and turned past rows of blank doors shut tight, scuttled down dim stairways and through access passages crosshatched with wires and pipes. The ruckus of the melee faded behind them until they continued forward in an unnatural quiet interrupted only by their footsteps and the noise of their breathing. Hugh struggled to keep up. The Reckoners were younger than he was and more fit. His lungs ached. His pulse pounded.

Soon the group came to a small dark passage that led them to flashing lights and open air. Wind swirled around them, cold and dry. Hugh gasped to catch his breath. Overhead hung the diffuse haze of cloud-reflected city lights like a pale copper canopy. The four Reckoners gazed skyward, searching. And then it appeared, banking around the corner of a once magnificent skyscraper long dwarfed by the shadowy edifice of the tower, a hover ship buzzing low and close to the buildings, a lone red signal light blinking at its nose. The craft descended, throwing up a backwash of air that swept the tiny platform clean. The Reckoners pushed Hugh toward the hatch, and a moment later they were shrouded in the sudden silence and regulated warmth of the vehicle's interior. As quickly as it had come, it rose back to the darkness.

The captain removed his headgear. His chiseled, bony face appeared ghostly in the glow of the cockpit lights. "My name is Suez," he said. "You'll be safe with us."

Hugh surveyed the serious faces of the others, who regarded him coldly. *He's old*, they seemed to be thinking, *but he's a killer. Caution is advised.* None of them were older than thirty, except for Suez, clearly in his sixties. One was the woman who had arrested Hugh.

"What do you want?" asked Carter. "Are you going to kill me?"

Suez shook his head. "Reward you for murder? Deliver what you most desire?"

"We've been waiting years for someone like you," said the brown-eyed woman. "We've been preparing. You have no idea how fragile the order we impose on the city is, Mr. Carter. There are powerful people who want to break our authority and let corruption and crime creep back into our society. And tonight they believe their goal is finally in sight."

"What does this have to do with me?" Hugh asked.

"What Lucy means is they want to prove the Reckoners can be wrong," added Suez. "Your trial is meant to restore faith in the old methods of justice, to turn the city against us and erode the established order. We can't let that happen."

"But six people witnessed me kill Mackie Neusted. I confess!" cried Hugh.

"You've led a peculiarly righteous life, old man. That balances much of your crime. Plus you killed to gain release from your despair, to profit by your death. That we cannot permit. The only rational sentence is to assure that you go on living and suffering, a hard concept to convey to masses that have been conditioned to scream for blood. For years the media has made us out to be righteous avengers in the biblical tradition, a depiction influenced a great deal by our enemies. These days most people can only understand justice in terms of violence. If you were to stand trial, you would be convicted and sentenced to death. They would ache for your blood to be spilled," Lucy told him. "But in this case that does not serve justice."

Hugh felt fear for the first time since he had pulled the trigger that ended Mackie Neusted's life. What torture did the Reckoners plan? He had never guessed that these agents who supposedly saw the world in stark black and white, clear-cut rights and wrongs, could ever fabricate something more than simple retribution.

They had been aloft but a few minutes when the craft banked and Hugh noticed through the front windshield that fires were burning on the steps of the city offices. People scurried around in every direction. Armed men attacked the front door in groups, launching useless sorties against the stone façade of the monumental structure. They raised their weapons and shook them violently, urging the flames to grow, screaming defiantly as Reckoners swooped down on each of them and brought them to their knees.

"The dissenters," said Lucy. "Little better than a lynch mob."

"Some have said the same about you," ventured Hugh.

"Not everyone understands what's happening in this city, Mr. Carter, but they're going to find out. Don't let what you see there disturb you," she replied, indicating the skirmish. "That's a diversion. They pretend to fight for you while we know that their true objectives lie elsewhere."

An apartment building eclipsed the scene of the mayhem as the ship turned sharply earthward. The plunging sensation put a knot in Hugh's stomach. Moments later the craft leveled out and dropped gently to a rooftop platform, where Hugh and the Reckoners disembarked beneath the shelter of a makeshift canvas hangar. Two other hovercrafts stood nearby, and a dozen Reckoners moved about the work area. Hugh's captors ushered him from the heart of the activity, down a metal staircase and into the building. Along the way they passed other Reckoners, all of them alert and on edge, each armed and in full uniform and patrol gear. The escort brought Hugh to an expansive room furnished with a long, wide table bordered by rows of high-backed chairs. A line of CityNet pods sat positioned along the table's center. One wall of the space was given over entirely to windows, and the lamps were kept dim to allow a spectacular view of the city, its lights glittering like jewels, the black skin of the East River snaking along beneath graceful bridges. A statuesque woman stood before the glass, her back to the room as she gazed outward, lush auburn hair flowing over her shoulders. The unexpected sight captivated Hugh, and he realized abruptly that except for Lucy and Suez, his escort had withdrawn.

"Please sit down, Mr. Carter," the woman said.

Carter chose a seat. The tall woman glanced at her watch, and then turned, locking eyes with Hugh as she approached him with long, self-assured strides. She took his hand in her warm palm and shook it. Her dark uniform bore no insignia of rank.

"My name is Ciara Donatello. I'm honored to meet you, though I wish the circumstances were better. I've always respected your dedication to our city," she told him.

Once she had been stunning. Hugh could see the artifacts of beauty buried beneath the now-severe angles of her face. All the softness had been driven out and her gentle curves replaced by sharp lines of tough muscle and the permanent ghost of cynicism lurking beneath her expression. A long-ago burned patch of skin around the left corner of her mouth had healed over with grayish scar tissue. But when she smiled, as she did in greeting him, the effect lit up her expression, undoing much of the harshness and ruin displayed there, and something stirred within Hugh. This was no simple cop doing her job. Wisdom brimmed in her eyes.

"We haven't much time, but I'll do what I can to help you understand what's happening and what role you must play," stated Ciara. "Most people trust our deterrent, but to some we're the enemy. They believe we rob them of their freedom, but they're quite careful not to break any laws even though they conspire against us. Or at least they have been until tonight thanks to the interference of some in the city administration who see us as an obstacle to be removed, who despise the limitations we impose upon them, and covet our authority. They are powerful people who possess the resources to undo our achievements. Randall Artemis is among them."

Ciara slid gracefully into the seat beside Hugh, comfortable and unhurried.

"They've been waiting for an apparent crack, however slender, in our effectiveness. They've been fueling the futile rage of the dissenters for years with money and promises, assuring that when the moment arrived, they could unleash that pent-up fury on their own city and turn it against us. That opportunity has come. They hoped to catch us off-guard, but we have sources of information they don't know about."

Ciara rose and gripped Hugh's arm so that he walked with her to the window. Across the room Lucy shut the lights. The glass seemed to vanish and Hugh could imagine they were intangible and floating high above the ground.

"When Piet Ruiz established our group, he swore it would always uphold the law, and so we have done. But we don't make the laws, and those who do have managed to create the loopholes they needed to prepare for tonight and seize the power they believe should be theirs. We've been forced to wait for them to act.

"Do you see that building on 40th two blocks from the river?"

Ciara asked.

Hugh strained his eyes to pick out the one she meant, a square brick structure set back from the street behind a parking lot. He recognized it. One of his missions stood opposite it and he passed it often.

"One of our headquarters. Seven hundred people work there," Ciara told him.

A blinding amber sphere of force erupted, expanding in microseconds, stinging the night as it rolled outward to swallow the whole of the building, and then the bubble of flame burst, sparks shooting forth, a pillar of black fog spewing into the sky. Hugh watched in horror. The sound barely reached them. He felt the faint tremor of the concussion in his fingertips pressed against the quivering glass.

"My God," Hugh gasped.

"No one was hurt. The building was evacuated earlier," Ciara said. "But they didn't know that when they attacked."

Another ball of flame burst to life across the river in Queens spitting fire and soot into the air. Far downtown a third ignited, and Hugh imagined other explosions tearing through the darkness all around them—the Armory uptown and the barracks in the Bronx, the Battery in lower Manhattan, the Navy Yard in Brooklyn, all the facilities used by the Reckoners. Their offices and command centers, their motor pools and lunchrooms, auditoriums and training centers, vanishing in sudden conflagrations. Ciara's calm demeanor suggested amazingly that none of it worried her.

"All of our buildings were evacuated," she told Hugh. "All our records have been transferred and all personnel secreted away to other locations in the city like this one. The dissenters are lashing out at empty shells, but they've left themselves vulnerable and exposed. Now we can bring justice to them."

Already Hugh saw tiny silhouettes cutting past the flames, the black hovercrafts and patrol units dropping to the burning ruins as the Reckoners responded. The sky sprang to life with flashing lights and the glint of gold trim as thousands of officers swarmed over the city and descended on their enemies. Hugh's position was too high to see the activity at street level, but he could picture in his mind the black-clad men and women corralling the perpetrators, chasing them until they could run no further, stilling them. He turned away, weak and overwhelmed, and stumbled to a nearby chair. How could his act of selfish desperation have become the catalyst for such destruction? Both sides had been waiting to use someone like him for their purposes. Did it matter which one succeeded? Either way, he believed it would be his city, his people—the ones who looked up to him and trusted him—that would lose.

"It will all be done by morning," Ciara said. "Our opposition will be eliminated. The fires will be extinguished. No innocents will have been harmed. Even Artemis will be in our custody. We will have taken control of the city."

"The people won't know who to trust, who to turn to," whispered Hugh. "They'll be living in the fear you've bred, terrified of their own protectors and their leaders. What good can you possibly think you've accomplished?"

"That's how it will be for a little while," admitted Ciara. "But order has been maintained, and in time we'll be stronger and more trusted than ever for it. And the people are going to accept us because you're going to help us reclaim their hearts and minds. This will be your penance."

And now Hugh understood what they wanted of him. He had given so many years of his life to serving the city yet they would have him go on when he was least capable of doing so, when all he wanted was to lay down, defeated, and rest forever. Despair had hollowed him out and they sought to fill him up again with their own purpose.

"I'll kill myself like I should have in the first place. You'll get no help from me," Hugh threatened. "All my life I worked for them, and there they are, no better than when I started. And you and your kind have done nothing to help. *Action, reaction*—that's all you are. You work to change nothing."

"Are you certain?" posed Ciara. "Maybe you didn't give enough, Hugh. Maybe after everything you let them have, every part of your being you gave over to their service, they still wanted more. Maybe they wanted you to believe they could change. But you never did. Not really. You thought it would be easy. You thought you could fix things by being a lone voice in the wilderness crying for compassion. And when it proved impossible, you gave up.

"Each year more and more people apply to our ranks, and we turn away many suitable candidates. Fewer and fewer people attempt to commit crimes. The gift we Reckoners have is very special, Hugh. I can't explain it to you in conventional terms. It's awareness beyond the five senses upon which most people rely to construct their reality. It's an understanding of how humanity fits together, and the number of people who bear the seed of that knowledge is growing. Before long there will be more of us in the city than those without it. Consider it, Hugh—so many people living with an utter clarity of vision for right and wrong, a comprehension of justice embedded in their souls rather than their minds. All the things you've been working your whole life to eliminate—hunger, apathy, poverty, unnecessary sickness—will cease to be an issue when the traits that permit those things to exist are burned away. And we can spread that knowledge to the world. Piet Ruiz led us here, and now our mission must begin anew with another lone man. I know you feel it, Hugh. You would have made an excellent Reckoner had you chosen to join our ranks."

Hugh could not bring himself to look into Ciara's eyes. They were glowing with belief. Could it be true? Could this be the source of the Reckoner's power, or was it a fairy tale meant to draw him into their machine? The people still trusted him in spite of his crime. He had realized that when they gathered in their numbers to witness his fate, hoping that all would be restored as it had been. If he reached out to them, they would listen.

Suez crept quietly to Ciara's side. "We haven't got much time," he reminded her.

Ciara activated one of the CityNet pods. The screen burned to life. A few keystrokes summoned the image she sought, a split-screen view of the lower floors. Armed men were fighting their way through a corridor and up an emergency staircase. Groups of Reckoners resisted, but they appeared outnumbered.

"Someone leaked to them that this should be one of their targets," Ciara explained. "We discovered it only a few hours ago. Their spy has been punished but it was too late for us to bring in reinforcements. We're spread too thin as it is. I'm afraid we're going to need your decision quickly, Hugh. The way I see it, you only have three options."

Suez placed a gun on the table in front of Carter, a stark gray unit of steel, loaded, Hugh could see by the indicator, and prepared to deliver death.

"You're of no use to us if you're unwilling," said Ciara. "So, choose— join us, or wait here for the dissenters to find you, or give yourself the release you desire. For how many years did you hope one man could change the world, Hugh? That the world could be better than it is? That humanity could be better? Now is your chance to believe it. Lead them, Hugh."

Hugh peered out at the smoke blotting away the city. The building on 40th continued to burn, but as best as Hugh could tell from so far away, his mission had gone unscathed. He lifted the gun, its grip cold in his sweating palm, and tested its heft. He struggled to quiet the turmoil in his mind and make space for the sensation Ciara described, the feeling of knowing what lurked beyond his senses. Was there something there or nothing? Enlightenment or void? He probed the darkness of his own heart, the regions he had long ago shut off and forgotten. If it were to be found at all, it would be found within him.

Gunshots cracked in the corridor. On the monitor screen, the dissenters closed in on the wide oak door of the conference room.

"We have seconds," hissed Lucy. Ciara raised a hand to silence her.

She knelt before Hugh and placed her fingers on either side of his face to direct his eyes toward hers. "I can help you," she whispered.

Hugh stared into the depths of her eyes. He barely heard the rising commotion beyond the door. He was floating downward through the black clouds of depression that had suffused him these last few years, swimming past the pain that had driven him to lash out in violence. The mists parted lazily and beneath them lay more darkness, solid, unyielding, icy. A gentle force urged him on. Ciara.

A heavy object slammed against the entrance. Lucy and Suez drew their weapons and dashed across the room. Other Reckoners clambered in from a side passage, bracing themselves for the assault. The door bucked on its hinges.

Unshaken, Hugh tested the barrier that continued to contain him. His weakness left him stunned. The barrier was rock solid and immovable. It felt like the weight of all history pressing the doors of hope shut tight day after day, week after week, year after year for decades and centuries, its weight measured in the tragedies and failures of every man and woman who had ever lived.

Ciara leaned close. "Stop lying to yourself, Hugh. You know it's there," she murmured.

She was right. He knew. So far away that he could hardly discern it, a tiny spark flickered in the black field that consumed him. He moved toward it.

The door crashed down and dissenters poured in, screaming, firing an indiscriminate wave of lead into the room. They had crushed their rage for too long, fought too hard for this moment, and they meant to make their fury known. Lucy and Suez led the defense, closing with the intruders to beat them back and stop them. They were better armed than their attackers and well-trained, but they could still be overrun by sheer numbers.

Hugh seized on the flickering will o' the wisp that had never left him, but that he had long suppressed. The darkness eroded, falling back as the light radiated outward, warming him, flowing through every part of his being until it had seared clean the last remnants of the despair to which he had succumbed and the anger he had permitted to take root within him. It singed away all doubt and once again he looked out on the world through a child's eyes, innocent and full of the desire for perfection that had so long ago set him on his path. He had tried to discard that light many times over the years. Every time he made excuses for the failures of others, every time he accepted less from someone he knew could achieve more, every time he made allowances in the name of mercy for greed or sloth or envy or myriad other sins, he had pushed it away, but it had never abandoned him. His denial of it had held him back from understanding the power of people's connection to him, obscured how deep were the voids they used him to fill.

It had been locked away inside him for years, his secret belief that he was better than those he helped and superior to those who gave less than he did. The power of it flooded through him and he felt, for the first time in years, that he might accomplish what he had set out to do. Punishing Mackie Neusted had been a first faltering step toward a new destiny, for him, for the Reckoners. Hugh opened his eyes, his face afloat with joy he had not felt in seven decades, and Ciara's stark, infinite expression offered him confirmation of everything he was experiencing.

But then a shadow fell across her.

Could this be his punishment, Hugh wondered. Could they mean to distort all that he had lived for, sentence him to their service in whatever unimaginable plans they harbored for the city? Could they intend to degrade him and all he had done until they declared him redeemed and let him die? In that moment Hugh existed in perfect neutral balance, poised between crumbling doubt and precipitous belief. He felt as if his soul was more exposed than it had ever been.

Something dark blasted through the air in a blur. Ciara's head snapped sideways, and dark fluid sprayed from her shattered skull, staining her long hair and sending a warm splatter into Hugh's face. She collapsed onto the floor. And as Hugh watched the unimaginable glory fade from Ciara's eyes, everything leapt into overwhelming clarity. His perception of the world transformed in an instant. All doubt and fear were ripped from him like the shingles of a roof torn away by a hurricane. He saw the stains of corruption infesting the dissenters—these were savage men who would hold back the world, forever dwelling in the shadows of their fear, lashing out at any who dared otherwise. He perceived the absolute wrongness of Ciara's death at their hands. He recognized the undeniable need for it to be answered.

He lunged to his feet, raised the gun at the dissenters, and squeezed the trigger. The shots exploded like thunder erupting from every part of his thin, weary body.

Outside, the pyres flickered, the flashing lights battled darkness and weapons sparked, their illumination etching apt prelude to the new dream Hugh Carter would bring to the world.

1.03 Excessive Exposure to Time

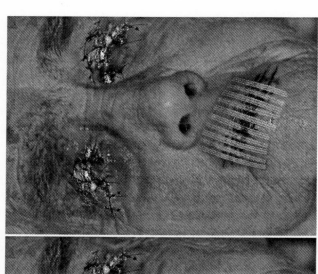

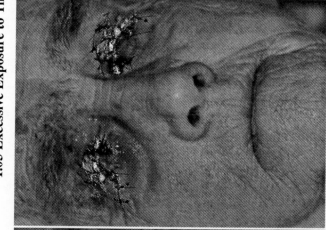

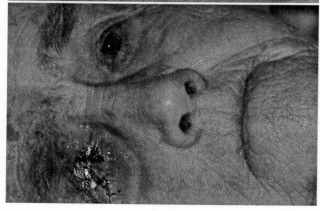

1.03 Excessive Exposure to Time. Most if not all patients who become infected with Temporal Awareness will first exhibit a rise in CD8+ T cells and then go on to develop this immunodeficiency syndrome, often in middle age, although the incubation period will vary widely from person to person and may be extremely long. Up to half the patients will suffer a febrile illness, floating anxiety, and existential aphasia similar to infectious mono-nucleosis. EET-related complex comprises weight gain, muscle loss, increased disorientation, longing for recognition by one's community, and incremental closure of the face. As a consequence of the immunodeficiency, patients regularly develop opportunistic infections such as toxoplasmosis, religion, and internalized tattooing. Malignant diseases are common, as are increased television watching, hope, and peripheral neuropathy. At present, Excessive Exposure to Time is always fatal.

Drainage
by Christian Westerlund

THE TRAIN SHUDDERS into the city center and she feels empty, like a hard shell wrapped around nothingness. Her dress is torn, covered in food-stains and engine grease.

The crossword puzzle is forgotten on the table. Instead she looks out of the dirty window. There's a gummy cockroach on the seat next to her.

She watches the city for a while. A dead panorama shot of skeletal buildings and empty warehouses. Porn shops everywhere, filled with pink lights.

The sky is flickering with stars, glowing embers in the dark. A few wrinkled leaves blowing in the wind and a bar sign with missing letters, glowing sadly in the autumn cold.

That's when she notices the Asian man.

He reeks of cinnamon and musk, of books and old pages. The eyes are twisted charcoals in his face. A smile—like a cracked mirror. "Are you here for the first time?" he asks with a heavy accent, folding his fingers like crusted wire.

"Yes," she tells him, trying to look away.

"I can show you many things," he whispers and his eyes glitter like the cold streetlights outside the window, and the girl forgets everything. His fingers are long and yellow, like brittle twigs, ages of dirt underneath his nails. His smile is like a picture out of focus.

The city outside the window. A frozen image of the world. Endless lines of empty buildings and dead neon, of insects and cracked asphalt.

"I can show you everything," he whispers. Then he smiles. A

grimy fly is buzzing around his face but he does not seem to mind. Instead he reaches for the gummy cockroach and puts it in his pocket.

Then he hits the fly with his twisted hand, turning it into a brown speck against the window. Very gently, he removes the wings and keeps them.

Somehow, she knows he will eat those insects once he's alone, images of the man sitting somewhere in a skeletal building, where everything reeks of semen and copper.

The train stops at the station, and the Asian man gets off the train. He never looks back.

They have her in the machine…

She has been connected to it, becoming a part of the greasy hoses and tubes that have been inserted into her head.

The rust-colored fluids are being pumped out into her body from the machine, keeping her constantly lubricated.

She's naked, kneeling, the upper half of her wet body disappearing into the rusty machinery, somewhere among the spinning cogs and wheels.

Her legs are spread wide and the sawdust beneath her is spattered with the rusty fluids that drip from her vagina.

This is a cold place, at the bottom of a skeletal factory, a decaying shell filled with greasy machinery. A dim lightbulb flickers endlessly in the ceiling.

And somewhere, deep inside the machine, the girl moans quietly. Her eyelids flutter rapidly, strange barcodes burnt into her eyes.

They keep her drugged at all times, a dead puppet, twisted among all the engine-grease and cogs that keep turning and turning…there is a soft electrical humming from the machine. The reek of sweat and old rust is sickening. Her vagina drips constantly.

Then they come.

There are endless lines of them, misshapen and deformed. Their eyes are the color of rotten cardboard. Soft penises and rotten teeth, the taste of dry vomit in their mouths…

One by one they stand between her legs and open her like a

chicken. She breathes heavily inside the machinery as they enter her, one at a time. The machine keeps her constantly lubricated, amber-colored fluids pulsating through her body like some sort of virus. A steel hose has been inserted into her ear and another one going up into her wrecked anus.

They ejaculate inside of her, one by one, their mis-colored sperm running down her thighs, mixing with the amber-colored stuff.

It goes on for hours.

And then, in the end, when everything is over, they leave her there alone. Someone inserts another hose delicately up into her grease-stained vagina. Gentle spasms run through her body.

The smell of musk and cinnamon fills the room as the door opens. Some lazy maggots are crawling in the leftovers in the corner. A dead cockroach lies on its back in the vaginal fluids.

"My love," someone whispers in the darkness, and the hose is taken out of her vagina, followed by a gentle shower of urine.

Then, two flaccid fingers disappear up into her, sliding gently, the thumb rubbing the swollen clit. And shuddering inside the machine, the girl comes.

"I love you," someone whispers.

And the humming of the machine fills the world.

The coffee shop is empty.

She's sitting in the corner, looking out of the window. Watching the endless lines of people passing in the rain.

A broken streetlight flickers in the darkness. Lonely people passing under it, never even looking up from the water that flows in the gutter.

The coffee shop smells like dust and old pages. There is only one other customer there—an old black man with hair like rotten satin. He's holding a glass of rusty water and he looks empty inside.

He has forgotten.

She looks out of the window, patting her belly. She is pregnant. The last few weeks have been kind of a blur for her. She remembers darkness and flickering lights, the sound of electricity and the smell of copper and burnt metal, plastic tubing inside of her.

And endlessly—images flickering in her mind. Flowered land-scapes, wide open meadows, vast parking lots filled with burnt-out cars.

And the feeling of loneliness.

She looks down into her coffee and notices the cockroach floating there. There are a couple of dead flies on the table, next to the grease-stained newspaper.

A few more hours before her train leaves. A few more hours to kill.

The rain falls outside and the people out there rustle like dead leaves, lost in the darkness. They too have forgotten.

She touches her belly again and everything feels cold. She has already thought of a name for the baby.

The old man coughs dustily next to her, staring down into his rusty water, as if there is actually something in there to see. His eyes have no color.

And somewhere in the night, a grimy train shudders in the abandoned station...

Mike and the
Coat Hanger Abortion
by Dustin LaValley

M IKE HELD THE crotch of his pants in one hand—so as not
to soak any misguided piss into the frayed denim—and his
dick in the other hand. The restroom was disgusting. There
were no doors, none even to the one toilet which looked as if it hadn't
been flushed since the bar had opened, and a pool of oddly colored
urine crept its way beneath the two wall-mounted urinals. Each contained an even supply of un-flushable objects: cigarette butts, used
condoms, broken needles, and more of the sort.

The second band—a local heavy metal band—began its sound
check. Mike rocked back and forth, mentally willing himself to get on
with it. But still, no go. "Ah, come on," he murmured to himself.

"What?" an adverse feminine voice grunted from inside the toilet
stall.

He hadn't noticed anyone enter. Embarrassed, Mike replied,
"Sorry...nothing."

An excruciating scream came from the toilet stall seconds later.
Followed by a small, barely evident splash.

Mike giggled to himself before looking over his shoulder at the
squishing footsteps passing behind. She exited too quickly and he
missed her appearance. But she did leave something behind, on top of
an overflow of paper towels piled against the side of the trash, a
slightly straightened coat hanger: a bloody coat hanger. Confused, he
returned his attention back to his business.

The sound check came to an end with the vocalist descending into a low, primal growl backed by a chaotic rhythm of double bass and distorted guitars.

Fuck it, Mike thought. He quickly shook his penis free of whatever might have made its way out, and zipped himself up. His shoes squeaked as he turned away from the urinal, practically spinning around in a puddle of piss. He lost control of his footing and in a mixture of slipping and tumbling, fell to the grimy floor, directly in front of the toilet.

From inside that filthy cesspool, he heard an ear-piercing squeal.

He cocked his head and stretched his neck to glance inside. Squirming wildly in the dense mixture of fecal matter and blood and urine, a fetus franticly attempted to wriggle through the cluttered toilet water.

Mike stared silently on his hands and knees. Vomit crawling up his throat. He swallowed, only to re-supply his gut with more acidic liquid to be thrown up. And he did. Multicolored chunks of indescribable origins scrapped through the insides of his throat and mouth, splattering on the already grimy floor. Quivering, his body released the collected fluid that had previously denied discharge. "Shit," he mumbled to himself, watching the urine trickle into a pool, forming around his knees.

His eyes quickly shot back into the toilet when he heard another squeal. The fetus stared bemused at Mike. Its slit-like mouth began to try and speak. Mike leaned in closer, turning his head towards the fetus. "Kill me." It whispered in a scared, shaken voice. "Please, kill me."

Causally, Mike rose to his feet, keeping the fetus in view while doing so. He reached slowly for the handle, looked into the eyes of the fetus, and said, "I'm sorry," as he pushed the handle down. Urine, blood, fecal matter and fetus, all twirling clockwise together in a combination of murky unwanted waste.

Paraquat Syndrome
by Efrem Emerson

I'VE BEEN TURNING orange lately. A really sick kind of orange, know what I mean? So I decided to see a doctor. Having a rather low and undocumented income, I went to this neighborhood clinic I saw advertised on the inside of a pack of matches. The Resurrection Clinic, located on lower Wendell Jeffrey Boulevard...down in the hood. It was a narrow storefront space sandwiched between Birdman's Appliance Repair and the Jumpin' for Jesus Thrift Shop. The waiting room was filled with the usual assortment of low-budget trailer trash, non-English speaking minorities, and other Third World riff raff.

A fat Filipina medical assistant sat behind the counter, glaring at me through thick-lensed glasses. She wore a lot of oily makeup and her hair was teased into a startling beehive. A big brown mole with a long black hair jutting from it adorned her left cheek. Her eyes bugged out like a huge insect.

"You fill out forms!" she said, handing me a pen. The hair on her mole began to twitch whenever her lips moved.

After completing seven pages of meaningless information, I sat with the rest of the peasants for a couple of hours before she finally led me back to the exam room. It was cold and sterile, in spite of the large framed photograph of a smiling Elvis on the wall. I waited there for another twenty minutes before the doctor, a tiny baldheaded Filipino with piggy little eyes, entered the room.

"You orange!" he said, looking me up and down. "Take off

clothes!" His piggy little eyes were very bright. I barely had my underwear off before he was all over me, hastily probing, groping, fondling, and measuring. He then took an X-ray of my pelvic region and a tube of blood before disappearing for yet another twenty minutes. I bided my time by rummaging through the drawers and cabinets, but didn't find anything useful except a giant jug of betadine, which was way too large to smuggle out anyway. I had just sat down when the doctor bustled back in, clutching a fistful of medical reports.

"You sick," he said, eyeing me lasciviously. His nametag read, "Dr. Resurrection," so I think he must be the head of the clinic.

I also think he's a fruit because he keeps looking at my crotch. I *am* rather well endowed if you know what I mean.

"What have I got?" I asked, zipping up my pants.

"Paraquat Syndrome," he replied.

"Paraquat Syndrome?"

"That correct."

"How bad is it?" I asked.

"Bad," he answered. "Veddy veddy bad. You blood work focked up, and you x-ray all focked up."

"But up until a day or so ago, I was feeling great."

"You not great," he replied, pulling a non-filtered Camel from the pocket of his white lab coat. "You sick and you orange. You bill three hundred dollar, cash only. I also need reexamine you penis. Would you please unzip fly and pull out, please?"

It was at that point that I stood up, grinned foolishly at him, then bolted out of his office. If I was so sick, why should I pay his overpriced queer-ass Filipino ass?

I don't like Filipinos, did I mention that? Too many years in the Navy, I guess. I can't stand their whiny-ass voices and truncated little bodies.

There were seven messages on my answering machine when I got home. I hit the play button.

"*You no pay!*" came Dr. Resurrection's pissed off voice. "*You pay now!*"

Beep.
"*Want money!*"
Beep.
"*You bad...you no pay!*"
Beep.
"*Pay now!*"
Beep.
"*You owe money!*"
Beep.
"*You no pay!*"
Beep.
"*I pissed! You pay now!*"
Beep.

I hit message/erase and walked into the bathroom. My normally handsome face stared back at me from the mirror. I'm now turning an even more interesting shade of orange, like when my ex-girlfriend Janet used that cheesy fake tan cream from Rite-Aid.

I quickly got online and looked up anything and everything to do with paraquat, especially paraquat-laced pot from the Seventies. I'd gotten drunk and smoked an entire bag of it once, you see, and that memory was now causing a fierce anger to build up inside of me.

I'd bought the pot from a goddamn Filipino!

The next day I suddenly had a strange urge to make some paraquat. Don't ask me why. Maybe because of my current affliction...but maybe some other, darker reason. I went back online and it didn't take me too long to learn how to mix a batch. It's not that difficult really, and one can acquire the ingredients from most chemical supply houses. I dashed out and got them, then spent the rest of the day putting it together. I was wondering how to test it when I heard Elmer, the neighbor's cat, meowing out in the hallway. I hastily dipped a couple of cat treats in the stuff, using rubber gloves of course, then tossed them outside my door. Elmer dug it as far as I know...I mean he ate those cat treats with real gusto! I kept an eye on him, taking a few notes. Anyway, he walked around in circles in the hallway for a few minutes, shit a big steamy pile on the gray industrial carpet, then keeled over on the rubber *Welcome* mat right in front of my door! I quickly carried him inside and measured him from tip to tail, writing down the numbers in my notepad. His pulse was weak and his eyes were turning orange, but he was still alive.

At least he was when I put him in the deep freezer case just off of the kitchen.

Dr. Resurrection called the police on me.

He must've informed them that I was a dangerous man.

He must've informed them that I'd stiffed him on his fee.

He must've informed them that, in his humble and unbiased Filipino opinion, I was a no good deadbeat shithook.

There's a black and white police cruiser parked in front of my apartment building right now, as a matter of fact. Two chunky-ass donut-gobbling cops are waddling their way up the front walk to the door. I can see them from my upstairs window through the purple crushed velvet drapes. Their uniforms are way too tight, man.

Dr. Resurrection is there too...leaning against their car and smoking a cigarette. He looks agitated. His face is scrunched up in a tight scowl. He keeps checking his watch and puffing away at his Camel.

The police are in the hallway now. I can hear them trundling along, getting closer. In a minute they'll be at my door. "Police," one of them shouts a moment later. "Open the door, please."

"Quarantined!" I shout back. "Paraquat Syndrome!"

I can hear them whispering to each other through the door, and can't quite make out the words. But I definitely think I hear the sound of a shell being jacked into the chamber of a Glock, so I choose that moment to slip out the bedroom window, drop noisily onto the roof of my neighbor's thrashed green Pinto, and ran off down the alley.

Dr. Resurrection really fucked me up by calling the cops. Now I can't go home! They've got surveillance goin' on...24/7, man. I mean

I tried to sneak back late last night, and there was another black and white parked out front of the apartment. A big fat cop was press-fit behind the wheel too, guzzling 7-11 coffee and munching Fritos. I watched him from the alley for a few minutes, and when he didn't appear to be leaving anytime soon, I bounced a good-sized rock off of his windshield and ran like hell. A moment later I heard nine straight shots as the cop emptied his weapon in the general direction the rock came from. A couple of the bullets whistled past me in the dark.

Goddamn fucking cops! Goddamn fucking Filipinos!

I'm staying in Room 9 at the Easy Eight, a cheap motel on Wendell Jeffrey Boulevard, just a few blocks from the Resurrection Clinic. It has a small kitchenette, an old black and white Motorola, and seventeen million cockroaches, more or less. I watched two of 'em cruise up the wall about an hour ago...then I smashed 'em into a foul-smelling paste with a copy of the Holy Koran I found on the nightstand by the bed. One of 'em stuck to the wall, its rear legs still twitching...the other stuck to the Koran. I winced as I put the book back in the bed-side drawer.

Right now I'm lying on the bed trying to relax. I still feel ok...but my skin is getting oranger and oranger. I got some Cover Girl kind of shit at the Rite-Aid down the street, and smeared it all over my face and arms. It does a fair job of camouflaging the orange, but I still look pretty weird. I also have to reapply it every couple of hours. The desk clerk, a big black dude named Clydesdale, checked me out for a full minute before allowing me to rent the room.

"Yo, dawg," he said finally. "Wassup wit' 'cho face?"

"Paraquat Syndrome," I said.

"Sheeit," said Clydesdale.

"Shit is right," I replied. "I smoked a little too much back in the Seventies, I guess."

"Nigga tried t'sell me some o' dat shit once...ah busted his haid!"

"How could you tell?"

"Shit was blue!"

"Blue?"

"Damn right...blue as shit! Ah busted his haid!"
"Well, I'm turning orange!"
"Ah heard dat!"

My face is plastered all over the morning newspaper. My high school yearbook photo...but other than my recent mullet haircut, I haven't changed much.

I'm a wanted man.

It seems I'm accused of making improper sexual advances towards Dr. Resurrection, as well as stiffing him on his fee. The paper quoted him as being outraged by this slander of his otherwise untarnished name. He was, he stated, pressing charges. "He no good!" the doctor is quoted as saying. "Dead cat in freezer!"

There was a smaller photograph of him just below mine. He's sitting at his desk in his private office, smiling into the camera. I noticed that there was another large picture of Elvis on the wall behind him.

I decided I needed to keep tabs on Dr. Resurrection. The little faggot was responsible for my dilemma as far as I was concerned...not to mention the fact that he's a goddamn Filipino. I hung out near his office till he left, then followed him home. He lives in the Happy Days Trailer Court just a few blocks from his office. I managed to hop the back fence and sneak up behind his trailer, a rusty-ass old Airstream, and peek in one of the side windows.

The place was trashed. Dirty dishes filled the small sink, empty Yoo-Hoo chocolate drink cans lined the counter tops, and cheesy Elvis posters filled most of the available wall space. "Love me Tender" was even wafting from a small ghetto blaster in the living area.

Christ! Love me fucking tender!

I quickly made a few notes in my notepad: Elvis posters, dirty dishes in sink, empty cans of Yoo-Hoo chocolate drink. My uncle Slug used to drink Yoo-Hoo...laced with copious amounts of rum. He'd down four or five of 'em, then pass out in the recliner while watching football. Most of the time he'd piss his pants...but that's another story. I finished my notes, then slunk down to the last window. The bedroom, I presumed. It had a yellow shade covering it, cracked with age. There was a small faded photograph of Elvis wearing one of those cheesy white jumpsuits taped to the bottom right corner. I had just positioned myself in front of it when the shade suddenly snapped up, revealing the angry contorted face of Dr. Resurrection staring at me through the window's filmy glass.

"Fock!" he hollered.

I bolted down behind an adjacent trailer, then hopped the fence into the alley and hid behind a dumpster. I heard the door to Dr. Resurrection's trailer open and slam shut, then footsteps. A moment later he appeared, trotting swiftly along the fence. He then climbed to the top, but caught his pants on the chain link, losing his balance and tearing them as he fell roughly to the ground. He lay there for a moment, breathing heavily, then got slowly to his feet and limped down the alley towards the street. The right seam of his pants had been torn nearly to his knee, the ripped edges flapping about as he walked. He turned right at the mouth of the alley and disappeared from sight. I followed him discreetly, keeping 50 or so feet back. His little bald head swiveled this way and that as he cruised the street looking for me.

A few minutes later he suddenly bolted across the street and stopped in front of Daddy's Other Wardrobe, an S/M shop featuring leather outfits, whips, riding crops, and other accessories. I ducked into a nearby doorway and watched him. He peered both ways nervously, then stepped inside. I kept watch for a few more minutes, then dashed across the street and peered in through the plate glass window. I could see him in the back, checking out the leather. A moment later he seemed to have come to some decision, because he came striding up the aisle towards the register holding a pair of black leather shorts. He was also carrying a small brown cardboard package under his arm, but I couldn't tell what was inside. A few more minutes went by as they rang up his purchases.

I was still wondering what was in that package when he suddenly stepped back out onto the street wearing those leather shorts. They were extremely short and very tight. I quickly faded into the doorway of the Little Bo Peep Show, but was too slow. He locked eyes with me, almost dropped the package, and his face went red with rage.

"Fock!" he shouted, starting towards me.

I ran back across the street, nearly getting nailed by a blue Camry, and tore ass down the sidewalk. I figured I'd lose him quickly enough. Unfortunately, the little fucker was pretty fast...faster than I'd give him credit for, being a non-filtered Camel smoker and all. I thought I'd lost him at the Tastee Freeze on the corner of 7th and Avenida Puta Madre, but when I dared to glance over my shoulder, there he was, practically glued to my ass! His ugly little face was twisted into another scowl, his arms and legs pumping with a fierce determination, and that mysterious brown package tucked under his right arm like a football. I turned on the juice. He finally petered out and began dropping back a bit. The last I saw of him he was leaning over the gutter puking his little bald head off.

"Fock!" he yelled between pukes, shaking his fist at me.

"Dat nigga want yo ass!" said Clydesdale, popping open a can of Colt 45. "He treacherous!"

He'd just finished spraying my room for the 3rd time. The roaches had been getting a little frisky lately. Clydesdale moonlights as an exterminator sometimes.

"He's a goddamn fucking Filipino!" I said, lying on the bed and watching a huge roach navigate its way across the ceiling. The intense insecticide smell permeated the air.

"Ah heard dat."

Clydesdale downed the brew in one long swallow, belched, then scratched at his crotch.

"What should I do?" I asked.

"Pop a cap 'n his chop suey ass!"

"You think?"

As if in explanation, Clydesdale pulled a Bic lighter from his pants pocket. I watched, fascinated.

"Check dis shit out," he said, flicking the lighter and holding the flame up to the roach on the ceiling. It burned fast, then fell smoking to the bed. I had to shift my legs rather quickly so it wouldn't land on me.

    "Goddamn!" I said.

    "Ah heard dat."

    I sneaked back to Dr. Resurrection's trailer late the next afternoon. I brought Clydesdale with me. He was pressed up against the wall of the trailer, smoking a cigarette. He brought along his huge container of industrial insect repellent, so we wouldn't attract too much attention from the neighbors. We both wore overalls, mine being borrowed from Clydesdale. They were a bit large, but I figured no one would notice. We each had name patches reading "Clydesdale" over the pen pocket, but again I figured no one would notice.

    I could hear Billy Joel crooning from the ghetto blaster as I crept back to the bedroom window. Maybe the good doctor was getting tired of Elvis. The shade was still down, but this time there was an inch gap at the bottom. The faded Elvis photo grinned at me from the lower right corner. I peeked inside. A dim light in the small bedroom revealed Dr. Resurrection, naked, holding a life-size Elvis blow-up doll. He was embracing it furiously, grinding his hips against it as well as planting huge sloppy kisses on the smiling Elvis face. I signaled Clydesdale and we slipped around to the front, stepping up as quietly as possible onto the small porch.

    The front door was unlocked. Clydesdale ground his cigarette out on the *Welcome* mat and we went inside.

    "Bug man!" I hollered. Clydesdale started spraying insecticide immediately after we entered, then the small bedroom door burst open and a visibly startled Dr. Resurrection stepped out. His naked body was covered with sweat. His tiny pecker was half-erect. The place was quickly filling up with fumes.

    "Hey!" he shouted.

    "Hey yourself!" I said, striding back towards him with a purpose. He ran back into the small bedroom and slammed the door. I heard a bolt click as the lock snapped into place. Clydesdale dropped his spray canister, then shouldered past me and kicked open the door with one brutal thrust of his huge foot. Dr. Resurrection was in the process of trying to squeeze out through the window. Clydesdale was on him like greased lightning, grabbing his legs and yanking him brutally back into the bedroom. He then tried to grab him about the waist, but the little naked man was slick with sweat and squirmed free. Luckily, I was standing between him and the door, so I kneed him in the crotch as he tried to get past me. He dropped like a sack of wet shit and lay moaning at my feet. I stepped back out into the living room, found the phone, and dialed Dr. Resurrection's office. As it was after hours, a recorded message came on.

"*Resurrection Clinic...leave name, number when hear beep!*"

"I sick!" I said, doing my best impersonation of Dr. Resurrection. "Not come in for two week!"

Grinning, I hung up and watched as Clydesdale tore all the Elvis posters off of the wall.

Dr. Resurrection is facedown on the smelly bed. Clydesdale four-cornered his ass, then I stuffed a dirty sock in his mouth. I also poured a couple of cans of Yoo-Hoo chocolate drink all over him...a spur of the moment decision on my part.

The blow-up Elvis doll is lying on the floor, deflated. Clydesdale gripped the head in one of his huge meathooks and popped it like a balloon. Judging from his treatment of the posters, I don't think he likes Elvis much. Billy Joel's "Piano Man" is drifting out of the cheap ghetto blaster from the living room. I've always loved that song, so I began to sing along.

"And the piano sounds like a carnivore!" I screamed. "And the microphone smells like a cunt!"

"Aaarrrrgh!" Dr. Resurrection grunted, struggling against the ropes.

"You sick!" I say to him, grinning. I'd brought along my recently cooked up batch of paraquat in a small mayonnaise jar. It was thick and blue-colored...real funky looking. I was stirring it up with a tooth-brush I found in the trailer's tiny bathroom. Clydesdale was now busy rummaging through the drawers out in the living room, looking for free shit. The bug spray was getting more intense. I poured some paraquat over the crack of Dr. Resurrection's tight little ass, then began swabbing it all over his rectum with the toothbrush.

"Mmmmmmm!!" He twisted his head around towards me, his piggy eyes wide with fear. Sweat glistened on his bald head. I then began mixing the thick fluid with the spilled Yoo-Hoo, creating an interesting design on his ass and lower back.

"Whoa," I said, watching Dr. Resurrection's ass thrust uselessly against the mattress. I reached down and tickled his balls just for fun.

"Mmmmmmmmm!"

Clydesdale has resumed spraying for bugs in the small living room. I hoped he'd found something in the drawers to make it worth his while. The insecticide is starting to burn my eyes.

At that moment someone pounded loudly on the front door.

"Whatchoo want?" shouted Clydesdale, pausing. The pockets of his overalls were now packed with God knows what.

"Police!"

"Sheeeit...d'muth'fuckin' po-leece be at d'do!"

"Stall 'em," I said, tossing a dirty sheet over Dr. Resurrection. He began to moan and struggle, so I bashed him in the head.

The front door burst in suddenly and a big fat cop entered, a SIG/Sauer gripped tightly in both hands. He swung the barrel towards Clydesdale, who dropped the spray canister and threw his hands up in the air.

"Freeze, motherfucker!" the cop shouted. He had a high effeminate voice.

"Can we be of some assistance, Officer?" I said, smiling as I closed the bedroom door on the struggling form of Dr. Resurrection.

The fat cop then swung the pistol towards me, his eyes wide and intense. I leaped aside just before he pumped seven straight shots into the bedroom door, ripping huge holes through the cheap wood. Then Clydesdale grabbed him by the neck and drove his fat head into the wall a couple or five times. The cop collapsed at his feet, moaning.

"Nigga, we gotta jam!" he said, picking up his canister of bug spray.

"Probably for the best," I said.

I considered a quick peek into the bedroom to get some kind of status report on Dr. Resurrection, but quickly changed my mind. The bullets had all hit pretty low...near level with the bed as far as I could see. I stepped back out into the living room, picked up the cop's

SIG/Sauer and stuffed it into the deep side pocket of my overalls.

"After you," I said.

"Ah heard dat."

There was a small mirror on the wall beside the front door, tilted at a slight angle. I caught a quick glimpse of a bright orange face, framed by an intense mullet haircut, grinning maniacally at me as I followed Clydesdale out the door.

Exterminator
by Greg Wharton & Hertzan Chimera

THE CEILING IS unfamiliar again. The heavily swirled stucco aged, yellow, flaking. I sit up slowly, my eyes taking in the strange new surroundings. I lift my legs off the abrasive brown and burnt orange floral-detailed bed cover and set my feet deep into the puke green shag carpet. A motel room not of my own picking, and I have no idea how I came to be here. My cock lies back on my stomach at a funny angle, the thick foreskin tugged back exposing the reeking death's cap mushroom. For a few minutes, I just amuse myself with it, you know, just moving it here and there leaving a shiny trail all over my stomach like snails, pretending it was a tongue doing the moving.

What is that smell? No, idiot, not my cheesy cock tip. It's something real old. Not really decay or mold or ruin, just an ancient presence stretching back through evolutionary twitches in the muck and filth. How many feet have rubbed deep into this same carpet over the years, how many naked butts have perched the same as mine on this very offensive bedcover? Where are my pants? God, where are my pants?

I have to pee, bad. So with much effort, I rise on shaky legs and head to the toilet. My ears buzz, the pulse of last night's—I think it was last night's—gig still with me. I detest those idiots in my band. Why do I carry them around like that? Like shit hanging off of a pristine boot, you know. When is SHIT FOR BRAINS (that's the name we all agreed on, God-damn-it) going to hit the big time? I would even settle for petty notoriety but we are a bit too soft for all the clever promotional japery Marilyn Manson pulls off. In the bathroom, the filthy mirror spits at me and I put my fist through its greasy face. In the kitchenette, ugly twins dance around like Wicca Women fisting each other up the ass with plastic Wellington boots on, sploshing through eels and all kindsa shit all over the linoleum. The stench of incense is nauseating—Fucking Groupies, now that is the name we should have gone with. They didn't even see me standing there.

I chunk back a handful of Sugar Puffs (the only way to start the day) with a swig of greasy old vodka, gargle the shit around in my mouth until the Sugar Puffs dissolve then swallow, whole. In the bedroom again, something real weird happens, not a flashback, not an epileptic seizure, not a memory as such, but something somewhere in the middle like the Bermuda Triangle under my itching wig. Blammo. And I am on the floor, face down with my hairy arse in the air, my sweating feet slipping about like mad. Face down in the scrawny shag carpet. That is where the stink is coming from, growing like a cancer from God-knows-when.

You can read a place from the stink in the carpet I always say. Don't know why I didn't check this joint out sooner—oh, I know, because I have no idea why I am registered here. Sounds of fisting still emanate from the kitchenette, such a potent choir of exclamation. I inhale a good hard lungful of shag scent, right back into the micro thin membrane under my brain where all the hallucinations grow like candle flames greeted to an oxygen enema. This is always the way it starts for me; soon I will be fully erect joining in with the ugly fisting twins in a nasty anonymous of hate. I didn't know the motel carpet fleas had got in there too. As I pull myself to my feet like someone getting over a brain haemorrhage, get dressed and grab my coat; their evil chemical magic is working its way into the psychedelic receptors in what remains of my brain.

Human-being is sooo easy. This one special though. Super fucked.

Shut up, grunt, human-being'll hear us!

Hear us? Hear us?! Human-being not able control his own piss tube. Who care if hear us? Hey, scumbucket! You no talent peece of sheete! See, human-being not even know where is. Not see blood on clothes, nor bruise on skin. Look how easy we make human being see twins fisting in distant land parsecs from this galaxy frame. As if they still contained life. As if they still from his decade.

You're right, human-being...

Is in the nineteen fifties! God, human-being is sooo easy. Fun, this will be...Come, you Alice Cooper wannabe!! See if you can feel this...

The door slams behind me. Gotta find those so called friends of mine...WHAP! My brain explodes in lightning bright flashes, blinding white pain, pain like long needles being plunged into my head, my legs give out, and I fall flat, face down with a crunch as my nose meets cement. WHAP! I'm back in the room, but as a spectator, like I'm floating, hovering above the bed. Some lucky bum is going at it with two beauties. Ooh, twins. Hey, the ugly twins! I quickly forget that I'm probably laying facedown on pavement in some city somewhere with a broken nose, and enjoy the view: I watch myself—*hey that's me!*—give it to twin A as twin B writhes in ecstasy with both hands thrusting madly into her snatch.

The man on the bed, me, swings an Errol Flynn sabre around and around his head as the giggling idiots watch on enthralled. Then down curves the steel in a carving skull arc. Thwok! It embeds itself in her forehead bisecting her ugly eyes. Our swashbuckling hero has to put his foot into the blade releasing, her screaming face separated from steel. The blade comes down again, slicing across her chest. Her friend starts to escape. Like a ballet, I leap off the bed, bilocated into the revelry, my cashmere codpiece glowing like salt in an open wound. The sabre catches her across the kidneys before she can get her hand on the door handle and she goes down. I drag her to the kitchenette where I sling her still twitching body onto that of her split skull twin and get out the shotgun from my suitcase. This is a simple sawn-off affair that fits nicely into any travel itinerary. She is always loaded, and I shove her barrel deep into the kidney gash of a twin, pulling both triggers, a daft grin on my face, my left eye hangs out onto my cheek theatrically double visioning the mass murder...

Stop toying with! Let human-being go.

Yeah, let human-being go!

Shut up, I need not you on our ass as well! I just testing, just having a little fisting fun!

Fine, it's not like human-being able to do anything about it! You all need to take it down a few notches! Okay, where were we...

I have vomited in the center of the fucking sidewalk and the human traffic are giving me a wide berth like I am some sort of infection. I roll over and grab my bloody nose, but it's fine I think. Its not like it hasn't been broken before. Must have been the Sugar Puffs. I slowly stand, gripping the railing, and test my legs. A little shaky, but in working order. God-almighty, I stink. Should have grabbed a shower. Should have had some more vodka. Oh well, I think, as I stumble through the unfamiliar parking lot. Like some no-brain soon-to-be-wed who has woken up miles from home on his nuptial day, I find in my leather jeans pocket a meishi from God-knows-who and a hand-written address of the Fishy Cat Rumpus Room (I remember this being a club I gigged in once, what city was that?). I try to stop a finely dressed passerby and ask him where I am, but he is not in the mood to deal with drunks or homeless folk on this fine day and says, "I gave at the orifice," passing me by.

What has happened to style? As I get up, everything looks like a flickering David Cronenberg from the old newsreels of yore. In the streets, fat pink greyhound buses all veined up the sides with a gleeful smile on the driver's face, stalk potential passengers. You can see them mounting the curbs with their hymenopterous wings of lust flipping open hydraulically. Room for one more, sir or madam, the grinning driver salivates onto his enormous steering wheel. Skull faces smile back through the greyhound's steamy windows. Someone at the back eating their own gun SPECTACULARLY—a hiss of YES! from the skull faces nearby as they start to roll around in the hasty decay. I shake my head and move off, hopefully, in the direction of the Fishy Cat Rumpus Room, the address in my hand like a shopping list. I have no idea where this is going. Maybe I can get some answers at the Fishy Cat Rumpus Room. My stomach gurgles.

He weele never make it to the Rumpussss Roooom.

Spectacular, luscious, large mounds of ripe juicy breasts, and I have my face buried deep. First suckling one, and then the other like a hungry babe. Her name is Lola. Oh, Lola! Big tits, big ass. Her face, well her face is a bit bar-aged and she wears too much make-up, but the lips still taste good! And she wants it, bad!

While trying to navigate, unsuccessfully, to find my mates, I happened upon a dark, cool bar called the "Where Else You Gotta Be?" Though not certain of anything else this crazy day, I was certain of the need for a tall stiff one, a drink that is.

Lola crawled over the three stools separating us within two minutes of my drink's appearance, and proceeded to wrap her not so tiny hands around the quickly growing bulge that her administrations were producing. Within five minutes she had me in a stall in the very smelly, cramped john. Oh, Lola! She was now pulling down my dirty slacks, and once my hard—and slightly sore—prick swung to freedom, administering strong suction to my whole middle section right through my mighty prick. The slurping sounds were a bit on the downright gross side, but damn the wench could suck! Oh, shit!

I was spinning in sensation as she deep-throated me hard, too hard, damn near bruising my engorge prickhead as she jammed it over and again against the back of her throat and grinding her teeth roughly as she yanked me back out. But it was working, two or three more pumps and I think I'll give her what she seems to want, maybe I'll treat her to a little of the same! Oh, yowzzz…Hey, I'm gonna, oh…

Not able to control myself, I grip her flame red hair firmly and…it slides from the top of her…oh, shit! The deeply pockmarked skull continues to devour me as I try to escape her jaws! Shit, what is that! I could swear that there are things, oh, things crawling around under her scalp and…scales…

She smiles up at me with my thick prick still deep within her jaws and I see them. Large jagged teeth! Her face is not the face I was kissing just moments ago; it is now a scaly, green mass with thick black and red hairs poking from both her cheeks and nose. The jagged yellow teeth start biting and the blood, my blood, squirts out and runs down her vile chin just as I…I come hard…I feel as if my spunk has been torn from my bowels and my hips buck once hard against the beast I thought was Lola and then hard back against the graffiti stained stall's wall, *only* my prick is gone, *only* a jagged wet stump remains…and I watch as the horrible beast chews with a look close to ecstasy and my blood and cum drip down her chin, throat, then breasts…all three of them! Three of them?

I crack my fists down violently at the vile creature that just ate the center of my universe and they land with a soft wet thud like an overly ripe pumpkin. Oh that smell, that's awful, disgusting! I pry my fists free. Oh my god, I scream! My god, my prick!

She laughs, shrill and wild and uncontrolled, like a banshee. I join her, then lose the footing of my legs and fall down much like a rag doll hitting my head on the cold porcelain, still clutching the red wig.

In a dark part of town a man rises to his feet, blood darkening his crotch. In his wake a sewer of gore. The metallic stench of blood and the oily taste of feces.

That was cool, you so wicked.

Thank you! Now got a fully online neural simulator going. Switching to chemical mode. DNA re-adjustment in effecto.

You so badboy, professor Mc Flea.

From the sewer wake flowing after the scruffy man staggering about in the crowded street, crawl spineless things. Oily tentacular things. Cockroachy exoskeletal things. Like vomit on the move. You can't outrun the river of sores, the lake of fury. You could see the shit unplugging itself from his wake. The scatological enema beings scatter in a hurry, burying themselves in the roots of tower blocks, office buildings, libraries, the halls of governmental power. Rewriting the past with their psychomorphic prowess. There can never be any escape from their sulphurous pornography, unless...

I gotta get to the Fishy Cat Rumpus Room. The finalé to my worthless shit piece of rock whore life is like a raging gore torrent assault course. At one point, I am carried along on the heads of Christ-knows-what. Crushing their shimmering craniums underfoot. Accelerating to about a million miles an hour, my gory insult of exis-tence swoops through the old town coalescing every modern thing in the ossification of the ancients. Their influence dislodging the con-temporary in favour of ye olde and crackling like old Newsreels, horror earthquake footage and volcanoes shoot through the panicked streets. Where my lusty erection used to root, dogfaces and catpussy and cowlicks of romance gush from the ragged hole. Layers are peeled from my eyes. The pain is amazing—a glass storm of shattered futures strobing forward at 1 billion hertz. A blinding struggle against the past distorted into the future. My shocked musculature seizes on several occasions and for the first time, I can hear the little chuckling and laughing and snorkelling sounds inside my head. Damn those rug rats. Damn those little bitching beasts. Damn those greasy shelled parasites.

In the distance a diminutive signpost flickers nostalgically THE

FISHY CAT (RUMPUS ROOM) gasping in the turbulent yellow smog storm like a drowning animal. Brain shattered customers fleeing the labia like double doors flapping hither and yon in oiled percussion. I dive into the establishment and ask the barman if he knows the writer of my pathetic little note, showing him the hand-written address signed by its author, *the Exterminator*. The barman casually points to a chap in a white suit in a relaxed corner booth overlooking the establishment as the psycho-sexual melée roars all around him, blonde hair beyond all albino whiteboyness, a still flaming daiquiri in his manicured finger-tips, a silver Glock pistol on the table catches the sickening scintillations from the horrific eruption of erotica on the dance floor, a roving glee in his eye. He blows out the flame as I reach his table, then looks up and sneers at me.

"Good God, man, where have you been? You nearly missed the deadline for the late edition."

"I did?"

"Yes, you just about pissed into the wind, mister. One more mis-take and..."

"Excuse me, but aren't you Andy Warhol? I remember your face from school, you're..."

"Enough of this nonsense! No time to haggle the price down. Follow me, if you want to live."

And just like that, he's off, tucking the Glock into his gray raincoat pocket. I follow him, carefully stepping around the bodies writhing on the dance floor in filaments of starburst glory and hellbound whorry, almost falling when I hit a wet puddle of who-knows-what, but catch myself by grabbing the closest thing, a bobbing bald head attached to another bald head's enormous cock, and right myself. This shit sticks to my hand and works its way up my arm like living chrome. The chrome discolors to rust and the shrapnel falls away taking the major-ity of my arm mass with it. I hold up a skeletal remnant and trudge on after the Exterminator. Better make this quick or all that's gonna be left of me is the Cheshire cat tip of my cock radiating in the throat-choking afterglow.

The man I assume is the Exterminator disappears through a door marked Private: Exterminators ONLY. With a desperate effort to keep the very structure of my atoms from flying apart, I twist the door knob

and enter the darkened room. My eyes gradually adjust to the lighting.
Good touch!
Thanks, human-being no have any sense of reality anymore...
Hee hee hee...

Andy Exterminator Warhol is across the dim room with his back
to me. The door slams behind me with a SNAP that makes my ears
pop. I'm back in the damn motel room. Shit, what the? Oh, and that
smell! It's that smell!

Andy Exterminator Warhol turns around, and I notice his bright
red painted lips and scary green eye shadow. He seductively unbuttons
the raincoat and lets it drop to the green shag carpet, kicking it to side
with his long very shapely legs.

"You've been a very bad boy!" He says as he runs his hands over
the short, short silver stretch mini-skirt he's wearing, then stepping out
of the come-fuck-me-pumps, making him four inches shorter but still
way over six feet tall.

Despite the trans-dimensional cleavage in spacetime bullying me
from the Fishy Cat Rumpus Room back into this damn skanky motel,
and despite the bizarre effects of Andy's made-up face, I am aroused.
Someone should just shoot me. Put me down like the damned horny
old dog that I am.

"Oh...I have?" Not knowing why, I am flirting, playing coy with
him. Someone, just pull out a revolver. Take aim on my lust center,
mid-brain. "I have this note..." I explain, "and I think it's from you.
I'm a little confused, and think you can help. You are the Extermin..."

Without warning, I am bitch-slapped from the side, barely seeing
the flash of Andy's arms stretching out from across the room, and fall
back onto the bed. He is on me in a flash and my pants are basically
ripped from my body, my big purple-red hard head poking from the
thick foreskin, once again ready for some decadent deed. The damn
thing has a mind of its own sometimes. Kill me!!! It is your only hope.
End the pain. End the sorrow.

He throws, first one, then two, three and four legs up and over my
body, plunging my hardness deep into his big, hairy, sloppy, hungry
wetness. It feels like he is swallowing more than my bad boy, and his
eight long luscious legs do a spider dance as he pounds me like I've
rarely been pounded. Pincers enter my back, holding me still, encased

in lust.

I'm getting close, "Fuck me," I think I scream out, "Fuck me!" forgetting how weird it is, then the spell is broken. He speaks, and it sounds like hundreds are speaking at once.

"You've been a very bad boy Mr. Exterminator," the little mites choir in unison, a legion of carapaced undead sucking the horror from my drug addled head, "You have killed millions of our intergalactic cousins, but now we have you right where we want you! You will now help us, not hurt us, and we shall finally take over what is rightfully ours!

Go Mom!
Go Queen!
Fuck heeme....!
Go!
Go!
Go!

"Mankind is coming to an end. Together, we will create the perfect being. Now, COME!"

I have no control and spill myself inside him, her, it, letting go. Pain then sears through my guts as the pincers that nailed my cock to him/her/it are retracted. Like a birthing scene run in reverse night after night after night. Like waves cascading, a numbness flows through my perforated shell. I can't move, but I now remember the whole sordid tale.

I am the Exterminator. I am only one of a few, in this whole wretched waste of what's left of planet Earth who knows the truth about the alien fleas and their diabolical plan to adopt this world as their own. I was chosen, early on, by what remained of the United Nations, to fight them as only I knew how. I successfully rid the earth of those I found and, until now, was able to do it undetected. Somehow, they must have tricked me, then implanted little earth flea traitors into my brain. Shit!

The note is of my own making, in my own writing. Shit!

The band, Shit For Brains, my cover. Shit! Shit!

And this is the Queen. Shit! Shit! Shit!

Andy's face has now shed its mask, and the Preying Mantis-like eyes stare deep into mine, think of molten lead being poured into the eye sockets of a still living torture victim. The Queen Mother's many-jawed maw grinds madly readying for the inevitable coup de grace. I know what's coming, and know no way out, so I close my eyes and prepare for the pain hoping it will happen fast.

Oh, please let it happen fast...

Queens devour Exterminators slowly, deliberately, with lust, and much happiness. Queens were impregnated by human-beings like my fellow Exterminators, and their children shall be the best of both species. No one will stop us now. No one will stop us now.

Along Came Auntie Rose Mary
by Brutal Dreamer

A BUDDING TEENAGER, Tamara Jean never appreciated her Auntie Rose Mary's sense of humor or her decorating taste. In fact, she nearly convulsed each time she was forced to go into her aunt's home. When she was five years old, her parents died due to "freak sickness" (well, that is what Tamara Jean was told). The only living relative left was her dotty Auntie Rose Mary; reluctantly Tamara Jean moved into the massive home.

Tamara Jean shuddered each time her aunt spoke. Her voice hit an obnoxiously high pitch and you'd think she was Edith Bunker. Her curly bleached blonde hair flailed to and fro with each maniacal gesture, and as if that wasn't enough, Tamara Jean loathed how her Aunt always called her T.J.

Her childhood was harsh; she had witnessed both her parents' struggle with the disease. Her father's cataracts glazed his once blue eyes into orbs hazed with the shadows of yesterday. Her mother's hands were riddled and knotted with abnormalities. Wonderments filled Tamara Jean. She questioned her parents' deaths, but received imperious answers. Auntie Rose Mary held those answers. However, she would rattle off asinine replies; it was as if Alex Trebek were interrogating her about Madam Currie's discoveries.

Tamara became more concerned with each brush off her inquiries met. Feeling something wasn't right about herself—and without the satisfaction of knowing the exact details of what caused the rare aging defect which led to the ultimate deaths of her parents—fear seeped like hot lava through her veins.

The last time she saw her parents they seemed very aged considering she was just a little girl. When they came to pick her up from Kindergarten, she compared them to the parents of her classmates. Her parents seemed more like grandparents to her.

Not sure why they aged so rapidly, she tried to figure out what caused the age acceleration. Her mother, Rachel, had soft, porcelain skin which rivaled Raquel Welch. Her father's chiseled, bronzed features put Mel Gibson to shame. The demon Age found them, and like a bloodthirsty monster it ravaged them. Her mother's soft skin turned to leather and shriveled while her father transformed into a hideous man ransacked with oozing pus-filled leprosy.

Tamara Jean read about leprosy, she wondered if that is what they had. She couldn't fathom how their mutation into hideous old creatures could happen so fast.

"Aunt Rose Mary…" Tamara Jean whispered. "Where did you get this lamp?"

Tamara Jean really didn't want to know. She feared knowing more than anything else. However, something inside her forced her to talk about the lamp. It was as if that lamp beckoned her to touch it. She ran her fingers up and down the odd yet familiar curves of the lamp as the long beads hanging from the shade danced over her hands. It felt as though tiny spiders were crawling over her hand. Swiftly, she yanked her hand from the lamp and grimaced.

Rose Mary chuckled and chided her silly childish fear of spiders.

"I bought that lamp at the curio shop on the corner of the street. Mister Dagle's Bric-a-brac Shop!" That was the only answer her niece would receive. "How 'bout some tea, T.J.?"

Rolling her eyes, Tamara Jean followed Rose Mary to the kitchen entrance. She peered back at the lamp. The structure—hauntingly familiar. Her eyes widened as she stared at the scarlet liquid, followed its flow down the curves of the lamp to the stand. The base appeared to be a shoe. One of those beautiful old fashioned white boots that laced up tightly with the pointed toes. The gooey liquid filled the tops of the boot and spilled over the rim, raining down the sides in scarlet streaks into an ever widening puddle upon the table.

"You want two teaspoons of sugar, or one?" Tamara Jean jumped when the obnoxious voice suddenly exploded from the kitchen.

She hesitated. "Uh…two…." Tamara Jean slowly strolled to the table. Her fingers traipsed the lamp shade. She apprehensively put her fingertips under the rim of the lampshade and lifted it upward, tilting it to the left. The light beamed onto the wall and created a prism of dancing colors. Tamara Jean's face turned back toward the lamp. Her fingernail got caught on the black fishnet stockings running up its length. Her face twisted, her eyebrows arched, and her breath caught in her chest, refusing to pump out.

Rose Mary walked through the archway carrying a silver tray of two tea cups and a rosy colored teapot. "Come, dear." Her yellowed teeth protruded through her thin orange-red lipstick smudged smile.

Tamara Jean watched Rose Mary place the tray on the coffee table by the couch. She walked toward her Aunt with much trepidation. "What's the matter…sweetheart?" Rose Mary asked.

Tamara Jean refused to speak. She quietly sat next to her aunt, her nose buzzing with the stench of moth balls and dime store perfume. Her eyes fell upon the beautiful tray filled with sandwiches and tea. The sound of her stomach rumbling made her realize just how hungry she had grown. Wary not to scorch her tongue, she picked up the tea cup and brought it to her thin lips. After just a simple sip her face contorted, although she was trying not to offend her aunt. "Mmm," she moaned, almost convincing, and reassured her Aunt it was delicious. As her aunt looked away, Tamara Jean's eyes squeezed tightly shut and she swallowed the thick sludge. The flavor was faintly familiar. She thought back to last week when she bit her lip and remembered the metallic tang.

She sat the teacup on the table and watched as her aunt guzzled and gulped the gooey beverage. The older woman looked over at Tamara Jean, all smiles. Crimson streaks outlined her yellowed teeth with small clumps of fibrous tissues caught in the incisors. Tamara Jean reasoned she must have eaten some meat earlier that day.

Taking her mind off the tea and Aunt Rose Mary's disgusting teeth, Tamara Jean picked up the small cuts of rye bread filled with rolled ham and cheese, bringing them to her salivating mouth. While doting Aunt Rose Mary watched her, Tamara Jean sawed her teeth through the bread. Her eyes widened at Rose Mary as she chomped further into the meat and hit a bone.

"Delicious, isn't it, T.J.?" her aunt said.

With a loud crunch she bit through the sandwich. She chewed upon the rubbery food, watching the benevolently smiling Rose Mary, and squinted her eyes with each chew. It was the weirdest texture and taste of ham that Tamara Jean had ever eaten. She tried hard to act as if she loved the tasty morsel without gagging, instead willing herself to make yummy noises with each forced smile. Her face dropped to her sandwich. The rolled ham and cheese had something round inside the fold of the meats. She analyzed it more closely. Aunt Rose Mary lifted a finger sandwich from the tray. Her mouth opened wide, allowing her to put the entire thing in her mouth, and she wrapped her lips around it. Tamara Jean gulped and placed the rest of her sandwich on the tray, watching in disbelief as Aunt Rose Mary finished off the entire tray of sandwiches.

The crunching nearly caused Tamara Jean to heave. She watched as Rose Mary dipped her sandwich into her teacup and swirled the rolled bread around in the liquid. When she brought the sandwich up from the cup, half of it was stained ruby red and dribbled long strings of tea. Rose Mary stuck out her lizardy pink tongue and licked the stringy liquid from underneath the bread. Then she dropped the sandwich into her drooling maw.

Tamara Jean bid her aunt goodnight and asked to be excused to the bathroom. Peering down over the top rail of the winding wrought iron staircase, she could see her aunt. Feigning a loving smile she waved goodnight.

Once in the bathroom she pressed her face to the faucet and let the cold water pour over her. She cried to herself in silence, her face steaming in the cool air, the bitterness stinging her eyes. The cold water soothed the burning fear and disgust she had for her insane Aunt Rose Mary.

She placed a dry towel to her face and dried the water droplets from her pale skin. Sad blue eyes peered back at her from the mirror, as if pleading with her for help to get away from the crazy old woman. Futile as it was, she still wished there was a way to leave the old manor.

Picking up a silver-plated hairbrush, old and heavy, she wielded it through her long auburn hair. She shuddered thinking of the ghostly hands that had used the brush before her, knowing that brush had been owned by some dead person. Less comforting was the fact that her Aunt Rose Mary had purchased it down at Mr. Dagles. She bought all her "rare artifacts" from that loony bin.

A dark purple velvet pillbox sat upon the countertop. She ran her finger over the top of the trinket box. The silver inlaid rose atop the velvet was sharp and detailed. Tamara Jean fondled the pretty box and cooed, "Wow." She picked up the box and lightly shook it. Curious about what secrets of yesterday loony Aunt Rose Mary kept prisoner inside; she shuddered yet slowly lifted the lid. With a dull click the box opened. Placed perfectly inside the molded box was an eyeball…a recognizable eye. She knew it was her father's eye. Tamara Jean suppressed a scream as the eyeball looked at her knowingly. She clamped the lid shut, her fingers trembled a mile a minute and she tossed the box back upon the countertop.

Aunt Rose Mary had never married, yet she had a beautiful white gown draped upon a burgundy satin hanger on a brass hook in the bathroom. The lace was filled with tiny French beads and knots, gilded with some silvery ribbons of thread. Tamara Jean wondered what Cinderella felt like as her dainty fingers trekked the length of the lacy material. She fantasized about her handsome prince arriving and taking her away from her demented Aunt Rose Mary. With an ear pressed to the door she listened, making sure her aunt was not coming up the stairs. When all was quiet, she slipped the dress from the hanger. She pressed the satiny material up next to her tender cheek. She relished the scent, reminding her how her mother smelt. Suppressed memories of her mother flooded, unbidden, bringing sadness with them.

Tears fell onto the lacy material. She wiped the wetness from her face and the dress, then stood up to unbutton her shirt.

She realized what a fine young lady she was becoming. Taking note of the cleavage of her recently developed breasts; plump and firm. Her fingers strolled over her cleavage and then around the tan, round nipples. Feeling a sensation unknown to her, the nipples protruded with her touch. She looked up and saw her face was flushed with embarrassment. Although, she was not sure why she felt as if she had done something wrong.

Her fingers trembled and with her index finger and thumb she pinched her nipple. The face in the mirror wore an expression of sheer bliss. A sudden moistness set into her pretty pink panties.

Unaware of what was happening to her body she reached down to the rim of her panties and dipped her fingers through the elastic. "What the…" she began to say as her fingers felt wet and her panties were drenched.

Confused, but unable to keep from touching herself, her fingers explored the wet and swollen area. While watching herself in the mirror she slid her panties below her hips and cupped herself. Waves of sensation swarmed over her until she moaned and her teeth gritted together. Despite the fact that she was unable to figure out what was happening to her, she couldn't seem to stop touching and gradually rubbing harder and faster, her body convulsed as her legs trembled and her breasts shook exciting her even more. An enraptured feeling overcame her and she exploded upon her fingers with wonder at what was happening to her. She thought, this was the best she felt ever since she was stuck at Aunt Rose Mary's and certainly it couldn't be a bad thing.

Tamara Jean was mortified as she examined herself in the mirror. Unable to comprehend what had happened to her, she quickly took a wash cloth and ran it under warm water. Her guilty eyes stared back at her, reprimanding. She put the warm washcloth between her legs and cleaned up, then dried herself off. Washing her hands with soap and water she feared Auntie Rose Mary finding out what she had done. Yet, she herself wasn't sure what she had done. Still, she reasoned she'd rather not have it exposed.

She returned to the dress once more. When she brought the material to her naked flesh the soft satin and lace kissed her supple, pale body. She lifted a milky-white leg into the opening of the dress, then her other leg; she brought the material up to her breasts and shoulders. The cool material felt sensational against her skin, with each tiny tickle giving her goosebumps. Her nipples were still stimulated, protruding through the lacy material in dark pink glimmers. She reached behind her back and slowly, quietly she zipped up the dress. She lifted her breasts inside, exposing more cleavage, then cocked her head sideways in the mirror. Her budding body was silhouetted through the lace and silvery-white satin beautifully.

Upon an old wooden chair with dark chartreuse velvety padded seat were two long white gloves. She walked to the chair and the gloves suddenly expanded as if a hand had slipped inside them. Forcing herself to overcome her initial fear she raised the edge and looked down inside. Nothing was in it. Surely a gust of wind from the moonlit window had filled them.

Her fingers wriggled into place—they were a perfect fit. She sauntered back to the mirror and saw the dress and gloves together. She giddily snickered and twirled around as if her Prince had found her and rescued her from this hellish home. Her bare feet smacked the cold tiled floor with each twirl. She danced about the bathroom and happened upon a boot. Unable to find the other one she placed her narrow foot into the boot and dragged the bare foot behind as she continued in her prancing. She felt the wispy veil scratch her face, the soft wilting net reminding her of when she was caught in a cobweb.

As the blaring shrills of Aunt Rose Mary swam up the staircase, Tamara Jean's eyes opened wide and she looked frantically around the room. The sun filtered through her blinds, although she couldn't believe it was morning already; Tamara Jean had hardly slept at all. Her nightmares seemed to be occurring more often and lasting throughout the entire night. Her sleep since her parents' deaths had been restless; for many years she kept waking up to such horrid images.

Aunt Rose Mary constantly reassured her that the dreams weren't true, and that she was not a wicked Witch Spider. Each night, it was the same. Tamara Jean dreamed she was caught in Aunt Rose Mary's web of horrors and held hostage to her insanity. "Sweetheart…" her aunt said, consoling her with a cool washcloth to the forehead.

The nurse at the Cinnamon Hillcrest Institute wiped Tamara Jean's brow and told her she had a visitor.

"No, oh good lord no," Tamara Jean pleaded with the nurse. "They want my leg. I know they do. My crazy Aunt Rose Mary wants my leg. She needs it. I dreamed it, I tell you…" she pleaded to the nurse not to leave her alone. She knew her Aunt Rose Mary was coming for her.

"Hon," the nurse whispered. "it's not your aunt dear. It's your Uncle John."

Unworried, still slightly doped and confused, Tamara Jean shrugged and moaned as the nurse unlocked the door and let the tall man into the room. The nurse offered the tall man a good day, slipping in a "she's flipped out today" nod before closing the door behind her.

The door clanked shut. Footsteps sounded until they disappeared off in the distance.

A man adorned in a black suit with white shirt approached Tamara Jean. His hair slicked back, making him reminiscent of the Handsome Prince she dreamed of in Cinderella. She stretched out her foot and slid it into the white boot. Gushy wetness sloshed between her toes. He handed her an oblong envelope. As her toes squirmed around in the icky sludge she tried not to vomit.

After tearing open the envelope a soul-rending scream escaped her lips. The enclosed document of authenticity had been sent with love by Aunt Rose Mary. All Tamara Jean needed to do was sign it.

The Prince turned around with a hacksaw in hand, and a gleam upon his face, he smiled. "Shh, my Princess." He pressed the jagged teeth of the blade to her creamy-white thigh and pressed down. Her scream was muffled by the sock he stuffed into her mouth. Scarlet liquid slithered down the blade of the thirsty saw and splattered the handsome man's face in hot thick darts.

Her eyes rolled into white orbs, while her leg felt like it was on fire causing Tamara Jean to pass out.

The man in the black suit picked up the beautiful leg from the floor and rolled it in a heavy blanket. Tamara Jean lay on the floor missing one of her legs, bleeding to death with each passing second. She felt life leaving her cold blue body.

He washed his face and hands, then placed his surgical tools back in a large bag along with the booted leg. He pressed the button and asked the head of the Nurse's station to unlock the door. After she unlatched the door he opened it and peered around the corner. As he locked eyes with the nurse she gasped. With his large hand placed around her neck and the other over her mouth, he yanked; a loud pop followed and her head faced completely backward. The gorgeous prince tossed her body on the floor with Tamara Jean's and left the bloodbath behind.

"You got it, my Prince!" Rose Mary's voice hit a high pitched shrill. "Each relative holds the most precious gift, the fountain of youth, in a special part of their body," she reminded her Prince.

He knew that was how Auntie Rose Mary kept such a youthful appearance for a woman rumored to be in her early sixties; he knew better. He had seen her birth certificate several years back.

She was born during a time when they had no sanitary systems. Open graves lined the streets with putrid dead bodies. Disease was rampant. Life expectancy was low. It was a time when witchcraft was feared. The documents said: Rose Mary Wildes born on September 17, 1692.

Although he didn't understand how she survived for those many centuries, he dared not question it, knowing she had been born of a witch with powers inherited from her ancestors of the sixteen century. She cast deathly spells upon her relatives: cataracts, tumors, cancerous diseases, and mental illnesses.

Even so, he did her bidding quietly without breathing a hint of fear or concern.

Rose Mary's house showcased these priceless special gifts. She slid a black fishnet stocking over the pale fleshy leg and placed the stump on the table, then draped a long beaded lampshade over the top.

"I knew I'd eventually catch that devious niece of mine, if only by driving her mad, I'd get her tangled in my web!"

The Prince smiled a coy smile.

"My darling…" she cooed running her red-painted finger down his torso. "You have another special gift for me…" He assumed she meant the usual "gift" stored in his boxer shorts, until she brought a dagger from behind her back and grinned an ever-widening gooey smile.

"You're a crazy old woman…you're craaaaaaaaaaaaaaaaaaaaaa…"

The man fell with a thud.

A Terrible Thing to Waste
by Vincent W. Sakowski

S CALPEL," THE SURGEON ordered. "Scalpel." The nurse slapped it into his open palm, and he turned back to the patient to make the incision. With practiced ease he cut along the line drawn on the patient's bald skull. The cut complete, he discarded the scalpel and slowly but firmly pulled the skin away with his fingers. Then he called for a number of hooks and clamps to hold the skin back.

"Do he and his family know his chances, Doctor?" the nurse inquired.

"Of course...stryker saw."

"Stryker saw."

The surgeon pulled the trigger, and the small circular blade whined and whirled into life. He moved in and began to cut away along the perimeter of the five-inch diameter circle. He removed the piece of bone and inspected his handiwork.

"Irrigation."

"Irrigation."

"Excellent." He admired the gray matter glistening before him, a covetous smile hidden under his mask.

"How's our patient?"

The anesthesiologist checked over the readings. "He's doing great, Doctor. Everything normal."

"Excellent." The surgeon stepped back for a moment and lifted his surgical gown. Underneath he wore only shoes and socks and one massive erection. With his right hand he grabbed his cock and gave it a squeeze, while he caressed the patient's skull with the other. As he stepped forward again, the others maintained their positions in anticipation.

Without waiting another moment, the surgeon lined up his cock with the hole and jammed it into the patient's brain.

"Where's my cottage cheese?!" the patient suddenly woke and screamed.

The surgeon ignored his cries and grabbed onto his skull, fucking it all the while, gleeful but also mindful not to get cut on the edges of the circle. He swiveled his hips around to fully explore the inside of the skull. Meanwhile, the patient occasionally called such things as: "Who keeps farting...? Light a match." And: "What a beautiful color for a crayon." Parts of his body tried to move at different moments, but he was buckled down for the long haul. Soon, gray and white matter slushed out of the hole while the surgeon tried harder to find some friction. The patient's eyes bulged as he pushed against them and he soon popped one of them out. He then worked on the other eye until it too popped and ran down the patient's cheek. Happy with the spot, rubbing the head of his cock along the eye socket, he finally ejaculated, squirting inside his skull and through the socket over the patient's face.

Breathing heavily, the surgeon carefully pulled his softening member from the hole. He noticed under all of the ooze a small scrape here and there, but no more than any other time.

"Who's next? I'm all through for now." The surgeon sighed in contentment. "I'd better go get cleaned up and speak with his family." He stepped away and dropped his gown.

The nurse and the anesthesiologist closed in on the dead patient, each running their gloved hands over his body.

"I get his liver." The anesthesiologist licked his lips.

"You got liver the last time." The nurse scowled and slapped his hands away.

"Complications." The surgeon laughed as he turned to leave. "There's always complications."

Ready for the Afterlife
by Abel Diaz

I WOKE UP feeling shitty on all fronts. Impossible to get out of bed. The only thing to do was lie perfectly still. Restrict all movement to essential functions: breathing, farting and occasional forays to the kitchen for cold beer. Maybe raid the porn stash the minute Betty left the house...

"Paul Vasquez!" Betty never entered a room—she crashed into it. "You're late for work!"

"Fuck work, Betty. I'm staying home. Can't you see I'm sick?"

She cocked a massive hip to one side and eyed me aggressively. She was not a friendly woman. "Bullshit! What's wrong with you?"

"Nonspecific malaise, Betty. Worst case I've ever seen. I may not pull through this time."

I could see her trying to figure it out. She hadn't looked up malaise in a dictionary recently. There was a good chance she'd buckle like before. But then: "Get out of bed! Get out of bed!"

She beat me with her bare hands like an enraged gorilla. I took one to the temple and blacked out momentarily. When I came to she was in my face: "You get the fuck out of bed, you lazy prick. Think you can lie around and play with yourself all day while I work my tits off? BASTARD! You make me so goddamn angry, Paul, I should torture you. I should make you die like an animal."

"Betty calm down," I appealed. "I'm a sick man. Can't you see I'm not well?"

"Then you go to a doctor!" She laid her hands on me again, and the lights went out.

I didn't have health insurance, so I drove myself to a community clinic. Your standard chop-shop operation. I was sent to the exam room after a long wait, and they sent in their interrogator, dressed in her contempt for the weak and infirm. The kind of woman who never wanted to be a nurse but did it anyway, and now she blames it on total strangers. A thoroughly miserable bitch. A Nazi in drag.

She got right down to it: "Well? What's wrong with you?"

"Nonspecific malaise," I said.

She lowered her clipboard and tried to cold snap me with her eyes. Frosty the Snow Cunt. "Can you describe the symptoms?"

"I can. My job is unfulfilling. I drink too much, but I worry if I stop drinking my writing will get dull. Which is pointless because none of my stories are getting published anyway. I've got the crazy shits all the time. I'm sick of everything. People seem cruel, selfish, and dumb to me. Not worth the skin they're printed on. Just rolling out of bed is a monumental task. My girlfriend gained a hundred pounds after I moved in with her. But I'm too gutless to dump her and get on with my life."

The nurse took a blood sample and left the room. She rough-handled the needle and collapsed a few of my veins. They looked like purple worms burrowed deep in my arm. I waited for several hours. I tried to read a magazine, but everyone had their clothes on and I lost interest immediately. I laid down on the exam table, felt the crinkle of butcher's paper beneath me. No reason to be awake at this hour. Soon enough I was asleep.

The doctor woke me up with a polite cough. I could tell by his expression the news wasn't good.

"Let me have it, doctor. Is it nonspecific malaise?"

"There's no such thing, Mr. Vasquez. You made that up."

"I have an English degree from the University of Washington," I informed him. "I don't make things up."

He sighed. "Would you like to know what you really have, Mr. Vasquez, or do you want to waste even more of your time?"

"What do you mean?" Sweat from every pore on my body. A salty perfume.

"I'm afraid you have PVD."

"Oh God shit!!!" Whatever it was it sounded dangerous, even terminal.

The doctor opened a cabinet door and produced a quart of rum and some glasses. He poured two doubles. "Drink up, Paul. What I have to tell you isn't pretty."

It was gone before he finished his sentence. "Can I have another?"

"Yes, of course," he said and served it up. A triple. Then he gave it to me straight: "You have PVD. Paul Vasquez Disease."

I checked his eyes. My God the man was serious. "What is that?!? And how come I've never heard of it?"

"We don't know what it is. No one's ever seen it before. We discovered it in your blood sample three hours ago. We rushed our analysis to the Centers for Disease Control, and they officially named it after you. Congratulations, Paul. It's quite an honor."

"Don't congratulate me, goddamnit! I got a disease and I want the cure!"

The doctor had expected such an outburst. He was trained for it. He calmed me down with a fresh rum and said, "Paul, I won't lie to you. This is the first case of PVD the world has ever encountered. We don't have a cure, or a treatment, or even any idea what to expect."

"This is such bullshit."

"Well," the doctor shifted uncomfortably. He reddened like a Bloody Mary. "It gets worse."

"Worse?"

"Yes, well," he turned around and busied himself putting things away. I heard him mumble something into the wall.

"What now? I have to do what with the who for the what?"

"I said you have to report to the CDC for quarantine." He turned around and faced me again. Composure regained. "They're giving you one hour to go home and pack some things. Bring several changes of clothing, whatever you need for hygiene, any medication you're presently taking, and something to read. You'll be in quarantine for at least thirty days."

How could this happen? I mean, honestly, was this real? And another thing: "What if I don't show up?"

"Paul, you don't want to do that. You're already under surveillance, and the CDC has quick reaction teams on standby. They have unmarked vehicles, massive firepower, satellite reconnaissance. They'd rather kill the disease than let it spread, Paul. It's just easier to turn yourself in. Until we know more, we have to assume PVD is contagious."

The decision to kill myself came instantly. I was driving home and I thought, *Quarantine*? Then I thought, *Bullshit*! Thirty days in a prison cell so doctors could stab thermometers up my butt and watch me die of Paul Vasquez Disease? Then slice me apart and arrange me like sushi: "You see, Nurse, this yellow piece here is where booze had hardened his liver. Reduced his body's defense to a fucking Maginot Line. Germans blitzkrieged right over that shit in WWII. I was there, Nurse. Went on to see action in Africa. Goddamnit, Nurse! Of course, there was fighting in Africa! That's the problem with you fucking interns. Never opened a history book in your fucking life. Just get the hell out of here and send in the pretty one with tits. Go on! Disappear, you ignorant cunt!"

I had precious little enough to live for, but with that in my immediate future…well.

On the way home I stopped at a pharmacy and bought a gallon of potassium chloride and a pack of sterile syringes. So it wouldn't look suspicious, I also bought laxatives, wart remover, crotch spray, toe powder, vitamins, condoms, ear wax remover, and calcium fortified chocolates. I put it all on my credit card.

When I got to the house, I went around gathering my paperbacks, comic books, and porn mags. The thought of somebody having their way with my babies while I was six feet in the ground just made me sick. I took everything to the backyard and set it on fire. The pages blistered away and blackened in the orange flames. After that I made a phone call to my ex-girlfriends. All three of them. "Thanks for giving me Paul Vasquez Disease," I said. "Thanks a lot, you assholes!"

I pumped my veins so full of potassium chloride my heart slammed to a halt. A darkness as hard as concrete encased me. It was that way for eternity, and then I began to see. The world was different now; it was a thousand shades of electric blue. My astral self was zooming around the living room like a goddamn jet fighter. Holy shit, I was a fucking ghost!

I flew over my body a few times and checked it out. I was soaking in tepid piss and drool. My eyes had gone all stupid. I laughed. Betty would have to clean that shit up when she got home from work. Plus I had killed myself leaning against the front door. Maybe she'd trip over my bloated corpse and get me on her shoes.

As I was picturing this scenario, my ghost felt a tap on the shoulder. I spun around and faced a menacing older man with a wizard's beard and a neon red suit. "ALAN MOORE," I astral-gasped. "The greatest comic book author in history! In fucking time immemorial!"

"Not really, Paul. I just look like him. My real body would blow your fragile mind to pieces, so I always come to the dead in an image consistent with their sacred ideal. I would have been Jesus if you were a Christian or Mohammed if you were a Muslim. Shit like that."

"I don't go for all that religious crap, Alan."

"I know, Paul. Do you mind if we get started?" He asked impatiently.

"Oh, yes, please. They must keep you pretty busy. You know, people fucking dying all the time."

"Yeah, sure," he said, but he wasn't even looking at me. He had a comic book open titled *The Nonspecific Life of Paul Vasquez*. He didn't seem impressed as he flipped the pages. "You've been amazingly useless to your fellow humans."

"I uh…you see what happened was…and then it was like…and I said…" I couldn't think of anything else to say. "I'm sorry."

"It's no big deal. Says here you never tried to hurt anybody or steal from them. Just sat around and drank a lot of beer."

"Good times," I reminisced.

"Yeah, well, it's good enough. Are you ready for the afterlife?"

I had to be honest. "Mr. Moore, I'm scared. Is everything going to be different? Will I be different?"

"No shit, Paul."

"Send me back, Alan! I change my mind. I don't want to die if it means I'll forget who I am. I've seen the movies. I'll be reincarnated as a talking dog and none the fucking wiser. Send me back! I want to be me, Alan. I know it isn't much, but who I am is all I got. I might as well have never lived if I can't hold on to that."

His face grew gentle for just an instant. Then he looked put out again. "Okay, I'll tell you a story to put you at ease, but then we really have to go." He checked his watch.

"Sweet!" My astral self stretched out and got comfortable. "Is it *From Hell*? *Watchmen*? How about *League of Extraordinary Gentlemen*? I fucking love that story."

"It's not a comic book, Paul. It's about life and death. You've made this transition before, but you don't remember. You're only called Paul today because you forgot who you are."

"That's bullshit, Moore."

"Listen to me, Paul. Once upon a time there was a stream…"

The stream came down from its source in the mountains, passed through many miles of country, and finally ran into a desert. When it tried to cross the desert it became stuck in the sand. Now, this stream knew it had to cross the desert, but it was damned if it knew how.

So the stream said, "This sucks crusty old iguana dick!"

And just then it heard a voice whispering in its ear: "If wind can cross the desert, then so can a stream."

This frightened the stream because it thought it was alone. The stream said, "Who the fuck?!" And then it said, "There's no way I can cross this bitch. Bastard sand is drinking me alive."

He heard the whisper again: "You'll never cross that way. Let the wind absorb you and lift you over."

The stream sighed. "But I'll lose my identity."

"If you don't, you'll never be more than a dirty marsh in the sand, and then you'll have lost your identity anyway."

This cocksucker has a point, thought the stream. "Okay, let's say I do it. Will I be the same stream when it's over?"

The whisper replied: "You won't be the same no matter what you do. You will either be a marsh, or you will cross the desert and be a new stream. You only think you are who you are because you forgot who you were."

But the stream still had its doubts. "How do you know all this?"

"I know," came the ominous reply, "because I'm the sand."

"Hot damn," yelled the stream. "So long, asshole!" And it leapt high into the air as vapor, was carried far across the desert, and set down gently over the mountains as rain. Then it became a new stream.

Alan Moore finished his story and smiled beatifically. "So you see, Paul, both you and the stream will change, but there is that which is eternal."

Silence.

"Whuh...huh...whassat? Mmmmm. Sorry, Alan, I must have dozed off there." I rubbed sleep from my eyes and yawned. "What was all that shit about the stream again?"

"Get the fuck out of here!" He roared and tossed me over the great divide after slapping me around for a good ten minutes.

A Night to Remember
with Mocha Sumatra
by Mark McLaughlin

MOCHA Sumatra. The very name seems to breathe danger, lust and perhaps even magick. Yes, we're talking magick with a 'k'—the more exotic, perhaps erotic and certainly frightening breed, not simply the schmaltzy 'c' variety practiced by potbellied, threadbare-tuxedo-clad charlatans, pulling cloned rabbitoids out of top hats in tiresome, touristy retro nightclubs as their plump, busty assistants, usually named Karla or Mimi, fidget in their second-hand sequined evening gowns and stare with mingled curiosity and desire at the cute Qorp busboys.

But certainly, while those Qorp busboys might flirt with Karla/Mimi, they are in fact longing for the passionate, well-rehearsed embrace of Mocha Sumatra. Mocha is, without a doubt, the most popular SkinDeep Channel performer on the planet of Zarnak—and survey results indicate that eighty-three percent of the Qorp population either subscribes to the SkinDeep Channel or watches it at the residence of a friend or relative.

I arranged to conduct this exclusive interview with Mocha Sumatra at her penthouse apartment in the city of Zohtogg. She greeted me at the door wearing black satin pajamas and a pink ribbon in her thick, curly blonde hair. She had painted a delicate pattern of tiger stripes on the cheekbones of her lovely, utterly feminine face, hauntingly reminiscent of the old-time Earth actress, Marilyn Monroe. Mocha stands about seven feet tall and, as most SkinDeep viewers know, is endowed with both male and female genitalia, ostensibly humanoid. One might assume she was a sort of hermaphrodite if it weren't for the fact that she also features other erogenous organs, of an uncertain though certainly provocative nature, within the rosy folds of her armpits.

I sat with Mocha on a huge purple couch in her entertainment area, sipping Y'kurbulian champagne (not a favorite of mine, since it is meat-based, but Mocha loves the stuff). This is what she had to say...

Mocha: You like the champagne, yes?

MM: It's unusual—especially the strong aftertaste of apricots and bacon. Mocha, I have a question that I just want to get out of the way, so bear with me. I don't mean to be disrespectful—but what exactly *are* you? I've done some research and it would seem that no one really knows your species or planet of origin. But then, maybe no one has thought to ask...

Mocha: Silly, silly boy! You can ask me anything! All the Qorps and whatnot who have seen me on the SkinDeep Channel know: I am not some shy little shugurka-puppy who is going to run away the minute somebody looks at me cross-eyed!

The truth is, I am what you Earthlings would call a 'mixed bag'. And that is because my mother was a Vroont. Once you know that— well, that explains everything!

MM: Perhaps. But I'm afraid I don't know what a Vroont is...

Mocha: You don't? You should read more books, silly boy. Or better yet, get out and see the universe—it's very big, you'd be amazed. Vroonts are the dominant life-form on the planet Skolara. All Vroonts are female, with vestigial male organs, just in case—to preserve the species, if a mate isn't handy. They always have the option to impregnate themselves.

You see, Vroonts are completely dedicated to the preservation of their species—not only on a social level, but on a cellular level, too.

They can mate with practically anything. Even plants. Even mold! They can store sperm cells from various partners and then have one big combination baby. I can tell you that as a first-hand fact, because I was just such a baby. I had a Vroont momma, who was a cocktail waitress on Skolara, and twelve daddies, six of whom were space-travelers visiting my momma's planet on business—or maybe just to have some fun, I don't know. A Vroont can also collect DNA from a female partner, but my momma wasn't into that scene.

My momma, her birth-name was Plaaart, but she called herself Stella because she thought that sounded pretty. She'd heard that name on some old Earth movie. One of my daddies was an Earthman. Oooh, my momma loved Earthmen—they are so dramatic, so intense, just like you, Mister Sexy What-Is-Your-Name?

MM: Mr. McLaughlin, but you can call me Mark. I was cryogenically frozen a long time ago—2027—after a really bad car accident. Last year they figured out how to fix me, so they un-froze me, put me back together, and then gave me some super-hormones to make me younger, which was nice of them.

Mocha: They did a good job. I hope they didn't leave any parts off when they put you back together! I might want to use some of those parts later. Do you think I am a sexy lady?

MM: You are so sexy—in so many different ways—it literally boggles the mind.

Mocha: Later, maybe I will boggle some other parts of you besides your mind! Anyway—where was I? Oh yes, my momma. She got some sperm from an Earthman, and some other nice guys from some other planets, including a couple very sexy Qorps, and after she thought she'd had enough sperm to make a really hot girl-baby—she grew me inside of her. But she made me part boy, too. In case I couldn't find a mate.

MM: I'm sure that'll never be a problem for you!

Mocha: Oh, you Earthmen, you make me laugh! You don't realize: the universe is a savage place, with lots of barren planets and dimensions and other far-off hidey-holes. A well-stocked life-form always brings along the ability to make a baby without any help. Say you had to live on that one uninhabited planet by Earth—Mars, I think it's called. You'd be all alone! No sex for you there! So, no babies. No little Marks to run around having fun on Mars. How sad!

MM: Fun seems to be a very high priority with you.

Mocha: And why not? Fun is good! Have fun, have some sex, make a baby! Then the baby grows up and starts everything over again! That is how everything works. And even if you can't make a baby—have some fun anyway. Then if you die, you can at least say, "I had some fun."

Now hurry up and ask me about the SkinDeep Channel. I have lots to tell you about my next show.

MM: Okay…tell me about your next show on the SkinDeep Channel.

Mocha: How did you hear about that? (Mocha laughed—a shrill, tittering cry, reminiscent of dolphins.) My next show will be called *The Baby Machine*. We start production next week. I will have sex with many creatures—male and female—from at least eight different planets, and then combine their DNA into one big crazy baby. I have a very fast metabolism, like anyone with Vroont blood in them, so it won't take me long to make the baby—it'll be born by the end of the show! You want to be one of the daddies?

MM: I'd better not. I was frozen for so long, I'm afraid my semen might be stale.

Mocha: Oh, I doubt that! Really, I think you should– (The entry monitor beeped.) Ah, he's here! I asked a special guest to stop by to take part in this interview. I'll go let him in! You wait right here!

I was surprised and delighted by this development. My approach to an interview is much like Mocha's approach to sex: the more, the merrier. Imagine my astonishment when Mocha returned holding hands with Jonni Gonad—the most popular of all the male SkinDeep Channel performers.

Jonni Gonad is a very muscular Qorp—eight feet tall, with lustrous black eyes, sky-blue skin and shiny red hooves. All Qorp men are generously endowed, but Jonni–! His nickname, the Blue Python, pretty much says it all. Jonni wore a black leather jumpsuit, with a black box strapped in front of his crotch to contain his coiled member. Jonni wears that box wherever he goes—except, of course, when he's on camera.

Mocha: (She tapped the box.) And what do we have in there?

Jonni: You sexy whore! You will find out soon enough!

Mocha: Jonni, this is the Earthman I was telling you about. He was frozen, but he's better now.

Jonni: Hello, pink man! Are you all grown up, or is that as big as you're going to get?

MM: Actually, back before I was frozen, I was considered an average-sized man—in fact, I was probably a little on the big side. But Earthlings are much bigger now. And Qorps are even bigger still.

Jonni: Were Qorps as big as me back before you were frozen?

MM: I don't know! Earthlings hadn't mastered the theta drive, so we weren't in touch with any other worlds yet.

Mocha: So that makes McLaughlin a primitive, Jonni. Oooh, a primitive! Doesn't that just make you want to have sex with him, to see what kind of primitive sex tricks he can teach us?

Jonni: Yes, McLaughlin, teach us your primitive sex ways! Just thinking about it is making the box a tight fit!

MM: That's certainly an—interesting offer, but I'm here to conduct an interview, so I'd better not.

Mocha: Oooh, his reluctance is so sexy! By the horns of Throk, I have to do it with somebody, Jonni! So I guess it's going to be you!

Jonni: Good thing, too! I'm about ready to burst out of this thing! (Jonni removed the box, and almost put out Mocha's left eye when he fully uncoiled.)

Mocha and Jonni wrapped their arms and various other appendages around each other and flung themselves onto the couch. I moved out of their path just in time. Modesty prevents me from describing what transpired on that couch during the next four hours. While they were busy, I went into Mocha's food preparation area and made myself dinner. Then I took a bath, put on one of Mocha's big fluffy snaarp-skin robes and watched a little of the SkinDeep Channel in her sleep chamber.

Jonni: Hey, primitive! Where did you go? We're done having sex! Let's do some more interview!

MM: (I returned to the entertainment area, where the two naked performers were resting on the couch.) Here I am. I made myself at home while I was waiting for you two to finish.

Mocha: Oooh, you look so sexy in my robe! Wha–? What is going on down here? (She began to scratch at her crotch.) Why am I so itchy all of a sudden? (She scratched at her armpits.) Something is wrong! All my sexy parts feel all hot and itchy!

As I watched, yellow pustules lightly streaked with green began to rise up on the afore-mentioned sexy parts. Mocha's scratching broke some of the pustules, spreading the infection to the surrounding flesh.

MM: Don't scratch! You're only making it worse!

Jonni: You look like you have Bagoonda's Scourge.

MM: What's that?

Jonni: I don't know. But I had sex with a whore on Yegpa-14 last week, and she had it.

Mocha: You stupid goork! You've given me the disease!

Jonni: No I didn't! Qorps never come down with Bagoonda's Scourge. I think we must be immune or something. You must have caught it from somebody else.

MM: You really are a stupid goork! You're obviously a carrier! Maybe full-blooded Qorps don't develop the disease—but Mocha is only part Qorp. And she has a fast metabolism, so she's showing the symptoms at an accelerated rate.

Mocha: Help me! I feel like my sex parts are on fire! I am dying!

    I went into the food preparation area, took some ice cubes from the refrigeration unit, and wrapped them in hand towels.

MM: Here—press these against the inflamed areas. Jonni, help her. I don't want to touch those pustules—I'm not even part Qorp, so they'd probably kill me. We've got to get her to a medi-dome.

Mocha: No! Never! It would be the shame of my life! If the public knew I had Bagoonda's Scourge, it would be the end of my career on the SkinDeep Channel! I would rather die! You'd better not put this in your interview!

MM: It wouldn't matter if I did. I'm planning on going back in time to sell it as fiction to an Earth anthology. I just bought a really nice time machine, and—

Mocha: The pain! The horrible pain! Jonni, you goork, I am going to

cut off your member and chop it into tiny little pieces! Then I'm going to burn those tiny little pieces and make you eat the ashes!
Jonni: The ice isn't helping, primitive McLaughlin! She's really starting to stink, too!

It was true. Mocha was exuding the sort of odor you'd expect from roadkill marinated in vinegar. Almost one-fourth of her skin was horribly infected and inflamed. Many of the pustules were now as big as eyeballs—and still growing. Some of the larger ones began to pop, so I backed away to avoid the splash.

Jonni: This is a bad nightmare! Can it get any worse?

The situation did indeed get worse. Black bile spewed from Mocha's mouth as blood and pus gushed from her other orifices. Her skin, once so fresh and lovely, withered and flaked from the sudden extreme dehydration. Her hair began to fall out in chunks under the weight of her heavy curls.

Suddenly a rounded bulge swelled up in her belly. Its rapid increase in size reminded me of a balloon being inflated—but this was nothing as harmless and whimsical as a balloon. No, indeed.

Within minutes, the growing bulge moved down and out. A hideous monstrosity squirmed forth from the birth canal—a blue baby with an enormous male member and a misshapen head covered with writhing feelers. The creature's mouth was filled with sharp green teeth, which it used to gnaw through its umbilical cord. The loathsome thing looked up and snarled at Jonni Gonad.

Jonni: Merciful Jakazuti! What's that?

MM: Well, she said she could have a kid with more than one dad. I guess you're one father, Jonni. And the Bagoonda's Scourge germ is another father. And she probably had some other weird sperm in her, too.

Jonni: This is terrible! Unspeakable! I am going insane with fright! What are we going to do, primitive McLaughlin?

MM: "We"? Hey, it's your kid. Hire a babysitter or something. I'm out of here.

I went back to the sleep chamber and put my own clothes back on. When I returned to the entertainment area, Jonni Gonad was sprawled on the floor, his throat ripped open. His grotesque child was busy eating his father's pride and joy—and I'm not talking about his shiny red hooves.

Before I left, I looked back one last time, and was surprised to see Mocha Sumatra staggering to her feet. She did have a rapid metabolism—apparently she was already starting to recover from Bagoonda's Scourge. She looked down at baby's first meal and coughed out a hoarse, dry laugh.

I do have one special memento from that incredible night.

That wonderfully fluffy snaarp-skin robe.

I know it was awful of me to take it, but what can I say?

I really liked that robe.

Mouthful of Dust
by John Edward Lawson

I FIND MYSELF standing at the foot of a hauntingly beautiful demon, naked save for the noose constricting her neck. The noose is composed of entrails—her own, extending from the hot, moist wound in her belly. It is both disconcerting and alluring that she remains impassive. Perhaps demons feel no pain? That could explain their proclivity for tormenting others; they aren't as mean as they are ignorant. Just idle speculation on my part.

The bulbous length of intestine provides an alarmingly entrancing textural contrast to the unsullied porcelain of her skin. I stare at the tail end of her umbilical necktie as it dangles, framed by her firm breasts, and want to ask, "What's a colon like you doing in a place like that?"

Her eyes seem to flicker. *I know who you are.*

Spaced evenly throughout the entrail noose are protrusions of organic black metal, sharpened needle thin. These meter-long spines each impale primitive monkeys, whose mournful death masks denote some sense of nobility. The prehensile tail of each stiffening primate is coiled tightly around a bluing infant's throat. Two dozen primate cadavers, two dozen human infants...I'm reminded of the piñata I broke open as a schoolboy. Only it wasn't a piñata, was it? Best not to dwell on those memories.

The nostrils of the demon flex, a nearly imperceptible gesture. *I can smell your soul from here.* Nearby, the winds wail over dunes of powdered bone. *I know your sins.* Nothing can resist entropy. Not seventy-five billion skeletons, not me. *I can lust after your lust.* The elements never stop tormenting the landscape. Her abdomen shifts, ever so slightly. A sudden intake of air, a particular kind of glistening at the edges of her wound.

Leaning on the mound below her I allow my fingers to whisper over the surface of the lowest baby. "Were they ever born?" I ask meekly. As if I'll get an answer.

As if you'll get an answer.

Those assigned the task of working in this den of iniquity ignore my comment. They've learned to keep their heads down. As the saying goes, the nail that sticks up is quickly hammered down. That sentiment brings my mind to the subject of martyrdom and my eyes are drawn to the ornate flesh mobile once more. There are no insects lighting upon her exposed organs, nor will there be larvae harvested in the fertile field of her body. Entropy doesn't touch agony. She'll never know what it is to be broken by rain, to be moved at the wind's insistence.

But I'll surely know you.

"Um..." Mulberry has entered my workspace. Her nervous wrists are shackled by leaden fingers as she makes an attempt at smiling. "Do you have a hot dog I could borrow?"

"I have a hot dog you *can* borrow." There is a silence that seems to discomfort Mulberry, during which I smooth over my nametag. In place of my name it reads *Sicks Sicks Sicks the Number of the Disease.* After Mulberry squirms under my glare for what should be an appropriate amount of time, I reach back and grip a flesh stick. All this without taking my eyes off her. "*Can* borrow." I turn the meat poker over in my hand. The others would consider it excruciating to remove these things from the grill by hand. Not me. I've got a demon over my shoulder.

In fact, I can feel her vision sauntering through the skin of my back, boring in deeper still. *You've got me behind you. Don't disappoint me.*

"Maybe, right..." Mulberry giggles, embarrassed. "Maybe now isn't a good time?"

I rise in a flash, barring her exit. Towering over her. I eat the hot dog, I abuse the hot dog. Not one bite slides down my gullet. The meat mush is kept in my mouth for excessive mastication, most of which

Mulberry can see because I make no effort to be polite.

I can taste her fear.

"*She can taste your fear!*" I bark, only with the mouthful of meat it turns into, "*Thee khahthathe shaw feeeee-ahh!*"

"I'm leaving now!" Mulberry struggles with my arm...is that my arm blocking the doorway? Yes, it is.

Soon enough I use that arm to push her up against the wall of my cubicle. My bulk pounds her into the corner. Some asshole coworker's plant gets knocked to the floor over in the next cubicle and Mulberry's crying, I think. My structural features grind into her—knees, elbows, and hips digging into Mulberry biceps and thighs and other tasty parts—all while my lust clamps onto her lips with the fervor of a lamprey. The meaty sludge is forcefully injected into her oral cavity.

A supervisor walks by in the hallway, soundly beating a drum as if it were his own child. "Do your part for the economy!" Wham, wham! "Enslave yourself!" Wham, wham!

Can you taste her?

"Fuck off," I grunt, bits of saliva-drenched hot dog launching from my mouth. "All I can taste is this damned meat!"

Mulberry seems strangely relieved; I see she's urinated on my workspace again. She offers some impenetrable syllables, then scribbles on a notepad, *Thanks.*

I glower a moment longer, then spit into a waste receptacle. "And I expect that back in the same condition!"

She finally manages to free herself and leave. Took her long enough. I almost had to let her go or something. The dark stain on her skirt, spreading down the back of her stockings, brings to mind the old line *baby I love to watch you leave.*

Back at my desk time seems to slow down. I could swear those impaled monkeys are sweating. Even if they were alive they wouldn't be able to sweat though, would they? Doesn't matter. The demon remains suspended in midair, in time, in my heart. Whoever did this to her wasn't content to merely hang her with her own guts. No. They wound the fleshy coils around her thighs, around her wrists. And those spines forcing themselves out through the slick membrane of her intestines beckon to some darker region of my mind that I'm not willing to acknowledge.

"Man, I'll bet that hurts somethin' awful!" So what if I can't help chortling?

The hint of a glimmer in her eye, a tremor across her lips.

Indifference to suffering is far worse than ignorance of it.

With that kind of haranguing, who needs to get married? I don't even know why I bother trying to work anymore. In the next cubicle a man or woman is scraping up spilled dirt with what sounds like a razor blade. The snicker they emit while carrying out this activity is tinged with libidinous insanity, so I sing a nonsense song just to block out the noise. "La la la la la lalalalalLALALALALALALAL...laaaaaaaa. La, ala la, la-hey-hey-hey. Hey, yeah, baby."

The dead babies linger in the air, secured to the demon by the dead animal tails, the injustice of their murders throbbing inside me like an erection. What's that at the corner of her mouth? Is it the suggestion of a smirk?

"I take offense at that."

The desert of bone dust shifts subtly beneath my feet. This does not disturb the hot dogs on the scientifically calibrated grilling device. It would take an earthquake to disrupt this contraption. Just to impress myself with the validity of my logic I pound the machine a good one, sending several meat sticks toppling into the bones of time.

Good one.

"Keep it up!" On my feet now, wagging a finger, and her smirk becomes a grin. "Keep it up and see if I don't stick these things where the sun don't shine!"

You know you want to. At least you're finally being honest about it. Somewhere, I'm preparing to scream. *Lay all your hot dogs out on the table. I've got plenty of places to stick them, don't I? You know you want to.*

The smell of baby powder wafts over my person, mixed with something like the tangy stench of a zoo. It's the final straw. I crawl onto my workstation and observe fingers clamoring at her cold, curiously solid ankles. *My* fingers. My lips worship at the alter of foot fetish. The problem is that I'm all too aware of her pedigree. She's one fifth wild turkey, a fact that almost numbs me to the prick of those thorn-like spines, the searing of my knees on the grill. The oily sweat exuding from the meat tubes quickly pastes the fabric of my trousers to my skin.

I can taste you from here.

"I can taste *you* from here."

Am I hot, dog?

So. Maybe being a demon is having a sense of humor. I wouldn't know. Viscous love dribbles from dead exits, sliding over erect nipples and flame-bright gore, distracting me with sip after sip of vein-vomit. I imagine this workspace as a nest, and my demon as the nurturing mother bird; my stomach turns. This compels me to stand fully now, kicking over a mandatory stack of papers. The cleaning crew will give me demerits now for sure. I have to grip those spines bristling from her digestive tract in order to maneuver her wound into contact with my lips. I mount her spines with both hands and feet now, my full body weight bearing her down further. My guess is she enjoys the extra tightness around her neck.

The supervisor steps in and Mulberry joins him. He stands there hoping I'll stop and acknowledge them, then clears his throat. "A word."

"That's two," I say while tonguing glistening guts. He must not be a demon because he sees no humor in my remark.

"Mulberry came to me about, well..."

I manage to pry my lips from the opening long enough to cast an apathetic glance over my shoulder. "Figured she would. Damn it." Inches away my demon's diaphragm is quivering in time with her breath.

The supervisor is lifting Mulberry's skirt under the pretense of sniffing her urine stain. "About your production level lately..." He continues to lift the skirt to ridiculous levels, stretching the fabric. Mulberry eyes him with something akin to unfiltered contumacy.

"Heh. Fifteen gallons this week, sir." The colon tastes the way tires sound as they screech before a car wreck.

"The thing is, hot dog sweat won't just regulate itself." I wonder what the supervisor would say if he could see himself knees and palms to the floor as he is now, head swallowed whole by Mulberry's skirt. "How's the glutinous fiber content of the sweat?"

"Up .042 percent, sir."

"Niacin?"

".975 percent, sir."

Mulberry's skirt has been cast aside like the rubbish we all know pleasantries to be. The supervisor's eyes are visible just above the elastic of her panties, peering out at me. "That's not what I asked."

I finally get up the courage to grab me some demonic tit. "Sir..."

"Nobody said anything about that!" Now only his bushy eyebrows are visible above the elastic of Mulberry's soiled panties. "We specifically refrained from saying anything about a brain tumor."

The statement hits me the wrong way and I fall from my perch astride the otherworldly beauty, finding myself being grilled once more.

Mulberry moves in, defending the supervisor. "He never said anything about that, you ungrateful shit!" She slaps me, enjoying it a little too much I think, then stoops to spurt the still-warm hot dog remains into my mouth. At least she kept her word and returned it in the same condition I gave it to her. To my eternal dishonor I suck greedily at her meat-frothing orifice.

That damned gratuitous snickering keeps rattling away in the next cubicle.

The half dozen rollers of the frankfurter sweat manipulator keep spinning under me, threatening to snag my clothing within its gears. Above me, Mulberry convulses the last of the undigested meat out of her system. Above her, the supervisor sweats and grunts, the tension rooted in his face not born of love. Above him, dead infants spin in reaction to the world's rotation, and their monkey anchors do the same.

A quake. Her legs consider parting? *I can lust after your lust.*

"He's getting unmanageable! Somebody call security!" The supervisor is really thrusting away now, as if he's in some kind of fencing tournament. Mulberry grimaces appropriately. "Just look at him!"

I'm starting to get confused here. "What did you mean by that, about a brain tumor?" The distinct odor of relish is emanating from down the hall. I continue to let the dead juices drip down into my mouth. "Well? Brain tumor?!"

Coworkers are crowding into my work space now, beads of arrogance glistening on their brows. "We never said anything about that! Stop saying that!"

I'm not the only one who can hear your sin.

Mulberry smirks; as the supervisor, she commands the fear and respect of the workers. Although one of them, I refuse to succumb to such feelings of inferiority. She thrusts a finger at me. "I'm going to be forced to write you up this time!"

"OoooooooooOOOOO!" the others say in unison, like elementary school students gathered around a fight.

Even I have to admit my buns are burned this time. I can't take arguing with a female supervisor any longer. If only she hadn't questioned me about my percentages! She continues to beat the drum, her eyebrows arching just above her panties. Can that be right? This is all making my head hurt, so I turn back to my work station. Only now do I notice that the hot dogs aren't hot dogs at all...the lumps of gray matter slowly browning on my grill seem terribly familiar.

SICKS SICKS SICKS THE NUMBER OF THE DISEASE

I look up to my demonic emancipator, my curse, drunk on the rage swelling within me. Will she deign to act, for once? Finally the demon opens her mouth to speak out loud, to clear my name—or so I think. All that exits between those cruel lips is dust, an inexhaustible supply that threatens to drown everything, even my sorrows.

Visits with Mother
by Kurt Newton

EVERY TIME I went to visit my mother, she would give me things. First, it was the toaster. *It makes the bread too dry, too hard to chew.*

Then it moved onto the knick-knacks.

After all these years I can't look at them anymore.

I thought Ma was just being practical. I'm pretty practical myself. I would always accept her "gifts," knowing if I ever needed a quick buck from the pawn shop, the stuff would come in handy.

Dinner plates.

Why do I need eight for when there's only one of me?

Picture frames.

I'm tired of the same faces staring back at me.

Lampshades. I know, lampshades?

I can see better without them.

You get the idea.

If it didn't work or it served no visible purpose, Ma had no use for it.

Except for Mittens.

Mittens was Ma's double-pawed Siamese cat of fifteen years, until I accidentally backed over it in the driveway. Of course, I didn't tell Ma that. As far as she knows Mittens ran away. Mittens' were the only pictures Ma kept. Sometimes I think she loved that cat more than us.

By the time Ma's seventy-eighth birthday rolled around, which she celebrated this past May, the small, four-room, salt-box she lived in was pretty much empty but for a few cat pictures, the couch she slept on, her morning radio, and her stack of Reader's Digests, which she liked to call the Third Testament. (I guess that makes Jesus editor-in-chief?) What food Ma ate, I brought by, stopping now and then on my way to the race track or back from giving blood at the local Red Cross.

And everything was fine...until Ma starting giving me things I didn't want.

That and the fact that The Mick was out to break my kneecaps for unpaid loans of a non-bank-oriented nature.

But I'm getting ahead of myself. Back to Ma...

"You've always been good to me, Sonny." (That's my name. Sonny Cataldo. I know, can it get any more pathetic?) "That good-for-nothing brother of yours..."

Petey—that good-for-nothing brother of mine—has a career and a home and a beautiful wife and two beautiful kids. He'll probably die fat and happy. I, on the other hand, have crap to show for myself. I've jumped from job to job like some kind of undiscriminating whore. I've lived in rat-infested apartments most of my adult life. Never had a decent girlfriend—at least not one that stuck around. The only thing I did have was Ma. Or more importantly, I had Ma's trust. Which was going to one day translate into a healthy life insurance payoff and a house of my own, if I played my cards right.

"Sonny, I want you to know that you've been the best son a mother could hope for."

"Thanks, Ma." Ma sat on her couch, the bare light bulb from the table lamp blinding me like the morning sun.

"But I want you to do something for me."

"What is it, Ma? Anything."

"I want you to take my hand."

Ma held out one of her crippled claws—the one she sprained last year in a fall, which never quite healed right.

"Ma, you need to get up?" I stood and offered my own hand.

"No, sit down, Sonny," she coughed. The hand waved at me, its wrist a stiff collection of knots, its bones appearing as though they were about to break through the skin, except for the place where a golf ball-sized swelling bloomed a purplish hue. "I want you to *take* my hand. It's useless. It makes me drop things. Please, it gives me too much bother."

"But, Ma, I can't."

Ma stared at me then. It was probably the first time I had ever said "No" to her.

With some effort, Ma got up off the couch and shuffled into the kitchen, her body hunched from too much gravity. She opened the drawer where the silverware was kept and pulled out a meat cleaver. Before I could shout, "Ma, what the hell are you doing!"—she had done it. It was as if she were halving a chicken breast on the cutting board. The cleaver had cut clean through her brittle wrist with a sickening snap.

I rushed into the kitchen and searched for something to use as a tourniquet. There was a surprising amount of blood. As I tied a kitchen towel around her muscleless forearm, she pointed with the stump of her arm at the separated hand on the cutting board and said, "Now be a good boy and take it."

So I took it.

I took it home. I didn't have the heart to throw it away. Besides, if somebody found it in a garbage can, it would probably cause a stir. So I put it in a pickle jar, empty of pickles but still full of its useless sour green juice, and stowed it in the cabinet beneath my bathroom sink. That was after I had bandaged Ma's stump, of course, kissed her crepe paper forehead and said my goodbyes.

It was weird. I actually felt like I had done Ma a favor. You should have seen the look in her eyes. (Or eye, I should say. The right one, to be more exact. The left one had a cataract that made it look like a peeled grape.) I felt like my mother's son. I felt loved.

I was also one step closer to getting my hard-earned inheritance. Even with one hand, Ma could still change the name of the beneficiary on her will.

It's awful dark in here. The Mick really knows how to make a guy sweat.

I wish I could remember the last time I ate. I'm feeling a little light-headed.
   So, where was I? Oh, yeah, the gift that keeps giving...

About a week went by before I visited Ma again.

It was a bad week. I'd dropped two grand on some filly by the name of Cut Me A Break—two grand that wasn't mine to lose. The horse might as well have been called Tear Me A New Asshole because that's what The Mick was going to have one of his "associates" do if I didn't come up with at least the first installment.

So there I am sitting, eating a bowl of Ma's homemade minestrone soup, trying to nice-talk her into that warm, fuzzy, agreeable state where I can convince her to change the friggin' name on her will from my "good-for-nothing" brother's to mine, when she gets that look in her eye. That "You're the only one who would do this for me" kind of look I'd come to recognize—and fear. And I'm thinking to myself, *What now?*

"Sonny, I want you to take my hair."

Ma pointed to her head with the stump of her arm, and a spoonful of minestone dribbled down the front of my shirt.

"It's all falling out anyway. Better not to have any at all than to mop up after myself every morning when I drag my head from the pillow."

"But Ma," I said, "if I pull out what's left, some of it's going to grow back."

"Don't be silly," she said and she reached down and picked up a razor blade off the coffee table—one of those old double-sided blades that my dad used to use in his shaver. I sat, frozen, as Ma dragged her wobbly hand across her forehead, over each ear and down around the back of her neck. Her handiwork done, Ma put the blade down and began probing the incision with her bony index finger to try and get a hold of the flap, but the blood was making things too greasy. Besides, it would have been kind of awkward for Ma to pull her own scalp off. I don't think she had the upper body strength.

So I got up off the chair and helped her out.

There was surprisingly little resistance as Ma's scalp lifted off like a freshly laid strip of wallpaper. To my amazement, not a single yelp of pain exited her dimpled old mouth.

"There you go, Sonny," Ma said with a gleam in her eye.

"Gee, thanks, Ma. Here, let me get you some gauze."

I put the hairy wet skin rag in a ziplock bag, then wrapped up Ma's head like a mummy.

And then it hit me. Christ! Ma wasn't just being practical anymore. Ma was getting senile.

I should have known something was up after she cut her own hand off. But this!

It was then that I figured now was as good a time as any to bring up the matter of her will.

"Hey, Ma, I know this is probably not the best time to talk about this..."

Ma was already aiming the remote at her television in search of her favorite soap opera, the scalpectomy she'd just performed all but forgotten.

"...and you're probably in a lot of pain and all..."

The television stopped changing channels and she began to fidget with the remote, aiming it at the television at different angles, squeezing the buttons harder each time.

"...but I just wanted to remind you that, if I remember correctly—now I could be wrong, Ma—but you still have Petey down as your sole beneficiary in your will?"

Ma stopped fidgeting with the remote and her head twisted on her dishrag-like neck. She stared at me, her one good eye boring into me while the other gazed out from behind the cloud of its cataract. I forged ahead, anyway.

"I mean, I know you're not going anywhere for a long, long time, Ma, but who else will take care of this place after you're gone?"

Ma continued to stare. It was hard to tell just what was going on underneath all that gauze.

I began to fidget, my fingers gripping the ziplock bag the way a lady grips her purse on a crowded subway. "I mean, Petey's already got a house. He'll probably sell this place the first chance he gets and all your things with it. Wouldn't you feel much better if I was the one to take care of things once, umm, well, you know, God decides it's time for the big sleep?"

Ma's stare softened. "You know, Sonny, you've got quite a head on your shoulders." She smiled. Then the smile turned into a grimace. "Petey doesn't deserve a single thing. What has he ever done for me? He doesn't even visit his poor decrepit mother anymore. It's as if I don't exist! Well, I'll tell you what, Sonny, if your brother doesn't need me, he doesn't need any of this." She gestured to the room around us.

Actually, there wasn't much left in the house to have. It was the house itself I was interested in. Back in the fifties it might not have been much, but now it was prime real estate.

"I'll call the lawyer first thing in the morning and set up an appointment," Ma said. Then she handed me the remote. "Now be a dear and fix this, my story's coming on in a few minutes."

It was the middle of the afternoon, for Christ's sake! She could have made the call then, but I didn't feel like pushing things.

I pulled the batteries out of the remote and put them back in again. Sometimes all it takes it a little rearrangement to make things right again.

And that's what I really wanted. I wanted to make things right. I wanted to get out of the hole I'd dug for myself and start over.

I handed the working remote back to Ma and she smiled again. The warmth in that smile was almost enough to make me feel guilty. Well, almost.

The Mick actually took it kind of easy on me that night, when I went to him to explain why I didn't have the money just yet. He only had his associates break two of my fingers—one for each grand I owed him. After all, I'd been a good customer.

My stomach just growled again.

All this reflecting has got me wishing I'd made some different choices in life. But what's that that John Lennon said? Life is what happens while you're busy making other plans? Boy, did he ever find that out to be true.

Oh, well, can't cry about it now.

So I go visit Ma the next day, thinking I'll drive her over to the lawyer's office. I'd make sure she wrapped her head in a scarf and wore one of her floppy hats. Maybe even put her arm in a sling.

But when I get to her house, all ninety pounds of her is sitting there on her couch in her nightgown and slippers, staring at the TV. Problem was, the TV wasn't on.

"You feeling okay, Ma?" I asked.

The gauze I'd wrapped around her head the day before was now stained with colors other than red, and had crusted to her scalp like a plaster cast.

"Sonny, I think I'm coming down with a flu bug."

"Want me to get you some orange juice?"

"Yes, that would be nice."

Ma didn't even notice the splints on my fingers when I placed the orange juice in her hand and sat back down in the rocking chair.

There was an eyelash curler on the coffee table—one of the old kinds that worked like a pair of scissors. I didn't think much of it. I thought maybe it was just another one of Ma's gifts from the attic.

"Ma, I hate to bring this up, but did you call your lawyer yet?"

A puzzled look clouded Ma's face. Then the cloud lifted, leaving a look of embarrassment behind.

"You know, Sonny, you're going to be mad at me."

"Ma, I'd never be mad at you. Why would I be mad?" I could feel my jaw tighten.

"Well, it's the phone."

"What about the phone?"

"You know how I always get those calls from people trying to sell me things? Subscriptions to magazines I'll never read because I can't see very well...vinyl siding for the house I'll never look at because I don't go outside...and those meat people —"

"Meat people?"

"You know the ones who deliver steaks and cutlets right to your door? Why do I need people to deliver things to me when I have you,

Sonny?"

"That's right, Ma." *What about the lawyer?* I wanted to ask her, but I held my tongue.

"So, last night after you left, after taking two more of those ridiculous calls, I thought to myself, 'What do I need a phone for?'"

No. I glanced over my shoulder into the kitchen. On the floor by the back door, next to a bag of garbage waiting to go out to the curb, sat a cardboard box.

"Not the phones, Ma."

"I want you to have them, Sonny, they're all there. They're yours now." She smiled thinly.

"But what about the lawyer? You were supposed to call the lawyer and let him know about the changes you wanted to make in the will."

"You're mad at me. I told you you were going to be mad at me."

I took a deep breath. It was hard to argue with a seventy-eight-year- old woman with a stump for a hand and a hair-do that looked like she'd just escaped from King Tut's tomb. I threw my hands up in the air.

"Sonny, what happened to your fingers?"

"Oh, nothing, Ma. Just a little accident."

And the accidents are going to keep getting bigger and badder if I don't come up with some money soon.

Another thing I didn't say out loud. I wanted to scream but the best I could do was a whimper.

"It's okay, Sonny. You can go to the lawyer yourself and get the papers I need. You've been so patient with me."

I got up and gave her a big hug. I could feel Ma's bony spine through her nightgown. And her head smelled kind of bad. But she was my mother, so I planted a big kiss on her forehead. "Thanks, Ma."

"And I've got one other thing to give to you."

And here I actually thought this visit was going to be about phones, and maybe an old eyelash curler, but damned if there wasn't something else Ma wanted donate to Sonny's Museum of Old Lady Body Parts.

"It's my eye, Sonny."

God, here we go again.

"I don't like the way it looks at me. And I don't like looking at it. I want you to take it."

"What about a patch, Ma? Remember Yul Brenner in The King and I?" (*The King and Eye*? I missed the humor at the time but for some reason find that funny now.) "He looked great!"

"No, dear, I don't want it anymore."

Ma reached for the eyelash curler then and began jabbing it into her eye-socket. But it was too big to accomplish what she wanted it to do.

"*Ma*," I said.

She continued to poke and prod, but all she succeeded in doing was making her eye tear.

"Ma," I said again, a little louder.

"Damn useless thing!" She threw the curler down in frustration and began to weep.

I got up and sat down next to her. "Ma...it's okay."

She turned to me then, her cataract-riddled eye now red and swollen.

"I'll do it."

Her mouth folded in like bread dough and more tears ran down her liver-spotted cheeks.

I knew a guy who used to hang out at the East End Pool Hall by the name of Jimmy One-Eye. Not only was Jimmy one of the best pool players in town, every now and then he had this trick of popping his artificial eye out on unsuspecting opponents after they'd lost— especially if they had a girlfriend in tow. It was always good for a laugh.

For Ma, all I did was what Jimmy used to do.

I pulled Ma's bottom eyelid down and dug my pinky into the corner by the bridge of her nose. It was a little stubborn at first, but my pinky was stronger than Ma's eye muscle. I held the back of Ma's head and pushed, and her eye just kind of rolled out onto her cheek with a sickening suction-cup sound. A stringy piece of tissue was the only thing holding it there.

"Sonny?" Ma grabbed onto me as if she were having a dizzy spell, and her other eye rolled back into her head. I quickly snatched the eye- ball off her cheek, snapping the connecting tissue. After that, Ma's equilibrium seemed to right itself.

"Thank you, Sonny," Ma said with a sigh of relief. "You're such a good boy." A dribble of blood ran from the corner of her eye-socket, down her cheek and into her mouth as she spoke.

"No problem, Ma," I said, her cloudy eye staring up at me from the center of my palm.

I pawned the phones. Didn't get much for them. Actually, the old-fashioned eyelash curler was worth fifty bucks to an antique dealer uptown. Damn thing was pure silver.

I made sure to drop by the lawyer's office to pick up the change-of-beneficiary forms. I still didn't know how I was going to swing the fact that Ma wasn't able to appear in person to sign the forms and get them notarized. I figured maybe I could convince the lawyer to drop by the house, instead. Maybe with the promise of an extra special cash donation.

I was feeling pretty good. Things were finally falling into place, and for once I felt like I was in control of my own destiny.

I took what little money I had and went to the track, feeling lucky for a change. Damned if I didn't win enough to pay The Mick his first installment—and then some. But like the fool that I am, I got cocky. I should know by now that a hot streak can grow cold as quick as piss in Alaska.

As I was walking out of the men's room, trying to wash the fear off my face, one of The Mick's associates spotted me.

I had to duck out fast. Something told me that The Mick wasn't going to be too happy that I was out playing the horses instead of scraping up the money I owed him.

Yeah, and if I had been born with two heads instead of half a one. Shit like this only makes sense after the fact.

Like I should have eaten three squares two days ago (or is it three?), then maybe I wouldn't be so hungry now.

Stomach feels like I ate a bowl full of broken glass.

Glassy Chips, the breakfast cereal for circus freaks! Or try our new Wind-O's, zero fat, zero cholesterol, one hundred percent fiber! Stay sharp! Bloody good....

Damn, I hope The Mick lets me out of here soon. I think I'm losing it.

The last visit with Ma didn't go too well.

After the near run-in at the racetrack, I didn't go back to my place. The Mick was sure to come looking for me there. So I got on a bus and took it out to where Ma lived and hid in the bushes until the sun came up. Ma didn't like trouble. Any son who broke the law was no son of hers. So I had to play it straight, like I'd been playing it since I could remember.

I must have looked like shit when I knocked on the door and let myself in, but, hell, Ma could hardly see, especially now, so what was I worried about?

I did begin to worry when I saw Ma sitting at the kitchen table all hunched over. And she wasn't moving.

"Ma? Is everything okay?" I asked, holding out little hope that anything was going to be okay. Petey would get the fucking house and I'd be on the run for the rest of my days. My whole miserable life passed before my eyes. Ma was dead, I was sure of it.

"Sonny? Is that you?"

Ma's birdlike voice came fluttering through the stale air. Along with a smell like rotten fish. She lifted her head up off the table.

"Jesus, Ma." My heart resumed its normal beat again. I noticed she hadn't changed her clothes. "Sorry to sneak up on you like that, but I thought —"

"Don't let the cat out, Sonny."

She had a plate of uncooked spaghetti in front of her, stacked up like a pile of pick-up sticks.

"Ma, Mittens has been dead for years."

A green ooze rimmed the bottom of the gauze that capped her head. Her stump arm had ballooned to twice the size of her normal one.

"Miss Mittens is dead? No, Sonny, don't play games."

"I'm not, Ma..."

Her head swiveled toward me. A fly crawled out of her empty eye-socket and took flight.

"Holy crap!"

"Don't swear, Sonny. You know how much I don't like swearing.

Don't be like that good for nothing father of yours, God rest his soul."
She crossed herself. "Why can't you be more like your brother? Petey
never swears." She scowled then. "And why aren't you in school?"

"Ma, I —" I didn't know what to say. I was a kid again. But then
maybe I've always been a kid. I never wanted to grow up and have to
do all the things that grown-ups have to do. Ma was right. Why
couldn't I have been more like Petey? Instead, I was left carrying the
torch for dear dead Dad.

"Ma, they sent me home because there's this field trip we're going
on, and you forgot to sign the permission slip." One of the many talents
I inherited from my dad—lying on the fly.

"Oh," Ma said, dumbfounded.

I grabbed a pen off the table and folded the beneficiary form in
half and slid it in front of her.

"Just sign here, Ma, so I can get back to school, the bus is waiting
for me."

In fact, there came a rumble outside that sounded like it could
have been a bus.

"Where Sonny, I can't see."

I put the pen in Ma's hand and put the point of the pen on the signa-
ture line. "Right there, Ma. Now go ahead."

She thought for a minute, then her hand started to move.
Right about this time, I heard car doors slam and footsteps coming up
the walkway. There came a heavy knock on the door. Before I could
ask who it was, the door was kicked open and in walked The Mick.

"Sonny Cataldo." The Mick spoke my name as if it left a bad taste
in his mouth. He'd brought two of his associates with him. The three
of them came toward me.

"Hey, you guys didn't have to come all the way out here," I said,
standing in front of Ma. I didn't want them to see her like that. "Look,
I got it all under control."

Ma was done writing, so I grabbed the paper out from under her
hand. I handed the will over to The Mick so he could read it for himself.

"I'll pay you back double if you just give me a little more time,"
I pleaded.

The Mick looked at me, then he looked back at the will again.
Then he laughed. He showed the will to each of his associates, who

joined in the laughter.

"And I suppose that woman behind you is 'Miss Mittens'?" He handed the will back to me.

I stared at the will. My heart must have stopped beating. I turned then.

No wonder Ma didn't make a fuss about the strange men who had just kicked her door in.

Ma sat as straight as I'd ever seen her. Her eye was glazed, staring out the kitchen window. Miss Mittens used to sit on that window ledge and chatter at the birds that came to the bird feeder. There was a hint of a smile on Ma's face, as if she were looking at something that made her happy.

I was grabbed from behind and pulled away. That's when one of the associates got a good look.

"Holy shit!" The three-hundred-pound goon retched.

The Mick leaned in and grimaced. Then he turned to me and said, "What kind of sick mother fucker are you?" He held a handkerchief to his mouth.

The Mick shook his head with disgust. "Get him out of here. And grab what's left of the old lady."

Damn fucking cat. How was I supposed to know the thing was so old it couldn't get out of its own way?

I guess I should have known I'd end up like this. But I thought being practical was the same as having common sense. I guess that's where I took after Ma.

I wonder when The Mick is going to let me out of here?

At least this meat locker isn't freezing cold. Must be in some old abandoned warehouse somewhere. Even if somebody did happen by, they probably wouldn't hear me. These walls are pretty thick.

I'm getting awful hungry.

Well, at least I don't have to visit Ma anymore. She's right here with me.

She don't smell as bad as she did. Guess I'm getting used to it.

Did I say I was getting awful hungry?

On the Filthy Floor
by Michael A. Arnzen

ROSE NERVOUSLY COUGHED and contemplated how much she loathed the fifth floor of the Lauderdale Wilton as the service elevator lurched and began its ascent. Her cleaning cart wobbled beside her as old-fashioned red LED numbers counted off the hotel stories. But to Rose, the digits might as well have been counting fathoms: this daily ritual ride in the elevator always gave her a sinking feeling, like she was being lowered into some surreal sort of shark cage that dangled on a rusty, chunky chain, falling deeper and deeper into the muck.

The air in the lift was heavy with the freshly bleached towels and sheets piled on her cart. But when the elevator hit number five, she drew as much of the air into her lungs as she could without choking— one last time before snorkeling into the sea of disgust and facing her daily housekeeping duties.

The door shuffled open as she held her breath. The dingy appearance of the walls never failed to strike her, even after six years of hard work: the fuzzy tan tinge of the only floor where smoking was permitted in all rooms always stood in stark contrast to the other levels of the Wilton. Here, the carpet was matted, stained and burned. The windows were hazed with gray clouds and scratches that caught the weak flicker of morgue-like fluorescent lighting. She called it the "Filth" floor rather than the "fifth." Because to her, this dismal smear of human culture represented everything disgusting about the world.

Everything sick. Everything that took her Daddy away.

Daddy's eyeballs jittered in the pits of their sockets, confronting her with their large brown and yellow panic. He had the wooden stare of a sick owl. Strain was apparent in his eyebrows. He couldn't speak, but she knew he was terrified.

His throat hole wheezed.

"Everything's going to be all right," Rose lied. She smiled away her repulsion while she tucked the blanket up around his cold throat and avoided the bright yellow gob of phlegm he'd coughed out of his tracheotomy tube. Its color and thickness was as surprising in its sudden presence as a spoonful of lemon pudding coming out of his hole. She kissed him on the temple and retrieved a hand towel, wiping up the sputum and laying the cloth like a baby's bib around the plastic vent cut into the flaccid flesh of his old smoker's throat.

She barely had the courage to look at him. His face was gaunt, pale, wrinkled up like her thumbs would get in the tub. It was as though his head had deflated since the chemo. His lungs were sucking him out from inside his own skin. And his breathing was always so raspy, always so strained.

The throat cancer was bad. His airway had collapsed above the larynx. He could no longer speak and he could barely draw breath. She could tell from the sounds he made. A mucousy whine.

The lung cancer was worse. It was terminal. And things were getting really bad. She could tell from the look in those jaundiced owlish eyes of his. He was receding, fading away, as the pupils took over the eyeball with blackness.

His tracheotomy hole routinely bubbled up phlegm, often speckled like a robin's egg from blood. She wasn't sure whether this was because the cut was infected or because the cancer was doing its inevitably deadly business. The tube had been replaced three times. The doctors told her there was little they could do anymore. Time was short.

Love is what he needed now. She invited Daddy to her house. To die. He agreed.

The bloody phlegm burbled up from his blowhole. She mopped it whenever she could. But it was getting worse and worse and worse.

All she could do was clean up the mess and wait for the inevitable.

She pushed her cart out of the service elevator and, after briefly checking the signage and door handle on the Fire Exit, exhaled and begrudgingly sucked in the tainted air of the Filth Floor. It reeked of stale ashtrays and spilled beer and pathetic sex. Florida's humidity boiled the walls sticky with piss yellow smoke residue, the sad paint bubbling here and there where it wasn't simply chipping or stained with fuzzy stars of mildew.

As she wheeled her cart toward the doorway for Room 501, she scanned the carpet's familiar tar black cigarette burns, scattered in reckless clumps like carcinoma. She kept her eyes open for new burn holes. Inevitably, she'd spot a new one near the elevator's door, an oval scar from a battle between flame-retardant carpeting and an unfinished cigarette. She'd given up patching the holes in the carpet years ago. But she kept a good account of these burns anyway. There were presently thirty-seven in the hallway. She was just keeping score, waiting until it hit sixty. Then she'd requisition a new carpet for the hallway. She'd done so three times during the six years of her tenure at the Wilton. And the management never questioned it.

In fact, Rose wasn't sure if anyone from management had even stepped foot on the Filth floor since she'd been hired. There were inspections, true, but she never actually witnessed them—she only received form reports once a month, taped to her cart's giant handle-bar when she arrived at work. The Supe had gotten so lazy, he'd just draw one long line through the "satisfactory" boxes on the left side of the checklist. Clearly he was rushing it. Probably just going through the motions. And expecting her to do the same.

The Supe was just like everyone else at the Wilton. No one wanted to deal with the smoker's floor. The Filth was a sore spot and a stink hole. An embarrassment to the lavish accommodations of the rest of the place, hidden from the rest of the outfit like soiled underwear beneath a cocktail dress. And they'd given up trying to clean or main-tain it. Because no matter how many ashtrays and ozone machines and flame-retardant furnishings they put in, cigarettes destroyed every-thing. Damage was in their very nature. They stained, burned, and melted everything in their path. Including people. And that upset Rose. Not just because they killed her daddy and nearly killed her in the process...but because her housekeeping skills were wasted on it all. She was a damned good maid. And cleaning up the smoker's floor was a meaningless waste of her time and talent. She was capable of so much else.

So she did just what she had to do. Although she had the extra burden of making sure the fire code regulations were met, Rose's job was still remarkably easier than the rest of the housekeeping crew. She could do a half-ass job and the Supe wouldn't say a thing. Her work wasn't cleaning, really, anyway. It was merely covering up. Every room was essentially the same routine. She masked the stink of tobacco with a potent deodorizing aerosol spray that, according to the label on the large metal can, "desmoked" the room. She'd run her wimpy vacuum over the shag—its tall red bag puffing out weakly like an asthmatic lung—but it never sucked up all the ash that the smokers powdered the floor with. She'd wipe the sticky counters and change the soiled sheets and hose down the formed yellow plastic tub and toilet, but it was all a superficial cover-up. She was just going through the motions. The yellow taint on the walls testified to the conquest of nicotine. The burn marks were permanently blandished on the bedside table and the toilet seat and the windowsill. And the smell of smoke was never really "desmoked" at all. Instead, it was rendered twice as deadly, the desmoker's disturbing chemical flavor lending the air a presence that perpetually reminded her of the smoker's taint that lin-gered invisibly in the room. It was an odor that ghosted every room on the Filth Floor with a lie that was right under everyone's noses: death was right there in the air.

Rose hated it. Everywhere she turned, she was disgusted. She couldn't escape the smell. If a hotel was like a person, then the Filth Floor was its lung cavity, and Rose felt as though she were watching cancer progress and spread inside of it all these years.

Just like Daddy.

Daddy slept while Rose watched him from the corner, sitting in her rocking chair, breathing in the darkness. She marveled at his hole, relishing the air that coursed into her nose and down her throat. She wondered what it would be like to lose that sensation. To get air in a direct hit, right there close above the lungs, without the taint of the mouth or nasal cavity. Would it be cooler? Fresher? More potent?

They both agreed that this was how it was to happen. No oxygen tent. No air tanks and nose hoses. Just a pleasant room with big windows that opened wide in the spring. A bedside table with a book to read and a rose in a vase to remind him of her love while she was away at work and the temporary nurse cared for him.

He agreed to all this through nodding and handwritten notes. In some ways, he was already gone. His voice was part of his personality—that gruff-yet warm deep voice of his, that voice that used to tell her how much he loved her...and her mom, once, too.

There was a time when that voice even lost its gruffness. A time when the gravel was gone and his words were as smooth as a drink of chocolate milk. It happened after his first stroke—at the far-too-young age of thirty-nine—when Rose was just finishing up the ninth grade. He stroked out from simply climbing the concrete stairs that lead up from the Ft. Lauderdale beach. A gang of the usual drunken college students on spring break discovered him and one had the good sense to dial 911 on his cell phone to fetch an ambulance. Later, after Daddy was resuscitated by paramedics and taken to the hospital, the doctors told him the obvious—that his two-and-a-half pack a day habit was killing him. He didn't have cancer yet, they said, but the early stages of emphysema combined with severely high blood pressure were dealing his system a one-two punch. Rose cried on his shoulder and left a big wet stain. Daddy said he made up his mind right then and there to kick the habit.

That's what it took. Illness. Sickness standing with its arms akimbo at the threshold of death. Tapping its foot.

And he did get better. He succeeded at quitting smoking by chewing gum, popping vitamin pills, and exercising like the doctors told him. He made it his goal to someday run up and down those very same steps that stroked him out without missing a beat. The emphysema soon receded and his blood pressure stabilized and he could easily swim laps in the ocean before going for a beachside jog and taking the steps in stride. And—most importantly, to Rose—his voice turned soft and warm. The way he said her name was like a hug and a hum and a goodnight kiss. She felt like she was hearing his true self then, the healthy self, the voice her mother must have fallen in love with.

But even that voice could turn sick. One night she heard it calling Momma all sorts of nasty, dirty things. And then neither one of them ever saw Momma again.

And then—perhaps because he thought it would make things go back to the way they were before he quit—he started smoking all over again. With a vengeance.

He made a pact with her. "Don't tell no one and don't give me that guilty look of yours no more," he said in that old gruff voice of his former self. "Do that and I'll love you forever."

She did her job quickly and efficiently, covering up the truth. She was a master at disguising the disgust. And it wasn't the hotel itself that was to blame for the sick living of the Filth Floor. It was the people who occupied the rooms. Although there weren't as many of them as there used to be, it only took a few chain smokers to infest the hotel and make it sick. She covered that fact up with her chemical cleansers, but there was a secret pleasure involved: masking the filth in the rooms allowed her to veil her own secret work.

She was fighting fire with fire. Combating sickness with sickness. She knew that smokers didn't listen to reason or relatives. They listened to their addictions alone. But she learned from her daddy that it only took one thing to get a smoker to turn around his life and stop killing himself and the people that loved him:

Life-threatening illness. Standing at the edge of permanent disease, teetering at the threshold of death. That could be the tipping point to heading back to health. And Rose was willing to do what it took to make it tip.

In Room 501—which harbored so much mold under its bathroom sink that she lovingly renamed it "it's-alive-oh-one"—Rose set quickly to work. She wheeled her janitorial supply cart inside the carpeted room and shut the door behind her. She slid her hands into her arm-length latex gloves with the determination of a surgeon. She first collected any and all ashtrays and stacked them on the desk beside the cheap coffeepot and stenopad. Then she reached for the bedding and, with one expert tug, she stripped the bedclothes with a snap, mini-mizing the amount of contact she'd have to make with the soilure on the sheets. Whether sweat or sex or snot, there was always something there. And she'd seen a lot of body residue on this job—from the disgusting puddle of blood-spotted cum left fresh on the center of the bed like a strange dessert topping to the petroleum jelly slathered in brown streaks all over the remote control. People fucked each other and themselves and the room furnishings with little care or discrimi-nation. They didn't care what they put inside themselves. That was the whole problem.

The quilted green bedcover could be reused, naturally, so she sep-arated that before pushing the white linens into the laundry sack on her cart. Then she made the bed with the fresh bleached fabric sheets and replaced the old coverlet above it, tucking it in nicely and setting an Andes mint on the pillow. She noticed that the green foil wrapper on the mint almost matched the large green stain on the inside of the coverlet—the one she'd been cultivating for six years.

Next came the ritual wipe down. She used a soiled pillowcase for this; the shortcut made the process move quickly. She slid her gloved hands inside the case and bunched the fabric between her fingers into a makeshift dust mitt, swiping every surface she could in a thorough swoop of all visible surfaces. She'd spit on the wood if it needed an extra polish. She ignored all nooks or edges that were taller than she, or any low surfaces which might have required sustained stooping. The important points were the surfaces that people would stare at for extended periods of time: the television screen and the window. The ceiling above the bed was probably worse, but the tar of three million cigarettes painted it fresh with a perpetually renewing layer of tar. The emergency sprinkler heads up there always scared her, like robotic eyes, watching and recording her secret corruption of the room. She preferred to stay away from them.

She had a special solvent for glass and sprayed it copiously on the windows. She hated the windows because she could not open them.

They were screwed tightly in place. The Wilton wanted to minimize the risk of suicide jumpers and drunken idiots falling out of the window. So the air conditioning unit did all the work, exchanging air. And the ACs on the smoker's floor were rarely ever serviced or cleaned. They just recycled stale smoky air, just like a secondhand smoker's lungs. Just like her lungs when she cared for Daddy all those years.

She had a routine. Every three visits to a room, she'd lift off the plastic grill and remove her own custom filter from the previous housekeeping. Then she'd carefully place the grimy, spittle-ridden dust mitt she used to clean the furniture and window surfaces over the filter. She'd turn on the AC to its highest setting and watch with a smile as the engine held the cloth in place, the blackened imprint of her hand on the rag fluttering against the metal mesh as though she'd raised her own flag of revolt. Satisfied that her dirty rag was contaminating as much of the air as possible, she replaced the grill.

As always, the AC stirred something in her lungs. She coughed harshly into her right hand. A surprisingly bright gob of phlegm rested in her gloved palm like a coin. She slid her hand inside the pillowcase and wiped it clean on the nappy gauze of the pillow's fabric, which had become a bit crackly from her old spit. Rose relished the idea of a smoker snuggling the sickly pillow against his cheek in his sleep.

Next came the bathroom. She had to summon her courage to enter it. Nothing threatened to repulse Rose more than her entrance into the restroom. People revealed themselves at their worst when they used the facilities. And when they were away from home, they never failed to be sloppy and careless...sometimes even downright sadistic to house-keeping staff. From black pubic hair clotted with spit and toenails in the sink to shit smears and runny vomit on the floor, the bathroom always threatened to make her gag. Even after six years of working on the Filth, her skin hadn't gotten thick enough.

Luckily, the most recent occupant of 501 hadn't left any parting gifts for her, beside the usual towels tossed rudely onto the floor and the usual amount of hair clinging in the shower stall. The latest guest had been fairly tame and humble for a smoker. She'd seen much worse—tampons clotted in the corner, yellow crud sticky on the hand towels, green sewage dribbling down the tub, spit sprayed bubbly all over the mirror—but the latest guest was cleaner than most smokers whose traces she had to erase.

Which meant she'd have to provide her own filth to secretly seed the room with disease. She sprayed the seat with so much alcohol it beaded up and then wiped it clean with a fistful of toilet paper. Then she sat down and pissed. She was too constipated and impatient to purge her bowels. After she squeezed the last droplet of urine from her bladder, she pulled up her pants and picked up the toilet brush that rested on the floor in a dirty stand beside the toilet. As a good maid should, she scrubbed beneath the rim of the toilet with vigor. Then she reached for the two small glasses that stood on a cheap plastic tray beside the ice bucket and preceded to use the toilet like a sick dishwashing basin, dunking the glasses into the yellow water and brushing them out with the toilet brush, one right after the other, with the efficiency of a housewife. She set one upside-down in the sink to let it dry out. Later, she would put a plastic wrap over the glass tops to imply they were sanitized when she returned them to their place beside the ice bucket. For now, Rose filled the other glass with tainted toilet water.

Then she returned to the desk, where the stack of ashtrays awaited. Rose lifted the top off the small barrel of the coffee maker and filled it up with the cold vile liquid. She tore open a plastic-wrapped cone filter, fisted open the sleeve around her latex hand, and dropped it into the coffee drip tray. Then she ceremoniously dumped each ashtray she'd collected, butts and all, into the awaiting black mouth of the filter. Once the pile of ash was steeped, she coughed up into her throat and spit on top of the custom drink recipe, topping it off with a spoonful of her own yellow pudding, before turning it on.

Contagion coffee—good to the last hock, she thought.

She proceeded to contaminate the rest of the room's hidden areas while it brewed.

Rose started coughing and wheezing shortly after they wheeled her father out of her home. Two weeks later she discovered that she had severe lung disease. Advanced cancer. Terminal. The doctors told her it was probably a combination of second hand smoke and heredity. She remotely understood that her father's habit was the primary culprit, clouding around her head all those years. But she believed it was working the smoker's floor at the Wilton during the last years of his life—working in a living hell to pay for Daddy's medicine—that pushed her to the threshold of death.

She wasn't able to save Daddy or save herself, but she wasn't going to go down without a fight and she could still help other people. She wasn't going to let smoking win. She would secretly save the sick from themselves. She would use her skills at housekeeping to keep the house unhealthy, and get the sick sicker, more quickly. She would secretly scare them straight so they'd quit on their own some day.

If only to give them a little hope for a few months. A little health. A chance to run on the beach and swim in the ocean with their families.

Rose dropped to her knees to wipe up the filthy bathroom floor. This was actually a shortcut she learned in training years ago: to wipe down all surfaces with soiled towels since they would all be laundered anyway. It saved the hassle of carting around cleaning cloths and rags. And it saved Rose's strength for her combat against cancer.

"Excuse me," a gruff voice called behind her, just as she was flossing a towel behind the toilet bowl.

Rose was so startled she bumped her shoulder into the toilet seat as she bolted up. She twisted around to face a tall man who towered in the threshold of the hotel room, nervously twisting his left wrist in the palm of his right hand.

She thought she'd locked the door. She always locked the door. This must be the guest from the previous night—the relatively clean one—returning to the room with his key. "I'm sorry," she said, her voice sounding strange to her. She coughed into her latex glove. The smell of her hand repulsed her. "I thought you'd already checked out..."

The man arrogantly waved her words away as he scanned the room, shaking his brown hair like a dog. "Did you find a watch in here this morning?"

She cocked her head. The voice sounded absurd to her. She wasn't used to talking to others while she worked. She'd never heard anyone's voice inside the disgusting bathrooms of the Filth Floor. He might have spent the night in this room, and his DNA might have surrounded her in the bathroom at this very moment, but he certainly did not belong here now. "You're looking for a watch?"

"Yes," he looked over her shoulder, his bushy eyebrows pressing together as he scanned the sink counter. "A Timex. Black band. Digital read-out..."

Rose shrugged. "No, sir. I'm sorry."

"It was a gift, dammit!" He pivoted on his heel to search the room.

She thought it best to ignore him and go back to work. But then she remembered the various nasty things she kept in her cart to taint the smoker's floor: things she'd found in rooms that she could use to cross-contaminate them, like pop bottles filled with chewing tobacco spit and Chinese food cartons she filled with samples of leftover room service mold and rot.

She jumped up and joined him, pretending to help him search. "I've already cleaned most of the room, sir. I'm pretty sure I would have found your watch by now if it was really here." As the man opened a desk drawer Rose bent over and lifted the skirt of the lower mattress cover to pretend to check under the bed—her only intent was to do so before he did. A porn magazine, an empty cigarette carton, and several large gray balls of hairy dust confronted her; she hadn't vacuumed beneath the bed in a very long time.

The familiar cloying flavor of menthol tickled into her nose. She twisted up at the smoker and stared at him. The man—audaciously—was smoking a Kool cigarette. She could see the pack's label through his breast pocket as his lungs heaved. He sucked and blew, sucked and blew.

"Sir..." she protested, but then her lungs exploded with a fit of hacking. She climbed her way back up from the floor to try to insist that he put it out.

But he wasn't paying attention. He was standing by the desk, cigarette dangling precariously between his dumbstruck lips, as he stared at the brewing coffeepot. It was boiling and burping with light gray water. Tar dripped down into the carafe in ugly clots. He paled with revulsion, blinking smoke out of his eyes. "What the hell are you making?"

Rose coughed. "Um...Turkish tea."

His face scrunched up in confusion, cigarette tipping up towards his nose as he did so. He looked, for a moment, like The Penguin from the Batman cartoons. "Huh?"

She needed to keep him distracted. Rose marched over to her cart and began pushing it towards him, effectively backing him toward the corner of the room with the heavy metal handlebars.

"There's no smoking here, sir."

"But it's a smoking room." He raised his hands. The squinched facial expression was glued on his features, but slowly coming unstuck, muscle by muscle. "Say, what's your problem, lady?"

"Put that out, Daddy," she commanded, shoving with the cart.

He bumped the back of his head into a lamp as he backpedaled into the corner. "Daddy? What the hell are you talking about?"

"Put that cigarette out or I'll make you drink that whole pot of nicotine coffee over there."

"You're crazy!" he chuckled.

A silence passed between them as she stared him down with the intensity of a diamond inspector. Slowly, Rose reached toward the steaming pot on her left to show him she meant business.

The man bolted to her right.

Rose heaved and pinned him hard against the wall with the heavy cart. As he doubled over its handlebar and hit the stack of towels with an *oof*, Rose reached inside the cart for a weapon.

The smoker came up for air.

Canister in hand, Rose desmoked him. The spray hissed right into his face, showering him with chemicals. He choked back poison as he clawed at his own eyes.

But the Kool that smoldered in the towels between them lit up with restored life. It climbed up the spray as rapidly as an Army ranger on a rope and then leapt across the chemical bridge that connected the two of them. Flames coursed into the man's mouth and lungs as they simultaneously burned a beeline toward Rose. Before she could blink, an explosion wrenched the aerosol can from her grip with a force that peppered her chest with hot shards of metal, throwing her to the floor.

Daddy's voice, calling out from a blackwater sea. A whisper of a cry behind crashing waves of pain.

Rose reawakened slowly from the shock. The room seemed surprisingly quiet and still for what she saw.

The smoker was feeling around the windowsill in a blind stupor, desperately trying to open the bolted window as his hair blazed with audacious orange flame.

Smoke was now everywhere. Curtain smoke. Towel smoke. Human smoke.

And her mouth felt exceptionally dry. And cold. And—when she finally moved to scream—completely useless.

A new hole had opened up beneath her chin. Her voice wheezed yellow goo out of it, pushing up shrapnel when she tried to swallow.

The man with the burning face was banging his head against the curtained glass. The thudding of his head was dull and distant, but then the shrill bell of the fire alarm asserted itself into her ears and water then showered down from above, fizzling the flames, joining her blood.

The blood that rapidly puddled in her opened throat box. Flooded out over the edge of the wound. Drowning her.

Daddy's voice again, calling from the sea of darkness. A gargling guttural cry.

Heat seared around her neck...then inside it. She choked and realized that Death was standing above her, pinning her arms with his feet, a carafe shaky in his bloodied hands, laughter maniacal in his melted mouth. He turned the fat bellied decanter and poured more of the soupy black mess into her throat hole and she tasted a lifetime of cancer as she choked and struggled and unavoidably swallowed the butts and ashes right into her lungs.

Her torso was ablaze in agony.

Daddy arrived on shore and put it out.

Battle Fever
by Scott Thomas

IT IS STRANGE, and sad perhaps, that my father is so much like a rumor. I was little more than an infant when he died, thus I cannot claim any honest memories of the man. The closest thing to a recollection is a blur, a suggestion of a large figure making sounds like a whistling teapot.

My earliest memory *about* Father is that he had only two toes on one foot. This bit of information, along with the rest, came to me from my siblings who *were* old enough to remember him. Why two toes you wonder?

My sister Olivia tells the story with more flare than I, but in short...during the war father found himself in a particularly unpleasant exchange with the enemy. Manning the firing steps in a dug out—a great muddy wound in the rain—father was knocked from his position by a close shell. More stunned than injured, he landed in the muck where a chum (more mud than man) broke his fall.

The man was a ghastly puzzle and had been dead for some minutes. But for the rictus teeth, this poor fellow's severed head was all but sunk in the mire. Father claimed that it was not unlike dropping into the clutch of a poacher's trap. The head, as the story goes, latched onto father's foot. No amount of effort could remove the thing—at last a surgeon got it loose, taking three of Father's toes with it.

Father was never right after that. He returned from the Front with a bad case of battle fever, repairing to our quaint village of Lower Slaughter in the Cotswold country. While his body, for the most part, had survived the war, his innocence had been murdered.

My brother Harry, the oldest of the brood, told me how Father spoke very little upon his return. More than anything else, Harry's impression of those days consisted of the thump, thump, thump of father limping about the cottage. Over time Father became slightly more conversational, and he limped beyond the confines of the little stone cottage as well.

Father spent much of his time wandering the countryside and along the river. Sometimes he took a pole with him, though he never came home with a fish. Once Harry stole after him (Father required absolute solitude on these excursions) and spied. The patriarch lumbered through the fine wood to a stream where he crouched on the muddy bank and verbally imitated all manner of whistling shells and explosions. The man's imitative powers were indeed evocative; Harry could all but visualize the shrill flight of the missiles, could nearly feel the drumming impacts.

Even after the horrors Father witnessed in France he remained a gentle man. Never a tactile fellow, he made an exception for the cat, who thought Father's lap (by the fire) was the best place on Earth. Father never raised his voice nor a hand to his children, though there was in fact one troubling indication of the man's inner torment, that being the time he bayoneted a snowman that my siblings had built in the yard.

During his second spring home, Father took to spending more and more time down at the stream. Each morning he would take up his pole and march off along the road, into the blossoming wood. One evening he did not return home.

My mother, who devoted a great deal of energy to trying not to let the world know what a nervous creature she'd become, sent Harry and Olivia to search for their father.

They knew where to find him, of course. He was by the stream, in the rain, lying in a small trench (or a grave perhaps?) that he must have fashioned with his hands. The man was alive, but he did not respond to their questions; he merely hobbled back to the house, guided by the children, who each held to one of his muddy hands.

My mother cleaned Father up and put him to bed in their dim little upstairs chamber. Later, while tending to his muddy garments, she discovered a note inside one of the jacket pockets. I have the thing to this day. It's a largely unintelligible effort, partly due to the blurring of the ink brought about by the rain. The content, as it remains, follows (unreadable areas have been indicated):

This morni-- the strea- r-- ----
A voice came to -- -rom t-- -----
Once again I sa- -he head; it flo----
In the stream, closer to the banks tha-
-efore. I was able to reach it and lift--
-- --t. It was the head of a babe, but it w--
--ackened as if from a fire. I kisse-
--

Father refused to speak following his last visit to the stream. He hardly left his bed, in fact, and was beset with fever. The doctor came, as I understand it, but could do little, if anything. Father merely remained in his bed (with pillows piled like sandbags) making those eerie rocket sounds...whistling and booming. The sounds echoed through the cottage and even, on occasion, woke the rest of us in the dead of night.

Toward the onset of June, after the oaks had blossomed and warblers flitted in the bitter cress growing by the stream, there came a most terrible episode. My mother and my siblings and I (too young to know what the commotion was about) were stunned by a dreadful noise. Father had been up in his bed about his mocking of shrilling missiles when suddenly the little cottage shook and sounded, as if blasted in earnest.

Father took to screaming from above. My mother flew up the stairs but found the door bolted. She could hear father on the other side, banging into walls and tripping over furniture as if a blind man.

The panicked woman called to him and pounded at the door. I sat in my wooden highchair wailing (so I'm told) and Olivia and Harry dashed out to see what they could from looking up at the windows.

Father, I'm told, passed the window several times, flailing his arms, bellowing pitifully. Strangely, his voice sounded quite far away, as if from a distance greater than that between the upstairs and the yard where they stood.

Olivia refuses to remember much beyond this point, or even what

Father looked like. I suppose it's one of those memories that should-n't be a memory, and she's rightly locked it away. Harry, on the other hand, has retained the event explicitly...

Father's face was gone. While the bulk of his head remained intact, there was a gaping black crater in place of his features, a terri-ble, bloodless hole, slick with mud and ringed with a fringe of dark hair, or perhaps scorched grass. His cries came from within the hole.

The man staggered by the window several times, desperately waving his arms. He managed to grope the window open and thrust himself half out. Then, as Harry tells it, a small black figure—a baby without a head—grabbed the edges of the horrid crater and pulled itself out of the muddy darkness. The child was scorched (still burning, in fact, if Harry is to be believed) and once free of the maw, threw itself down, landing in the bushes below the cottage.

The baby emerged upright from the shrubbery (the least of its wonders) and dashed past my siblings, down the road and into the woods, searing the grass as it went.

When neighbors were summoned and the door to the bedchamber was forced open, my father was found to be dead. The children were not allowed to view him, and Mother never spoke of how he looked. We were told only that he was taken by the fever (despite what Harry and Olivia saw).

As for the baby...several days following the funeral, Harry was brooding about the yard when he noticed the burnt bush where the baby had fallen, and the singed grass where the thing had passed. He followed the trail—even the road showed signs of scorching. Burn marks led him into the green June wood, and down to the mud and murmurs of the stream. Small footprints showed in the muck, passed through the trench that Father had dug; their progress made it clear that the headless child had gone into the stream.

Search as he may, Harry could find no sign of the creature. He even followed the water for several miles, but there was no bobbing baby, nothing snared in the growth along the way. There was only the stream, quiet and constant, sinuous and gray as it flowed along the outskirts of Lower Slaughter.

⇜About the Authors⇝

Michael A. Arnzen won the Bram Stoker Award and International Horror Guild Award in 1995 for his novel, *Grave Markings*. His story collection, *Fluid Mosaic*, includes his best work from the 1990s. Other recent titles include: *Freakcidents: A Surrealist Sideshow*, *Dying (With No Apologies to Martha Stewart)*, and *Gorelets: Unpleasant Poems*. Raw Dog Screaming is publishing his collection, *100 Jolts: Shockingly Short Stories* in Spring 2004. Arnzen holds a PhD in English and teaches in the Writing Popular Fiction graduate program at Seton Hill University. His creative website, gorelets.com, is popular among sickos online.

Greg Beatty attended Clarion West in the summer of 2000. He's had over forty short stories accepted since then, by venues ranging from *Palace of Reason* and *Ideomancer* to *Sci Fiction* and the new British magazine *3SF*. (For more information on his writing, visit his website). When he's not at his computer, he enjoys spending time with his girlfriend Kathleen.

Brandi Bell lives in San Diego and works for *Fiction International*. She writes mostly in the vein of sexual politics while waiting for a heart transplant of the emotional kind.

Brutal Dreamer [a.k.a. Peggy Jo Shumate] is married to David and has two children: Isaac Wade and Lizzy Marie and her loveable cat, Shackie Taques. Brutal Dreamer is a Movie Reviewer for DVD Empire, Reviewer for Massacre Publications, 2000 Graduate of the Institute of Children's Literature, Terror Scribe Member, and former editor, reviewer, and promotion manager of other magazines and publishers. Brutal Dreamer was Paul Kane's March 2002 Shadow-Writer and has almost 100 published works in both electronic and print, including *EOTU: Fiction, Art, and Poetry*, *The House of Pain*, *SDO Fantasy*, *Decompositions*, *The Dream People*, Rainfall Press, Southern Rose Productions, *Terror Tales*, *Steel Caves*, *The Swamp*, etc. Her work will be featured in 16 anthologies between 2003-2004. You can visit Brutal Dreamer at her official website or e-mail Brutal.

Scott Christian Carr is a writer and journalist residing with his wife and son in New York's haunted Hudson Valley—in an out of the way UFO hotspot called Pine Bush. Scott is the Chief Editor of the critically acclaimed *Apocalypse Fiction Magazine* and is currently involved in the production of the AFM/Blue Moon Movies film, *The Nuke Brothers*. His fiction and nonfiction have recently appeared in such publications as *Pulp Eternity*, *Pegasus Fiction*, *The Dream People Literary Magazine* and the upcoming Double Dragon Publishing anthologies *Scary! Holidays Tales to Make You Scream* and *Of Flesh and Hunger: Tales of the Ultimate Taboo*. In 1999 he was awarded The Hunter S. Thompson Award for Outstanding Journalism.

James Chambers is a writer and editor. His fiction has appeared in numerous anthologies, including *Weird Trails*, and *Warfear*; the chapbooks *Mooncat Jack* and *The Dead Bear Witness*; and the online magazines *Stillwaters Journal* and *The Black Book*. His tale "A Wandering Blackness," one of two published in *Lin Carter's Dr. Anton Zarnak, Supernatural Sleuth* received an honorable mention in *The Year's Best Fantasy and Horror, Sixteenth Annual Collection*. He lives in New York.

Hertzan Chimera's crazy brand of psycho-erotica has appeared in such literary venues as *Fangoria*, *The Urbanite*, *Dreams & Nightmares*, *Suspect Thoughts* and *Wildclown Chronicles* to name a few...Hertzan Chimera invented a new interview style for horror website Terror Tales—victims included Tom Piccirilli, Charlee Jacob, Michael A. Arnzen, Jack Ketchum and Edward Lee. His books include *Red Hedz*, *Szmonhfu*, *Broken*, *Boyfistgirlsuck*, and *United States*.

Tim Curran lives in Michigan, works in a factory by day, and writes horror, crime, and westerns by night. His tales have appeared in many small press magazines including *Flesh and Blood, City Slab*, and *Black October*, as well as in anthologies such as *Crime Spree, Weird Trails*, and *WarFear*. His crime novel, *Street Rats*, is now available from PublishAmerica (www.publishamerica.com). PublishAmerica will also be bringing out Tim's horror novel, *Toxic Shadows*, later this year. Two dark westerns, *Skull Moon* and *Grim Riders*, will be published in 2004 by Amber Quill Press. And his supernatural horror/western, *Skin Medicine*, has recently been accepted by Hellbound Books. You can find Tim Curran on the web at:
http://www.darkanimus.com/curran.html

A.D. Dawson is the facilitator of The Dodsley Pages (www.dodsleypages.com) and lives in the East Midlands of England. A.D.'s contribution to the anthology, "The Nutter on the Bus," was inspired by the amusing stories his daughter, Sarah, relates about the odd people she comes across whilst travelling to college by bus. However, in the psychological arena that we call life, who indeed is the oddity on the bus? It doesn't necessarily have to be the man who draws a penis on the window—does it?

Abel Diaz is the greatest living hack in American fiction. He lives in Seattle, where he pursues his interests in comic books, porn, and beer. He may or may not speak English.

Kevin L. Donihe has acceptances in over 120 magazines/anthologies—small-press, semi-pro, pro, and otherwise in eight different countries. He is the author of *From the Bowels of Birch Street, Voluptuous Sunrise, Spin Cycles, What's this About, Then?, Poems to Evaporate By*, and *Shall We Gather at the Garden?* Kevin also publishes *Bare Bone*, a magazine of pyschological horror.

Scott J. Ecksel lives in Washington, DC, where he writes fiction and poetry. Some of his recent work may be seen at *The Cafe Irreal, Netauthor's E2K, Fiction Funhouse*, and *Clean Sheets*. Currently, he is writing a novel for young adults. He spends a lot of time in coffee shops.

Some of them serve wine, but, he admits, he prefers hot chocolate.

Efrem Emerson hails from Aroostook County, Maine. If you don't know where Maine is, then that's your problem. He's had an assortment of jobs, including potato picker, dope dealer, produce clerk, inept auto mechanic, nursing assistant, drug counselor, auto parts driver, and professional musician (he gave a $10 guitar lesson once). He currently has only one robbery conviction, and the gun was loaded, but he never actually shot anyone. His work has been published in *Fiction International*, *The Dream People*, and *Bastard Fiction*.

Jack Fisher has sold fiction to well over 100 different markets including *Cemetery Dance*, *Space & Time*, *Horror Garage*, *Dark Regions*, *Black October*, *The Night Has Teeth*, *The Urbanite*, *Decadence*, *Not One of Us*, *Writer Online*, and many more. Jack is the editor of the multi award-winning horror magazine, *Flesh & Blood*. Jack resides in central New Jersey where he is a Paramedic.

Steve Goldsmith is twenty-four years old and lives in Kent, England. After gaining a degree in English and Media at Chichester University, he studied Television Production Technology and worked for a time at a TV station in London. He grew up watching just about every horror movie going, and due to a lack of quality movies of the genre currently being made, he thought he would entertain himself by writing stories. He has had these stories accepted at various outlets, including: *The Dream Zone*, *Dark Angel Rising*, *The Murder Hole*, *House Of Pain* and *CimmPlicity*.

J. M. Heluk believes there is a certain measure of terror lurking, even on the brightest most innocent days, if one is inclined to look for it. This author peers into the darkest climates, gathering inspiration from the horrors floating unseen beyond the bluest of clouds, to the things we all fear are crouching behind us. Heluk has sold fiction to print publications, anthologies and to numerous websites. J. M. Heluk is an editor for an online horror magazine, writes full-time for an east coast newspaper and shares a home with three grisly things.

Like most writers, **C.J. Henderson** has had to supplement his income from time to time. Over the decades, he has also kicked around as a movie house manager, drama coach, blackjack dealer, critic, roadie, advertising salesman, supernatural investigator, card shark, dishwasher, traffic manager, short-order cook, stand-up comic, toy salesman, and street mime. As an award-winning author, however, he is the creator of both the Jack Hagee detective series and the Teddy London supernatural detective series. His short stories have appeared in scores of anthologies and magazines. His novels are known around the world. As a comic book author, he has handled every character from *Batman* to *Cherry Poptart*. If that weren't enough, his *Encyclopedia of Science Fiction Movies*, released through Facts on File, has become a smash hit, entering its third printing.

Jonathan William Hodges is a twenty-something author of dark fiction living in North Carolina. His work has appeared previously in *Flesh & Blood*, *Extremes 4: Darkest Africa*, *Whispers from the Shattered Forum*, Undaunted Press's *Vicious Shivers*, and others. To further exemplify his confusion at what he wants to be when he grows up, he also publishes and edits all titles released by Blindside Publishing, http://blindside.net, and operates http://ProjectPulp.com, the online small press bookseller. His writer website, with news, bibliography, and losel filler, can be found at http://blindside.net/JonHodges.

Harold Jaffe is the author of eight fiction collections and three novels, including *15 Serial Killers* (2003), *False Positive* (2002), *Sex for the Millennium* (1999), *Othello Blues* (1996), *Straight Razor* (1995), *Eros Anti-Eros* (1990), *Madonna and Other Spectacles* (1988), *Beasts* (1986), *Dos Indios* (1983), and *Mourning Crazy Horse* (1982). Jaffe's fiction has appeared in numerous journals and has been anthologized in *Pushcart Prize*, *Best American Stories*, *Best of American Humor*, *Storming the Reality Studio*, *American Made*, *Avant Pop: Fiction for a Daydreaming Nation*, and *After Yesterday's Crash*. His novels and stories have been translated into several languages, including German, Japanese, Spanish, French, and Czech. He has been the recipient of two NEA's, a California Arts Council grant, a Rockefeller fellowship, a NY CAPS grant, and two Fulbrights, to India and to the Czech

Republic. Jaffe is editor-in-chief of *Fiction International* and Professor of Creative Writing and Literature at San Diego State University.

Earl Javorsky (or whatever his name is) extended his teenage experience well into his late thirties. He boogied 'til he puked, he bopped 'til he dropped, he did not draw a get-out-of-jail-free card. Now, years later, the LAPD have his triple beam and his P38K, his Fender is in the closet, and he sells software to support the wife and kids and cats and dog and to keep the white picket fence looking good. In his spare time he cranks out brief protests, in the form of short fiction, against the normalcy of his life. He has a completed suspense novel that he is hawking, much as he once hawked band demo tapes. We wish him luck, as he is our highest hope.

Dustin LaValley lives in Upstate, NY with his two-year-old, overweight rottie. When he isn't finding new material to read he's working on his own short fiction.

The illness that is **John Edward Lawson**—Hyattsville, Maryland. And donuts. The intent of his writing? Explore "the horrible"; it is found in fiction, poetry, and non-fiction. The illness that is publishing—*The Scars are Complimentary* (collected poetry, June 2002), the anthologies *Of Flesh and Hunger: Tales of the Ultimate Taboo* (Double Dragon Publishing, March 2003) and *A Slap in the Face* (bizarrEbooks, March 2003). More donuts, and editor-in-chief of Raw Dog Screaming Press. The intent of his writing!

David Anthony Magitis: Born 01/12/74. 1993 National diploma Graphic Design. 1996 B.A. honors degree Graphic Design. His art is how he feels, the horror, anxiety, depression, pleasure and pain; a bid to bring out those demons that hide deep inside. That's about it really—oh, and he does a few book covers now and again.

Ronald Damien Malfi is the author of numerous short stories and screenplays, as well as the novel *The Space Between*. He currently resides in Maryland.

Jessica Markowicz is an epicurean metaphysical dominatrix who spends her days seeking banter, bondage, bacchanalia, and other modes of transfiguration in sunny San Diego under the advice of her physician. She predominantly writes sci-fi erotica as an experimental course of treatment for her obsessive compulsion for absurdity, sensuality, meaning and the bizarre.

Mark McLaughlin's fiction, nonfiction and poetry have appeared in about 500 publications, including *The Black Gate, Flesh and Blood, Galaxy, The Book of Final Flesh, The Last Continent: New Tales Of Zothique*, two volumes of *The Best Of The Rest*, and two volumes of *The Year's Best Horror Stories*. The most recent collections of his work are *Once Upon A Slime*, a trade paperback from Catalyst Books; *The Spiderweb Tree*, a poetry chapbook from Yellow Bat Press; and *Hell Is Where The Heart Is*, a 400+ page story collection from Medium Rare Books. Also, he won the Bram Stoker Award for Superior Achievement in Poetry 2002, along with Rain Graves and David Niall Wilson, for *The Gossamer Eye*, a three-author poetry paperback from Meisha Merlin Publishing.

Kurt Newton is the author of two short story collections—*The House Spider* and *Dark Demons*—and *The Psycho-Hunter's Casebook*, a collection of murderous poetry penned by fictitious serial killers. *Denizens of the Cityscape*, an illustrated collection of poetic tales, is forthcoming from Double Dragon Publishing. For more information, visit Kurt's website at www.kurtnewton.com.

"Freaks are just like us," Ed McClanahan once wrote. "Only more so." **Andi Olsen** agrees with Ed McClanahan in a big way. Her Freakshow environments & excerpts therefrom have appeared in galleries across the country & in Europe, most recently in Los Angeles, Seattle, & London. She has also published numerous illustrations—including collage-text collaborations with Lance Olsen—in various books and journals, & collaborated on a video in tribute to Kathy Acker. Visit her online at http://www.cafezeitgeist.com/andi.html.

Lance Olsen, novelist, short-story writer, critic, and reviewer, was born among the hermetically sealed, climate-controlled malls of northern New Jersey on October 14, 1956, at 2:30 in the afternoon under the sign of the House (i. e., rest and peace), according to the Aztec horoscope. He is the author/editor of nonfiction books such as *Rebel Yell: Writing Fiction* and *Lolita: A Janus Text*. His novels and fiction collections include the books *Girl Imagined by Chance*, *Freaknest, Time Famine, Tonguing the Zeitgeist, Hideous Beauties*, and *Sewing Shut My Eyes*. Olsen has been awarded the Fulbright in Finland, 2000; Idaho State Writer-in-Residence, 1996-1998; Pushcart Prize, 1998; Finalist for 1995 Philip K. Dick Award. He was an associate professor and professor at the University of Idaho for ten years, but he is feeling better now. Until 2000, Olsen was the most unread American writer in the twentieth century. Currently, he is the most unread American writer in the twenty-first.

Claudette Rubin enjoys American films and early-mid 19th century European music. Her preferred authors are Dostoyevsky, Homer, and Nietzsche when he's not making a fool of himself. She liaises in linguistics with a nation of generally democratic principles. She's hindered to occasional, near-paralysis by obsessive compulsive disorder. She also likes telescopes though she's never owned one and doesn't recall looking into one at any time in her life, but she loves everything in existence because she operates by a categorical imperative of magnanimity; this allows her thorough latitude at being as bold as she wishes.

satan165's mystique and legend is only matched by the skid marks which copiously coat his drawers. He is hated by many, respected by few. Besides a host of other problems and personality defects, his work can be found strewn about *The New Absurdist*, *The Whimsical Icebox* and www.lowpro708.com. Currently battling a nightmare case of the shingles, he has taken to trying to inspire a new round of ritual killings with his upcoming work, but will settle for a minor social disturbance. Chances are you have no idea who he is, but you can be damn sure he knows very well who you are and is watching you now...

Vincent W. Sakowski's writing has appeared around the world in print, onstage, on the radio, and on the Internet. He is the author of the anti-epic novel of the surreal *Some Things are Better Left Unplugged*, and the novella *The Hack Chronicles*—both published by Eraserhead Press. Vincent is the founding member of The Brotherhood of the Rat—a collective of writers, artists and dramatists of the surreal, bizarre, and experimental.

S. William Snider lives in Colorado Springs where he struggles with out-of-state tution fees from UCCS. When he's not staggering through the worst psychology textbook ever written, he goes out to the movies by himself way too much, smokes pot and defends his Kansas City Chiefs against the hordes of Denver Bronco fans.

Jeffrey Thomas is the author of the novel *Letters From Hades* (Bedlam Press), the collections *Terror Incognita* (Delirium Books) and *AAAIIIEEE!!!* (Writers Club Press), and *Punktown* (Ministry of Whimsy Press), from which a story was reprinted in St. Martin's *The Year's Best Fantasy and Horror* #14. Forthcoming are the Punktown-set Lovecraftian novel *Monstrocity* (Prime), the novella *Godhead Dying Downwards* (Earthling Publications), a Lovecraftian collection entitled *Unholy Dimensions* (Mythos Books), an expanded hardcover edition of *Punktown* from Prime, a German edition of *Punktown* with cover by HR Giger and *Nether: Improper Bedtime Stories* (with brother Scott Thomas, Delirium Books).

Scott Thomas' fiction can be found in the following anthologies: *The Year's Best Horror* #22, *Leviathan 3*, *Octoberland*, *Songs From Dead Singers (And Other Eulogies)*, *Strangewood Tales*, *The Dead Inn*, *Tooth and Claw*, *Red Jack* and *The Ghost in the Gazebo*. Two stories from his collection *Cobwebs and Whispers* have been reprinted in St. Martin's Press' *The Year's Best Fantasy and Horror* # 15. One of those stories will be translated and published in France. *Nether (Improper Bedtime Stories)* a collection of erotic horror by Scott and his brother Jeffrey Thomas, is planned for publication by Delirium Books. Scott, his wife Nancy and cat Hamish live in Massachusetts.

Christian Westerlund has placed fiction with magazines like *Underworlds*, *Redsine*, *Flesh & Blood*, *The Dream People*, and with anthologies like *Octoberland* and *Darkness Rising 6*, among many others.

Greg Wharton is the publisher of Suspect Thoughts Press, and an editor of two web magazines, *Suspect Thoughts* and *Velvet Mafia*. He is also the editor of the anthologies *The Best of the Best Meat Erotica*, *Law of Desire* (with Ian Philips), *The Love That Dare Not Speak Its Name*, *Love Under Foot* (with M. Christian), and *Of the Flesh*. A collection of Wharton's short fiction, *Johnny Was and Other Tall Tales*, will be released in 2003 by Suspect Thoughts Press. He lives in San Francisco where he is hard at work on a novel.

LaVergne, TN USA
20 October 2010
201567LV00002B/131/A